THE UNDEAD.
TWENTY TWO

RR HAYWOOD

rrhaywood.com

Disclaimer: This is a work of fiction. All characters and events, unless those clearly in the public domain, are fictitious, and any resemblance to actual persons, living, dead (or undead), is purely coincidental.
The inclusion within this story of the character "Anja" is used as a prize in a competition and although to a degree they are based on the real persons they remain fictitious characters within a work of fiction and the author asserts his full rights to amend, delete or change those character(s).

Design, Cover and Illustration by Mark Swan

CHAPTER ONE

Day Twenty-Two

'Done?' Paula asks, her face shining with sweat and her hair plastered to her scalp.

'Yeah, we're done,' I say quietly, looking at the array of weaponry taken from the army base by Maddox and now sorted and cleaned. Three general purpose machines guns. Twenty assault rifles. Pistols and crates of ammunition, grenades, flashbangs, tear gas and one longbow with a bunch of arrows salvaged from Roy's van.

I look round at the others all beaten to hell. Broken noses, broken ribs, black eyes, swollen ears. Reginald's hand splinted with broken fingers.

Those things are on the outside though. Those things are the superficial wounds to the carriages that contain our souls and hearts, and that's where the most damage has been done. That's where it hurts more than we can really take because the way we lost Blinky wasn't right.

I look up at the night sky, at the thousands of stars shining and think never before have I seen them so clearly, and so many too.

There's no light pollution now and no smog either. No factories churning out fumes or cars and trucks belching smoke. No planes in the air, no trains, no anything.

'We won't all fit in there,' Paula says, bringing my attention back to see her staring at the Saxon.

'Could go tonight,' Maddox says.

'Sorry?' I ask.

'For a van,' he says. 'I could go get one tonight while you rest. Take Mo with me...'

I mull it over for a few seconds, weighing our needs up against the security of the whole.

'No,' Paula says firmly.

'Take me an hour or two...' Maddox says.

'I just lost one,' Paula says cutting across him as a fresh tear rolls down her cheek. 'I'm not losing another one today...'

The lad nods, rendered silent by the emotion pouring from her. She coughs, clearing her throat. 'Nick? Can I have a cigarette please?' she asks with a glare at Roy tutting as he steps away. 'Problem?'

'Stinks,' he mutters.

'We all stink,' she snaps. 'We all stink and we're all filthy...'

'Cigarettes won't help then will they.'

A silence settles. An uneasy quiet where none know what to say. Where none have the words to give. We said nice words at Blinky's grave. We wept, and we even smiled a little but that raw power that made us gel to give thanks in prayer has lessened now.

'Get some rest,' I say, breaking the quiet. 'I'll take first watch. Clarence, you sleep tonight. Maddox and Mo can...'

'I'll stand my watch,' Clarence says, his deep voice rumbling and hoarse.

'You should sleep,' Paula says, looking from him to me. 'Both of you.'

'Let us do them,' Marcy says.

'Said I'll stand my watch,' he says, ending the conversation abruptly.

'Come on,' Blowers says, motioning for the others to follow him. 'Charlie? You coming?'

'Minute,' she says dully.

Cookey stops and turns back, looking like he's about to say something as Nick brushes his side, pushing him on.

'I'll get some drinks,' Marcy tells me, following after the others back to the long low house Maddox found for us.

Charlie holds back, her arms folded across her body. Her head lowered.

'You okay?' I ask.

'Not really.'

'Stupid question.'

'Sorry, Mr Howie,' she says, easing her tone down a notch.

'Don't be. Is there anything I can do?'

'No...thank you.'

'Get some rest.'

'Will do,' she says, holding her ground as she swallows and bites her bottom lip. 'How do you deal with it?'

'With what?'

'Your sister...the others you lost...'

I stare at her, not knowing what to say. Not having the answer to give and while I search for words of comfort she simply nods once and walks off towards Jess grazing peacefully on the lush grass.

Ten minutes later, Marcy walks back with two steaming mugs while glancing over to Charlie brushing Jess by the rear of the horse box trailer thing.

'Didn't she already brush her?' Marcy asks quietly.

'Twice,' I reply.

'Maybe I should speak to her.'

'And say what?'

She thinks for a second then shrugs and sits down next to me on the back step of the Saxon. We sip in silence, watching Charlie brush Jess from head to toe, vigorous brushing too. Not that Jess seems to mind, she's not tethered and could just walk off if she wasn't enjoying it. Meredith lies near them, her head up and her tongue hanging out as she pants in the hot night air.

Charlie then disappears into the horse box trailer thing. Minutes pass. Long minutes until Meredith rises to her feet and trots silently over to lay down on the grass outside the back of the trailer.

'She sleeping in it?' I ask Marcy.

'Looks like it,' she murmurs. 'Want to me to go and look?'

'No. Maybe she just needs some alone time.'

'Maybe,' Marcy says thoughtfully. 'Howie?'

'Oh god,' I groan and look at her.

'What?'

'You said my name like mid-conversation which means you want to talk about something.'

She blinks at me, all gorgeous and sultry and more gorgeous. 'Yes,' she says.

'Fine,' I say glumly then frown at realising we can't have sex with Charlie being so close in the back of the horsebox trailer thing. Then I remember we buried Blinky just a few hours ago and here I am thinking about sex, which makes me hate myself.

'We can't have sex now,' Marcy whispers, which makes me feel a bit better that I wasn't the only one thinking it, but I doubt Marcy hates herself.

'Is that what you wanted to talk about?' I ask hopefully.

'No.'

'Oh,' I say, back to glum.

'I want to end it.'

'Eh?' I ask, sputtering coffee. 'Why? What did I do?'

'Pardon?' she asks me, looking for confused for a second. 'No! Not us, I meant...oh bless, did you think I meant us?'

'Er...no, I mean...did you mean that?'

'Aw, you're sweet.'

'Patronising.'

'Bless you, no that's not what I meant. I mean the infection thing.'

'The infection thing?'

'Yes, the infection thing. You should let me end it.'

'Right. I see. So...just to be clear on that?'

'Ah okay, yes so I leave you all and go off and...you know...*find* some hosts of my own and then a few more and...off we go...'

'Right.'

'You wait in the fort and I'll be back in no time. Good idea?'

'No. It's a terrible idea.'

'Really? I thought it was a good idea.'

'Seriously, it's the worst idea ever.'

'Okay,' she says slowly in a tone that I know means she doesn't mean *okay* at all. 'And why is it a bad idea precisely?'

'It is a bad idea precisely because it means you killing a bunch of innocent people and making them into fucking zombies to fight the other fucking zombies. Which is shit. Like...like really shit.'

'But Reggie said to be what I was. He said that.'

'I think he meant to get us out of the shit yesterday. Which you did and was awesome by the way...maybe a little bit excessive with killing three hundred people but...'

'I was angry.'

'Yep, totally get that. Angry, yes. So...I mean...it was a good idea then but as a tactic to fix the world? Um...not so sure.'

'Why?'

'I just said why. It'd be like...I don't know what it would be like... other than it would be bad.'

She pouts and huffs, sips her drink, swallows and looks at me again. 'I disagree.'

'Cool,' I say. 'No.'

'Just go back to the fort and wait for me.'

'I said no.'

'They're my friends too, Howie.'

'Who are?'

'Everyone here. They're my friends too.'

'What's that go to do with it?'

'They'll die if they keep going. We felt Blowers die and now Blinky and Mo is just a kid...'

'Mo? Have you seen him fight? He's like a mini-Dave.'

'He's still only sixteen.'

'Okay, no I get what you're saying, I really do...but no.'

'But...'

'It's not the right thing. We can't take people against their will to fight something they didn't ask for.'

'It's not like that. Listen, Howie, the bit when they turn isn't nice but after that...well, they don't feel anything, no pain, no suffering, they won't know anything...and anyway, Reggie turned back and your ex-girlfriend who you had sex with in that filthy dingy room on the table while we all listened also turned back...so...'

We both stop as a flash of blue goes past my eyes making me blink and pull away sharply while instinctively bringing my hand up to protect my face.

'No! hold still,' Marcy says, reaching out to push my hand down. 'It's just a moth.' It dances in front of my eyes for a second, too close to focus on until settling on Marcy's outstretched finger.

'That's a butterfly,' I say, gaining focus to see electric blue wings framed with white and black edging.

'Beautiful colours,' Marcy says. 'I wonder what it is.'

'It's a butterfly.'

'I know it's a butterfly. I meant what kind.'

'A blue one.'

'Idiot. Anyway, back to...'

'No.'

'You're not listening.'

'I am and I did and it's still no. Thank you for getting us all out of the shit but that's not the way for us,' I say while staring at the fragile creature resting on her finger. The wings beating softly, opening then closing. So beautiful too.

'Right. And your way is the right way yeah? Getting them all killed?'

'Oi!'

'Sorry, I didn't mean it so harshly...' she sighs and watches the insect, lifting it closer to her face. 'Will you at least think about it? Just say you'll think about it. Talk to Reggie and see what he thinks...we'll ask Paula and...'

'Okay just slow down. I'll think about it.'

'Thanks.'

'I thought about it.'

'Dick.'

'Yep.'

My eyes open to a room filled with the first rays of a new dawn that should give fresh hope, but it doesn't. The world is just as shit and broken as it was yesterday.

'Let me end it.'

'I literally just woke up,' I say gruffly, looking over to see Marcy lying on her front with her head turned towards me and her dark eyes staring intently.

'I can finish this,' she says.

I push up from the bed but she grabs my wrist to make me turn back and so we stare with eyes locked and I know, in the depths of my heart that she'd do it. She'd leave here today and bite, cut or even kiss the poor first fucker that crossed her path and send them off to build an army. I smile at the thought of it, at the image in my mind of an all-powerful Marcy and wonder if Darren had any idea what would happen when he bit her arse.

'What?' she asks, seeing me smile.

'Nothing,' I say gently and her smile spreads as she frowns.

'What's funny?' she asks. I drop down onto an elbow and reach out to trace a finger down her cheek. She closes her eyes at the contact, reaching up to hold my hand as I lean in to kiss her lips. So soft, so bloody soft and warm and even now it makes my heart beat harder and suddenly we're back on the plains outside the fort with the seasons changing around us and the world spinning.

'I can fix it,' she whispers, pushing her body against mine. 'Go to the fort and wait for me...'

I don't reply but savour the warmth of her, the press of her body and the soft kisses she gives while her hair falls over my face.

'Let me finish it...then we can go somewhere...find our own fort and make little Howie babies...'

'Yeah?'

'I want to grow old with you...' she says, moving deftly to straddle me with her legs either side while her breasts brush my lips with a new tactic that she has obviously thought about since last night with an attempt at seducing me into submission. Not that I'd fall for such a cheap trick.

I stiffen and grow hard, opening my lips to take the nipple of her right breast in my mouth as she reaches down to free me from my boxers and guide me inside her.

Yeah great willpower there, Howie.

'I can end this,' she says with a gentle gasp, moving forward and backward as the urge within me grows. Her body angles a touch, robbing the breast from my mouth as the other comes over, lowering to be kissed as the soft nipple stiffens between my lips.

We breathe harder, moving together while the bed makes quiet noises in reaction to the weight of our bodies. A shift of the frame, gentle and rhythmic. The rustle of the sheets beneath us. The hot air between our forms that we inhale deeply. Her eyes flutter open and closed, watching me through heavy lids and she lowers, bringing her mouth to my ear and my body tingles from the soft air blasting across. 'Let me end it.'

I shake my head. Just a fraction of motion but enough for her to detect and she moves a little bit faster, pushing a little bit harder to take me a little bit deeper.

'Let me end it,' she urges.

I shake my head again, unable to speak from the boob in my mouth.

'Tell me you love me,' she demands.

'I love you,' I say, somewhat muffled.

'Tell me you trust me.'

I nod instead of trying to talk.

'What I had before...I can use it...all their minds were in mine.'

I shake my head this time so she pushes harder with a sudden show of irritation. 'Let me,' she says, her voice a notch deeper, huskier, harder, her fingers curling just a little to give me the feel of nails.

'No.'

'Let me end it,' she says almost petulantly, thrusting down so hard it makes me gasp a bit.

'No,' I say, hoping she'll do the thrusting thing again.

She lowers to stare into my eyes, her body building to orgasm, shuddering then spasming harder. I grip the cheeks of her arse and run my fingers over the scar made by another man's mouth. She reaches back, pushing my hand into the bite, gasping at the sensation. 'Fuck me,' she urges, pushing my hand into the bite. 'I'll end it...I'll finish it...' the words spill out on a rush of air.

'You won't,' I gasp, opposing her wishes, refusing compliance or to be swayed by the feel of her body.

She thrusts down, taking me the deepest yet while forcing my hand to push into that bite.

We come together. Powerfully and deeply with a battle of energy that flows from one to the other until it ebbs away, easing as our bodies relax and we lie entwined and coupled, clasped together but the fleeting pleasure we gained soon slides away to leave the harshness of the new day ahead of us.

'They're my friends too,' she whispers softly. 'Don't kill them all...'

The day is as shit as I thought it would be, only shittier, and hot too. Damn hot.

'It's damn hot,' Paula says, dropping from the Saxon in the nearest town centre an hour or so after waking up to some messed up semi-aggressive morning sex while being cajoled into letting my zombie infected girlfriend go off to build a zombie army to take on the other zombie army. Is she my girlfriend? Are we a couple? What a surreal thought.

'You know where to go?' I tune into the now and look over to see Maddox talking to Anja at the side of her car, which is a Volvo, which is Swedish, but she's Danish and I drift off into another surreal moment.

'South on the motorway towards Portsmouth then off at the junction you said...' she repeats his directions while I look through the windscreen to the newborn baby asleep in the car seat and wonder what kind of life he has in front of him and decide it will be a shit one where something bad happens every half an hour, but I really hope not. Genuinely I hope he gets to live peacefully and never see or do the things we see and do.

'Don't stop moving, not for anything,' Maddox says. 'You've got the pistol?'

'Yes, yes it's here,' Anja says, patting the holster on her hip. 'I feel like a twat carrying it but...'

We needed Anja's car to get into town as there was no way we'd all fit in the Saxon but now she needs to leave so we can carry on being the heroic fighting unit we are. Apart from the fact we're all withdrawn and quiet and being overly polite to each other in a snappy, biting, snipey, big-family-row kind of way.

Charlie travelled in the horse box trailer thing behind the Saxon. The one she slept in all night and then woke up to do hard physical training while Mo and Dave beat each other up on their watch. She didn't join in with them, but just kept to herself doing pull ups, push ups and stuff on her own.

Clarence said Marcy gave him a small carrier bag of biscuit packets for his watch, which Jess nicked from the back of the Saxon and ran about with it in her mouth while Clarence chased after her, until Charlie came out, stopped Jess, took the bag of biscuits from her, gave them to Clarence then went back in to sleep without saying a word. I did ask Clarence why he had a bag of biscuits in the first place, but he said he couldn't tell me, at which point Paula blushed and walked off to shout at everyone.

We all say goodbye to Anja, hugging and shaking hands one at a time, apart from Dave who moves swiftly away in fear of another human being touching him, and Charlie who nods and lifts her hand while moving away on Jess.

Then she goes, driving off in the Volvo while we stand about in that weird strained silence. All of us looking battered to hell, apart from Dave and Mo, and Maddox, and Marcy and Paula of course, and Charlie. Okay, so a few of us look battered to hell. Including Reggie who has also stayed silent and pensive and is currently sitting in the front seat of the Saxon staring at his splinted hand that Roy fashioned to keep his broken fingers straight.

Awesome. Another great day in the new world. I look round expecting to see a horde charging us right now. Like a super big one armed with swords and ninja sticks.

'Ninja sticks?' Paula asks.

'Huh?' I blink at her, realising everyone is looking at me. 'What?'

'What's ninja sticks?' she asks.

'I thought that,' I say, peering at them suspiciously.

'You said it...' Paula says. 'You said...*a super big one armed with swords and ninja sticks...*'

'Didn't. I thought it. Stop reading my head thoughts. Right, what are we doing again?

'We're getting new kit, Howie,' she says.

'Okay. From here?' I ask, looking around the tiny town centre filled with the big brand name retailers that could afford the prime positions. It's the same wherever we go. The same shops. The same signs. The same everything. If the infection didn't come and kill us the boredom of the same shit in every town across the country would have.

'They are all the same aren't they,' Roy says as a few nod and grumble in agreement.

'Stop reading my head thoughts,' I snap, glaring at everyone. 'Weirdos...right. On with it...er...where can we get coffee from?'

'No power, boss,' Nick says. 'We used Roy's van for that.'

'Fuck's sake,' I grumble. 'Fine...everyone stay here. Dave, me and you will check that side...Clarence, you check that side. Charlie, range out a bit but not too far...and shout if you see a coffee shop that's like open and has power on...'

I head off with Dave towards the nearest building line, peering into stores and shops. Stepping through broken doors and windows to sniff the stale air and view the ground, looking for recent motion or foot traffic. We do one side, steady and thoroughly, crunching over broken glass, senses ramped and heightened. I reach for my radio, thinking to ask Mo if he's getting any weird vibes then remember we don't have any radios.

'All yours,' I say to Paula after meeting back in the middle with Clarence to the same awful weighted silence.

She sighs heavily, looking as weary and beaten as everyone else. It's still early morning but the energy has gone from us, like we've got nothing inside to give.

'Right, come on then,' she says without enthusiasm. 'Best get it done. Marcy? Give me a hand?'

'Mo, go with them,' Blowers says.

Cigarettes get passed round in that awful weighted silence and time passes until they come back with armfuls of clothes, bags, torches and batteries. The things we had before Blinky was killed, but it doesn't feel right now. Nothing feels right now. I wonder over to the Saxon, heaving up onto the driver's step to peer in at Reginald still staring at his broken hand.

'You alright?' I ask.

'No. No, I am not alright. My glasses are broken,' he says in a tone which is perhaps the saddest I have ever heard.

'Do you still need glasses?' I ask. 'Hasn't the infection thing fixed your eyes.'

He just looks at me like I suggested we share bodily fluids with a bottle of massage oil. 'I like my glasses.'

'Right. Okay...we'll get you some new glasses.'

'I am very happy at this news,' he says in a way that suggests he isn't very happy at all.

'Great. Should we doing anything today? I mean...like a plan or something? No? Right. Great chat. Er...catch you in a bit then.'

I drop down and walk back just as Charlie dismounts to take a bottle of water from a case on the ground.

'Could have passed you one up,' Cookey says.

'It's fine,' she says dully without looking at him. 'Hot,' she adds, as though needing to fill the awkward silence that follows.

'I could fan you?' Cookey asks, making a valiant attempt at a joke. 'I'm your fan...yay...'

She doesn't reply, she doesn't even look at him but walks off with an obvious act of placing distance between her and everyone else and the lad shuts down. Turning away to walk off and stare down the street.

'Okay, at least we've got some kit again,' Paula says, sorting through the now packed bags. 'Underwear and spare tops inside. Water, batteries, torches...same as we had before basically. Nick, you got a smoke please?'

Roy tuts, shaking his head and making a point of moving away again.

'What?' Paula snaps.

'You're smoking more and more,' he points out.

'So?'

'Weapons,' I say, cutting in before a row can develop. 'Axes, knives...'

'We'll need a DIY store,' Paula says tightly, taking the cigarette from Nick while giving Roy a look of daggers.

Silence again. Paula glaring at Roy. Roy shaking his head. Reginald on his own in the Saxon. Maddox off to one side, watching us all intently. Clarence rubbing his neck. The lads pensive. Mo and Dave standing side by side and I catch Marcy staring at me with a loaded expression. 'No,' I say bluntly.

'What?' Paula asks, looking from Marcy to me.

'Nothing,' I say.

'Mr Howie, can I take a few minutes to get changed and cleaned up?' Charlie asks.

'Yeah sure, want someone to go with you?'

'I will be fine, thank you,' she strides off towards the building line with her new bag as Paula gives Marcy a look.

'Well go on,' Paula prompts.

'Just leave it,' I say.

'Oh is it a thing between you two?' Paula asks.

'It concerns everyone,' Marcy says.

'What does?' Paula asks as the street fills with the sound of smashing glass. We spin round, hearts booming, hands lifting rifles and already striding out to see Charlie slamming the butt of her rifle into a plate glass window.

'Fuck me,' I mutter, my heart in my mouth.

She looks around, hearing my utterance. 'It was locked...'

'Need a hand?' Clarence asks.

'Done it,' she says, raking the glass out before stepping through.

'What were we saying?' Paula asks as everyone calms down from the fleeting panic.

Marcy looks at me without hostility, without anger. Open, sincere and honest. I do what everyone does and sigh heavily while reaching up to rub the stress from my temples that already feel grimy with sweat. 'Marcy said she can end it,' I say, snapping every head over.

'Right,' Paula says tightly before inhaling on her cigarette as the tension in our group ramps even higher. 'I see,' she adds in that Paula way of expressing extreme displeasure. 'And how exactly would you do that?'

'You know how,' Marcy says quietly, looking around at everyone. 'I can end it.'

'Genocide again?' Maddox asks.

'At least I'm asking this time,' she says quietly.

'That's something,' he snorts under his breath.

A crash makes us all jump again. 'SORRY!' Charlie shouts from inside the shop. 'I KNOCKED A...A THING OVER...'

'YOU WANT SOMEONE WITH YOU?' I call out, my heart once again going like the clappers.

'NO.'

'Listen, just go to the fort and wait for me,' Marcy says earnestly.

We start making noises to show our disagreement but she carries on. 'Please! Just listen...'

'Marcy,' Blowers says.

'No, Simon. I felt you die. We all did. Same with Blinky. I can't go through that again. None of us can...look what I did yesterday, I can end it. Go home. Go to Lilly. Let me...'

'No,' Nick says firmly, giving the first solid voice despite the offer of going back to see Lilly.

'Nick, see sense...I can infect and I can control what I infect. I can end it.'

'Jesus, Marcy. Have you heard yourself?'

'Fuck off, Maddox.'

'Innocent people,' Paula says, her voice flat and hard. 'Children...'

'Can you do it without turning kids?' Roy asks.

'Roy!' Paula snaps.

'I have the right to ask questions, Paula,' he says angrily.

'Yes,' Marcy says. 'I...I can try anyway...'

'Try?' Roy asks.

'We're not having this conversation,' Paula says.

'If the kids are with their families I can't just leave them,' Marcy says. 'Maybe I could get loads of the kids together with some adults and leave them somewhere or...'

'What the fuck?' Paula asks. 'A creche? Are you being serious? Hey excuse me, I need your mummy and daddy to help rid the world of evil by infecting them with a fucking disease but don't worry, stay here with this old...'

'Paula,' Marcy cuts in, an edge to her voice.

'That is fucking sick,' Paula says, inhaling again to blow the smoke away in a cloud that rolls up into the sky. 'Sick as fuck...sicker than fucking sick...'

'You wouldn't let Maddox go yesterday because you lost one...' Marcy snaps.

'Don't you bloody dare!'

'I will dare, Paula...they will all die if they keep going. Mo is a child...'

'I ain't a kid,' he snorts, too high-pitched and quickly clearing his throat to speak deeper. 'I ain't a kid,' he says again.

'Smooth, Mo,' Nick mutters.

'Point right there,' Marcy says. 'I love Mo like a little brother and by fuck am I letting him get killed when I've got the thing that can finish it.'

'You'd have to kill more to do it!' Paula shouts.

'BUT IT WON'T BE THEM DYING,' Marcy fires back, waving her hand at everyone. 'And Reggie told me to be what I was...'

'TO GET US OUT THE SHIT,' Paula shouts. 'Not to...to...'

'Go back to the fort. Protect Lilly and the children there. That's where you should be...'

A crunch of broken glass and we look over to Charlie stepping out of the shop now changed into clean clothes. I hear Marcy draw air with intent to keep going and move in swifter than Dave slicing a throat.

'Enough for now,' I say firmly like the leader of men that I am. And women of course. And a dog. And a horse.

'All I'm saying is that there's no need for you to suffer anymore,' Marcy continues, ignoring my valiant leadership skills.

'Orders, Mr Howie?' Charlie asks, reaching Jess and obviously wondering whether to mount back up or not and at least one person here recognises my authority.

'We need to find a DIY store or an electronics place for radios and drones and...'

'Can we discuss this first?' Marcy asks.

'Talking of drones,' I say, giving a little smile as I look round at the grim faces. 'Drone joke? No? Right, awesome...'

Paula squeezes her eyes closed and pinches the top of her nose, sighing long and heavy. 'Can we just load up and find another town?'

'In what?' I ask.

'In anything,' she snaps.

'Like what?' I ask again. 'There's nothing here...' I cast my arm out at the street that other than the Saxon is currently devoid of all vehicles.

'Just find something.'

'Okay...I shall cast my magic invisible fuckstick and make a van appear down that bloody road shall I?' I say while waving my magic invisible fuckstick at the end of the road, from which comes the screaming noises of an engine stuck in low gear accompanied with a squeal of tyres which all come a second before the bloody great big armoured cash in transit van goes stonking across the road into the shop front on the other side with a resounding crash. 'Wow,' I mumble, looking from the van to my magic invisible fuckstick.

'Ask for coffee,' Blowers whispers.

CHAPTER TWO

Day Twelve.

Maybe he is gay. Mind you he did have a good stare at her boobs last night when he thought she wasn't looking, but then it could have just been the sight of it that drew his eyes rather than a lustful look, so yes, maybe he is gay. No. That doesn't seem right. Men like Gregori are not gay.

She blinks at herself, realising she just thought the most un-PC thought ever by assuming a rugged cold-blooded serial killing psychopathic freak *must* be heterosexual. Who was that gay serial killer in America? Was he gay or did he just kill gay people? She stands upright, thinking hard while the water from the shower beats down on her chest.

'Casssceeeeeee?'

'What?' she calls out.

'Need a wee wee.'

'I'm behind the curtain.'

She hears the door open and peeks out to see the boy peeking in through the bathroom door. 'Morning sunshine,' she beams.

'Morning,' he grins back, all toothy with his blond hair all tussled and sleep creases on his face.

'Have a wee then,' she says, disappearing back behind the curtain to carry on shaving her legs while pondering why the hell Gregori didn't try and fuck her last night despite literally showing him her tits. The top she wore was so low cut and she bent over like a hundred times in front of him, lingering and pausing, looking up and waiting, and waiting, and bloody waiting.

'Sleep now,' he said after eating.

'Yeah?' she asked, winking at him with what was a very clear open suggestion for him to say *Hey Cassie, why don't you come to bed with me so we can fuck all night.* Except he didn't say that. He just went to bed leaving her wearing a stupidly low cut top on her own.

'Is this our house now?' the boy asks.

'Er...dunno,' she calls out. 'Why? Do you like it?'

'Do you like it?'

'I don't know. Do you like it?' she asks.

'I don't know, do you like it?' he replies, giggling at the sudden game developing.

'No,' she says bluntly. 'It's boring.'

'I don't know, do you like it?' he asks, thinking the game should still be going.

'Go and get some breakfast.'

'I don't know, do you want some breakfast?'

'Go on, sod off...let me shower in peace.'

'Okay, Casseeeee!'

She peeks out to see him running out of the door that he leaves wide open then looks over to the splashes of urine on the toilet seat that he didn't bother lifting up and the other splashes all over the floor. 'Door's still open,' she says under her breath, going back under the shower to rinse off before switching the shower off and stepping out while wrapping the towel around her body.

A noise from the hall and she turns to see Gregori emerging from his room with the bright sunlight streaming through the windows giving light to the scars on his face as he turns to fix those emotionless eyes on her standing in the bathroom. She swallows, holding the towel in place while he simply stares without expression.

'Shower's free,' she says.

He nods once.

'The boy's already up.'

He nods once again then walks off.

'Gregori?'

He stops and looks back.

'I er, I forgot to ask last night but has the boy been bitten by a dog?'

'Dog?'

'We were reading a story and he said he hates dogs and he wants you to make the dog's brains come out.'

'I know nothing about this dog,' he says while she shifts a bit to make the towel ride a bit lower.

'Oh okay,' she says lightly. 'Maybe he didn't like dogs before or something.'

Gregori looks at her, then down at his feet while she frantically wriggles but he catches sight of the motion in his peripheral vision and looks back as she pretends to scratch her side. 'Bit itchy...so no dogs then? That's so interesting...' she lifts the arm holding the towel pressed against her body enough for the material to slide down and away while she yelps and tries to catch it but misses and fumbles as she steps and tries ever so hard to cover her modesty before glancing up to see he has gone then stands upright with her hands on her hips. 'Definitely gay,' she grumbles, slamming the bathroom door closed.

'What this?' Gregori asks, picking the box up in the kitchen.

'Frosties,' the boy replies. Crunching away on the golden flakes as Gregori takes a few to eat then grimaces with distaste.

'Is sugar.'

The boy carries on eating, watching Gregori closely.

'Is too much,' Gregori says. 'Make sick, make fat...'

'I like Frosties. Tony the Tiger likes them...'

'Who Tony?'

'Tony!' the boy says as though the answer is obvious, reaching up to tap the picture of a cartoon tiger on the front of the box that Gregori studies closely.

'Tiger no eat sugar. Eat animals.'

'Like dogs?' the boy asks hopefully.

'Cassie say you no like dog.'

'It bit Jennifer.'

'Who Jennifer?'

'And Mohammed and Kate and Rachel and Oliver and...' a stream of names flows from the boy. English, Indian, Polish, men and women. He stops to chew, swallows and carries on while Gregori watches him with a scowl.

'The things? The dog bite things?'

'It bit Paco.'

'Paco? Who Paco?'

'The man from the movie.'

Gregori gives up and puts the box of cereal down to look round for healthier food. They need fruit and vegetables. Good nutritious food. Not sugary food filled with chemicals. He looks to the window and across the grounds to the treeline in the distance. 'You no bring things?' he asks.

'No, Gregoreeeee.'

'Boy, look at me. You bring things here?'

'I said no, Gregoreeee!' the boy sing songs the reply, spooning more dry cereal into his mouth.

'I check. I see and I kill,' Gregori says, pulling his pistol from his belt to show the boy who just shrugs and eats while swinging his legs as Cassie strides in and heads for the kettle, flicking the switch down and staring for a few seconds before cursing under her breath.

'No power,' Gregori says.

'Yes, thank you,' she says, stepping to the gas hob to light the pan of water. 'Go to bloody Ann Summers at this rate...'

'What this?' Gregori asks.

'What?' she asks.

'Who Ann? The dog bite Ann?'

'What dog?' she asks, turning to scowl at him while he scowls at her while the boy eats Frosties.

'The dog, it bite Mohammed and...'

'Oh that dog,' she says. 'No Ann Summers is a shop...doesn't matter.'

'What shop?'

'Just a shop. Coffee?'

'Coffee shop.'

'No, Gregori. Would you like a coffee?'

'I like coffee yes. I check now.'

'Check what?' she asks.

'Outside. For things. Make sure boy no bring here.'

'Right,' she says. 'Go do that.'

'I do that.'

'Go on then,' she says, shooing the hardened killer away while she rattles mugs to plonk down a little bit too loudly.

'We need the fruit,' he says, unlocking the back door. 'And vegetables.'

'Great,' she says, smiling at him with a lot of teeth showing.

'Sugar,' he says, aiming the gun at Tony the Tiger.

'Okay,' she says, showing more teeth.

'I check now.'

'Fine. Go check,' she says in a way that suggests he either goes and checks or drops dead. He goes out to check, scowling at her scowling at him while the boy eats Frosties.

She takes a handful of Frosties to eat and tussles the boy's head.

'Get fat,' he says with a giggle.

'Then we'll get fat together and be big fatty fat faces waddling after Gregori,' she says, mouthing more Frosties. The boy giggles more, his legs swinging harder as she puffs her cheeks out and holds her arms out from her side. 'I'm a fatty fat face,' she says deeply, waddling on the spot as the boy laughs harder. 'GREGORI SAID NO EAT SUGAR...' she affects an accent as she bellows, hearing the boy squeal with laughter from his chair at the table. 'I GREGORI...I EAT CLOUDS AND HEALTHY GRASS AND...' she stops on turning, freezing at the sight of him in the doorway, the pistol in his hand at his side. 'Coffee?' she asks lightly.

It is in the nature of the world that doing anything with a child takes an inordinate amount of time and the boy eats the Frosties slowly then drinks water slowly before going upstairs with Cassie to wash and dress slowly while Gregori prowls the ground floor then finally stands at the base of the stairs glaring up until they come down.

'Day is gone,' he says gruffly.

'It's still early,' she replies, waving a hand at him.

'We go.'

'Yes, we're going. Where's the sun cream?'

He shrugs, scowling.

'He needs sun cream, it's blazing hot.'

He shrugs, scowling. 'In car.'

'In the car? Okay, we can do it on the way.'

'We go.'

'Yes! We're going. Sorry, I didn't realise we're on a tight schedule.'

'Come we go,' the boy sing songs the words, skipping from the house across the parking area to the car.

'Come we go,' Cassie says deeply, affecting the accent as she puffs up to being fat again, trying to get through the door with Gregori standing stony-faced behind her. The boy bursts out laughing, clapping his hands in delight. 'I fat. I stuck,' Cassie rumbles.

'We go,' Gregori says from behind her.

'Just having fun, Gregori,' she says, walking on and turning to watch him lock the door then go round the car, visually checking the wheels

'What's that for?' she asks, pausing with her door open.

'Check,' he grunts.

'For what? Gregori? What are you checking for?'

He opens the back door, nodding at the boy to get in. 'Belt.'

'Yes, Gregori,' the boy skips round to clamber in, twisting to pull his belt over while Gregori watches to make sure he fastens it properly.

'Sheesh, hurry up,' Cassie says, wincing at the heat in the car as she sits in the passenger seat. 'Get the engine on it's bloody boiling in here.'

'Cassie said bloody.'

'Don't say that word you little snitchy pants,' she twists round to waggle a finger at him, pulling a face to make him laugh as Gregori gets in. 'So, handsome...where are you taking us?'

Gregori glances over, the scowl ever-present. Pistol into the central console, another one in the pocket of the door that he closes securely. Keys turned, check the warning lights, turn again, start the engine, listen for any noises that shouldn't be there while reminding himself the vehicle is a diesel estate with front-wheel drive.

'Okay,' Cassie says brightly. 'Great chat, mystery tour it is then.'

'Town,' he says gruffly. 'Belt.'

She tuts, pulling her belt across. 'There's no police now.'

'It make noise if no belt.'

'Oh, and there was me thinking you cared,' she says sweetly, giving him a big grin. 'I'm so going to make you laugh one day.'

He doesn't react but pulls away, driving gently from the parking area down the long drive towards the old country road that feeds to the main carriageway. Forested treeline in all directions stretching away for miles. A natural clearing in which the house sits. Tranquil and gorgeous but dull as dishwater.

'Have you ever laughed?' Cassie asks after a few minutes of near silence that carry on when he doesn't answer. 'I hate it when you do that.'

'What?' Gregori asks.

'Ignore me. Have you ever laughed?'

'I watch road.'

'There's no other cars. Have you ever laughed?' she tuts again and twists to look at the boy, 'have you ever seen him laugh?'

'No,' the boy shakes his head in the way of a child, rotating fully side to side. 'He cried at the park.'

'What?' she asks.

'I no do this.'

'He cried?' she asks, then twists to look at Gregori. 'You cried?'

'I no do this,.'

'At the park,' the boy calls out. 'He fell down.'

'You fell down?'

Gregori stiffens in the seat, tightening his hand on the steering wheel as he thinks back to pushing the boy on the swings while losing his mind as the things came out of the houses. He shot a few before lying down to let them take him. Except they didn't and when he sat up the boy was running around their legs while they watched as docile as ever.

'I can't imagine you crying.'

'I no cry.'

'Everyone cries. It's fine.'

'I no do this.'

'Okay okay. Take it easy.'

'No say I do when I not do this thing.'

'Okay, Gregori.' He snaps his head over, glaring hard. 'Watch the road,' she says, pointing forward.

'I no cry,' he mutters, turning to watch the road.

'Maybe you hurt your knee,' she says quietly, lightly.

'I no hurt knee!'

'Joking! It was a joke. Lighten up for fuck's sake...'

'No say...'

'Okay. Yes, Gregori. No swearing.'

Silence. Then a small voice from the back. 'Cassie said fuck.'

'Don't say that word,' she says.

'No say this word,' Gregori says at the same time.

Silence.

Cassie prods the radio knobs, turning dials and wishing modern cars still put CD players in their music systems. She hums softly, turning the hazard warning lights on for a few seconds to watch the switch blink with the tick tick noise until Gregori reaches over to switch it off.

She hums, turns a dial, plays with the air vent then turns the hazard warning lights back on, watching it glow on and off with that ticking noise until he reaches over to turn it off.

She checks her nails, opens the glovebox, mooches through the contents and turns the hazard warning lights on as Gregori slams on the brakes, making Cassie and the child lean into their seatbelts.

Silence.

Tick. Tick. Cassie sits back, shifting to get comfy. Tick. Tick. Gregori grips the steering wheel, his knuckles turning white. Tick. Tick. The boy stares at the button, then at Cassie, then at Gregori.

Gregori goes to speak but before the words come out she flashes a hand out to turn the hazard warning lights off before sitting and staring around at the countryside as though nothing happened. 'Are we going then?'

'You are child,' he pulls away, building the speed up on the wide road as they pass a road sign for whatever god-forsaken shitty northern town they'll end up in.

They reach the outskirts of whatever god-forsaken shitty northern town this is, and Cassie lifts her upper lip at the signs of death and carnage strewn about the streets as Gregori slows the car to gain watch and study the angles, junctions, doorways and windows. Scenting the air like a dog. His head cocked and his mouth open to listen. Every sense straining.

She winces at a mangled corpse covered in writhing maggots then up to the smear of blood on the wall above it. Another body a few metres away. Bloodied footprints and a wake of damage that speaks of the route the infected took as they charged through. More here and there. More death. More broken bodies. A woman in a plaid skirt with her left leg but a bloodied stump. Her mother had a skirt like that.

The thought sparks a flood of memories. Thoughts of her home and life. Her mother and father. Images in her mind of her house and friends. Pain rushes in, sudden, overwhelming and unseen by Gregori or the boy as they both study the world outside the car.

She grips the door handle, hardly breathing, her body tensing. Grief and loss hitting with the utter realisation that the world is over and in ruins. Broken windows. Broken buildings. Broken bodies. She thinks about what she did yesterday. She took life. She masturbated in the shower thinking of Gregori taking life. She is just as broken. Just as corrupt and tainted. She can't breathe. She can't see. She clamps her eyes closed while her head spins. She killed. She took life. She is a freak and the reaction to her own evil is stark and powerful. An insight of the beast within. A view of herself and what she sees is black and rotten until something inside reacts to her own introspection. Another voice that grows louder and rises up as a weird feeling comes over her, like the time she was injected with a sedative that spread through her body like a strange heat. It's like that now but coming from within to blossom and radiate out until but seconds later there is just a deep calmness that dilates her pupils and makes her sink into the seat with a low groan that goes by as unheard as the turmoil she felt but a minute before and when she looks out she does so with new eyes to see a world that isn't broken or ruined at all.

This is a new world. A brave new world and theirs for the taking. She locks eyes on the boy in the wing mirror and sees the flash of the thing within him that makes her heart skip a beat.

'Know what?' she asks, laughing sudden and bright. 'We, my lovelies, are going to have a nice day today...'

CHAPTER THREE

Day Twenty Three

Danny was exiled yesterday. It was his own fault.

'I'm sorry but he's got to go,' Keiron told the two dozen or so people taking refuge in the ruins of the old castle at the edge of their town. Danny knew Keiron wasn't sorry at all. Danny was a reminder of a life his mum had before she met Keiron.

The old castle wasn't that old either. It was built in the last century by a wealthy American who decided he wanted a castle on his land. Then the American died, and the castle fell into disrepair and ended up looking more of an *old castle* than real old castles.

It did, however, have a working drawbridge and a big moat full of deep water so when the end of days came the locals rushed across the drawbridge, plugged the gaps in the walls with scaffolding boards and took refuge.

They'd done well too and lasted without serious incident for twenty-two days, but Danny's behaviour was isolating him and in such a closely packed environment it stood out too much.

'He's too angry...too weird...' Keiron said while his mates stood flanking Danny, holding their bats and lengths of wood ready. Danny glanced over to his mother who just looked away while holding Danny's step-brother and step-sister to her skirts.

'Don't look at your mum,' Keiron snapped. 'You keep telling me you're a man now...'

'I am,' Danny muttered.

'Good. Then you can fuck off and be a super soldier then...'

Danny hated hiding. He'd been an army cadet and was just about to join the military when the world ended. He kept saying they should be out there fighting and taking back their town. He said his dad wouldn't hide like a coward. Then Keiron and a few of his mates pinned Danny down and threatened him with a hiding if he didn't pack it in.

Then on the dawn of the seventh day, Danny became increasingly agitated until he was pacing up and down clenching his fists without knowing why. If that wasn't bad enough he suddenly broke down and wept, then surged up with a wild look and ran for the drawbridge.

'I'LL FIGHT...I'LL FIGHT...' he screamed until Keiron and his mates dragged him back in and locked him in a tiny storeroom where they heard him muttering the Lord's prayer. They left him in there for two days.

It happened a few more times after that. Odd times when Danny would suddenly tense and become agitated, his eyes hardening and the veins in his forehead bulging out, but then Danny had always been an angry *difficult* child, so his mother just put it down to stress and didn't intervene when Keiron and his mates locked him away.

'You're a fucking coward,' Danny told Keiron as he was shoved in the storeroom.

'What did you call me?' Keiron demanded, pushing through his mates to grab Danny round the throat.

'Coward...you're a fucking coward...' Danny couldn't help it. The anger inside was too strong, the rage was too powerful.

Keiron punched him the belly. It was a hard punch too and Danny bent double, gasping for air. 'Little cunt,' Keiron told him.

'Coward,' Danny said, standing upright with a glint in his eye.

Keiron was big too. A builder with solid arms and shoulders, and a gut to match from nights spent in the pub and he'd always used that bigger size to keep Danny in check, threatening him constantly, hitting him often and the beating that followed only ended when Keiron got too out of breath to continue and leant against the wall while Danny stared up at him with that wild glint still in his eyes.

Then, on the eighteenth day, it came back stronger than ever and Danny once again tried to leave, and once again Keiron and his mates tried stopping him, except this time, Danny put Keiron on his arse. Not only did he put him on his arse, but he took him off his feet with a huge punch before Keiron went down on his arse, and Danny then proceeded to take on Keiron's mates, knocking them left, right and centre.

'STOP IT!' his mother screamed at him, rushing in front of him while all around him the men stood shocked and bloodied.

The beating that followed that was the worse one by far. They used sticks to do it as clearly fists and feet weren't enough for Danny. Keiron even made his mates hold Danny down and used his leather belt across Danny's back for a few minutes thinking he'd finally bring the boy to heel, but Danny started raging again so they scuttled out and locked the door.

Nobody questioned the fact a bunch of white men were whipping a young black man into submission. It didn't help that Keiron couldn't stand that Danny's dad was a big black man either. Danny's mum was white, but she had olive skin and dark hair, so Danny looked black, *you look proper black* Keiron used to tell him when they were alone. *You don't even look half-caste, just black, like from Africa...like a monkey.*

As Danny got older and transitioned from boy to man he finally started to understand why Keiron had so much hostility towards his dad. Danny's father was everything Keiron wasn't, handsome, strong, tall and broad and he looked tough in his army uniform too.

They were going to let him out on the twenty-first day and exile him then, but Danny became increasingly agitated throughout that day until he suddenly broke down in tears with a rush of pain inside, but without knowing why. Without reason or cause. Danny's mum thought he was showing remorse at first and suggested to Keiron that maybe Danny was finally seeing how bad he was. Keiron told her she was a stupid cow.

By the twenty-second day, Danny was calm enough to come out of the small storeroom and was made to stand in the centre of the courtyard inside the castle walls while Keiron told everyone that Danny had to go. Danny didn't argue. He didn't really say anything but looked around at the men holding weapons and eyeing him warily.

'I done my best by you, Danny. I really have,' Kieron said as though full of regret. 'Everyone here knows I tried with you, son...'

'I'm not your son,' Danny muttered.

'No you ain't, no son of mine would ever behave like you done... you got something wrong in your head. Don't matter now anyway. You gots to go.'

That was it and at the age of eighteen, Danny Arnold was exiled from the castle and forced to walk across the drawbridge.

No food. No water. No weapons. Just the clothes he was in. Jeans and a filthy torn blood-stained t-shirt. Old trainers on his feet that had holes in them because Keiron refused to buy him new shoes. *He's fucking off into the army soon, they'll give him new shoes.*

The castle was only a few miles from his town, so he headed there first, walking through the deserted streets until he saw the first dead body outside the supermarket. The face was all chewed up and it looked rotten, but he recognised the name-badge on the apron and knew it was old Mavis who was always up early to work the bakery section. He'd always liked Mavis. She was nice to him and said he would make a fine soldier. She used to give him sweets when he was a kid and pulled sad faces if she saw the bruises on Danny's face or arms.

Danny went home to his semi-detached house and his tiny room at the back. He took the box out from under his bed, opened the lid and spent an hour staring at photographs of his father, smiling to himself at the sight of the *big black man* that Keiron hated so much.

It was while staring at the photographs that Danny made the final decision. He already kind of knew what he was going to do the minute he crossed the drawbridge but seeing his father sealed it in his mind.

Soldiers don't hide. They fight back. Danny wasn't a proper soldier yet, but he had thrived in army cadets and the mindset was there. The ideology of it. The essence of what soldiers do. They defend, and attacking is a form of defending.

Danny took a knife from the kitchen and went out to pick a fight. To do what his father would have done.

Danny tried to drive Keiron's filthy work van, but he'd never had any driving lessons, *I ain't paying for him. He's going in the army soon anyway, they'll teach him* Keiron had said.

Danny ended up smashing it into the garden wall, then panicked for a second at what Keiron would say before remembering he never had to worry about what Keiron said ever again. So, he drove the van through the rest of the garden wall and then through lots of other garden walls and all in first gear with the engine screaming.

He only stopped when the engine went bang, and thick smoke poured out but it felt good. It felt really good, so he walked home, went into the big front bedroom, opened Keiron's wardrobe and pissed in it, chuckling to himself while thrusting his groin forward and swinging left to right.

One idea leads to another and a few minutes later he was in the kitchen leaving a present in Keiron's super-sized *Sports Direct* tea mug.

Revenge taken, and he set off to scout his town out, but it was deserted. He found another car and drove that, stalling and hopping with gears crunching and much swearing into the next town but that too was deserted. By nightfall he had broken the gearboxes in two cars, crashed another one and searched five towns but hadn't seen a single person or one of the things, so he camped out in a house and ate tinned food scavenged from kitchen cupboards before falling asleep on the sofa.

He woke at dawn to a pain in his ankle and the squelchy noises of an old man with bloody stumps for legs slobbering away and screamed out, first in fright, then in horror, then in pain and finally in outrage at being outmanoeuvred by a legless old man using his one remaining tooth on his leg. He tried shaking him off at first, but the old chap clung on so Danny sat up and rained punches into the old man's head, which had no effect other than helping stab that tooth in a bit more.

Danny then threw himself off the sofa to roll over the carpet with the legless old man still clinging on with much gnashing and slurping.

He grabbed his knife from on top of his bag, the bag that he had left right next to the sofa, so he could *bug out quickly should enemy movement be detected,* and stabbed the old man in the chest. Several times. In fact, Danny wondered how many times he would have to stab the frenzied old man before he actually died and then, in the heat of the moment, he gained enough clarity of mind to stick the blade in the old man's throat and finish it quickly.

He then sat back in shock and awe, and fright and horror, of course, to wonder what the hell had just happened. He knew, as everyone did that saw it all happen on the first night, that being bit meant you turned into one, but Danny didn't immediately think of that due to the revulsion of realising the old man's tooth was still stuck in his leg. A filthy great thing that Danny stared at in grossed out horror before yanking it out to chuck away.

It was only then that he realised he wasn't a zombie, so he waited in silence for another few minutes but still didn't turn into a zombie and it was at that point that he heard the sound of running feet followed a second later by the thud of someone throwing themselves at the front door, and concluded, being a diligent army cadet, that it was enemy movement and he really should bug out.

Then the front window imploded from the heavy body sailing head first through it that dropped with a snarling thud and tried to rise fast but got tangled in the drapes and crashed into the big flat screen television and tripped over the legless and now toothless old man's corpse while Danny ran for the back door, pausing just long enough to call himself a twat for not seeing the now blood-smeared dog flap.

He ran out into the garden and over the back fence into a street, looking first right and seeing nothing then left and seeing dozens of the things running past the junction at the end.

'Fuck,' he whispered and set off, knowing he couldn't hide because the ones in the house behind him were still coming through. He started running but that motion was seen by the infected pouring past the end of the street who twitched direction with a staggering fluidity to give chase.

They gained on him too and Danny quickly concluded, being a diligent army cadet, that they weren't slowing down or getting tired, which in turn led him to realise that if he didn't find a way out soon he would get chomped and bitten way worse than by a one-toothed legless old man.

He reached the town centre, bursting out from a small side street to see infected people all over the place. Both sides cut off and the big horde coming up behind him. A second to find a way out. A second and no more. A beat of a heart. A blink of an eye and a flash of blue dancing in front of his eyes that made him flinch, but that flash of blue stood out. The colour so vibrant and so different to everything else around it and in the sheer chaos of that second he gained focus on the butterfly flapping and dropping on the thermals as it flew off towards a nice big armoured cash-in-transit van ditched in the middle of the road with the back door wide open.

He ran for it, concluding that it was the only chance of survival. What happened after he got inside he had no plan for, but in such times of life and death situations, one can only factor for the next few seconds.

The last twenty metres and he gave a surge of power to his legs, gritting his teeth with a glance over his shoulder and a wince at just how close they were. Then he was there and leaping up to stop dead and reach back to heave the door closed as the first infected reached out and lost his fingers from the door slamming shut.

'Gross,' Danny gasped, seeing the filthy digits drop to the floor of the van that rocked and thudded as the things outside threw themselves at the sides and back.

Danny looked around, heaving for air, spotting a cupboard section with lots of pigeon holes and a desk with a pop-up monitor fitted in it and banknotes thick on the floor forming a carpet of money. Another door to the front and he spied through the safety glass to see the cabin was closed and secure before opening the hatch to clamber into the driver's seat and crying out at seeing the keys stuffed in the ignition while the infected threw themselves at the windscreen, doors and sides.

After several false, lurching, jolting starts he finally got it going in first gear and pulled away. He tried to change to second gear but pushed the stick into fourth and stalled the engine. The infected caught up and once more threw themselves at the windscreen and doors.

That happened six more times before he finally found second gear and took the van from that town, after crashing into several parked cars, taking a few posts down and going over a roundabout, into the country lanes leading to the next town. He still didn't have a plan other than getting away and re-grouping, and by re-grouping, he meant hiding for a bit until he could figure something out.

The problem was that Danny focussed so much on the wing mirror and keeping watch on the horde behind him that he didn't really pay attention when he reached the new town, and he didn't pay attention when he flew across the junction where a group of people were stood bickering and where a man with curly dark hair was waving his invisible magic fuckstick as Danny drove the van through the plate glass window of the travel agent's.

'What the fuck?' Nick says, watching with everyone else as a young black man runs out from the broken shop front to stop dead before glancing up the street at the big army vehicle and the people stood near it and double takes with an obvious show of surprise.

'Saxon,' Danny mutters. That's a Saxon. Then he spots the men and women holding rifles. British Army assault rifles. Combat clothes. Combat boots. The army. Must be. He sets off, running towards them then slowing to march smartly with his arms straight and his chin high, looking from Nick to Cookey then to Blowers.

'Officer?' he asks politely. They point at Howie who finally lowers his invisible magic fuckstick while wondering why everyone is pointing at him and why a young man with a bruised and swollen face dressed in filthy clothes and carrying a high gloss travel brochure is coming to attention in front of him.

'Cadet Arnold! Permission to draw a rifle,' Danny says smartly, staring over Howie's head to a point in the middle distance while saluting with the brochure still in his hands.

'Permission to draw a rifle, *Mr Howie, Sir*,' Dave says.

'Sorry sergeant! Permission to...'

'Dave, not sergeant.'

Danny blinks, glancing once at Dave. 'Permission to draw a rifle, Mr Howie, Sir!'

'Right,' Howie says. 'Um...what's he looking at?' he asks, turning to look behind again.

'What happened to his face? Paula asks. 'What happened to your face?' she asks Danny.

Danny glances at her in the same way he did to Dave. Snapping his eyes over to look then staring ahead again at a point over Howie's head.

'What's that?' Marcy asks, peering at the catalogue in Danny's hand.

'Er...' Danny stares at it, not realising it was in his hand.

'Can I see?' Marcy asks, taking it from him. 'Ta...'

'What's your name?' Clarence asks, cocking his head over to the side.

'Danny Arnold...Sir, I know how to use one.'

'One what?' Howie asks.

'Rifle, Sir. I am proficient in the SA80 assault rifle, Sir.'

'Right,' Howie says slowly, looking down at the lad's torn shoes and filthy clothes. Cuts and bruises on his arms. Blood on his ankle and left shoe that looks fresh. His face swollen and as bruised as the lads and not the type of injuries that come from contact with the infected. 'What happened to you, Danny?'

Danny falters, hesitating for a second, his lips twitching as though to speak but without sound given then clears his throat to stand taller. 'I er...I fell, Sir.'

'Sure,' Howie says. 'That happens a lot...' he adds as Danny finally notices the injuries on him and the others. 'Is it okay if our medic takes a look at you, Danny?'

'They're coming, Sir,' Danny says, stiffening his frame again.

'Who are?' Howie asks.

'The...the things...chasing me, Sir. Loads of them...I tried getting away but I can't drive and couldn't get from second gear and...'

'Okay,' Howie says, cutting in gently. 'Mo? You feeling anything?'

'Nothing, boss,' Mo says, shrugging.

'Nick, Where's Meredith?' Howie asks, looking around.

'Licking her arse,' Nick says.

'Where's Jess?'

'Licking Meredith's arse.'

Marcy tuts softly, flicking through the brochure. 'I'd love a holiday...'

'How many were chasing you?' Howie asks Danny.

'Er, not sure, Sir...at least a hundred...I can fire a rifle, Sir. I know how to...'

'Slow down,' Howie says. 'You're safe now...'

'Ah it's fucked innit,' Mo snaps, twitching his head. 'They's comin'...'

'Blowers, get a firing line on that junction he came from.'

'On it, boss'

'Maddox, you're in Blowers team, Clarence, you grab a GPMG ... we've got no hand weapons, remember that... Charlie, mount up but stay back and Nick, keep hold of your dog...we're not fighting them close quarters today. Roy, have a look at Danny here please...'

'I got bit!' Danny blurts, dancing back a step as he remembers his ankle. 'Don't come near me...'

'We've all been bloody bit, mate,' Blowers mutters as everyone walks off, not paying the least bit of attention.

'Can I keep this?' Marcy asks.

'Pardon?' Danny asks.

'The brochure, can I keep it? Mind you we can get another one when we've finished...'

'Er...yeah sure...'

'Aw that's sweet,' she smiles, giving him a wink. 'Let Roy have a look at you.'

'Marcy. Fall in,' Blowers calls.

'I'll stay with Danny,' Paula says. 'Okay, young man. I'm Paula. How old are you?'

'I'm er....' Danny mumbles, watching everyone moving off to form a line facing down the road as a woman on a horse trots past with a huge dog running with them. 'Eighteen...I'm eighteen, Ma'am.'

'Bless, good manners. You sit down on the back step...are you thirsty? You look hot, let me feel your forehead...'

'I got bit!' Danny says again, lunging away from her hand.

'I'm immune, it's fine, yeah you're very hot. He's very hot, Roy.'

'It's a hot day,' Roy grumbles, stopping in front of Danny. 'Where were you bit?'

Danny leans over as Clarence stretches past him to lift a general purpose machine gun from the back of the Saxon and spots the other weapons stacked inside. 'Is it just you?' he asks, looking from Paula to Roy to the rest behind them.

'Just us,' Paula says, pushing a bottle of Lucozade into his hand. 'Have a drink.

'There's loads,' Danny says in alarm. 'Like more than a hundred.'

'We'll be fine. Drink...Danny...' she calls his attention in her *Mo* voice, gently lifting his chin to make him look at her. 'Drink. Get some fluids in your body.'

He nods and lifts the bottle, glugging the sweet contents while Roy grabs and lifts his leg.

'Ankle was it? Ah, I can see...broken the skin...definitely an infected was it?'

Danny covers his mouth from the belch, nodding quickly. 'Yes, Sir...didn't have legs and his eyes...'

'What about his eyes?' Roy asks.

'You know what he means, Roy,' Paula says. 'They were red?'

'Red,' Danny says. 'He weren't human...I stabbed him loads...in the chest. Why haven't I turned into...'

'HERE THEY COME!' A shout from the line. Paula and Roy

turn to watch as Danny stands up, hearing the drum of feet in the otherwise silent air. A sickening, fear-inducing sound that makes his heart beat faster. A rush inside. An intense worry.

The first one runs into view. A lean woman with long red hair sprinting fluidly who looks up the street and shows reaction at seeing the group. A visible change. A cocking of her head and she slows from the sprint to a run to a jog to a walk and finally stops to simply stare. Her chest heaving. Her arms at her sides.

The rest come behind her. Running with fury in their faces. Desperate for the bite to take the host. Wild and crazed and running hard but they too slow as though a message runs through them, as though a ripple effect of a thing within them bringing them down from a sprint to a jog to a walk.

'What the...' Paula whispers, moving out a step with Roy.

They look so human. So very human. Heads upright. Arms at their sides. Motion in their forms coming from breathing hard from running so far. The female in front starts walking up the street. Walking like a person would walk. Not ungainly. Not jolting or twitching. Normal and the horde behind do the same. Those still running into the street coming to a gradual stop to join the ones in front walking slowly.

'Reggie...get out here,' Howie shouts.

'Reggie,' Paula relays the call as Danny turns to see a small man in the front of the vehicle twisting round. His face as battered and bruised as everyone else. He clambers down stiffly, limping from the front past Danny, his eyes fixed only on the horde.

'Oh my,' Reginald whispers. 'Indeed...'

Howie stands in the middle of the group, his rifle lowered, his dark eyes staring from the woman with the red hair to the others behind her walking slowly up the street. She stops to stand still, seemingly watching Howie while her horde come to a slow stop behind her. All of them with heads up. All of them so human. Even the ones with awful injuries stand normally. A man with one arm gone from the shoulder. The gristle, meat and bone showing visible. Faces bitten. Necks bitten. Bite marks everywhere. Blood on their clothes. Some naked and unashamed.

Howie blinks, glancing left to Reggie now at his side then faces forward again and as the horde all come to a stop so the street falls into a silence broken only by the sounds of them breathing from running and the low, constant, deep throaty growl coming from Meredith who walks low and poised to stand in front of the pack leader. Showing the enemy her teeth. Her head lowered. Her eyes fixed. Hackles up.

Jess snorts, slamming a front hoof into the road surface. The jostle of reins and buckles. Charlie holding her steady.

That silence stretches on with two sides staring at each other. Reginald swallows, his broken hand now forgotten on seeing the change in the other side. The other player is making a move, but he doesn't know what it is. His own senses dulled from the beating he took. His own mind taken out of the game and a feeling inside that the other player kept going without them.

'Your kind are cruel...'

'Holy shit it spoke,' Cookey mutters in shock at the infected woman with the long red hair calling out in a clear voice.

'We're infected, and we can speak bellend,' Blowers whispers.

'Cruel,' she says again, lifting her chin as she speaks with a gesture so human it renders them all silent. 'We are not,' she adds. 'We are not cruel...' her voice drops in tone as she finishes, almost as though she is expressing shame at the people in front of her.

Silence again. Heavy and charged. Fingers on triggers.

'We,' the woman calls out. 'Did not kill Blinky...'

A shot fired from an SA80 assault rifle that spins through the air at nine hundred and forty metres a second and the woman flies back off her feet with the back of her head exploding in a cloud of pink mist.

'You don't say her name,' Howie whispers, looking down the sights.

A pulse. A thing inside. Danny stiffens, his lips curling back at the feeling he had before. The same rage but so much stronger now. Focussed and concentrated.

'Your kind killed Blinky...' Another shot fired and the male infected speaking out flies back.

'We didn't kill her...'

Another shot.

'Your kind killed her...'

Another shot.

'Your kind are cruel...'

Two shots taken together. Howie and Clarence firing at the same time.

'We are not cruel...'

More shots taken. Blowers and Cookey lifting rifles to join in.

'You will kill them all, Howie...'

Everyone shoots. Everyone fires and the street fills with gunfire as scores of infected standing passive and inert fly back from the rounds slamming through them.

Howie lifts a hand. The guns fall silent. Chests heaving. Ears ringing. The rage right there and if he had an axe Howie would charge. He barely holds himself back now from rushing in to kill with his hands, but his team are sore and broken from the beating they took, the beating that came from their own side and the words sink in. The truth of them stinging harsh and bitter.

'Your soldiers are cruel...' another voice calls out and the shot comes from behind that makes Dave spin with his own weapon aimed at Danny holding Roy's rifle left propped against the Saxon braced in his shoulder.

'My father was a soldier,' Danny shouts. His voice so deep yet so young and cracking with emotion. 'My father saved his unit...'

'PUT THAT RIFLE DOWN,' Dave roars.

'Jesus,' Paula says, moving fast. 'Danny, give me that...'

'MY FATHER WAS A SOLDIER,' Danny shouts.

'Give me the bloody gun, Danny...now!'

He complies at her tone, lowering the weapon to make safe before handing it over, his eyes hard.

'Your kind are...'

'Oh fuck off,' Howie shouts, opening fire as the street once again fills with the roar of gunfire and it takes mere seconds for the slaughter to be over. The ease of pulling a trigger to end scores of lives with bullets going through hearts, lungs and into brains. Bones shattering. Blood spraying and just another pile of what was once human form now dead and broken on the ground.

There is no order given to ceasefire. None is needed and as the last one falls so the rifles and the heavier thud of the GPMG fall silent and that mood they had before, the awful, crushing, soul-destroying emotional state grows only worse for the words said.

'My fault,' Roy says into the charged quiet.

'Fucking prick,' Blowers snaps. 'Do not leave a loaded rifle in...'

'Do not call me a fucking prick,' Roy says back.

'We could have been shot from the rear...' Blowers shouts. 'KEEP HOLD OF YOUR WEAPON.'

'I wouldn't shoot you,' Danny says. 'I'm a cadet...I was joining the...'

'You ever touch a weapon without my permission again and I will fucking hurt you,' Blowers snaps, striding at Danny. 'DO YOU UNDERSTAND? Soldiers have discipline. They follow orders. They don't grab guns and fire without being told...'

'I'm sorry...'

'SHUT UP,' Blowers roars from a foot away, his haggard beaten face twisted with anger.

Danny nods once, lowering his head as they all reel from the rage inside. The rage that isn't vented for the lack of a fight given. A simmering thing that makes lips pursed and brows drop.

'We'll give you directions to the fort,' Blowers says. 'Then you can fuck off...'

'Whoa hang on,' Paula says.

'What fort?' Danny asks, looking from Paula to Blowers then beyond to Howie. 'What does that mean?'

'It means you're going,' Blowers says.

'Going? I'm not going...I want to fight...I'm a cadet and...I was joining the army...'

'We're not recruiting,' Blowers snaps, cutting him off.

'Okay, Simon. Take a minute please,' Paula says.

'I said we're not recruiting...'

'Stand down, Blowers,' Paula says.

'We'll get you transport then you can go,' Blowers tells Danny.

'MISS PAULA GAVE AN ORDER, CORPORAL.'

Blowers stiffens to attention, standing upright. 'Yes, Dave.'

'Stand down. Check weapons. Ensure your team is hydrated.'

'Yes, Dave...my team with me...' he moves off towards the Saxon, not looking at Danny.

'We can't take someone else into this shit,' Nick says to Paula, walking behind Blowers with Cookey. 'Ain't fair...'

'Mr Hewitt, do we have an issue?'

'No, Dave. Sorry, Dave.'

Howie glances over, watching Blowers lead his group away while Danny stands with his head down next to Paula. He could interrupt and say something, but those issues are best dealt with by Paula, and besides, Dave has got it under control. Instead, he looks over the slaughtered infected. 'Well that was fun,' he says darkly.

'Indeed,' Reginald says.

'They didn't attack,' Clarence says.

'Oh, but they did,' Reginald replies. 'They most certainly did, and I rather fear that form of attack will have a far greater effect than a mere sordid scrap.'

'New tactic,' Clarence asks. 'Like psychological warfare.'

'Unfortunately, that is exactly what it is, and I should imagine now they have started they will only do it more.'

'We're already fractured,' Clarence says, looking at Howie. 'Few more comments like that and we'll be suicidal...' he trails off to look round, finally resting his eyes on Danny. 'What about him?'

'Maybe Blowers is right,' Howie says. 'Can't take another kid into this shit.'

'Alas but this is a war,' Reginald says thoughtfully, looking at Marcy for a long second. 'And right now I think we need all the help we can get.'

CHAPTER FOUR

Day Twelve.

They hunker down in the aisle of the supermarket as she presses her finger to her lips, urging the child to be quiet as the footsteps come closer. They can't make a sound. The consequences will be dire, catastrophic even, but now they are trapped and cannot move for fear of giving away their position.

The woman bites her lip, her eyes wide. She can hear her own heart beating and still those footsteps come closer. The heavy tread of a man hunting them. A bad man. An awful man. A most terrible killer with bulging eyes and pock-marked skin. A serial killer that stops at the end of the aisle to stare down at them crouched at the base of the shelf with an open bag of marshmallows held between them.

'Bugger,' she says as the boy giggles and carries on eating. 'Haff a smarshmallow,' she says, throwing a pink blob at Gregori who catches it deftly. 'Shreely nice,' she nods as Gregori sniffs the squidgy thing.

'Is sugar,' he says.

'Shnice shugar,' she says, chewing with a look of heavenly delight. 'Just try it,' she urges after swallowing. He flicks the thing away, disdainful and almost pompous in his manner. 'More for us,' she grabs another packet from the shelf, locking eyes on Gregori as she pinches the top to pull the seam apart as though daring him to stop her.

He shrugs, 'get fat,' he walks on pushing his trolley across the dusty ground. 'Fatter,' he mutters, going out of sight.

'Oi! I'm not fat,' she yells with a mouthful of marshmallow, leading the boy out of the aisle to follow Gregori. 'My god what an awful dreary place,' she stops to frown, looking down at the boy. 'I sounded just like my mother then,' she points at him, her eyes twinkling when he grins and laughs. 'Which is never a good thing as my mother was a hag...'

'What's a hag, Casseeee?'

'Hmmm, like a witch. But not a good witch, like an old woman that only ever moans about everything...'

Gregori falters mid-step, turning to look back before walking on.

'I am not a hag, Gregori.'

'I no say this.'

'I don't moan about everything,' she affects a reaction of deep insult and walks on while casting overly dramatic mean looks to Gregori that just makes the boy laugh again. 'Cheek of it,' she mumbles.

'Cheek of it,' the boy parrots.

'Well said. The cheek of it,' she says again.

'Dumbass motherfuckers,' the boy says, making Cassie and Gregori both stop.

'What did you just say?' she asks.

'Dumbass motherfuckers.'

'Okay, that's a bad word,' Cassie says, wondering what awful life he had before this that led him to know such terrible things. His mother was clearly a cunt. Not that Cassie would say that. She plucks the bag of marshmallows from his hands with a stern expression. 'Good boys who don't say bad things eat marshmallows.'

'Aw but...'

'No. You can't say rude things. Where did he learn those words?' she asks Gregori.

'I not know this.'

'Shocking really,' she says.

'Marcy's going to the fort.'

'Okay stop. Who is Marcy? Did she tell you the bad words?'

'He say this name before,' Gregori says.

'Bitten on the bum,' Cassie says, clicking her fingers at Gregori as she remembers. 'Marcy was bitten on the bum.'

'Bitten on the bum,' the boy says, staring at his bag of marshmallows in Cassie's hands.

'You,' she says. 'Are a very strange little boy. What are you?'

'Dumbass motherfucker.'

'Right. Stop saying those that.'

'Randall said it,' the boy blurts.

'No. Listen to me...'

'But, Casseee, Randall in the prison with...' innocence and honesty pour from his expression. His blue eyes so wide and open. She scowls, thinking to be cross, thinking to chastise but it's so hard to be angry at him for longer than a few seconds.

She holds a finger up to keep his attention, signalling this is not the time for him to speak. He casts a look at Gregori who stares on as impassive as ever, his senses tuned to the world around them while he waits.

'Who is Randall?' she asks. 'And who is Marcy?'

'Marcy's going to the fort.'

'Marcy was the one bitten on the bum, is that right? Who bit Marcy on the bum? Was it Randall?'

'Darren.'

'Darren bit Marcy.'

The boy nods.

'Who bit Darren? Was that Randall?'

The boy shakes his head. 'Darren wasn't bited.'

'Bitten. Darren wasn't bitten.'

'Bitten.'

'Good boy. How did Darren get...it,' she flaps her hands, unsure of what to say.

The boy points to his mouth, holding his finger on his bottom lip.

'In his mouth? Okay, so Darren got something in his mouth then Darren bit Marcy on the bum? Yes? And now Randall is in prison. No?'

'He got out.'

'Oh he got out,' she says. 'With Marcy? No? Great. This is all very clear. Is this clear?' she asks Gregori.

'Is not clear.'

It's not clear,' she tells the boy then kisses his forehead simply because he's so scrummy. 'You're scrummy, you know that,' she says. 'Even if you are nuts.'

'Nuts,' he says, giggling.

'Is the fort near here?'

The boy doesn't answer and his expression suggests the question is beyond him and the things he knows are not his but belonging to something else, the thing inside him, the aged thing that she keeps seeing but that isn't there right now. 'It's fine,' she says warmly, smiling at him. 'It's all fine. Go and run about.'

She stands slowly, watching as the boy runs off down an aisle. 'Was he bitten?' she asks Gregori. 'Did blood go in his mouth? In his eyes?'

Gregori thinks back to the boy stabbing the things attacking his mother, the close proximity and the microscopic fluids no doubt flying about in the air. Sweat, saliva, blood, even tears. 'I not see but...he use knife when his mother she bit.'

'He stabbed his mum?'

'Thing bite mother. Boy stab thing.'

'Oh, I see. Bloody hell, where did he get the knife from?'

He shrugs, 'I take him then. His eyes, they not the red.'

She goes to speak then spots the scratches on her arms made by the boy when she restrained him in the room as Gregori slaughtered the infected in the garden below. A feeling inside at the thought of it. An anger at Gregori that flashes up. 'Shouldn't have done that.'

'What?'

'Killed them,' she snaps. 'They weren't hurting you.'

'Who? Who I kill?'

'At that house. Why did you kill them?'

'What house? The men? They hurt you yes?'

'What? No! Not those...' another rush inside at the memory of Gregori killing the men she pulled to the floor while her breasts were exposed, at the heat of it, the frenzy of it and she smiles warmly, flitting from one mood to the other, 'it's cool.'

'You crazy woman,' Gregori tells her.

'All women are crazy my darling.'

'No. You have the problem. In here,' he taps the side of his head, walking after her while she turns to walk backwards, still smiling.

'Are you calling me mental?'

'Have problem. Need doctor, head doctor.'

'Says the serial killer...where's he gone? BOY? WHERE ARE YOU?' she listens for a second then tuts with a roll of her eyes. 'I'll find him.'

She sets off down the aisle he ran through, following the footprints made in the dust on the floor. To the end and left then on past the ends of the aisles. 'Where are you, you little monkey,' she calls out, hearing a giggle and the sound of running feet. She spots the tracks disappearing through a set of double doors that obviously lead into the rear storage area and runs fast with sudden fright at the thought of the boy going somewhere unsafe. 'Boy! Come back...'

She pushes through into an instant change of environment. Dark and gloomy. Shadows everywhere. Shapes of large wheeled cages filled with boxes of goods made ready to go out onto the shop floor when the end of days came. Smells hit her nose. The stench of unwashed bodies. Of decaying matter but those scents were prevalent in the supermarket too from the meat left to rot in the freezers and chiller cabinets. She goes to turn, to push the door open to call Gregori in fear of going further when she hears the giggle coming from nearby.

'Where are you?' she snaps, taking another step into the storage room. 'Boy! Where are you?' she wishes he had a name to call, a proper name and in that surreal moment she starts thinking of names when she hears him giggle again and spins this way and that, trying to see him. 'This is just creepy now...'

'Up here, Casseeeee.'

She snaps her head up to a wide shelf seven feet off the ground and the boy perched on the edge with his legs dangling down, laughing at her.

'How the...' she goes closer, following the line of the shelf to see it running the length of the room with no ladders or steps going up to it. Nothing to climb on either. 'How did you get up there?'

The boy smiles with his face half hidden in the shadows and lifts a hand to point. Cassie turns, frowning in confusion then stepping back into a box on sight of the tall man standing silently between two of the large wheeled cages. 'Jesus...who are you?'

'Daudi,' the boy says, stretching his hands out as the tall man moves out from between the cages to reach up for the boy.

'Don't touch him,' Cassie hisses, rushing forward but the man grabs the boy round the waist and lifts him carefully down, bending his upper body into the light for Cassie to flinch at the sight of his red eyes and his right ear bitten away. She snatches the boy from his hands, back-stepping while thinking to shout for Gregori as another shuffle comes from further in the room. A woman. Her arms limp at her sides. Her head cocked over. Her long brown hair hanging greasy and matted. Blood on her chin and down the front of her supermarket uniform. Another one behind her. More of them shuffling towards Cassie and the boy while Daudi simply watches on, inert and without threat or malice.

'BOY!' Gregori's voice. 'CASSIE?'

'WE'RE FINE,' she shouts, her heart thundering in her chest.

'I FIND VEGETABLES IN THE CAN.'

'GREAT!' she shouts back, staring as more come quietly into view.

'CARROTS IN THE CAN.'

'OKAY,' she swallows the fear, the shock and holds the boy in her arms who watches on with interest.

'GREEN THINGS IN THE CAN TOO.'

'OKAY, GREGORI,' she shouts. 'Do you know them?' she whispers to the boy who nods once. She leans back to look down into his face, seeing that look is back in his eyes, the thing that isn't him, or that is within him.

'I NOT KNOW WHAT GREEN THINGS ARE.'

'What do they want with you?'

The boy doesn't reply but watches as more shuffle into the muted and gloomy light. Snatches of red eyes seen in the rays of illumination. Awful wounds and terrible injuries.

'IS SMALL. SMALL GREEN THINGS IN THE CAN.'

Cassie blinks, frowning for a second. 'PEAS, THEY'RE PEAS.'

'YES. IT SAY THIS WORD. PEAS YES.'

She looks to Daudi standing so close. Seeing his features. His eyes so weirdly expressive but like a puppy, like a dumb creature that only wants love and she reaches out, not knowing why but only wanting to touch him, like she has never touched a person before but knowing this thing is not a person. Her fingers brush his chest, but he shows no reaction, he doesn't lunge to bite or hurt.

'OTHER SMALL GREEN THINGS IN THE CAN...THEY BROKE...'

'Broke?' she mutters, thinking for a second. 'MUSHY PEAS... THEY'RE DISGUSTING.'

'I TRY THESE MUSHKY PEAS.'

'SERIOUSLY, THEY'RE DISGUSTING.'

'I TRY YES. I TRY MUSKA PEAS.'

She prods Daudi in the sternum, lifting an eyebrow when he still doesn't try and eat her. 'WE'RE NOT EATING MUSHY PEAS, GREGORI.'

'I FIND THE OPEN THING. I TRY NOW.'

Daudi looks down at her fingertips prodding his chest as the boy giggles softly.

'IS OPEN,' Gregori shouts.

'He's eating mushy peas,' Cassie tells the boy. 'He'll turn northern...say bye,' she says, moving back to the doors.

'Bye bye,' the boy says, waving at Daudi then the others standing in the gloom.

'Bye,' Cassie says, pausing by the doors.

'I LIKE THESE MUSKA PEAS.'

'Don't let Gregori see you,' she whispers. 'Stay here.'

'That one,' she says again, tapping the window.

'We have one,' Gregori says, holding the can of mushy peas in one hand while pushing the white plastic spoon in to load up with a glimmer of excitement in his eyes.

'Jesus,' she says, watching him. 'How can you eat that?'

'Is nice,' he says eagerly with the most human gesture she has seen so far.

'Don't eat anymore. Seriously, you've had three cans, you'll be sick...right anyway, get that one.'

Gregori mouths the mushy peas, chewing happily while looking through the huge plate glass window. 'We have the car.'

'No, we have *a* car which is a crappy old thing...I want that car...' she says again. 'Don't we?' she asks, looking down for the boy then over to see him pulling his shorts down by the back of the Volvo. 'No wee wee in car,' she says.

'No wee wee in car,' Gregori snaps, spinning round to see the boy pissing over the back wheel.

'It's a Range Rover,' Cassie says, tapping the glass. 'Like the best Range Rover you can get...just shoot the glass out so we can get in... don't scowl at me...look I was held prisoner and tortured and...and awful things and I am very upset at all the bad things so let me have a Range Rover. I'll make you a nice dinner of pie and mushy peas.'

'Pie?'

'Yes. Chicken and gravy pie...shoot the window and I will cook your dinner.'

'You cook?'

'Naked.'

'What?'

'Nothing. Just shoot the window.'

Gregori sighs, checks the boy, pulls his gun and waggles it at Cassie, motioning for her to move away.

'Don't shoot the Range Rover,' she says.

'I no shoot Ranger Rover,' he says.

'Range Rover, not Ranger Rover.'

He stiffens, looking at her. 'You make pie.'

'Yes! Shoot the bloody window or I'll get the other gun and do it myself.'

He shoots the window.

'It didn't work,' Cassie says, staring at the intact window.

'Is safety glass,' Gregori says, smiling to himself while taking another mouthful of mushy peas. 'It no break by the gun.'

'Boy, cover your ears...you're a twat sometimes,' she says, earning the first-ever chuckle from the Albanian.

'Drive car through, it only way to break,' he says. 'I do this. Hold mushky peas. No eat mushky peas...'

'Trust me I won't,' she says, grimacing at the can.

'See,' she says half an hour later, sitting in the front passenger seat of the gleaming black Range Rover. She holds her hands out, flexing her fingers in a show of pleasure. 'Oh no...not a chance.'

'What?' he says, halfway into the driver's door.

'You're not bringing mushy peas in my new car. No eating anything in the new car.'

'Can I eat marshmallows?' the boy asks from the back.

'What! No! They're worse than mushy peas. Give me that packet. Are you getting in, Gregori?'

'I finish mushky peas.'

'You've got a whole crate of them in the boot. Just leave them...are your hands clean? Show me...show me...right yes, that's fine. Okay, look isn't it nice?' she beams when he finally gets in.

'Is okay,' he says, turning the ignition on.

'It's more than okay...' she says, pressing the switch to wind her tinted window down. 'Got air con, satnav...Bluetooth...ooh, Bluetooth! Ah damn, I don't have my phone. I had good tunes on that too. We need to find a dead body with an unlocked phone...or we need to find a new phone then a computer with iTunes so we can download some music. Actually, go back into town.'

'What?'

'Go back into town. That supermarket had an electrical section. We can find something to play music on this.'

Gregori looks at her, feeling the very first bite of frustration that nearly all adult men face at the prospect of *going back* into the town for more shopping. 'We do other day? Boy need rest yes. He sleep now.'

'I'm not tired, Gregoreee.'

Back to town. The Range Rover gliding serenely through the apocalyptic streets with a glum Gregori begrudgingly admitting to himself that the car is very good while also thinking of eating pie and mushy peas and wondering what Cassie meant when she said naked.

They park outside the doors and go back into the supermarket to the back where Cassie spends the next fourteen years perusing the phones and devices with Bluetooth while the boy plays in the toy section while Gregori leans against things and sighs and grumbles and rolls his eyes.

'It'll take longer the more you grumble,' she says with a sweet smile. 'I think I have a plan.'

'Good. We go now?'

'Go into the music aisle and grab one of each music CD...then we can download them onto one of those laptops then put them into a file and transfer onto this Android phone then Bluetooth it to the car stereo....'

He stares at her in mild surprise of a well thought out idea that makes complete sense.

'That caught you out didn't it,' she says with a grin. 'Not just a pretty face, Gregori...'

Gregori drives the car, enjoying the feel of it, the way it moves. The response of the engine and the incredibly high standard of engineering and in the silence of the drive, with the gentle thrum of the wheels on the road and the engine rumbling ahead of them, he thinks of mushy peas and everything that has happened and wonders why he couldn't kill the boy, and also wonders if he would have the same reaction if he tried to kill Cassie.

He glances at her and watches her blink slowly as though drowsy in the hot afternoon air. She yawns, covering her mouth while making a little yelping noise that brings moisture to her eyes.

He tells himself he is tolerating her. That her presence, in his and the boy's life, gives purpose to aid the boy's welfare. He tells himself that is the only thing he cares about. That he spent a life taking life. Killing. Hurting. Doing the very worst things and now, while the world is falling, he will repent and make sure the boy can be a child.

That's what he tells himself, then he wonders why he tolerated being dragged from the supermarket to every single other shop in that town. Opening doors with either skill or force so she could fill bags full of new shiny things. He wonders why he also tolerated her holding clothes against his body checking for size and colour while talking non-stop. She even put a baseball cap on his head then said he looked ridiculous and to take it off, and he didn't shoot her.

Maybe he should have shot her? Maybe he should shoot her now but then he'd get blood in the new car and she'd nag, and he wouldn't be able to eat pie and mushky peas tonight, so maybe he will tolerate her a little bit more, because it suits his purpose, which is to give the boy a good life. That purpose. Just that one and nothing to do with the fact that somehow, despite everything single thing she does being irritating, there is something about her.

He looks in the rear-view mirror to the boy sitting in the middle of the back seat reading a brightly coloured book. The boy is not hungry or thirsty, he isn't overtired either or sweating. Nor is he sticking blades in the bodies of the things or asking Gregori to make the brains come out.

'Ooh, slow down, slow down,' Cassie says, extending her arm an inch in front of her nose pointing to the side. 'Did you see that sign? There's another one...ooh, look.'

Hillside Luxury Boutique Hotel and Spa.

'We need a luxury boutique hotel and spa,' she says earnestly while nodding earnestly.

'We no need this.'

'We do! We so need this...come on, let's just have a look...why live in a house when we can live in a luxury boutique hotel and spa?'

An entrance ahead on the right. He slows the car as the next sign-board comes into view and spots the thick chains stretching across the driveway leading to the building in the distance. A handwritten poster nailed to a post.

No more survivors. We're full: You will be shot
Leave now

'Oh,' she says sadly. 'What a shame...I really wanted a boutique hotel and spa...' she looks at Gregori, pulling a sad face.

'Is no safe,' he says. 'Have guns.'

She shrugs gently, pouting a little while dropping her hand to the central console to lightly finger the butt of the pistol resting there. 'You've got guns too...'

'We no go this place,' he says firmly, holding her eye contact with that awful, terrible glare that makes her feel funny inside.

'Okay,' she says lightly. 'You're right, let's go home.'

He narrows his eyes, tilting his head.

'What? Don't scowl at me. It was just an idea...come on let's go home.'

He drives on, unsure of what just happened. Nothing just

happened but something just happened. It's all very confusing. People are confusing.

He checks the house before they go in. Listening, sniffing the air, checking for signs of movement then walking back and forth from the car to the house. *Those in the lounge...not them, they go in the kitchen... put the bags of clothes in the hall.* In and out. More bags and the day wears on with afternoon giving way to evening and when he goes to his room he finds his bed covered with new clothes laid out. New tops. Simple t-shirts, button up casual shirts, jeans, socks, underwear and boots.

After washing he goes down to a kitchen filled with music playing from one of the open laptop computers while in the lounge more stand open with screens lit from the power stored in the pre-charged batteries.

A rich smell in the air. Pastry and meat. A pan on the gas stove filled with mushy peas, others filled with tinned vegetables. Freshly made coffee on the side and Cassie pottering about in a new pair of denim shorts and a loose fitting baggy shirt. Her face rosy from working, strands of her hair stuck to her forehead. The boy at the table singing to the music, his legs swinging on the chair while colouring in a book open in front of him.

'We can find a DIY store and get solar panels to charge batteries,' Cassie says, rushing to the gas stove to stir the pans. 'New clothes okay?'

'Is good,' he grunts.

'Great, food won't be long.'

'I er...' he pauses, nodding manfully. 'Thank you.'

She looks over, frowning with amusement, 'it's fine, sit down... shame about that hotel. Would have been nice to stay somewhere with a pool...probably got a gym too.'

He sits down, not noticing the look between the boy and Cassie. The shared smile and the thing in his eyes showing clear for a second before he goes to drawing.

'Never mind, right...are you ready for pie and mushky peas?'

CHAPTER FIVE

Day Twenty Three

They sit in the Saxon. The mood heavy, the silence as oppressive as the crushing heat. Someone new is here. Someone different and Danny sits with his bag on his lap looking around at the others.

'Can we go,' Marcy says, fanning her glistening face. 'Can't breathe in here.'

'We are,' Howie says from the front, landing heavily in the driver's seat. 'All in?

Danny's father told him that the military is a strange place. From the outside looking in you'd think it was one big machine all working together, and to an extent that was true, but that machine is made of units and teams, all of which have their own issues and dynamics. Danny's father explained that moving into a new unit was hard, especially in times of war as it meant you were taking the place of someone that was killed or injured, and you had to step into all those emotions going on, while still doing your job.

You've got to get involved, his father told him when he first started cadets years ago. *Get stuck in, impress the nco's and keep your head down. Ask questions when you need to but stay polite. If you're unsure if someone is an officer then call them sir, they'll soon tell you if they're not.*

Danny felt like a spare part after the others killed the infected and got to work retrieving the van he'd crashed into the travel agent shop. Danny quickly worked out they were keeping the van then heard them saying they had one before and that all the kit from the Saxon had to be moved.

'Can I help?' he asked, watching as Corporal Blowers paused from hefting a crate of ammunition out from the Saxon.

'Boss? What we doing with him?' Blowers called over to Howie talking to Reginald.

Howie looked over with a quick frown. 'With us for a minute...'

Danny knew they didn't want him here. They said he should be sent to the fort. He didn't know what that meant and expected an argument to break out but then he saw the discipline of a fighting unit at work and within a second everyone was back to work.

'Take them over there,' Blowers told Danny, pointing at the crates and equipment. 'Touch a rifle and if Dave doesn't kill you I will...'

'Yes, Corporal.'

Blowers paused again, looking like he was about to say something else then carried on. 'Make sure you drink, it's hot.'

'Yes, Corporal.'

So Danny worked and he worked hard, rushing back and forth between the vehicles, carrying heavy crates until his filthy top became sodden and clung to his frame. His torn trainers slapping on the pavement while Clarence ripped the fittings out to dump on the road.

Charlie stayed on Jess, holding position at the end of the road to see down the junction where the infected came from. Her eyes up and watching, her mind repeating over and over the moments where she was pinned down in the army base. The faces of the soldiers so full of hate and lust. The terrified rage in them and the fact that right then, she was just a piece of meat to be fucked and used. She couldn't do anything. She wasn't strong enough to fight free and in a way she wished she'd done what Blinky did and gone out fighting, but thinking of Blinky only magnified the pain.

Cookey stayed silent, working hard and glancing now and then at Charlie, fretful and worried at the complete change within her.

To each their own and so everyone delved into thoughts while they worked. Each giving mind to what they went through, to working now, to the worries of the others. To Blinky, Charlie, to Marcy saying she can finish it and what that means. Too many issues. Too many problems.

'What about them, Corporal?' Danny asked, pointing at the spare rifles he hadn't touched or even dared look at. 'There's no magazines so...'

Blowers looked at him for a long second. 'Next to the crates.'

He worked on. Ferrying back and forth and taking care to only hold the rifles by their slings.

'Drink,' Blowers said, holding a bottle of water out when Danny went back to the Saxon.

'I'm fine, thank you, Corporal.'

'It's not a request.'

Danny took the bottle to drink, glugging deep as Blowers told him to finish it.

Blowers then gave him a rucksack and a pair of new boots and told him to go round to the front of the Saxon to get washed and changed. He told him to wash properly and to use the wipes in the bag. Everything was matter of fact, firm and direct.

He did as he was told and felt stupid and self-conscious walking back to the others when he finished. Like he was emulating them or copying, or pretending to be a soldier but no one batted an eyelid at him.

'Better?'

Danny looked up to the muscular young black man staring at him. 'Yes, thank you, Sir.'

'I'm Maddox,' Maddox said casually. 'You had a drink?'

'Yes.'

'Drink more, keep drinking.'

'I will.'

'You's alright?'

Another voice to his side. The young Arabic looking lad. 'Yes, thank you.'

'Mo Mo innit.'

'What is?'

'I am,' Mo said with a grin. 'You's Danny yeah?'

'Yeah...Danny.'

'Feels harsh now bruv, but we went through some shit the last day or two, you get me? They's good people though aren't they Mads?'

'If you say so, Mo.'

'Don't be a cunt, Mads.'

'They're good people, they won't hurt you,' Maddox said, tutting at Mo. 'Might get you killed though,' he muttered under his breath.

'That's Mr Howie,' Mo said, pointing at Howie. 'He's the boss. That's Paula, she sorts us out for clothes and food and like...all the stuff that Mr Howie doesn't do. Marcy, that's the fit one, she's the boss's woman, you get me? She's smart and funny...'

'Genocidal.'

'Fuck off, Mads.'

'Joking,' Maddox muttered, offering a quick grim smile.

'Nick, he's awesome. Fix anything. Cookey, he's funny as fuck but not right now cos one of our crew got killed...Blowers is in charge of our team, hard as nails. You get me? He's unkillable...listen to him and do what he says. Clarence is the big hench one, he's like the boss's right-hand man...that's Dave who I work with...he's autistic so he don't read social situations well. Roy is the medic and Reggie is like the brains. Charlie is on the horse, she's smart as fuck but her best mate Blinky was shot...so she's quiet yeah?'

'Yeah, yeah sure...sorry for your loss.'

'The dog is called Meredith...don't touch her if she's got anything in her mouth.'

'Like a toy?'

'Nah, like an arm or a dick.'

Danny blinked, trying to see if Mo was joking or not but he seemed serious.

'So you's staying with us then?'

'I want to fight,' Danny said earnestly.

'You's a fool, bruv,' Maddox said, slipping into the same street language as Mo.

'I was bit...Mr Howie said...'

'We's immune or...' Mo goes to say.

'Mo,' Maddox cuts in with a warning look, shaking his head. 'Not your place to say. Leave it for Howie or someone else.'

'I didn't turn into one of them,' Danny said. 'Got me in the ankle... I stabbed him but he wouldn't die.'

'Throat or head innit,' Mo said, matter of fact. 'They don't feel pain and they don't bleed like normal people.'

'Right, done,' Howie called out, striding with the others from the new van. 'Everyone gather in...Charlie!'

'Coming.'

'Everyone here?' Howie asked, looking around. 'Danny, sorry to put you on the spot but...' he stopped talking, looking up to a flutter of something moving above their heads. Something small and delicate. A flash of blue as it sunk down, flapping silently to land on Danny's shoulder to rest the beautiful electric blue wings ringed with white and black.

'We saw that,' Marcy said. 'Last night, Howie...'

'Yeah we did,' he said quietly as everyone stared at it.

'Reggie, what is it?' Marcy asked.

'Adonis Blue butterfly,' Reginald said, as captivated as everyone else.

'I've never seen one like that before,' Paula said.

'That is because they are exceptionally rare,' Reginald replied as Danny turned his head, trying to see the delicate creature resting on his shoulder.

'So pretty' Marcy said, moving closer to hold her finger out in front of the insect, moving a fraction at a time for it to lift first one leg then the rest as it transferred from Danny to her hand and there followed a surreal moment of two creatures so resplendent and perfect in form and design staring at each other before the butterfly flapped those gorgeous wings and took off back into the thermals. Flying away as everyone turned to watch it.

'Er so yeah, Danny,' Howie said, picking up his earlier train of thought. 'You can either stay with us or head for the fort...'

'I want to fight, Sir.'

'Actually, that's not your only choice at all. You can do what you want. You can go now or whatever, anybody here can leave when they want...'

'I want to fight, Sir.'

'You got bit?' Howie asked.

'Yes, Sir. On the ankle, Sir.'

'I saw it, definite bite mark,' Roy said.

'Okay,' Howie said. 'The dog hasn't eaten him so he's either like Maddox or like us...we'll talk about that later. For now, if you're staying with us then you follow orders, got it?'

'Mr Howie,' Blowers said, shooting a look at Danny as Charlie cleared her throat, clearly about to speak out too.

'We'll discuss it later,' Howie said, looking around at everyone.

'Boss,' Blowers said, nodding once.

'New van is ready...we need radios, a drone...axes and all the shit we lost...that's the plan for today...Maddox, I want you in the new van guarding Reginald. That's your primary role from now on. Anyone goes near him that you're unsure of then deal with it. You're smart enough to work that out...'

Maddox frowned, slightly taken aback at the change then realising very quickly that it meant he didn't have to sit in the back of the oven-like Saxon arguing with Blowers. 'On it,' he said firmly, earning looks from everyone. 'That wasn't sarcastic.'

'Sounded sarcastic,' Marcy said.

'Did a bit,' Blowers said.

'Wasn't,' Maddox said.

'I'd prefer to travel with Jess...' Charlie said. 'So I can respond quickly...'

'Mate, don't do that,' Cookey said but Charlie ignored him and stared at Howie.

'No. In with the rest of us,' Howie said.

'Boss,' Charlie said quietly.

'Roy, back with Reginald in the new van...everyone else load up.'

Now the small fleet moves out. The Saxon in the lead. The new van behind with Roy driving and Maddox in the passenger seat feeling very relieved.

Reginald in the back trying to think while constantly finding his mind stuck in the loop of being beaten and hurt. Being tied to a chair for no reason other than sadistic delight. He thinks of Marcy and the temptation to release her on the world. She'd win, of that there is no doubt. But using her now would be an act of spite driven by vengeance and those emotions must be tempered because if Marcy is used in that way there will be nothing left at the end. Marcy is the nuclear option to be used only if and when all hope is gone.

Reginald also knows he shouldn't have left it so long in the army base. If he'd deployed Marcy quicker then Blinky would still be here and his team now wouldn't be as fractured as they are. That hesitation will not happen again.

That unity is the single most important thing. Far more important than any of them realise because there is a risk Lani turned from breaking her connection to the group. Of course, there is also the possibility she simply turned back into an infected because of her genetic make-up, but without knowing what caused it Reginald must factor for all possibilities.

He worried before that Paula's relationship with Clarence could drive them apart, and that such a thing could mean one turning Roy against the team, which cannot happen. Reginald even contemplated arranging Dave to execute Paula should the need arise, such was the level of risk posed, but at least that issue seems to be suppressed for now.

'Reginald?'

He looks around, startled from his thoughts to see Maddox coming into the back.

'Need anything?'

'Oh gosh, well now...I need lots of things. New glasses, some tea, maps, writing pads, writing implements and perhaps even the option of wearing clothes that suit me rather than these awful sporty...military things...but other than that no, I am fine.'

Maddox listens while moving to sit down and lean against the side of the van. 'Was it your idea for me to travel with you?'

'Let us say it was a collaboration of ideas discussed with Mr Howie. Are you displeased?'

'Not at all. I'm not one of them so...maybe it's best.'

'Indeed, which is what we thought. Mr Howie is not your enemy, Maddox.'

Maddox nods, smiling at the man. 'Do you mind me in the back or do you want peace and quiet?'

'On the contrary, it is nice to have someone to talk with.'

'Who doesn't just talk about tits and arses,' Roy calls out from the front, making Maddox snort a laugh then look up to the blast of cool air rushing from a vent, he closes his eyes, feeling the temperature drop with a pleasurable shiver. 'Is the air-con okay for you?' Roy calls out with a chuckle.

'Just fine,' Maddox murmurs.

In the Saxon, they sweat and breathe the hot air in silence. The thrum of the engine and the big wheels rolling on the road. The vibration in the frame that Danny can feel through his new boots that he stares at for a few minutes before looking over at Meredith lying down with her head towards the back then up at everyone else. All of them so quiet and withdraw.

He looks out the open back doors to the van he drove and beyond it to the horsebox then glances at Charlie who sits with her head back and her eyes closed. She's really pretty, even with the scar and the chunk of ear missing. She shifts position, seemingly detecting his gaze so he looks over to Cookey then to Nick, Blowers and down to Dave and Mo.

'Got to be another storm coming,' Paula says to no one in particular.

'Hope so,' Marcy replies.

Silence again.

'Be good, clear the air,' Nick says.

Silence. Just the vibration of the vehicle's motion.

'Definitely,' Cookey says. 'You okay, Charlie?'

'Fine,' she says, her voice clipped and tense.

Silence again. Looks shared between Marcy and Paula, then from Paula to Clarence who turns in his seat, the two of them locking eyes for long seconds in a way that Danny doesn't understand.

'So who beat you?'

'Pardon?' Danny asks, looking to Marcy.

'Your face,' she says. 'All beaten...like them,' she adds, nodding at the lads.

Danny stays silent, not wanting to sound like a waif from a broken home or someone with baggage or issues. *Be strong and silent. Work hard and don't go blabbing your whole life story to everyone*, his father's words in his mind. He remembers all of them. Everything his dad ever said.

'Something to hide?' Nick asks.

'No offence, Danny,' Marcy says. 'But we don't know you...who beat you? What for? What happened?'

If you have to speak out then always be honest. Don't lie for anyone ever. 'I got angry,' Danny says.

'Angry?' Marcy asks as Charlie finally opens her eyes to look at him.

'Angry,' Danny says. 'In the place we were hiding...like...like this feeling inside...I'm not mad or anything, like I'm not...I don't have issues.'

'We all get angry,' Paula says. 'Go on, what happened?'

Danny shrugs, clearly uncomfortable at the scrutiny. 'Just odd times. Like when Mr Howie was shooting them in that street and I grabbed that rifle...like a feeling inside. I'm not nuts...I wouldn't have hurt anyone I promise...I er...I said we should be fighting back but they said no and I got angry and tried to get out and fight...Kieron he...'

'Kieron?' Marcy asks.

'Stepdad,' Danny says. 'Him and his mates...stopped me going out.'

'I see,' Marcy says, nodding slowly while studying him.

'I'm not crazy or anything.'

'I think we're all a bit crazy...' Paula says, her voice cutting off as the Saxon starts slowing.

'What's he doing?' Clarence asks from the front.

'No idea,' Howie says.

Everyone leans forward, peering down to see through the windscreen to the solitary figure standing in the middle of the road, blocking the junction to the High Street of the new town beyond him.

Mo feels the prickle inside. The sensation in his head. 'They's here,' he calls out.

'Make ready,' Blowers orders, everyone stirring to action. 'Mo, cover Charlie down to get on Jess...tell Roy and Mads we've got a contact...'

'Paula, be ready to drive this,' Howie shouts, pushing his door to drop out as Danny jumps out behind Blowers into the blazing sun, he spots Mo running with Charlie past the van then hears the clang of metal as the ramp drops then the drum of hooves and a snort as Jess comes thundering out.

'With me,' Blowers says, Danny stays close, going wide from the vehicle feeling horribly empty-handed while everyone lifts rifles to aim up and round, sweeping their eyes over doorways and windows.

A clatter behind him and Charlie goes flying past on Jess, aiming to get ahead of Howie, Dave and Clarence slowly advancing on the solitary figure standing in the road.

A man. Middle-aged with a pot belly and thin arms and legs. Short hair and a light coating of beard flecked with grey. His eyes red and bloodshot. A clear bite wound on his right hand. His clothes ill-fitting but strangely clean, as though new and hastily pulled on.

'Coming through,' Maddox rushes past, his rifle up and ready as he flanks Reginald limping towards Howie, Dave and Clarence at the front.

'Is it just him?' Reginald asks.

'All we can see,' Howie says.

'You are cruel,' the man says, his voice rasping and low from not speaking for days.

'Fuck's sake, we're back to that...' Howie says. 'Anything else?'

'You are...' the infected man cuts off with a strangled gargle as Meredith decides, at that point, to eat him.

'Right. I see,' Reginald says stiffly, watching the dog snapping her head side to side ragging the man over the road. 'I gather we are not communicating with him then?'

'We need a bloody leash,' Clarence says.

'Leash?' Howie asks. 'We're British, it's a lead.'

'Same thing...he's dead.'

'I can see he's dead,' Howie says. 'Reggie, was that opportune or did they know we were coming here?'

'I would suggest they knew given the proximity of this town to the last one.'

'Okay, load up...we'll try the random thing and find somewhere else.'

Five minutes later they set off with Danny once again in the same seat but this time staring down the Saxon to the dog lying down with her front paws over the lip of the back edge with a human foot dangling from her jaws. The foot she pulled off the man before jumping into the Saxon and growling with her ears down at anyone going near it.

'Drink,' Blowers says, passing Danny a bottle and the day wears on with a long drive out of the area into another town, then out of the Saxon to go with Blowers while the others loot Maplin's electronics store then cover Maddox smashing another window to run in to grab goods before coming back out a bare minute later.

Back into the Saxon. Into the heat and the strained silence and the lack of jokes or banter. 'Drink,' Blowers tells Danny.

In the back of the new van, Maddox lays the pairs of spectacles he grabbed from the optician's shop on the table in the cool air. 'I just grabbed what I could...'

'Oh now, that is a thing,' Reginald says, smiling for the first time since he woke up from being beaten unconscious. 'These are from the display units I gather?'

'They are, I know they're not real glasses but...I figured it's the wearing of them rather than the corrective lenses.'

'You, Mr Doku, are a dark horse.'

'Racist.'

'What!? Gosh no, I would never say a comment of such a nature...I meant dark horse as in...'

'Joking, Reginald. It was a joke.'

'I got it,' Roy says from the front. 'Good joke.'

'Oh well now, yes that did give me a fright. I would never be racist.'

'What do you think?' Maddox asks, putting a pair of horn-rimmed glasses on. 'Do I look smart?'

'Let me see,' Roy calls out, chuckling when Maddox leans through. 'Very good.'

The DIY warehouse on the edge of an industrial estate comes next. The Saxon used to batter the shutter down and punch an access hole through.

Dave and Mo go in first with Meredith while everyone else waits outside. Danny once again empty-handed and staying close to Blowers. No comments. No chat.

'Clear,' Mo says, reporting to Howie. 'No signs of movement. Dust on the floor is unbroken...no smells.'

'Okay, quick as we can...axes, torches, lights...tools, grab everything we need. Charlie, stay out here on Jess. Maddox, you too,' Howie says.

They go in quickly, jogging almost comically as one unit into the wide central aisle to stop and read the signs indicating the section before splitting up and rushing off.

'Danny, with me...' Howie says, running off towards the axes with Dave and Clarence. Danny goes with them, rushing into the tools section to see Howie clapping his hands together at sight of the axes. 'Thank fuck! Danny, hold your arms out...'

He does as told, standing still while Howie loads him up with long-shafted axes, some with single heads, others with double and all with carbon fibre composite handles.

'Take them out to Maddox then straight back,' Howie tells him. Danny runs off awkwardly, down the aisle then off to navigate the debris that was the door before the Saxon took it out then out into the heat and glaring sun to see Maddox aiming his rifle across the vast car park at a lone figure walking into view.

'Put them in the van then get Howie out here,' Maddox says quietly. He runs to the van, heaving the axes in before running back through the broken doorway to sprint hard back to the tools section but finds it empty.

'MR HOWIE!'

'Here, what's up?'

'Man in the car park...Maddox said to...'

He doesn't finish. A burst of action as everyone runs hard, bursting from aisles to vault through the door into the car park to see Charlie and Jess midway from them to the figure walking across the car park.

'Is that an infected?' Howie asks.

Meredith streaks out, a blur of black fur and legs flying past Jess towards the figure that doesn't flinch or falter. A second later she hits at full speed, tearing him apart.

'Bloody hope it was,' Clarence mutters.

'Okay, Clarence...you hold out here. Everyone else be quick. In and out...'

Danny goes with them. Running from the aisles with his arms full of gear to dump in the van, going out to see Meredith streaking across the car park to take another one down. A woman with long hair wearing a white nightgown.

In and out. More goods into the van. 'Tell Howie I said we need to go,' Clarence tells Danny.

'Mr Howie, Clarence said we...you...he said we should go, Sir.'

'Okay, everyone out...'

Shots fired as they head for the door. Single shots of assault rifles. They move fast, punching back out into the sun to see figures walking slowly towards them from all points of access. Old men and women. Younger adults. Some naked. Some dressed. Meredith running here and there taking them down while Clarence, Roy and Maddox fire single shots from rifles.

'This is just creepy,' Clarence shouts on seeing Howie coming out while Reginald peers from the back of his van, that thoughtful expression now etched on his face once more as his mind finally starts working properly again.

Ten minutes later they set off. The Saxon a tin can of high heat with everyone sweating and drinking water. Charlie still silent. The lads still silent. Everyone still silent while Maddox, Roy and Reginald enjoy their cooler air and cooler drinks.

Danny wants to ask why the infected people are doing that. They chased him earlier. They were crazed and wild. Why the change? What's happening?

You won't always understand everything going on, Danny, trust the officers to deal with the big questions and have faith they'll do it properly. You'll be a good soldier one day.

'You alright, Danny?' Howie shouts from the front, bringing Danny from his memories.

'Yes, Sir. Thank you, Sir.'

'Drink,' Blowers tells him.

Danny drinks.

Day to evening and as the first hint of a darkening sky appears overhead so the Saxon drives slowly over the pitted hardstanding next to a large open-fronted barn on a hill deep in the countryside.

'Check it's clear,' Howie says, cutting the engine off. Danny once again goes with Blowers and the others, checking inside the barn and behind the bales of straw then round the back. 'All clear?' Howie asks as they come back. 'Good work...Paula, all yours.'

'All mine,' Paula says, moving out with a clap of her hands. 'Nick, get a fire going. Cookey, brew duty. We're on cold tinned food but we've got plenty. Hose at the end, get washed and changed...' the orders fly out fast with everyone moving out and once again Danny is left without instruction or knowing what to do.

He gets wood for the fire. He helps carry the axes from the van to Dave and Mo working with whetstones to give them sharper edges. Lanterns and lights taken from the DIY store are turned on, bathing the yard in a soft orange glow that banishes the ever-darkening shadows.

'Danny?'

'Yes, Corporal,' he says, running over to Blowers.

'You know how to clean rifles?'

'Yes, Corporal.'

'Clean rifles then...you touch a round and I will...just don't touch any magazines.'

'Yes, Corporal.'

He works with Blowers, showing he is proficient while his belly rumbles from a lack of food as he remembers he last ate nearly a whole day ago.

Blowers walks off, coming back a minute later with a chocolate bar. Passing it to Danny.

'Thank you, Corporal,' Danny wolfs it down, savouring the taste and sugar rushing into his bloodstream as Nick, Cookey and Maddox come over to help. 'She's still not talking,' Cookey says.

'Just lost her best mate, give her time,' Nick says.

'It's not healthy,' Cookey says.

'Paula will step in if it goes on,' Nick says.

'Done?' Blowers asks Danny.

'Yes, Corporal.'

'Go and wash...hose at the end. Wash properly, use the wipes.'

'Yes, Corporal.'

Blowers watches him go, biting his bottom lip then marching out into the hardstanding to Howie stood talking to Reginald. 'Boss? Got a minute?'

'Yeah sure, what's up?'

'Danny, he's young and...'

'Mo's sixteen,' Howie says.

'Yeah but...Mo's Dave trained...'

'He wants to fight,' Howie says, rubbing his jaw.

'Mr Howie?' Charlie asks, walking over. 'May I talk to you?'

'Sure, this about Danny?'

'It is,' Charlie says, her tone formal and clipped.

'I think you've both got the same view, that he should go?'

They both nod, Blowers looking to Charlie who keeps her gaze fixed on Howie.

'Think of it like this,' Howie says. 'He grabbed a rifle and shot at them earlier...that tells me he's up for it and he wants to fight...so he'll find a way but at least with us, he'll get some training and be safer. Otherwise, he'll get in the shit and crash another van and we won't be there to dig him out the crap...'

'I didn't think of that,' Blowers concedes. 'Sorry, I wasn't questioning you but...'

'Fuck off, Blowers. Jesus mate, you've earned the right to question anything. Train him up for me, if he's no good then we'll cut him loose okay? Listen, we just lost Blinky and I know taking someone else on means they're at risk...but every person here has a choice. Go and get cleaned up and eat, get some rest. Charlie, are you okay?'

'I'm fine.'

'Talk, Charlie. To me, to Paula...Clarence...Cookey...to Meredith if it helps.'

'I'm fine,' she says. 'Thank you.'

She walks off leaving Howie and Reginald sharing looks. 'I'll get on,' Blowers says. 'Cheers for that...'

He walks off, going to the Saxon to his bag, pulling a fresh top out then walks up to the hose at the end and Danny round the corner out of view washing.

'Mate, you decent?'

'Yes, Corporal.'

'Got a spare top here for you,' Blowers says, stepping round to see Danny in his underwear rinsing himself with the hose.

'Thank you, Corporal.'

'It's just Blowers mate...I'll leave the top here. Make sure you wash properly...' he turns to walk off, catching sight of something that makes him turn back to look harder as Danny spins quickly to face him. 'Show me your back.'

'It's fine, Corporal.'

'Danny, show me your back...'

Danny hesitates, not wanting to turn, not wanting for it to be seen, not wanting the questions that will come.

'Turn around,' Blowers says again. Danny turns reluctantly to stand in silence for long seconds and when Blowers speaks his voice comes out low and hard. 'Who did that to you?'

'It's fine, Corporal.'

'Wait here...Roy?'

'Corporal, I don't need...'

'What's up?' Roy calls out, walking over.

'Take a look at Danny's back.'

'His back? Why what's...oh, I see, bloody hell, how did that happen? Are those whip marks? Jesus, Danny. Someone whipped you?'

'What's going on? Paula asks, walking around.

'Danny's back,' Blowers says.

'What about his back? Oh my god...'

'He's been whipped by the looks of it,' Roy says.

'Howie, come here,' Paula calls.

'Please, it's fine,' Danny says.

'What's up?' Howie asks. 'Fuck me...has he been whipped?'

'They've gone deep too,' Roy says, gently fingering the welts and lacerations. 'Does that hurt?'

'It's fine, Sir,' Danny says, standing in his underpants while more people come round to stare at his back.

'Holy fuck,' Cookey says.

'Jesus mate, who did that?' Nick asks.

'He worked all day with a back like that?' Paula says. 'You poor love, you should have said...'

'It's fine,' Danny mumbles.

'There's a risk of infection,' Roy says.

'But he's got what we've got,' Nick says.

'We don't know that,' Roy says. 'He might be like Maddox...we'll need some antibiotics.'

'Grab some in the morning,' Howie says.

'What's like me?' Maddox asks, walking over to join the crowd with Clarence. 'Has he been whipped?' he asks sharply.

'Leather belt I'd say...used the buckle end too,' Roy says. 'You can see the shape of it in his skin...'

'He said in the Saxon that Kieron and his mates stopped him going out to fight,' Marcy says.

'Who's Kieron?' Maddox asks.

'His stepdad,' Paula replies.

'Stepdad? His stepdad and his mates did that? Are they white?' Maddox asks.

'What?' Paula asks.

'Why does that matter?' Marcy asks.

'Danny, are they white?' Maddox asks.

'Maddox, I don't see how...' Paula says.

'Danny, are they white?' Maddox asks again.

'Yeah but it's not like that,' Danny says quickly, pulling away to turn round.

'Where are they?' Maddox asks.

'Okay slow down,' Paula says firmly.

'White men pin a black boy down and whip him?' Maddox asks, his voice hardening more by the second.

'Maybe it's not like that,' Marcy says.

'He just said it,' Maddox snaps.

'It's fine. I got angry...I said...'

'They whipped you for being angry?' Maddox asks, clearly seething. 'I'll go get angry and see if they whip me...'

'I'll go with you,' Blowers says.

'Stop speaking over him!' Howie snaps. 'We're not a fucking lynch mob...'

'Lynch? He's been lynched...'

'Mads, mate...just slow down a second,' Howie says. 'Let Danny talk.'

This isn't what Danny wanted. Not like this. He wanted to work and be a soldier and fight back, not stand in his pants with everyone feeling sorry for him. 'I'm fine,' he says again with a stronger tone to his voice. 'I got angry and tried to get out to fight...Kieron tried to stop me so I hit him...then his mates too...'

'That's a stick mark,' Roy says, absorbed with looking closely at Danny's injuries on his naked torso. 'See that? Right across his ribs and another one on his arm...and there on his stomach. You can see the imprint...'

Danny closes his eyes, feeling the situation spiralling out of control. 'Please...I just want to fight.'

'Okay okay,' Howie says, waving Maddox and the lads obvious anger down. 'Paula, speak to Danny and find out. Everyone else just slow down and let us get the facts first...get washed and eat...go no now, no point throwing questions at the lad. He's been through enough by the looks of it.'

The dynamics change instantly. The group moving as one with Danny and Paula in the middle, the poor lad still in his underpants wishing he could at least get dressed. A sharing of worry and shock, of outrage and a new topic to talk about and discuss and what they'll do to whoever this Kieron is when they find him.

Reginald joins in, heartily agreeing at the disgusting behaviour of evil men pinning a young man down to whip and beat with sticks, while giving silent thanks for a new thing that can bring a combined sense of righteousness back into the whole.

Only Charlie stays isolated. Still lost and trapped in her own mind at also being pinned down by men who only saw her as a piece of meat and those thoughts, those memories and feelings transmute into a dislike for her own appearance. That she is feminine and pretty. That if she was masculine it may not have happened.

She brushes Jess, washes Jess, feeds Jess and finds reason to stay out of the barn, cleaning the horsebox, checking Jess's feet, trimming her tail, all of which are essential and must be done, but are all also physical and make her move and sweat.

Night proper comes. The sky a deep inky black filled with a million stars but the heat stays. That crushing humidity.

Danny gives Paula his story, slowly, reluctantly and only wanting to be accepted for who he is and what he can do rather than the experiences he had before. Eventually, they eat and settle down on beds of straw as the fire burns low and the lights are turned off.

Danny sleeps fitfully, waking to see Mr Howie and Marcy by the back of the Saxon talking quietly. Then again later when he looks out to see Clarence, the dog and the horse all engrossed in eating something with Danny's mind-boggling a little at the size of them all and when he rolls over he spots Paula awake and lying on her side staring out at Clarence. Roy a few feet to her side but not close.

He drifts off again then wakes to see the first hint of light touching the sky and stares in utter awe at Mo and Dave and never before has he ever seen such a thing, never before did he ever think such a thing was possible. The two of them fighting with a speed he can barely track. It's only when they break for water and look away that Danny follows their gaze and moves a touch to see Charlie doing pull-ups from the back of the horsebox then dropping down to do press ups. He thinks to get up and exercise too but detects it would be an imposition, so he stays silent and once more drifts back off to sleep as the new day creeps towards them.

CHAPTER SIX

Day Thirteen

Cassie runs fast, sprinting with her arms stretched out and just catches the frisbee as it flies past. 'Ha! Got it.'

In the garden of the isolated house. A large lawn bordered by the thick tree line of the forests in all directions. A glorious sun shining down. A glorious day in the new world where the birds sing and the insects buzz. Where the flowers bloom and the treetops sway with a gentle breeze.

She swivels slowly from left to right, the frisbee ready to be launched, aiming first at the boy then off towards Gregori then back to the boy. A feint, a rouse, an obvious show that she is going to throw it at the boy but sending it towards Gregori instead, a hard throw too that sends the disc soaring at him and she waits, watching with delicious delight as he simply plucks it from the air and feels the tingle in her groin at the way he moves.

'Good catch,' she says.

'Me...me me me....' The boy shouts, urging Gregori to throw the disc.

Gregori huffs, tuts, showing great disdain at such an immature game, shaking his head and aiming at Cassie before flicking a perfect throw for the boy who runs off with his hands held out as it flies overhead.

'Ah you almost caught it,' Cassie says. 'Very close...'

Getting Gregori out here to play was far easier than she thought it would be. She simply didn't ask him. The same as yesterday, she just pottered about with the boy, listening to music on the laptops they took from the town, ripping them onto files ready to be transferred onto an Android phone. She noticed Gregori stayed close. Always nearby, always watching them. She noticed too that he kept looking at her when she danced with the boy but rather than pulling her top down to show her cleavage or doing anything to flirt she just carried on as normal.

She went to bed too without making any comments or lingering about. She masturbated in the night, but she went slowly, building up to a deep orgasm while clamping her mouth closed to prevent the noise being heard.

Then, this morning, after breakfast, she smothered the boy in sun cream and took him out into the garden to play. Gregori soon followed, as watchful as ever and eventually, she threw the frisbee at him, expecting to miss but gasping slightly when he snapped a hand out to catch it.

'Okay,' she calls out. 'So...tell me again what happened.'

'Is not real,' Gregori mutters.

'Oh pooey, it's interesting...go on,' she looks at the boy, watching as he throws the disc which hits the ground a few feet in front of him then runs over to boot it hard.

'CUNT,' he screams at it.

Cassie folds her arms, Gregori the same. Both of them cocking their heads over as the boy seethes for a second before noticing their looks of displeasure. 'Sorry,' he says quickly, back to the child. 'It fell down.'

'It didn't fall down. You threw it badly...you say that word again and we'll stop playing.'

The boy nods, grabbing the frisbee to throw again, slamming it down into the ground then struggling to control the rage, visibly clenching his fists and going red.

'Don't swear!' Cassie warns.

He tries again, finally throwing it properly towards Gregori who runs a few steps to catch it and the rage the boy had fades instantly, like a switch pressed and he's back to normal.

'Right, anyway, so go on...Howie's sister is Sarah? And she's dead now?'

'Dead dead dead,' the boy sings.

'And who killed her? Howie?'

'Nooo, Casseee, Dave did kill Sarah.'

'But he's Howie's friend? Is that right?'

'Yes, Casseee, and Blowers and Cookey and Nick and Clarence and Lani too but Lani was bitted by...'

'Bitten.'

'Bitten by Marcy but then she got better and Marcy and Howie wanted to cuddle but the doggy pushed them in the sea and Dave cut April's head off and...'

'And all of this happened in this fort?'

'Yes and...'

'Is the made up story,' Gregori says, throwing the frisbee at Cassie.

'That was too high!' Cassie says, running after the frisbee. 'Got it... right, so what happened to Randall?'

'He got deaded and his brains came out and the lady showed her boobies to Dave.'

'She did what?' Cassie laughs.

'Showed her boobies,' the boy says, laughing too.

'Why did she show her boobies to Dave?'

The boy thinks for a second, 'maybe he was thirsty and wanted the milk from her boobies...'

'Maybe,' Cassie says, still chuckling.

'But Dave killed her.'

'Aw, for showing her boobies? That's mean. You can't kill a woman for showing her boobies,' she says, still chuckling while giving Gregori a strange look before launching the frisbee as hard as she can at him. He still catches it though. Running backwards with perfect grace to stretch up and pluck it from the air. 'I hate you! Stop catching it.'

'Is easy,' he says casually, giving a shrug.

'For you maybe...'

'You catch yes?'

'Don't be a...' she stops herself from swearing with a glance at the boy. 'Don't be a naughty sausage.'

'Haha! Sausage...Gregoreeee is a naughty sausage...'

'I throw, is easy....' He flicks his wrist, sending it gliding serenely up and over her head. 'Run...catch....'

'I AM RUNNING,' she goes fast, sprinting while the boy laughs and leaps high thinking she'll grab the edge but whacks it on to bounce off a tree deep into the undergrowth. 'GREGORI!'

'What? I throw. You catch.'

'It's gone in the woods now...bloody twat,' she grumbles to herself, stomping into the treeline. 'Frisbee? Where are you? Making me run... I bet he thinks I'm fat. I'M NOT FAT, she yells.

'I NO SAY THIS.'

'Bet you did,' she carries on muttering, searching for the red plastic disc. 'Ah, there you are...' she rushes forward to the base of the bush on seeing the flash of colour, dropping onto her knees to reach in, her fingertips groping for the disc then pulling back on feeling the soft warm material of a shoe. She throws herself backwards in fright, landing on her arse and about to scream when she spots the face through the leaves. A child. Ten, maybe a little older. Dark haired and pale. Blood on her cheeks. Her eyes red and bloodshot.

Cassie's heart booms in her chest, the scream still there, ready to come out. A shuffle further behind the girl. A man with the same red bloodshot eyes. More behind him and the more she looks the more she sees. Faces staring. Red bloodshot eyes everywhere. Creepy and awful, macabre and sinister but she feels another reaction too. An instant worry.

'You can't be here,' Cassie gasps.

'YOU NEED THE HELP?' Gregori shouts.

'NO!...you can't be here,' she whispers again, seeing more of them. 'He'll kill you...go back.'

They stare at her inert and unmoving. She rises to her feet then spots the frisbee a few feet away, running to grab it. 'Go back...don't let him see you.'

'You no find?'

'Casseeee?' the boy runs in ahead of Gregori, making her panic and rush back towards the lawn, grabbing the boy to heft up into her arms.

'Make them go back,' she whispers urgently. 'Found it!' she adds in a bright voice, throwing the frisbee out to Gregori at the edge of the undergrowth. 'Come on, time for lunch I think...then how about a drive in our new car? We can listen to music...'

She strides on, marching out onto the lawn to put the boy down so he can run then glances back at Gregori standing stock still and her heart whumps at the sight of his pistol in his hand.

'What's up?' she asks, forcing her tone to stay light.

'Hear something,' he grunts, holding a hand out to silence her.

'Fox, I saw it...it ran off, come on, are you hungry? Tin of mushky peas maybe?' she braves the risk of a reaction and goes back to loop her arm through his, pulling him on while chuckling and making a game of it. He falters, unsure of the close contact, frowning at her but seeing the smile and the ruddy complexion in her cheeks.

'I like mushky peas,' he says, allowing himself to be turned.

'I like mushky peas,' she copies his voice, barging her hip into his to keep his attention on her. 'Your arm muscles are like rocks,' she says, squeezing his upper arm. 'You're so strong...I was thinking about doing some exercise? Would you help me?'

She breathes a sigh of relief at getting him inside the house, glancing back to the treeline as though expecting to see them all edging out into view. 'Come here, my lovely...you need a wet flannel to cool down,' she lunges after the boy, laughing and joking as she gets him to the sink to rinse a cloth that she starts wiping over his face as Gregori goes out and a second later she hears the toilet door closing. 'They can't be here,' she whispers. 'Gregori will kill them.'

'But...'

'No buts, make them go further back...right back...' the toilet flushes, the sound of running water as Gregori washes his hands. 'Are more coming here?'

The boy nods, his blue eyes fixed on Cassie. She kisses his forehead, sighing quickly.

'I can't stop them,' he whispers.

'Okay,' she hears the door to the toilet open. 'We'll think of something...'

Music on. Noise made. Food prepared. Coffee brewed. Food eaten then out the house into the car. Gregori goes with it. His senses sharp and he felt the prickle of something when he reached the undergrowth in the garden earlier but then Cassie said she saw a fox then grabbed his arm, pressing her body into his.

The only sex Gregori ever had was with women supplied by his masters. A reward for a mission completed. Not all the time but now and then. The women were always silent and sullen. Either on a trafficking route or already at their end destination to be passed around and used as reward, payment or for simple income. He only ever kissed one, but she tasted like an ashtray. After that, he never bothered, and it was always over within seconds. No passion, no comfort, an act for the sake of it and one that he wasn't all that fussed about.

His mind was so mission focused and he was always caught up in the kill. In being the *ugly man.* Flying into countries, into states, into places to be taken to the target then exfil out.

Now there are no missions and so his mind can think of other things. Things like mushy peas and pies. Things like the music that Cassie plays on the devices. Things like the boy playing frisbee. Simple things. The sway of her hips. Things other than killing. Other than hurting and suffering. Other than driving fear into the hearts of men. The scent of her perfume and the strands of hair that stick to her forehead when she's hot.

'Oh my god that's so good,' she groans pleasurably in the passenger seat as the big engine of the Range Rover sends ice cold air flowing through the inside. Gregori grips the steering wheel a bit harder in response to the noise she makes. Shifting in his seat. His eyes staring ahead at the road. 'Isn't that nice?' she asks, gasping a little.

'Is good,' he grunts, his voice even deeper and more gravelly than normal. She groans again, stretching out and lifting her hands above her head in a way that makes him glance over to see her nipples straining against the inside of her top.

'Whoa! What happened?' she asks, jerking up from the car swerving to the left.

'Is rabbit,' Gregori lies quickly, correcting the vehicle. 'It ran...I swerve yes...rabbit...is rabbit.'

'Wow, lucky rabbit...music?'

'Is good. Yes. Music.'

'Really? You like music?'

'Yes. I like.'

'Ooh spot the serial killer being more human...'

'I no this thing.'

'Joking! Right...let's get this going...haha! Can't beat some eighties pop...You'll love this...Tiffany, I think we're alone now...'

The magic happens. The magic of driving just for the pleasure of it. Of seeing sights while music blasts out. The thumping beats rattling the frame. Eighties classics. Electro synth. Rock hits, modern pop and heavier tracks with a solid bassline that Gregori can feel in his bones.

No place to go. No place they need to go. They have everything they need right here. Food, drink, shelter and a man that can kill the world to make sure the boy is safe and right now, there is no place either of them would rather be.

Fields and meadows go by. Vast tracts of open land. Hills and valleys. Through villages torn apart from the end of the days where the corpses lie bloated and rotten and the flies rise when the Range Rover swooshes past with the music blaring.

They pass places of survivors. Even glimpsing the odd figure here and there, some that run and hide while others rush out to wave and scream for help but they don't stop because theirs is not a happiness or security to extend to others. What they have is theirs and theirs alone. Bought and paid for. Owned outright and Cassie stares out at them, her eyes hardening at the sight of mere people suffering in their dirty sordid lives. Scrabbling for life while she rides in a luxury car and sings with a boy and an Albanian serial killer.

They find their favourite songs, playing them over and over, learning the lines to sing out and she sees his lips moving and bursts out laughing in delight, taking the hand from his leg to move through his hair with an entirely natural gesture, running her fingers down the back of his neck while singing and laughing with the boy.

The gunshot comes as Gregori slows the Range Rover on driving into a village and spots the road ahead blocked with cars dragged out to form a barrier. A bottleneck made. Houses on both sides. Trap. Danger close. He brakes hard while the music plays, anchoring on to bring the speed down, intending to go into reverse and get out.

That's when the shot comes. The boom of a shotgun from the right side that peppers the bonnet and wing with hundreds of metallic strikes. Cassie screams out. Gregori brakes hard, opening his door and grabbing the pistols from the door pocket and the central console as he goes. A second shot comes. A shout. More shouts. Loud angry voices. Cassie jabs to release her seatbelt and scrabbles between the seats, diving to cover the boy with her body as Gregori spots the shooter in the first-floor window of the house and shoots him dead, the pistol in his right hand booming out.

He twitches fast, sensing movement and firing into a window on the other side. A scream. A gargled yell. Cassie lifts her head, scrabbling to get the sawn-off shotgun out from under the passenger seat, holding it ready while the boy stays silent beneath her.

'No! Please...please...stop...' a female voice screaming out. Cassie looks up through the open window to see the door to a house opening and a woman rushing out. She aims and fires the shotgun without thinking, without thought. Killing the woman outright who flies back off her feet through the door she came from then snatches a look to see Gregori standing in front of the car with his arms out, aiming his pistols left and right while the music still blasts from the stereo.

He comes back slowly, working a safe retreat to the car then into the driver's seat, sending a flurry of shots into windows and doors while reversing the car back down the road, slamming it round to face the right way before powering on and only then does he snap the stereo off.

'Hurt?' he asks, turning to look at them as he drives.

'My ears hurt,' the boy says.

'He hurt?' Gregori asks, alarm in his voice.

'No his ears, from the shotgun...he's fine, we're fine...are you...did they get you?'

'No,' he says in a way that suggests the question is entirely stupid.

Silence for a few seconds. The wind rushing past the windows. She pushes the hair from her eyes, shaking her head. A look to the boy then to the rear-view mirror where she locks eyes with Gregori. She smiles in shock, then grins in a way that makes Gregori frown slightly.

They should be terrified. They should be panicked and fretting but to Gregori, this is life and normal and to Cassie, it was just bloody exciting. Firing the shotgun. Hearing Gregori shoot. Hearing people scream out. The adrenaline. The feel of it. Besting people that had set a trap who now lie bleeding and dead. She wants to whoop and shout out, she wants to yell at their victory and then kiss Gregori but she stays silent, shaking her head and grinning at the boy.

Back home. Back to cold showers and food made. She watches the treeline, not seeing any of the things anywhere in sight while thinking of earlier, the fun of the drive, the music, the shootout. Oh my god it was so good. So fucking good.

'What this?' Gregori asks, looking down at the boy drawing on paper at the kitchen table as the sky darkens outside with the night coming.

Cassie looks over at the sight of the boy holding a crayon in each hand while drawing circles. His right hand working clockwise, his left anti-clockwise but both so close together with a bizarre symmetry of motion. He adjusts fluidly, drawing a flow one way then a contraflow the other while overlapping and creating incredible patterns across the sheets. His face a mask. His eyes focussed.

He gets faster and faster, looping circles with a speed that isn't quite right. A muttering from his lips that grows louder with a tune given that makes Cassie lean closer to listen.

'*Amaziiiing Grace...*' the boy sings in a whisper as though to himself. 'All the way up and round and round and round and...' he carries on drawing the circles while many miles away the infected run in dizzying circles on the top level of a multi-storey car park, ripping Howie from the others.

Faster and faster, his hands whirling on the paper that becomes thick with the lines. Then he stops with the crayons snapping in half as he pushes down. 'Howie's got a heart in his mouth...'

A blink and he's back to the boy smiling at the two adults. 'Can we play frisbee tomorrow?'

CHAPTER SEVEN

Day Twenty Four

Grief is a powerful thing and brings forth a range of emotions. Guilt being one of them. Guilt that you are still here when others have perished.

A virus has spread across the world and infected billions of people. Some are immune, and some, as in her own case, appear to be infected but not suffering the same effects as everyone else.

Charlie can compute that. She is highly intelligent. She can understand and grasp those things, and likewise, she can grasp that millions have perished and those deaths, although awful, are *understandable* in the context of the situation.

What Charlie struggles with, and the thing causing the ever-increasing surges of guilt loaded grief, is why Blinky died the way she did, and why, when the world is falling apart, men in uniform that swore an oath to protect, wished only to harm and rape and sometimes, every now and then, the mind won't let you move on from those thoughts, no matter how hard you try.

The morning after burying Blinky, Charlie exercised hard. She trained so hard she almost puked. Then she worked all day with Jess. Guarding her team. Ranging out when needed but isolating herself from the others.

Now, in the morning of the twenty-fourth day since the world fell, she exercises again. Harder than before.

'You's alright, Charlie?' Mo asks tentatively, taking a break from Dave training.

She pauses mid-pull-up, her body dangling from the edge, the muscles in her arms and shoulders showing taut and defined.

'I lost Jagger, he's my best mate too...hurts but...'

'Mo,' she snaps, intending to tell him to go away.

'I love you, Charlie but your crew need you, get over it yeah?' his voice hardens as he speaks, the street tone rasping and direct. The boy that broke *into* an army base to save them and she carries on doing pull-ups with a lump growing in her throat and the tears spilling from her eyes.

It wells up inside. It has to come out and vent. The grief is too much. The sheer overwhelming feeling of it. She starts to weep and fights to keep the sobs silent, feeling ashamed, embarrassed, angry and wronged.

Images in her mind of the men holding her down, their hands in her hair, dragging her along and in the rush of all the emotions that's the thing she keeps focussing on because a woman is defined by hair, that's the feminine against the masculine. Charlie knows she is pretty and knows part of the perception of her looks is her hair, the same hair the men dragged her by and used to pin her down, rendering her defenceless while Blinky lay dead.

She sobs again, suppressing the noise as she rushes inside the horsebox out of sight. Her hands wiping frantically at the tears. Willing herself to man-up and stop sobbing like a girl but it hurts so much she drops to her knees and grabs at her kit bag, pawing at the flap to get the box out, the box she took from the shelf in Boots when everyone was grabbing the things they need. She told herself she needed them for Jess. All horses have to be clipped now and then and having battery operated clippers on hand is a good thing.

That's what she told herself but the reality, deep inside, was for herself and so she rips the box open and sobs harder, fighting to stay silent while pulling the hairband from her hair and yanking the strands free before turning the hair-clippers on and pushing the bare blades over her scalp.

She won't be feminine. She won't have hair. She won't have the thing that men used to drag and pin her down or the thing that men say when they're trying to fuck you. *I like your hair, Charlie. You've got nice hair, Charlie. Let me fuck you, Charlie.*

That's all they want and if it's not given they'll take it. Not again though. She won't ever be in that position again. She'll be strong and fast. Hardened and not feminine and so she pushes the blades across her skull watching with choking sobs as the locks of hair tumble down.

Mo runs swiftly, vaulting a straw bale to land next to Paula, dropping to a crouch, his hand on her shoulder.

'What?' Paula blinks from sleep to awake, her heart hammering not at the sweaty sight of Mo but at the worried look on his face.

'S'Charlie...she's cutting her hair off...'

'What?' she moves fast, rushing to her feet as those around wake from the motion to see Paula jumping over the bale to run barefoot in trousers and a vest towards the horsebox.

'What's going on?' Howie asks, sitting up.

'Charlie's cutting her hair off...' Mo says.

'She's what?' Marcy asks, scrabbling free from her bedding, blinking awake to run.

Paula stops at the edge of the horsebox, her eyes widening to wake her mind quicker to take in Charlie on her knees bent forward sobbing her heart out while trying to yank the hair tangled in the blade of the clippers.

'Oh my love,' Paula rushes in. 'Oh Charlie...'

'It's stuck...' Charlie sobs, half her hair shorn away. 'It's fucking stuck...'

'It's okay,' Paula drops at her side, pulling her in.

'What the...' Marcy balks at the sight, rushing in to look down.

'They're stuck,' Charlie sobs the words out, trying to pull hard on the clippers while being held by Paula.

'No no no, you'll pull it out,' Marcy says, dropping next to her. 'Let me do it...let go, Charlie...'

'They were...they were...' Charlie heaves the words out, her mind fracturing, her heartbreaking while the fucking clippers refuse to work from being tangled in her fucking hair. She yanks again, vicious and hard.

'Stop, Charlie...let me get it free,' Marcy says,

'They were going to rape us...' she voices the fears inside and the weeping comes harder, her whole body heaving with the pain of losing Blinky, with the pain of everything. 'I can't stop thinking about it...Blinky and...feeling her die...holding me down...I couldn't move...'

Paula's face hardens as she thinks back to the first night in her office when Clarke pinned her against a desk to push his fingers inside her. She can still smell the stench of pizza grease in the air and his foul breath. She swallows the memory away, 'we got through it,' she says darkly. 'And they're dead...we're not. I know Blinky died but she went out fighting. Don't take that from her, Charlie...'

'I can't...I just...'

'You can and you will. Channel it...use it...that's what we all do...if you give in then those pricks win.'

Shame comes next. The feeling of being immature and having the reaction of a child and Charlie goes to rise, to pull free.

'No,' Paula whispers, kissing her head. 'You've done nothing wrong...none of us have...' she locks eyes with Marcy, messages given without words needed because Marcy can end this. She can finish it on her own and the seconds pass, becoming minutes as the venting is given to release the pressure inside. It works too. Not instantly but Charlie feels the lessening of the strength of the things she felt inside. A clarity of mind edging back as her breathing normalises and she sinks further into the hug, still crying but less now, softer, gently, the pressure easing.

'How bad is it?' she asks eventually, breaking the patient silence.

'Ah,' Marcy says, running her fingertips over Charlie's half shaven head. 'You know...'

A snort, a sob but the sound of a dry laugh.

'Um, so...you'll have to finish it,' Marcy continues with soft humour in her voice. 'Unless you want to look like a total spaz that is.' Another snort from Charlie. 'I mean, if the twat-look is your thing then just say...no judgement here...'

She finally moves to sit up, her face red from heat and crying, her eyes red and she reaches up to gingerly touch her partially shaved head. 'I'm so sorry...'

'Don't be,' Paula says. 'You've gone through hell...'

'So have you...so's Mr Howie and...'

'We're older,' Paula cuts in, her voice soft yet firm with authority and experience. 'Everyone is different anyway...you'll need to finish it off,' she adds, looking at Charlie's scalp. 'Don't worry, hair grows backs...'

'Grows quicker now,' Marcy says. 'Want me to finish it off?'

Charlie nods, 'please...'

'Go on, bend forward a bit...always wanted to do this actually,' Marcy says. 'Not on you, I mean in general...'

'I'll be back in a mo,' Paula says, pushing up to her feet. 'Desperate for a wee...'

She goes out to see everyone else gathered together just inside the barn. Worried faces, hard eyes. The same pervading mood within them all with the promise of another shit-filled day of absurd heat and humidity but Paula know more than anything that this tension between them all has to break. Howie can lead them into battle and rally them on, but this is Paula's job. This now. Fixing this. She didn't intend for this role or responsibility, but such is the way of life sometimes.

'How is she?' Howie asks, his voice gruff from sleep.

'She's okay...ish,' Paula says. 'Had a good cry, she needed it...'

'Mo said she's...' Howie trails off.

'Cut her hair off,' Paula finishes the sentence.

'Fuck,' Nick says quietly.

'It's my fault,' Paula says. 'Too much going on...I should have talked with her and...'

'No, that's not fair,' Clarence cuts in.

'It is fair...anyway,' she says. 'Marcy's finishing it off...'

'Anything we can do?' Cookey asks, his expression so full of worry, his blue eyes not twinkling now, the smile not there.

'No...I don't think there is...' she says heavily. 'Just get through it I guess...I need a wee...' she walks off then stops to think for a second, turning back to look at Cookey. 'There is something...sounds silly but...just be you today? Please?'

She walks off, leaving them all reflective of the words she just spoke and what they mean and of the great and awful danger she just invited into their lives.

'Did Paula just tell me to be me?' Cookey asks.

'No,' Blowers says quickly. 'She meant...er...be someone else.'

'She didn't. She effectively just gave me permission to be a complete dick.'

'You don't need permission to be a dick,' Nick says.

'Your mum does,' Cookey says.

'Oh god no,' Blowers says, groaning.

'That's what your mum says,' Cookey tells him. '*Oh god no*...cos it's so big.'

'Paula?' Blowers calls out. 'What did you do?'

'What did you do, Paula?' Nick shouts. 'Take it back...'

'And your mum says that too...' he trails off as the clippers stop buzzing and the horsebox creaks as Marcy and Charlie walk into view. Charlie with her head down and her hand running over her skull to feel the bristles of her dark stubble. It feels so weird, so light and strange.

'Let's have a look then?' Cookey calls out.

She looks up at him, at all of them. The scar on her face more pronounced from the lack of hair. The chunk missing from her ear so visible. The bruises to her neck from the fights. Her skin tone darker, mixed-race and nearer the tone of Mo Mo and it shows now with her highlighted hair gone. She looks striking and everyone holds still, caught in the second.

'Charlie?' Cookey says. 'Guess what?'

'What?' she asks, her voice still tight but at least her head is up and looking at him.

'You're a proper egghead now...'

'Twat,' Blowers says, 'can't believe you just said that...'

'Right well we're up now,' Paula says, walking back. 'Anyone else want a haircut while we're here? Howie, I'm looking at you...'

'Load up we're moving out,' Howie says, earning a few chuckles of weak humour. 'But seriously...no.'

'Why not?' Marcy asks, holding the clippers up.

'I'm er...doing that thing?'

'What thing?' she asks pointedly.

'The er...the thing with um...' he looks around, spotting Blowers. 'Blowers and er...'

'Danny,' Blowers says quickly.

'Danny,' Howie parrots, pointing at a slightly alarmed Danny.

'With Danny,' Blowers says, also pointing at Danny. 'Drill.'

'Drill,' Howie says.

'Right,' Marcy says eyeing them suspiciously. 'Nick? You're looking a bit bushy...'

'Fuck that...I mean...'

'Drill,' Blowers says. 'All of us I think?'

'I don't have hair,' Clarence says.

'Apart from Clarence,' Blowers adds. 'Or Roy cos he's a bit baldy too...and Cookey actually.'

'Eh?' Cookey asks.

'You need a trim,' Blowers tells him.

'You do,' Nick says.

'From Marcy? Fuck off...'

'Er excuse me?' Marcy says.

'Can you do it properly?' Cookey asks.

'Please? Are you joking? Have you seen how vain I am?'

'I hate you, Marcy...don't even laugh at me. It's not funny. Stop it... all of you...laugh at Charlie...' Cookey huffs in his seat next to Blowers. Back in the super-hot tin-can Saxon leading their small fleet out the yard and back into the world. Sniggers and laughs from his sides and the seats opposite.

'Safety on?' Blowers asks, still chuckling.

'Yes, Corporal,' Danny says, smiling at Cookey. His rifle between his legs, loaded with a full magazine.

'The fucking safety should have been on those clippers,' Cookey scoffs, earning a fresh round of laughs. 'Would have done a better job with a rifle...'

'Oh stop whining,' Marcy says, waving a hand at him. 'It's not that bad.'

'Fucking is,' Nick snorts, bursting out laughing at the sight of Cookey's butchered hair. His blond locks cut uneven with tufts poking up here and there and shorter patches where Marcy used the clippers with her tongue poking out and one eye closed in focus.

The mood still hard. The tension still showing in the lines of their eyes. Moments of silence now and then but less so now. Charlie still stays quiet and pensive but she's here with them, and no longer avoiding eye-contact.

Danny keeps glancing at her shyly, a little mesmerised by how she looks with a shaved head. He has the same response with Marcy too so stays focussed ahead to the lads and thinks of the drill they did before moving out.

Danny knew it was a test. *Try hard and always keep trying. Don't ever give in.*

Blowers started off easy enough, making him dry fire the rifle then showing what he'd do with a blockage and how to reload the magazine. Fire. Blockage. Re-load. Again and again. Running up and down. Fire and manoeuvre. Down and fire. Run and fire. Watch the angles. Watch your sides. What is the objective? How do we get there? What is in the way? Blockage. Re-load.

'No time to clear the weapon, draw your pistol...down...up...run, cover that corner...face out. INCOMING...FIRE...work a retreat...'

The others joined in too. Even Mo who had already trained with Dave at dawn. Then Mr Howie gave permission for live firing.

'This shit just got serious,' Cookey told him while the others rolled their eyes and called him a twat.

'Good aim,' Blowers told him after watching his rifle skills. 'Bit shit with the sidearm though...'

Then Charlie mounted on Jess so Danny could feel see what it was like with a horse thundering past at speed while Roy fired arrows past his head while rifles were fired while Blowers shouted at him to clear the blockage and re-load.

After drill, he had to see Dave who sorted his kit out. Fixing his holster just so. Adjusting the sling on his rifle. Making sure his boots were laced properly and nothing on him could snag or come loose.

'Knife,' Dave said, giving him a spatula. Danny expected to hear everyone laugh at that point, but no one did. 'Strike and move...stab don't slash...'

It was bloody hard work, but it was also one of the best things Danny has ever done, once he got over the self-conscious weirdness of everyone else pretending to be targets, attacking him at varying speeds while Dave told him how to stab, where to stab, how to clear an opponent back and gain space.

'Axe,' Dave said, giving him an axe. 'No lesson, just hit them with it. Strike and move. Hydrate. Questions?'

'Eat, Danny,' Paula said after.

'Drink, Danny,' Blowers said.

'Let me check your back, Danny,' Roy said. 'It looks okay I think, no sign of infection. We'll get you some antibiotics to be sure though.'

'Radio, Danny,' Nick said, showing him where to put it threading the wires under his top to the earpiece.

'Load up, we're moving out...' Howie said.

. . .

Now they stand in the centre of another town. Charlie on Jess. Meredith sniffing about as they wait for reaction, for the infection to see them.

'So, that's the plan?' Paula asks, looking from Howie to Reginald. 'We're using ourselves as bait so Reggie can observe them.'

'Um, pretty much,' Howie says, looking around the deserted street.

'Great plan,' Paula mutters.

'I've got a plan,' Marcy says brightly. 'You can all go to the fort and let me finish it.'

'We were heading north before the...' Paula says, trailing off into a second's worth of pained silence. 'Before the army base...'

'Indeed, and that may well be the case but right now I rather think we need to know what we could be going into' Reginald says, hovering near the back of his van with Maddox at his side.

'That's obvious mate,' Howie says. 'It'll be a shit-ton of angry fucked up zombies...'

'Living challenged,' Reginald says.

'Zombies,' Howie says.

'I prefer living challenged,' Clarence says.

Dave cocks his head over. Meredith next to him doing the same. Both of them wondering why people talk so much and don't listen enough. Noises to the left. They both turn to look. Noises to the right. Scrapes and scuffs. They both turn to look. A sense within their instincts telling them to turn and they look back to the other end of the street to see a flash of a body running out of sight. A calculation. To shout or to give orders quietly. The attack will come but it is not happening this second. Calmness must prevail. Positions must be gained. All in a second. All in the blink of an eye and the beat of a heart.

'Ambush, Mr Howie...'

A simple statement made that has every rifle snapping up to aim with hearts booming in chests.

'With me,' Maddox grips Reginald's shoulder, turning him towards the open door of the van.

Danny does as everyone else, aiming up while not knowing why. Not understanding why Dave said there was an ambush. What ambush? Where? It's calm and deathly quiet with just that one woman walking down the centre of the road towards them. He glances over to see Roy clambering deftly on top of the van to nock an arrow in his longbow and wonders how the hell a longbow can outfire an assault rifle.

'YOU ARE CRUEL,' the woman shouts the words, her voice rolling down the front of the buildings.

Then they come and Danny's world changes in a heartbeat. From a calm, almost serene street where they were discussing existential existence to an utter carnage of many things happening at once where he absolutely believes they will die because there ain't no hope in God's green earth that anything can survive what's coming at them.

Every window above them on the first floor blows out with a seemingly choreographed explosion of bodies flying out while every door at street level smashes down or pings off hinges and from every junction and alley they pour wild and crazed, then a hand grips his shoulder.

'RUN DANNY...'

Danny runs. He hears that order and he complies.

'FIRING LINE HERE...DOWN...MAKE READY...'

He drops to a knee, dumping his bag in front to access the spare magazines.

'FIRE...'

He fires at the coming masses because that's what they did in the drill earlier.

Courage is one thing, Danny, but when the bullets are flying, and men are dying, it's training and discipline that see you through. His father's words in his mind and so he picks his targets and burst fires. His aim wild, his heart jackhammering but he breathes, and he fires, gaining control, gaining order.

'MAGAZINE.'

He shouts the word without realising he does so, dropping one out to get a new one in, bolt back, make ready, aim and fire but there are still too many. They'll be overrun. He changes magazine again and snatches a look behind him to gain a split-second view that sears into his mind. Howie cleaving a man in half with his axe. Clarence lifting a heavy woman off her feet to launch at more charging him. Jess on her back legs with Charlie standing up in the saddle swinging her axe down. Dave spinning with a spray of blood arcing in the air. Mo behind Howie, going low to stab up into the groin of another one. Maddox at the back of the van stabbing one through the neck. Bodies everywhere and beyond them another small firing line with someone in the Saxon using the GPMG to fire down the other way.

Something swooshes an inch from his nose that makes him gasp and look to see Roy on top of his van holding his bow and staring at Danny while pointing at his own eyes then away. *Watch your front.*

Seconds pass. Minutes. Hours and days and it goes on and will never end. An image in his mind of his father sitting on the swing next to him in the park. His face bearing an expression Danny couldn't understand. *A firefight feels forever, Danny. Like it won't ever end...but it's over like that*...he clicked his fingers, emphasising his point.

'CEASEFIRE,' Dave's voice. Huge and bellowing and it's done. Over. Finished in minutes and Danny lowers his rifle to look down at the many spent casings on the ground and the many bodies lying dead.

'Up, on your feet,' hands to his shoulders, lifting him up. 'Look at me...look at me...' Blowers in his vision. The black patch over his eye. 'You okay?'

Danny nods, his hearing feels weird, his ears ringing. He goes to speak, coughing then clearing his throat.

'Are you okay?' Blowers taps the side of his face, not hard but enough to jolt Danny back to the now.

'Yes, yes, Corporal...'

'Good lad,' Blowers says, grinning for the first time. 'Clear your weapon, fresh magazine, hydrate...'

Into the Saxon. Drive to another town. Out and make ready.

'YOU ARE CRUEL,' a lone figure walking towards them, shot by Dave, then the rest come, charging and wild.

'FIRING LINE...MAKE READY...FIRE!'

'Guess who's back bitches,' Cookey laughs in the Saxon after the next one. The energy flowing again. Faces animated.

'Drink, Danny,' Nick tells him. 'Here, eat that, mate,' a snack bar chucked over. 'You're doing well, you okay?'

'Yeah, yeah good,' Danny says.

Next town. Out. Make ready. They come without warning this time. Simply charging. They still die.

Saxon. Drink. Eat. 'You okay, Danny?' Paula asks.

'Yes, Ma'am, fine...thank you.'

Town to town on a linear path with a balls-out show of aggression. Hundreds killed. Thousands even.

Afternoon battle in another nameless town. Everyone hot. Everyone working and even Danny feels the difference. There's far more now. Many times the number they had before and it's not long before they're fighting a retreat into a large collapsing circle with Danny once again thinking they'll be overrun.

'BLOWERS...' Clarence roars, standing taller than everyone else and seeing a narrower road beyond the lines of attacking infected. 'CLEAR THAT JUNCTION...WE'LL HOLD THESE...'

'ON IT...CHARLIE...GO...MY TEAM, OBJECTIVE IS THAT JUNCTION. HAND WEAPONS...MAKE READY.'

That's when Danny first sees the damage a horse can do, or rather, what Jess and Meredith can do with a vicious, brutal charge into the enemy. The huge horse battering them aside to clear a path into which Blowers and his team run screaming hell for fury. Danny with them. Terrified to the core with his axe gripped and swinging. *Axe. No lesson. Hit them with it.*

Blood everywhere, spraying all over them. He swings out wildly, not realising that Nick and Cookey work his flanks to keep him safe or that Mo stays at his back. Then it becomes too much, and he's gone too deep. Isolated and trapped. Swinging round with his axe and seeing only infected and none of his own team. A mistake made. An error given. He screams out to fight on but senses the end is about to happen and the infected close in for the kill as a man mountain roars past, driving them back with Clarence in full Berserker mode.

Howie goes past, slamming into the lines with a ferocity that make them wilt back. Danny sees it right at that point. The sheer animalistic nature of Howie and the absolute violence within him that makes him move with a speed that isn't right.

Fight little brother. An essence of a voice in his head. Not a voice. A being. A will exerted. *Pack fight*. The feeling he had before when he got angry and Kieron locked him in the storeroom, only a hundred times more powerful and he feels them. The dog, Howie, all of them. In his mind. Not their voices but their essence, their will, their energy from one to another.

A thing of unity. A hive mind.

Then it's over and he stands heaving for air with blood dripping down his arms amidst a sea of broken human forms. The stench of it. The metallic tang of iron mixed with shit, piss and sweat. Innards everywhere. Bones showing.

He pukes hard with hot bile burning his throat, bent over and thinking he will drop until strong hands grip to hold then someone presses a bottle of cool water to his lips while someone else pours more water over his head.

'Good work,' Howie's voice, close and hard from the bloodlust flowing. 'Good lad, one of us, Danny.'

Hands patting his back, ruffling his hair. *Good work. Good lad. You did well. One of us*.

'He's a squaddie alright,' Blowers laughs. 'Don't go so bloody deep next time, bellend...'

'Yes, Corporal,' Danny says, grinning widely.

CHAPTER EIGHT

Day Fourteen.

The second Gregori wakes he knows someone is up before him. The day is still early, dawn barely here as he steps out from his room and spots the boy's empty bed.

He moves silently to stare down the corridor to the back of the boy bent over the table. A box of Frosties open next to him. A bowl full of the crunchy cereal and a carton of juice with a straw poking out the top as the child hums quietly while drawing with his crayons.

Gregori goes back to his room and spots Cassie's door ajar and becomes trapped in a second's worth of thought before moving to peer through the gap at her sleeping form that makes him feel funny inside.

The night was incredibly hot. Close and sticky. A storm coming with a pressure pushing down that makes the air thick enough to chew. He slept in his boxers without covers and he can see Cassie has done the same, lying in just her bra and knickers on her back, her arms splayed out. Her legs open slightly, one knee bent up, her hair spread out on the pillows. Her chest rising and falling. Her mouth slightly open.

An urge steals through him. A lust to do what he did with the prostitute girls. His breathing deepens, his heart hammering so loud he thinks she will hear it and wake. Then he spots himself in the mirror above the dresser and repulses at the sight of his pock-marked skin and his awful bulging eyes and the sick, lustful expression that makes him pull back and away, turning swiftly towards the bathroom and the cold waters of the shower. He was called the *uglyman* for a reason. That's why they gave him prostitutes because no woman in their right mind would touch him willingly.

He washes quickly, soaking his hair in gel and feeling the shiver of cold water in the hot air. A tap at the door.

'I wash,' he says quickly.

'I'm bursting,' Cassie calls through, her voice heavy with sleep.

'I wash,' he says again but the door opens a crack and he peers around the edge of the curtain as she peers around the door.

'Need a wee, go back,' she says, waving him away. 'I'm going to burst...'

She comes in without waiting, rushing for the toilet as he pulls back, shocked that he saw the cheeks of her bum as she turned while tugging her knickers down.

'Boy!' she snaps, grunting with annoyance. 'He's pissed on the seat again...it's all over my bum. Disgusting...'

Gregori stands still under the flow, listening to her rustling and moving about.

'Unless it was you?'

'I no wee wee on the seat.'

'Good,' she mutters. Then he hears it. The tinkle of her urinating, and despite all the things he has done in his life, he finds it both mesmerising and appalling at the same time. Gregori can remove the internal organs from the human body with surgical precision. He has done so many times. From women too but right now he cocks his head over and stands with his mouth hanging open at the noise. And that noise goes on too. And keeps going on.

'Drank a lot of water,' she calls out.

He listens, it goes on.

'Stop listening...you're making me self-conscious...'

'I no...'

'Why is it so hot?'

'I not...'

'It's too hot. I'm all sticky...'

He stares at the curtain before glancing down at his penis and starting with shock at the physical reaction he is having.

'You okay?' she asks, hearing him mutter and move quickly.

'Is big...is cold! Shower...cold is good.'

'Right. Well, shout me when you're done so I can jump in.'

'Jump in.'

'Pardon?'

'I no say this.'

He washes quickly, willing his erection to go down then hops out to towel off while thinking of her weeing in the same room as him and the sight wedged in his mind of her bum when she turned to tug her knickers down. When he goes out he does so quickly, rushing past her room with a suppressed yelp at the sight of her standing in her bra and knickers with her hands on her hips.

'Are you okay?' she calls out.

'FINE...IS FINE...'

They meet again on the landing. Both dressed. Both cleaned and ready for the day.

'Breakfast?' she enquires into the suddenly awkward silence.

Into the kitchen. She aims for the stove, putting water on to boil while he moves to the back door, pulling the locks and bolts back.

'And how are you?' she asks, kissing the boy's head.

'Fine, Casseeee,' he mumbles, lost in his drawings.

'Stop weeing on the toilet seat...hmmm? Are you listening?' she pulls a sheet out, looking at the circles he drew last night and the precision of them, like something a machine would make. Then she spots the other pages. The ones he has done this morning. 'Jesus...did you do these?' she asks. Something in her voice catches Gregori's attention who turns from the door, moving back to look down at the sheets on the table and in her hands.

The first one she picks up is filled with stick figures holding what look like crudely drawn axes and a big dog. All of them drawn in dark colours, black and dark blues and dark greens. Red used to show the blood on the axes cutting into other stick figures drawn in lighter colours. Dozens of the same things drawn over and over on the page with battles and fights underway. Poorly drawn with a skill expected of a child his age.

Then she picks up another sheet, as Gregori shifts the pages on the table.

From crudely drawn oddly proportioned stick figures without joints or bends in their arms and legs to the ones that show elbows, knees, better-proportioned limbs and facial expressions.

She notices all of the people holding axes are angry with down-turned mouths whereas all of the victims in the lighter colours are happy and smiling with red only used to show blood and their eyes. That the lighter colour figures are infected is obvious.

The next sheets show a marked transition again with scale and depth used to reflect the fighting. The dark figures now given comparable size. The first one with a blob of curly dark hair. The one behind him much smaller. The one after that is huge with thick limbs. Women too given shape with bulges for boobs and hair on their heads.

Cassie looks from the pages in her hands to those on the table. Seeing where the boy has used softer, lighter strokes with an increase in skill. A huge explosion in one picture. Bodies flying through the air, all of them smiling and happy while the darker figures look up with angry faces.

'Jesus,' she murmurs the word when Gregori slides a sheet of paper out that shows a dog tearing a person apart. Deftly drawn and way beyond the level of competence on the others. The face of the victim tragic and happy at the same time. Not a stick figure either but more of an image captured by an angst-ridden teen skilled in art. The dog too, clearly a German Shepherd. The shades used to reflect the variances in fur colour.

'Paco Maguire,' she whispers, seeing a face peering from a sheet. The Hollywood actor drawn in crayon. 'Oh Jesus...' she spots the other sheets. So many of them all containing the face of a man with dark curly hair. His eyes deep, dark and brooding. The viewpoint from the front, from the left and right capturing his profile. Dark angry shades. His nose harsh, his jaw harsher.

Other faces. A man with blond hair and lighter eyes. A good-looking man. A huge bald man. A small man with close-cropped hair. The skill increasing with each one to that of an accomplished artist.

Gregori pulls another one out. A breath-taking image of a stunning woman. Thick lustrous hair. Plump lips, sensual and captivating. Cassie hates her on sight and with a surge of jealousy she snatches the page out from under Gregori's hand. More pictures of the same woman. All of them showing her beauty but a cruel beauty it is. A coldness there. A sadistic venom in her eyes.

The boy sits back, nonchalantly eating cereal and as he moves so Cassie and Gregori see the image he was drawing. The dark curly-haired man looking furious while surrounded by smiling men and women holding him down while a human heart is pushed into his mouth. The blood spraying out down the man's chin. The people surrounded him all with red eyes but earnest as though giving aid to a wild angry demon.

'Can we play frisbee today?' the boy asks.

Gregori looks back to the first picture drawn. The crude stick figures then to the last one and the deft skill used. It's not right. It's wrong. What he is seeing is wrong.

Cassie feels the same thing. A weird sensation inside. That the world is skewed and off-kilter. Each of the drawings is organic and if placed in a row you could see the development of an artist that would take years, more than a decade. Not a couple of hours.

'Is this Howie?' she asks, pointing at the image of the man pinned down with a heart shoved in his mouth. That he is the main focus throughout is obvious with the beautiful woman a close second.

The boy nods.

'Who is that?' she asks, prodding one of the pictures of the beautiful woman.

'Marceee,' the boy replies, reaching for a handful of Frosties.

'Marcy, she was bitten by Darren...which one is he?' Cassie asks.

'Darren is deaded.'

'Dead,' Cassie corrects him then spots Gregori staring at a picture of Marcy. 'Look at you drooling.'

He blinks, looking at her. 'What this?'

'You,' she snaps, 'dribbling all over it...'

'I not know this.'

'Wank bank yeah?' she asks, ditching the sheets on the table.

Gregori pauses, thinking she just said a rude word but not quite understanding the context or meaning.

She crosses to the stove, taking the pan of boiling water to pour into a mug then adds long-life milk and a spoon of sugar before turning to see him staring expectantly.

'What wanky bank?' he asks.

'Ask Marcy.'

'Can we play frisbee now?'

They won't play frisbee for three reasons. The first being that Cassie cannot risk the disc going into the treeline again, the second being that it's too hot to move, let alone chase things about outside and the third being that Cassie has a plan in mind. Plus the fact she's feeling a psychotic rage at the thought of Gregori staring at that picture.

'Come on, get washed and changed,' she tells the boy curtly. They go off together, the boy cooling off in the shower while Cassie sorts his clothes for the day. 'Finished?' she asks in the bathroom.

'Yes, Casseeee...we can't to the fort today.'

'We're not going to the fort any day,' she says, drying him off.

'We can tomorrow,' he says earnestly.

'Okay,' she says, thinking it's easier to just go along with it.

'When Howie doesn't live there.'

'Howie is moving out is he? Right anyway, you remember what we said about? Our secret yes? Daudi in the supermarket? Do you remember?'

He nods quickly, his wet head bobbing up and down.

'Is it done?' she asks quietly.

He carries on nodding.

'Are you sure?'

The nod keeps going.

'Good boy, let's get you dressed and hopefully we can have a swim later.'

Gregori drinks the coffee he made himself while looking at the pictures while also wondering why Cassie got angry at him for looking at the beautiful woman. She is beautiful though. He looks again, pulling one closer.

'Oh my god, you're like a dog on heat,' Cassie snaps, striding in as he turns away quickly.

'I just look,' he says as innocently as a serial killer can.

She arches an eyebrow, folding her arms and holding position in such a way that makes him squirm and think again about shooting her. 'Anyway, my handsome, we're going out today,' she says lightly, switching into nice Cassie with a big smile. 'I want solar panels, remember? And the car has air-conditioning...'

He scowls, thinking he does not want to go out today and maybe they should hang around the house and do normal things that are good for the boy.

'And I thought we could get a pool,' she adds.

'Pull?'

'Pool, for swimming. You know, one of those big inflatable things. Fill it with water and we can splash about...'

His mind fills with an image of Cassie splashing about and in that image she is wearing a bikini and strangely, he thinks of her weeing again. 'Yes,' he says deeply, seriously, 'is good for boy...exercise yes...'

'Good man,' she says, giving him a wink before sashaying off.

Into the car where all three sit and simply savour the pleasure of the air-conditioning bringing the absurd temperature down. The air so thick that even walking from the house to the car made them sweat. Still, she has a plan and if it works the effort will be worth it.

'Into town,' she says as he pulls away. 'Music?' she asks lightly, choosing a song she knows he likes. 'This weather? It's just crazy...' she pulls her top out from her body, wafting it a few times. 'Makes you want to sit naked doesn't it?'

She keeps the chat going, nice and easy, nice and light. Distraction without being obvious. The boy sits in the back, singing along to the music as the big vehicle goes through the country roads. She stays relaxed as they near the junction and reaches out to turn the volume down. 'Can you swim?' she asks.

'Yes,' he says.

'I'm not a good swimmer,' she says conversationally, her keen eyes glancing forward as the junction comes into view. 'It will be good in this heat though...oh look, what's happened there? Slow down...'

His eyes snap over to the junction, taking in the big sign.

Hillside Luxury Boutique Hotel and Spa.

A body in the road where the tarmac meets the gravel of the driveway. Another one a few feet away and a dead woman slumped against the post beneath the sign saying *no more survivors.*

Gregori slows, easing his foot off but ready to power on again. His eyes reading the positions and clues that tell him the people were taken down as they fled.

'Oh now that's awful,' Cassis says sadly. 'Pull over...'

'No stop here,' he says.

'Just pull over, they might need help.'

He looks at her, surprised at the show of concern that he wouldn't expect to see. 'They dead...'

'Just pull over, we're safe enough...it's not like the things ever hurt him do they?'

Gregori stops the car, easing into the junction but angling out so they can flee if needed. His pistol in hand when he gets out to view the bodies one after the other, walking from the road to the woman slumped against the post. Her neck bitten too deep and the blood thick down her front.

'Is it recent?' Cassie asks, standing next to Gregori as they stare down.

'More than one day,' Gregori says.

'Shame to let it go to waste,' Cassie murmurs, shaking her head at the sadness of it all.

'What?' Gregori asks.

'The luxury boutique hotel and spa...shame to let it go to waste...I mean they're all dead aren't they.'

'These dead. Others may be okay.'

'That's a good point. We'll go check and see.'

'No do this,' he says as she walks off back to the car.

'Why not?'

'We go. We get pull and swim...'

She pauses, midway into the car. 'They've got a pool,' she says, nodding at the pictures on the big sign.

Gregori looks at the image on the board and the gorgeous turquoise waters of the pool complete with a beautiful woman splashing about in a bikini. 'We check, yes...'

'Thought you would,' she murmurs.

The hotel is picture perfect. Modern, sleek and refined. One large central building and a car park filled with high-end sports and executive cars. Landscaped grounds, fountains and box-hedges cut perfectly and the Range Rover crunches noisily over the gravel drive towards the double front doors standing wide open. No movement. No motion and Cassie's heart flutters with nerves that Gregori will somehow realise what she's done.

'Can't see anyone,' she says, forcing a neutral tone. 'Are the things here?' she asks the boy.

'Daudi has gone gone gone...'

'Daudi?' Gregori asks with a scowl.

Cassie laughs it off, waving her hand with a roll of her eyes. 'More crazy names haha! Come on, let's go and have a look,' she says, pulling the sawn-off shotgun out from under the seat.

Gregori goes first, venturing inside the beautiful lobby filled with sleek glass and muted colours. Ultra-modern mixed with exquisite taste. A bar to the left. Deep leather chairs and sofas. A restaurant to the right. Gilt and golden.

The signs of life are clear. Empty bottles and glasses on the tables in the bar. The restaurant tables covered in used plates. Chairs turned over, tables too. Signs of a fight, of a massed panic that ripped through the hotel. Bloody footprints on the tiled floor and smears on the polished glass.

'Oh wow,' Cassie says, approaching the foyer to the luxury spa section. The double doors again wide open and they step through to see a fully equipped modern gym, steam rooms, saunas and then to the back of the building with huge picture windows overlooking the grounds and a beautiful large pool of turquoise water.

'Guess they all left,' Cassie says, one hand holding the boy while the other grips the shotgun. She shares a look with the boy, winking at the secret they share. He giggles softly, trying to wink back but closing both eyes.

Gregori frowns, wondering how the things got into a place where the survivors had taken the effort to warn people to stay away. Where are the bodies? Then he remembers the survivors would now be infected so would have left with the attackers, but why were three corpses were left on the entrance drive? A prickling of suspicion. His highly trained senses telling him something isn't right with what he is seeing.

She spots his expression hardening and the way he looks around. A flutter of panic inside. She thinks quickly, looking for something to deflect his attention but not seeing anything.

'Lovely pool,' she says but he shakes his head and it's obvious he's going to order them to leave. 'So hot,' she gasps, fanning her face.

'Come...we go...' he growls the words out, unsure of his environment, unsure of everything, the pistol gripped in his hand.

There's no other choice, she must use what she has. 'Just give me five minutes...'

'No,' he says then balks as she pulls her top over her head, stretching up with her arms high to let it drop before unbuttoning her shorts that she tugs down to stand in her bra and knickers.

'Quick swim?' she asks the boy, feeling Gregori's gaze on her, her heart thudding with pleasurably excitement. 'It's just so hot...' she looks up at Gregori, lifting her eyebrows quizzically, demure and sensual. A pause, a second worth of life frozen in time then she smiles and turns to dive gracefully into the water, sliding in with barely a splash and leaving the boy and Gregori staring after her.

'Can I do swimming please, Gregoreeee?'

He turns to look at the child with all thoughts of dead bodies and open doors now gone from the front of his mind. 'Yes. Is good. Swim. Yes.'

CHAPTER NINE

Day Twenty Four

Ten minutes after Danny's first close-quarters fight and Howie looks round at the mangled broken bodies as the energy eases back, the lessening of the flow between them that was needed to get through the battle. That Danny is one of them is now beyond doubt. They all felt him within the thing they have. Whatever that is they still cannot say, but then many things of this new world are beyond their understanding.

To kill is wrong but what they are doing is right. Howie knows that, but it's not enough. That pressure is there and growing. The feeling in his bones that they are trying to hold the ocean back with a sponge. A few days ago, he would have relished a kill-rate like this. Scoring hundreds per day, but now it just doesn't feel right. A niggle. A nag.

'It's not enough,' he says to Reginald and Clarence.

'It rather does feel that way doesn't it,' Reginald remarks thoughtfully, his mind whirring with thoughts, ideas, facts and knowledge.

'We need a plan, Reggie,' Howie says. 'If not then we'll just go north like Blowers said...'

'Understood,' Reginald says, staring around at the bodies then over to the others gathered around Danny and giving silent thanks the precious unity is coming back. Howie is right. What they are doing now is of no real consequence to the other side but it's bringing them back together, and right now that is the priority because without unity there is but one option left.

'What about Marcy?' Clarence asks, clocking the way Reginald is staring at her. 'Her idea...'

'No,' Howie say firmly.

'Not unless all else fails I would suggest,' Reginald says. 'I rather think of Marcy as being the nuclear option...she'll win, my god she will win but there will be nothing left...'

'Rather her than it though,' Clarence says.

'Wise words,' Reginald says genuinely.

'So if it comes to it then we'll have no choice,' Clarence says, looking at Howie who nods but stays silent.

'Which makes Marcy our secret weapon,' Reginald says. 'Which in turn will feed her narcissism and vanity and make her intolerable. But yes, my advice would be to protect her at all costs.'

'Hang on,' Howie says, a light-bulb illuminating in his head with a staggeringly simplistic realisation. 'We need to find the Marcy equivalent then...if she controls what she takes then there'll be one like her making them talk and writing those *he is coming* things everywhere. Why the fuck didn't we think of that before?'

'We did,' Reginald replies stiffly. 'Or rather, I did.'

'Then why aren't we looking for it?'

'What do you think we are doing? We are looking *for it,*' Reginald says. 'That is precisely what we are doing...are they smaller groups working independently of each other or one larger hive mind? What on earth do you think I have been studying and thinking about for the last few days? That is exactly what I meant when I complained previously about having sordid little squabbles here and there and that we needed to find the source.'

'Oh,' Howie says.

'Indeed. Oh,' Reginald says haughtily. 'What did you think I was doing in Roy's van?'

'Dunno, drinking herbal tea? That was a joke,' he adds quickly on seeing Reginald start to bite. 'Okay. At least we've got a plan now. We'll find the Marcy-equivalent and in the meantime, Dave, from now on you stick by our Marcy's and keep her safe.'

'Mohammed will be assigned, Mr Howie.'

'It's better if it's you, Dave.'

'I protect you, Mr Howie. Mohammed will be assigned. Simon should also be made aware she has VIP status.'

'Oh god, don't tell her she's a VIP,' Howie says quickly. 'Blowers, you got a minute?'

He walks over, breaking free from the others. 'What's up?'

'I can't even say it,' Howie sighs.

'Marcy has VIP status and is to be protected at all costs,' Dave says flatly. 'Mohammed will be assigned for close-protection.'

'Right,' Blowers says. 'Understood...does she know?'

'God no,' Howie says.

'Don't tell her,' Clarence whispers.

'Don't tell her what?' Marcy calls over.

'She's a fucking bat,' Howie mutters before calling out. 'I just said we should call it a day...this heat is too much.'

'Urgh, this heat is too much!' Marcy says, dropping onto the bench seat in the Saxon. 'I'd go and sit in Reggie's van if it wasn't so boring...and if Reggie wasn't in it.'

'Fact.'

She looks to her side at Mo nodding earnestly then leans forward to look down the vehicle to the back doors to see Dave and Nick now in the end seats.

'It's hot innit,' Mo says casually, smiling at Marcy then at Paula.

'What are you doing?' Marcy asks him.

'Nuffin','

'Mo,' Paula says, 'why are you up here?'

He shrugs innocently and full of that rakish boyish charm. 'I wanted to be closer to you...'

Blowers blinks his one good eye while everyone else finds something to look at.

'Didn't have no family,' Mo says sadly, looking from Paula to Marcy. 'You's like my sisters, you get me?'

Nick coughs. Cookey winces. Blowers shifts. Charlie rolls her eyes while Danny just takes it all in.

'Aw you are so sweet,' Marcy says, wrapping an arm around his shoulders to pull him for a hug.

'He is,' Paula says, leaning over to pat his knee. 'You sit up here with us, are you hungry? I've got some of those snack bars you like somewhere...'

'Why can't all men be like you?' Marcy asks him, kissing the side of his head while Mo grins down at the others all shaking their heads.

'Unbelievable,' Nick mutters. 'Can I have a snack bar?'

'There's some in your bag,' Paula calls down without looking. 'Here you are, sweetie, let me open it for you.'

'Thanks, Paula,' Mo says.

'Danny, one for you too,' she adds.

'Thank you, Ma'am.'

'You're a sweetie too,' she tuts at him.

'I'm a sweetie,' Cookey says.

'You're not a sweetie,' Marcy says.

'I am,' Cookey announces, thinking to pull Charlie into the conversation then spotting the distant look in her eyes again. A hardening in her expression that stills his tongue and the moment passes as that weighted silence comes back and suddenly the joke of Mo cuddling into Marcy seems flat and forced, awkward even and the fragility of their state shows once again.

In the new van Reginald also shakes his head in surprise. 'Well now, Mr Doku...I really don't know what to say.'

'Just say if you need anything else.'

'I will, yes...but gosh. I didn't even see you get them.'

Maddox decides to stay quiet and watch Reginald peruse his selection of scale maps, writing pads, notebooks and pens. A magnetic wipe clean white-board stuck to the side of the van next to his desk. Clips and fasteners for paperwork. Stationary of all types and all taken in the blink of an eye by a young man highly skilled in the arts of getting what's needed for the *bossman*.

Maddox isn't altruistic. They both know that, but Maddox and Reginald also both know he is a part of this, whatever this is, and Maddox wants to be in this van, so he'll do what it takes to keep his place.

'Unity is important then?' he asks conversationally.

'It is indeed,' Reginald says, unfolding a map. 'Vital I might add.'

'Did Lani turn because that was broken?'

Reginald leans forward as though trying to find their position while his mind runs fast. 'It is a possibility...along with many others.'

Maddox nods as though only half-interested. Both of them playing a game of which they are acutely aware. 'They made us do team-building exercises in young offenders...'

'Ah is that so? Did they help?'

'For some.'

'I should imagine you learnt skills otherwise unintended,' Reginald says, smiling ruefully. '*How to make others do as you desire* by Maddox Doku eh?'

Maddox grins, unable to stop himself. 'Something like that. I had an idea...it's just a suggestion but...'

Reginald listens intently and gives a little bit more respect to Maddox.

'Reginald to Howie? Can you switch to channel three for a private conversation?'

'Doing it now,' Howie transmits back as Clarence reaches over to switch his radio to channel three. *'Yeah go ahead, Reggie...a what? Really? How far? Okay...we'll do that.'*

'Do what?' Marcy asks. 'I thought we were finishing for today...'

'Just one more thing,' Howie calls back with a heavy tone. 'Sorry...'

'Fuck's sake,' Marcy mutters. 'We can't move in this heat...'

'It's fine,' Blowers says to the restless shifts coming from everyone. 'It's work...get hydrated. Drink, Danny.'

Danny drinks and wipes the sweat from his forehead. The air so hot and thick in the Saxon.

Paula rests her head back against the Saxon wall. She could be in the van with Roy enjoying cooler air, but it felt important to be with the team right now. Especially after losing Blinky and now they've got young Danny. Besides, the mood is still so fragile.

'Two minutes,' Howie calls out.

'Make ready,' Blowers says as everyone starts checking rifles, magazines and glugging water.

The Saxon stops on a wide country road just a few feet back from the junction with a dual carriageway. Only one building in sight, a huge sleek thing of polished plate glass windows.

Everyone gets out, rifles up and ready, all of them looking around wondering what they are doing.

'That building,' Howie says, moving off with Dave and Clarence as the rest follow behind with Marcy frowning at a smiling Mo walking at her side. 'Ah now, someone's opened it for us too,' Howie grins, stopping in front of a broken plate glass window.

'Hadley's luxury car dealership,' Paula reads the sign on the front. 'Why are we here?'

'All in good time, Miss Paula,' Howie says, leading the way in.

It's big too. A mini-warehouse of a building with a white tiled floor on which high-end cars rest on clean black tyres with doors open to show their exquisite interiors.

They go in after Meredith with Howie, Dave and Clarence pushing through to the back area, kicking doors in to check the offices, washrooms and workshops. Thick dust on every surface. The air stale and musty. All good signs.

'Everyone okay?' Howie asks, walking into the main display room.

'Fine but why are we here?' Paula asks.

'Downtime,' Howie says simply. 'Maddox's idea...too hot to work and there's a big open road right outside...'

'No way, are you being serious?' Nick asks as the others start grinning in surprise. 'Like not fucking about serious?'

'Not fucking about serious,' Howie says.

'Maddox,' Nick calls out, turning to look at him. 'You're still a complete cunt but best idea ever...'

'Ferrari 458 over here,' Roy calls out.

'Lamborghini Gallardo here,' Nick replies. 'Shit colour though... lime green?'

'Yellow one over there,' Blowers says.

'Maserati,' Cookey says, reading the small display plinth position behind one of the cars.

'Lotus over here,' Roy says.

'Got a Porsche,' Nick says.

'Which one?' Blowers asks.

'Which one,' Nick scoffs. 'There is only one...' he adds as Paula looks to Clarence who shrugs.

'You not into sports cars?' she asks him.

'I can't fit in them,' he says simply.

'Oh,' she says, looking up at him. 'Too big.'

'Too big,' he says, looking down at her.

'Yeah,' she says, caught in his eyes.

'Hmmm,' he says, unable to look away and wishing only to push the loose strand of hair from her forehead.

'Ahem,' Marcy says, moving between them.

'Right! Are we going?' Paula booms, clapping her hands as everyone looks over.

'We just got here,' Nick says in alarm.

'Eh, what?' Cookey asks. 'Aren't we driving them?'

'Er, yes, carry on,' she announces, blushing furiously. 'Cigarette I think.'

'Really?' Roy asks.

'Don't even start. It's too hot,' she fires back.

'So what's missing?' Nick asks, nodding at the empty space within the display line up.

'Er...' Howie says, walking over to read the information plinth.

'Ah, that's a shame.'

'What was it?' Nick asks.

'Bugatti Veyron,' Howie says.

'Fuck,' Nick groans.

'They've got a Veyron?' Blowers asks.

'They had a Veyron,' Howie replies. 'It's gone now.'

'What cunt nicked that?' Blowers asks. 'Selfish prick...'

'What are we doing then?' Cookey asks.

'We're not nicking them,' Blowers says. 'We're admiring...and even if we drive one we'll leave it here for the pleasure of other survivors...'

'What's a Veyron?' Paula asks, lighting a cigarette while standing just outside the broken window.

'Paula,' Marcy tuts. 'Even I know what a Bugatti Veyron is...it's like the best car ever.'

'Now nicked by some selfish thundercunt,' Blowers says.

'Oh,' Paula says, blowing smoke into the air. 'Ask Howie to wave his thing.'

'My what?' Howie asks to the sniggers rolling around the room.

'Dirty sods. I meant the thing he waved earlier...' Paula says.

'I haven't waved my thing at anyone,' Howie says.

'You've waved it at me a few times,' Marcy says to more sniggers. 'And in the armoury with Lani when she turned into a zombie and you had sex with her on the table while we all listened outside...'

'Fuck's sake,' Howie groans as Danny looks at Mr Howie in awe.

'I'm not on about Mr Howie's penis,' Paula says.

'Thank god for that,' Howie mutters.

'I meant earlier...' Paula says.

'What earlier?' Marcy asks.

'Earlier...in the street,' Paula says, huffing at herself. 'You know... the willystick...'

'Willystick?' Howie asks.

'Fuckstick?' Blowers suggests.

'Fuckstick,' Paula says, clicking her fingers at Blowers. 'He waved his fuckstick...'

'It was a magic invisible fuckstick,' Cookey says.

'Yes, that,' Paula says.

'What about it?' Howie asks.

'What?' Paula asks.

'I'm so lost,' Howie says.

'The Veyron car,' Paula says. 'It's not here...'

'Oh! Oh, I see...you want me to wave my magic invisible fuckstick to bring the Veyron back?'

'Yes! Oh my god I think this heat is killing brain cells,' Paula says.

'Either that or your explanation was shit,' Marcy says.

'So?' Paula says, staring at Howie.

'What?' Howie asks, looking around. 'I'm not doing it now...don't all look at me like that. Seriously, stop looking at me...fuck's sake...fine, okay...here is my magic invisible fuckstick that I shall wave to make the Veyron appear...tada!'

Silence for a second as everyone looks to the big hole in the window and watches the blue-winged butterfly flap lazily from right to left before the roar of a high-performance engine coming towards them sounds out. A screech of tyres and black and orange Bugatti Veyron appears in a screeching sliding stop.

'You really need to ask for coffee,' Blowers says, looking from the Veyron to Howie.

A gear change and the Bugatti engine whines as it reverses back into the parking space it held earlier. Crunching over the broken glass and coming to a stop with a few more revs coming from the front.

'REV IT AGAIN,' Nick shouts to the driver. Listening as the engine roars out in the confined space. 'SO GOOD...'

'VERY GOOD,' Roy shouts to many manly nods.

'HE'S A GOOD BLOKE FOR BRINGING IT BACK,' Blowers shouts.

'TOP BLOKE,' Cookey shouts.

'GOOD LAD,' Nick adds, his voice booming out as the engine finally cuts off, dropping into an awed silence of everyone staring at the car.

Then the door opens, and a slender tanned tattooed arm stretches out with a black pistol held by the barrel and the butt facing Nick who takes it without a word and hands it back to Cookey who passes it to Blowers who hands it on to Mo who gives it to Maddox who passes it on to Danny who doesn't know what to do with it.

The arm disappears from view for a second then reappears holding a black police issue G36 assault rifle by the barrel with the stock held towards Nick who takes it without a word and hands it back to Cookey who passes it to Blowers who hands it on to Mo who gives it to Madddox who passes it on to Danny who fumbles with his own rifle, the other pistol and now another assault rifle.

Only then does the driver get out and stand with her hands up and away from her body as though to show she is unarmed before moving to stand between Nick and Cookey in the silent line facing the car.

'So beautiful,' Nick whispers.

'Is,' the woman whispers.

'Work of art,' Roy says.

'Definitely,' the woman says.

'I almost don't want to drive it,' Nick whispers.

'Oh you do,' the woman whispers.

Dark blond hair pulled back, a stud in her nose, another two piercings in her left eyebrow. A simple vest top, tattoos on both arms and the empty pistol holster on her right side. She doesn't flinch when Meredith pushes her nose into her hand but glances down, smiles and strokes the dog's head before looking back at the car.

'Is this the group with Mr Howie and Dave?' she asks quietly, her mouth turning up and to the left when she speaks.

'Yeah,' Nick says, lifting a hand in the general direction of Howie. She keeps her eyes on the Veyron and lifts the front of her top up to show bite and scratch marks on her bruised stomach.

'I got bit by the zombie things and I keep getting weird moods...is that normal?' she asks as they all look from the car to her belly for a second.

'Nah, you're a freak,' Cookey says, looking back at the car. 'We'll have to shoot you.'

'Okay,' she says, pulling the top down.

'It's fine. We've all been bit,' Nick says.

'Cool,' she says, lapsing back into reverential silence for a few seconds. 'Fancy a drag race?'

'Fuck yes,' Nick says. 'Ferrari versus Lambo?'

She pulls a face, tilting her head side to side. 'How about all of them?'

The lads all turn to look at her with love shining in eyes as Paula sighs and shakes her head. 'I'll get another bag ready...and Mo?'

'Yeah?'

'Yes, not yeah.'

'Sorry, Dave. Yes, Paula?'

'You're not taking part, you're only sixteen.'

'What! That's not fair...'

'Or you, Danny...not after smashing the van into that shop.'

'Aw but, Paula,' Mo says, rushing after her. 'I'm a good driver. Ask Mads...'

'He's shit.'

'Fuck off, Mads! I can drive...Mr Howie lets me drive the Saxon... I'll just do a slow one at the back or something and I'll put the seatbelt on and everything...'

'No,' Paula's voice sails through from outside.

'So not fair. I invaded an army base on my own and rescued everyone and...'

'You had Maddox with you...and I said no...'

Mo stops rushing after Paula, his face screwing up like the sixteen-year-old boy he is, then he spots Howie and turns quickly. 'Mr Howie...'

'Oh no, don't bring me into this...'

'Cheeky fucker!' Cookey says, bursting out laughing. '*Aw but Dad...mum said no...*' he mimics, setting everyone else off.

'And you's can get fucked,' Mo tells him, flicking a middle finger which just makes them laugh more. 'Sorry, Miss, I ain't swearing at you,' he tells the woman. 'Just them bellends...Paula, please!'

'No!'

'Ah but but...Clarence...' he tries again, looking imploringly at the big man.

'Don't even try,' Clarence says.

'Fuck's sake,' Mo huffs, folding his arms and stalking back to stand next to Marcy. 'S'fine innit. I'll just guard Marcy with my life while's you's go and drive nice cars...'

'What?' Marcy asks.

'Mo!' Blowers groans.

'Fuck it,' Howie groans.

'What's going on?' Marcy asks.

'Not sayin' nuffin',' Mo grumbles. 'I'm too young to drive so's I be quiet.'

'Why is Mo guarding me?' Marcy asks, looking from Mo to Clarence to Reginald then to Howie who all burst to life at the same time, walking towards the woman stood with Nick.

'Hi, I'm Howie...' Howie says, holding his hand out.

'Clarence,' Clarence says, joining Howie's side.

'Blowers?' Marcy asks, her voice hardening.

'I'm Blowers,' Blowers says, turning quickly into the small group surrounding the woman. 'So er...you got bit? That's awful.'

'Awful,' Howie says.

'Must have hurt,' Cookey says.

'Looks painful,' Nick adds.

'Hello my dear, my name is Reginald, it is very nice to meet you...'

'I like your tattoos,' Cookey says.

'Is she still there?' Howie asks in a whisper that carries across the room.

'She's folding her arms,' Nick whispers as Marcy folds her arms.

'She's doing that angry pouting thing,' Cookey whispers as Marcy starts glaring.

'I can fight like the whole army, but I can't drive a Porsche...' Mo grumbles.

'Use your magic fuckstick on her...' Cookey urges.

'Er, not the thing to say right now mate,' Howie says, wincing at the new woman. 'He doesn't mean my penis...I just said penis...'

'You said penis,' Clarence tells him.

'The boss just said penis,' Nick says, covering his face with his hand.

'Stop saying penis to the new woman,' Marcy snaps. 'Leave the poor girl alone...'

'I'm fine, really,' the new woman says politely.

'What the...' Paula says, walking back in to see them all crowding around the new woman. 'What the hell are you all doing?'

'I said Mr Howie should use his fuckstick on Marcy, but he was worried the new lady thought I meant penis so he...er...told the...nice lady...' Cookey tails off into the silence.

'Jesus wept,' Paula says, marching through them. 'Go on, sod off and leave her alone...she doesn't need to know about fucksticks or...'

'Please, Paula.'

'I said no, Mo...you're only sixteen...right, you come with me,' she says to the woman. 'Honestly, they're awful round new people sometimes. It's just embarrassing...what's your name?'

'It's fine,' the woman says, looking around at everyone while being escorted away. 'Natasha...but everyone calls me Tappy.'

'Tappy? That's nice. Why Tappy? I said no, Mo...this is Charlie who will stop the idiots from pestering you. So yes, great. Why Tappy?'

'Er my er...my surname.'

'Your surname is Tappy?' Paula asks as Charlie smiles at the new woman who smiles back while staring at Charlie's shaved head.

'Drinkwater,' Tappy says quietly.

'Drinkwater?' Paula asks. 'Oh, I see...yes that makes sense.'

'I don't get it,' Cookey says.

'Someone better tell me why Mo is guarding me...' Marcy says. 'No? Really? I'll just ask Charlie then...'

'Me?' Charlie asks. 'Why me?'

'You know everything,' Paula says. 'Charlie knows everything,' she tells Tappy.

'I really don't,' Charlie tells Tappy.

'I love the shaved head thing,' Tappy tells her. 'Really suits you...'

'Thanks, only did it this morning.'

'Right! Fine. Charlie, why is Mo guarding me?'

'How would I know? Oh, hang on...ah yes, that makes sense actually.'

'Charlie knows everything,' Paula tells Tappy again, handing her a rucksack.

'Can I say?' Charlie asks, looking to Howie and Reginald who both shakes their heads frantically.

'Someone better bloody tell me,' Marcy snaps. 'Is this because I bit those soldiers?'

'What?' Tappy asks.

'It is isn't it? It's because I bit all those soldiers...'

'Honestly, it's really not like it sounds...' Paula says, opening the rucksack in Tappy's hands. 'So in here, you've got water and...'

'WHOA!' Marcy shouts, glaring from Howie to Mo. 'Is Mo meant to kill me if I try and bite anyone?'

'What?' Howie asks.

'Eh?' Blowers asks.

'No!' Clarence says.

'God no,' Howie says.

'Of course not,' Reginald says.

'Is that it? Mo, you little shit...you said you loved me like a sister...'

'Dunno, I'm only sixteen,' Mo says glumly.

'And some snack bars in case you get peckish,' Paula continues.

'It was only three hundred,' Marcy says. 'Not like before when I did thousands...'

'What?' Tappy asks.

'It's not that,' Howie says.

'It's not,' Blowers says.

'I'd say you're being protected rather than guarded, Marcy,' Charlie says.

'Don't say it,' Howie blurts.

'Like a VIP...' Charlie adds.

'Oh god she said it,' Howie says.

'What!?' Marcy asks. 'Why?'

'In case the infection goes for you...because you can do what it can do...only better...'

'Oh arse,' Howie mumbles. 'All hope is gone.'

'It's over,' Blowers says.

'Was nice knowing you all,' Clarence says.

'We had a good run,' Howie says.

'No, it was fun,' Blowers says. 'Ish...apart from dying twice...and losing an eye and a finger...'

Marcy simmers, her arms folded, her eyes hard but the words sink in and they sink deep. VIP. Protected. She can do what the infection can...but better. 'So I'm important then am I?'

'Okay,' Howie announces, looking around at the lads. 'Blowers, you shoot me and Clarence...then do yourself...everyone else find a shooting buddy and we'll just end it here yeah?'

'Pack it in,' Paula calls out testily. 'I'm so sorry, Tappy...it's not normally like this.'

'It is,' Charlie mouths. 'All the time.'

'Honestly, it's fine,' Tappy says politely. 'Er, why are you giving me a bag?'

'To keep your things in,' Paula replies as though the answer is obvious.

'Okay,' Tappy says, looking down at the bag then back up to Paula. 'Why's that then?'

'Where else you going to put your stuff? Oh, have you already got a bag? I didn't even think of that...of course yes, you can use your own if you want...'

'Use it for what?' Tappy asks.

Charlie clears her throat and offers a tight smile to Tappy and an apologetic one to Paula who she can see is looking more strained by the minute. 'If I may interject, I think Paula is assuming you may be joining us?' she asks as though making a gentle suggestion.

'Er, so...you guys having a big chat?' Nick asks, edging towards the Bugatti Veyron. 'Alright if I just crack on yeah?'

'Who said you're driving the Veyron?' Blowers asks, edging towards the car.

'Who said I'm not?' Nick asks, taking another step as Cookey, Blowers, Maddox and Roy all do the same.

'Stop,' Blowers orders. 'I'm the corporal so...'

'Fuck you!' Nick blurts, 'we're on downtime...'

'Can we do this in a minute?' Tappy asks, looking from Charlie to Paula. 'It's just that I...' she steps backwards while thumbing over her shoulder at the Veyron then turns to see the lads all staring at her suspiciously.

'This is stupid,' Maddox sighs heavily as though all of this is beneath him and starts to turn away before making a dash for the car. Tappy bursts to life, running for the open driver's door while Nick, Cookey and Blowers all plough forward, burdened by their weapons. An instant melee as they come together, jostling and trying to push forward.

'Ow,' Tappy cries out, clutching her arm.

'Oh shit, are you okay?' Nick asks as the lads all back-up with instant alarm.

'Sorry, was that me?' Cookey asks.

'Mugs,' she bursts out laughing, dropping into the driver's seat to flick a middle finger up.

'Cheating sod,' Cookey says with genuine admiration. 'Well played though...'

'I would like the bag!' she calls out with a laugh. 'After the downtime though...is that okay?'

CHAPTER TEN

Day Fourteen.

'Last room,' she says with a huff, not bothering to wait for him this time but pushing the door open and waving her sawn-off shotgun inside. 'Anyone there? No? What a surprise...that's because they have all gone,' she adds as Gregori moves past her into the room.

Cassie watches him check the sides and underneath the bed before opening the wardrobe and leans over to open the bathroom door with a sigh so he can check that too. The same thing he has done in every room of the luxury boutique hotel and spa.

'Done?' she asks, holding the shotgun while wearing a fluffy white *Hillside Luxury Boutique Hotel and Spa* complimentary gown and slippers. She did think twice about putting the gown on. Prowling around a hotel in your bra and pants with a shotgun might be sexy if it was just her and Gregori, especially given that every room has a bed in it, but with the boy present, she chose modesty over seduction. Besides, being overtly sexual to Gregori doesn't seem to be working so well.

'Is good,' Gregori says seriously, emerging from searching the bathroom and now at least feeling a little bit more at ease after checking every single room in the place and locking all the exit doors.

'Great, can we go back to swimming?'

'Yes,'

'Great,' she says again, holding still when he doesn't walk off and now knowing enough about the man to pick up the vibe when something is bugging him. 'What now?'

'I no have the thing.'

'What thing?'

'For the swim. I no have this.'

She blasts air, hot and sweaty. 'What thing, Gregori?'

'The clothes. I no have this.'

'Swimming costume? You mean like trunks? To wear?'

'Yes.'

'It's fine. Swim in your pants...you're wearing pants right? Boxers? Shorts?'

'Yes.'

'Great.'

'No.'

'Why no?'

'Is white.'

'Your boxers are white?'

'Yes.'

'And?'

'They look through when the water go on them.'

A pause, a moment to decipher. 'See-through?'

'Yes,' he says gravely.

'Right.'

'We go shop.'

'What? We've just spent all morning searching...'

'Okay. I no swim. I watch,' he says with that same gravelly voice while somehow conveying a great air of sadness.

'No,' she sighs. 'We'll find some...come on...'

Another search and she sweats on, letting the gown hang open as they back through the rooms where she tuts and scowls at the mess and state of those that were in use.

'Dirty pigs,' she says. 'Don't you ever be a dirty pig,' she tells the boy jumping on a bed while she roots through a suitcase as Gregori stands nearby trying not to look at shape of her arse through the gown. 'I know it's the whole of the world thing and they've been here for like two weeks but seriously? Basic hygiene rules still apply don't they?'

Ten minutes later she treads water in the pool, relishing the coolness of it as the boy splashes in the shallow end, jumping to catch the ball she just threw. Motion at the side and she glances over to see Gregori walking from the changing room wearing a white fluffy gown and slippers while carrying his clothes neatly folded and his pistols resting on top. 'The shorts fit okay?' she calls out.

'Got it!' the boy shouts out, grabbing the ball. 'Cassееее, I got the ballie ball...'

'Well done...Gregori? Did they fit okay?'

'Yes,' he says deeply, placing his things down before stepping free of the slippers then undoing the belt to slip the gown off and stare down at his bright pink flowery shorts. Cassie stares too. But not at his shorts.

'Jesus,' she whispers.

'Is bad,' he grunts, still staring down.

She swallows at the sight. She's seen him with his top off and caught glimpses here and there but now, in the pure light of the swimming room she can't help but gawp. Every muscle in his stomach doesn't just show but bulges out, pushing through the skin. The striations in his chest and the bulk of his shoulders. The shape of his arms and the veins here and there. The narrowness of his waist. The muscles in his thighs, not too dense, not too bulky. She's never seen anyone look like that in real life. Only in movies and magazines, on pop videos and telly programmes and she doesn't blink when the boy throws the ball that smacks into her forehead and bounces off.

Scars too. Puckered dots of flesh where the bullets went in. Jagged slashes now faded and old where the blades bit and when he turns she gasps at the old faded white lines on his back from where they whipped him as a child. A tapestry of wounds. A walking history of conflict and violence. He reaches the edge of the pool and stops and despite the muscles and the injuries, he looks vulnerable and exposed. That this is new territory for him and Cassie finally gains an understanding that he simply doesn't know how to be other than when he is guarding or protecting, or fighting, or being active in some way.

'Come in,' she says with a genuine smile. 'It's really nice.'

He nods once, pauses again then dives forward, moving like an Olympic athlete with perfect grace to slide into the water, going deep and far and she laughs at seeing him pass underneath and turns as he surfaces a few feet away.

'Gregoreeee, throw the ballie ball...'

They play catch in the pool. A simple thing. A simple game. The boy in the shallows with Cassie in the middle and Gregori at the deep end. Three people enjoying the coolness of the water while outside the sky darkens with the first hint of the storm clouds coming, and a few hundred metres away, in the treeline bordering the luxury boutique hotel and spa, Daudi, a former supermarket worker, stands with his arms at his sides and his red bloodshot eyes staring forward while behind him the people that were surviving in the same hotel do the same. A back door left open by one of the survivors who popped out to smoke.

A rustle and Daudi looks over to see another one joining them. A few minutes later and another one arrives. Only a few score now but more will come. A trickle feed from a slow march across fields and through thickets of trees. All of them staring ahead across the grounds to the big picture windows of the swimming room and the three people inside clambering out of the pool to wrap towels round waists before they go off to find food.

They eat in the restaurant. Food taken from the larder and stores. Tinned fish, crackers, cheeses. Simple foods but delicious after the exercise taken and Cassie continues the slow light-bulb moment of awareness she gained as Gregori stood at the edge of the pool.

She cringes to herself, thinking back to just a couple of nights ago when she wore the low cut top with no bra and how he glanced but didn't react, and how he did nothing when she pushed and rubbed against him. It was too much. Too full on. Whatever life he had before this formed a mindset that in many ways is incorruptible. The slightest gesture or word that puts him back into that mindset and he becomes rigid and stern to the point of an extreme.

Now though, when she is relaxed and doing nothing other than chatting and eating, she catches him stealing glances at the front of her gown sagging open as she sits, and he snatches those glimpses like a shy teenager rather than a filthy dirty pervert.

She flirts but softly. She smiles often, reaching out to touch his hand. 'Hmmm, try this,' she says, holding out a cracker loaded with cheese. He goes to take it, but she pulls back. 'Not all of it greedy,' she says, making the boy laugh. 'Take a bite...' she waits, watching as he frowns, and that vulnerability comes back before he leans forward to bite the cracker held in her hand and the temptation is to send the boy out of the room so she can fuck him senseless right now, but instead, she smiles and carries on eating and chatting with the boy.

'So is this a late lunch or an early dinner?' she asks.

'Early lunch and late dinner,' the boy laughs, swinging his legs.

'Silly,' she tells him. 'Look at that sky outside...I'm telling you now, we're not driving back in a storm. We'll stay here tonight. Fancy that? Staying here?'

The boy nods eagerly, 'can we do swimming and the ballie ball and...'

'Do we need to go back at all?' she asks, looking at Gregori and letting the question hang for a minute.

'Is things there,' he says. 'Computers. The drawing things for Boy...'

'We could bring them here, just a suggestion, we'll worry about it later...now, I don't know about you, but I am sweating my ti...I'm really hot so back to the pool? But no swimming for a bit. Can't swim after eating. Very dangerous...'

More wife. Less whore. That's what she tells herself as they clear the food away and head back to the spa. More motherly-type. That's what he needs. That thought makes her think of the boy and in turn, she feels her heart soften and a surge of love rush through. She never thought for one second she would ever have a maternal instinct, especially not for someone's else's bratty, precocious fucked up savant child but with the boy it's there in buckets. Just the mere thought of him being hurt prompts a sense of dread.

Back to the pool and back to the cool waters easing the heat from their bodies and back to Gregori and Cassie snatching glances at each other's forms and shapes. Gentle and easy. Nice and pleasant. A seduction by another method.

The first drops of rain hitting the window go unnoticed and it's only when the pattering grows louder that they look over to see the sky now filled with low dark clouds and that energy in the air ramping higher and higher. Static everywhere. The feel of it. The weight of the atmosphere pushing down.

'Oh my,' she says when the rain hits proper. Lashing the windows with a fury building outside. She bites her bottom lip in thought of the things she guesses will be nearby. 'I hope anyone out there finds shelter,' she says clearly, looking at the boy. 'Out of the rain and wind...'

He stays quiet, looking at her and there it is, the thing inside that's not him, that's not the boy.

Still the rain comes harder and the swimming room grows darker, but they stay in the water, bobbing up and down as they watch the storm building up outside. The big picture windows giving a perfect vista of the sky. The noise grows too. The sound of the rain hitting the roof, the edges, the eaves and drains, the waterfall as it rushes from corners and the drumming against the glass. Solid and sustained.

'Wanna drink,' the boy climbs out, going to the tables nearby to glug his juice while watching the windows. He sits down on a lounger, yawning and sleepy then lies back on Cassie's robe, seemingly content to watch the show in comfort.

'Bless him,' she whispers, still in the pool and turning back to watch the windows and listen to the wind howling with a ferocity that grows every few minutes. The light now nearly gone and in near darkness she moves closer to Gregori floating at the edge with his arms stretched out on the inner lip to keep himself still. 'Bit scary,' she whispers.

'Is just storm.'

The first crackle comes and makes her gasp. The searing bolt of pure white energy flashing across the sky followed by the long deep rumble of thunder. She looks around, thinking the boy might be afraid but spots him sleeping on the lounger and moves closer into Gregori's side. 'I don't like storms...'

He stays still, feeling her closeness while they watch the windows. The air still so hot. The water about them still so pleasant. Another bolt of lightning brings instant light and she pushes into his side, pressing her body against his as the thunder comes, filling the sky above them.

She breathes harder as though afraid and pulls his right arm in front of her chest, holding onto him rather than the side of the pool and the rain lashes the glass and the wind howls. Her heart beating louder and faster. His the same. Static in the air. Tension between them. A shared thing to look at and she lowers her head, bringing his arm up to gently touch her lips to his inner elbow as though absent-minded and doing it from familiarity and comfort. She feels him shift position slightly but doesn't know if that is good or bad, so she stays still, watching the windows as the storm grows louder.

The forked lightning comes again. Solid bolts that sear into their retinas, making both of them close their eyes and when the thunder comes she feels his arm drawing her in as though to protect her. An act of chivalry that she goes with. The brave warrior and the frightened lady.

Near darkness now. She pushes her arms down through the water to gently brush her fingertips across his thighs with small circles and light touches that edge closer towards his groin. Another bolt of lightning. Another huge clap of rolling thunder and his arm moves, lessening the grip and for a second she worries she's pushed too fast and he's moving away. Then she feels it. His fingertips on her belly.

Copying her actions. Small circles and light touches. She breathes harder, her own hands tracing a route across his thighs while his hand does the same but goes up across her stomach to the sodden material of her bra. Another bolt. Another clap of thunder and he slips a hand inside, cupping her left breast like a teenager having his first fumble but she's never known anything more erotic. He touches her nipple, his thumb moving back and forth as it stiffens and her hand finds the opening to his shorts, gently easing in.

It's happening. It's actually happening. Less whore. More wife. She goes slow, teasing and demure, pausing to lift his hand out of her bra to kiss his fingers before pushing it back in, all gently all slowly. Her own hand now inside his shorts, brushing his penis that responds instantly to her touch, growing in her hand and the bolts sear the sky and the thunder roars as she takes his hand from her bra and guides it slowly down into her knickers while gently rubbing his swelling cock.

'Oh my god,' she whispers, squeezing her eyes closed when his fingers touch her clitoris. She can't hold back. She can't. It's too much. She tugs his shorts down, exposing his erection then reaches to slide her knickers off. She's going to fuck him. Right here in this swimming pool. His hands are on her breasts, pulling her bra down, touching her, feeling her nipples. His hard cock pressing into her backside. She's going to fuck an Albanian serial killer in a swimming pool and has to force herself to remember to be more wife and less whore.

'Is this okay?' she whispers, hoping to hell he doesn't say no.

'Yes,' a delicious whisper comes back so she lifts in the water and reaches down to grip his cock while lowering and as the first sexual contact between them happens so the deep bang of the front doors being kicked in sounds through the hotel and she feels herself flying forward through the water as he turns to launch himself up and out.

'Stay with boy,' he orders, snatching his pistols up and running for the door. His feet sliding on the wet tiled floor. Another flash of lightning and a low rumble of thunder that builds louder and louder, filling the sky with a show of true power that mocks the mere mortals scrabbling on the surface of the planet.

Gregori moves fast and silent. His senses now ramped. His mind back in the world in which he was trained. He strains to listen, hearing noises coming from the front of the hotel. Footsteps, voices, males, deep and heavy. Three people. Four. More coming in. He sniffs the air, inhaling deeply through his nose to gain scents of tobacco, after-shave, body-odour and alcohol, the smells of the living rather than the smells of the infected.

Out of the spa reception to sweep along the connecting corridor to the hotel foyer and in pitch blackness he goes forward, his pistols up and aimed, his eyes fixed on the strobing light bouncing off the walls from the bolts of energy lashing the shy outside. Snatches of words reach his ears that grow clearer as he nears.

'...broken it you dumbass, Ditmer.'

'You tell me to kick it. I kick it, Behar.'

'Kick it in, not kick it off...'

'Too many steroids, Ditmer...' another voice, deeper, harder. A few laughs.

'I am sorry, Ylli...' instant subservience shown.

Gregori surges out, a second ago he was ready to fire and kill without regard but he heard the words in his own tongue, in his own language. Albanian men. Big, broad and holding automatic weapons that come up to aim as Gregori comes into view. Over a dozen of them that don't flinch or flee but they are not the types to flinch or flee. They merely aim and wait, as they are trained and told to do, as is the discipline of a trained unit.

'Hello, my friend,' one of the men closest to Gregori says in near perfect English. His eyes cold, his gaze hard. 'I suggest you lower your guns...' he says in the way of a man used to being heard and understood. A man used to authority but Gregori looks past him to the older man standing with a raincoat about his shoulders and the only one not holding a weapon.

'Ylli,' the older man says, his voice low and thick.

The man that told Gregori to lower his guns moves instantly back in a show of subservience as the old man simply stares through the gloom and darkness, waiting and watching. The lightning comes. A flash of pure white light. Less than a second but enough for everyone to see the pock-marked skin and the bulging eyes.

'Lower your weapons, Gregori,' the old man orders. 'You are amongst friends now...'

CHAPTER ELEVEN

Day Twenty-four

Paula smiles, feeling the bittersweet tang of complex emotional reactions from all that it is to be human. Simultaneously glad that her team seem to be enjoying themselves but feeling heartbroken that Blinky isn't here to join in.

The sound of it. The sight of it. The smell of it. The fumes of petrol and hot rubber on hot tarmac. The sheer power of the engines roaring out. Some so deep and throaty Paula can feel them in her bones. Others lighter, seemingly alive like animals. The speed of them too as they move from static to all-out charging down the dead-straight mile long stretch of wide road running outside the luxury car dealership.

'THREE...TWO...ONE...**GO!'** Dave's voice booming from the start line. The small man pressed into action to give the countdown and two more cars set off. Paula doesn't know what they are. She doesn't really care either but knows the red one is being driven by Howie and the blue one is driven by Maddox and as they roar from the start, rapidly accelerating with engines screaming up through the gears so she starts that half smiling, half wincing, half squinting and not wanting to watch while not being able to look away thing again.

'You're like a mother hen,' Clarence says loudly from her side, speaking over the noise of the engines.

'Put's my heart in my mouth,' she shouts as the two cars go thundering by and catches glimpse of Maddox and Howie grinning at each other then they're gone. Swooshing down the road and a few seconds later the brake lights show as they slow and turn and come back the same way, slowing to a stop amidst the excited chat as Howie and Maddox clamber out with Maddox grinning at the victory.

'Like a glove,' Paula remarks.

Clarence frowns at her words then follows her line of vision to Tappy in the middle of everyone, laughing and joking like she's always been there and Danny too, quieter and far more serious but in with them as much as anyone else.

'But then are we taking them to die?' Paula asks, giving voice to at least one of the conflicting emotions inside. She looks up to Clarence, both of them standing with their arms folded.

'Can't think like that,' Clarence says. 'Danny would fight anyway so at least with us he gets trained and some safety...as for Tappy? Don't know yet but she seems okay.'

'Okay?' Paula scoffs. 'She's more us than us.'

'True,' Clarence says with a deep chuckle.

'You know the lads will want tattoos now because she's got some,' Paula says. 'I guarantee one of them will mention it before tomorrow.'

'Probably,' Clarence laughs.

Reginald sits in his van, the back door open and facing out so he can watch the proceedings while studying, thinking and planning but at least now he can push his glasses up his nose and jot notes down.

He has to tell the others what he knows, or rather, what he thinks they need to know because the time is nearly here for him to place his few pieces on the board and play the game.

He also knows that to follow the path they need will certainly push them into the most peril they have ever faced and there is every chance they will not survive.

He sighs heavily and looks out the open back door through the sweltering heat haze to Paula and Clarence standing too close together and tuts before looking beyond them to everyone else on the road.

'Damn it,' he mutters, focussing back on Clarence as the big man leans down to hear what Paula is saying as two more supercars roar up the road. The chemistry between them is obvious, even to Reginald. The way they're both folding their arms as though showing everyone they are merely chatting while in fact, they're having to consciously resist the desire to reach out and touch one another. 'It's no good,' Reginald tells his desk, drumming his unbroken fingers on the table-top. 'No good at all...' he can't have it. He cannot tolerate a risk to his unity but what's to be done? The lure of people who wish to copulate and mate is powerful, and Reginald cannot always be present to dissuade them. He thinks again at manipulating a situation whereby Paula is killed but that would destroy them so soon after losing Blinky. 'Damn it,' he says again in frustration that not only has he got the future of humanity to worry about but also the dangers of Paula and Clarence behaving like blasted teenagers. 'Blasted people,' he grumbles, seeing Paula place her hands on her hips and shake her head.

'PLEASE!' Mo shouts from the road.

'I SAID NO,' Paula shouts, her hands still on her hips.

'AW COME ON...' Mo shouts, placing his hands together as though in prayer. 'I'LL BE SAFE...STRAIGHT LINE UP AND DOWN...PLEASE PAULA!'

'Go on, let him,' Clarence murmurs, smiling at the sight of Mo as everyone around him laughs.

She shakes her head but can't help the grin showing that makes Mo's eyes sparkle with hope. 'Yeah? Can I?' he asks, nodding eagerly.

'Go on, Paula,' Nick calls out. 'It's safe enough.'

That does it and within a second everyone is calling out for Paula to let Mo race. Tappy included.

'Fine,' Paula gives in, laughing at the sight as Mo bursts to a sprint, leaping over the railing to throw his arms around her, almost knocking her over. 'Idiot,' she laughs, kissing his head. 'Just go easy.'

'I will!' he runs back, leaping the barrier once more. 'THANKS PAULA...'

'I say, this all looks very exciting,' Reginald says, stepping next to Paula. 'Little Mo Mo joining in is he?'

'Er yeah, yeah he is,' Paula says, moving away a step from the uncomfortably close proximity of Reginald assuming the space between her and Clarence. 'Hang on a bloody minute,' she snaps, staring over at the cars lining up to race and seeing Mo rush to get inside one of the cars. 'Isn't that the fast one...the Bugatti thing...MO YOU LITTLE SOD!'

Dave shouts the countdown and a second later the cars go past with Paula grimacing at her little Mo giving a frantic wave while grinning from ear to ear behind the steering wheel of a Bugatti Veyron. What she, or Mo, don't notice is that Nick is driving the other car much slower than normal.

'He's taking it easy,' Tappy says to Charlie from the start line.

'Nick?' Charlie asks. 'He's lovely like that, they all are really. Very protective.'

'Cool,' Tappy says, detecting the pain in Charlie's eyes. The same with all of them, the same with her too, but then none can get this far into surviving and not suffer but she smiles and waves as the cars come back and Mo leaps out to run with his hands in the air at beating Nick.

Danny doesn't drive any of the cars, not given the fact he smashed a van into a shop in an otherwise quite deserted street. He does, however, sit in with the others as they drive. Laughing at the speed and sensation then taking his guarding role very seriously in between. Holding his rifle properly and looking round properly while hoping he is doing it all properly and feeling relieved everyone seems to have forgotten about the whip marks on his back and his racist stepdad.

The rain comes during another race between Nick and Tappy. The two of them having driven every combination of car to try and best the other with increasing competitiveness.

Nick in the Ferrari 458. Tappy in a Gallardo. Both hammering down the road to turn at speed, slewing round to face back the other way. Engines screaming. Hands gripping steering wheels. Wheel rubber burning and back they go to the finish line, Nick just edging in front to take the win and surging out to run over as Tappy pushes out of the Gallardo shaking her head.

'FUCK YES!' Nick shouts.

'Lucky,' Tappy says, holding her hand out. 'High five on that...' She drops the hand as he goes to high five, arching an eyebrow.

'Oooh, left you hanging,' Cookey laughs.

'Cheeky fucker,' Nick says, and the heavens open with an instant ferocity. From quiet to noise. From sunshine to the sky suddenly darker and full of low angry clouds but the feel of the cooling rain on their hot skin makes them gasp and turn their faces to the sky, drenched in seconds with the sweat rinsing away.

None of them move. None want to move. A moment in time that brings them all to silence. Grimy, hot and sticky but now suddenly cooler and so they stand and listen to the billions of tiny drums beating all about them.

Tappy opens her mouth to let it fill with pure clean water, drinking some then spitting more out and chuckling as it sprays up into the air. She does it again, standing with her head back facing the sky with her mouth stretched wide open to take the water in before spraying it up and laughing at the feel and sight. Charlie looks at her, feeling the strangeness of a shaved head in the rain and the way the rivers run over her scalp. She watches Tappy laugh and shake her head side to side then stamp her feet to splash more water with a weird happy yelping noise that makes the others look over.

'SO NICE,' Tappy yells out, grinning widely with her mouth turned up slightly to the left. 'SO BLOODY NICE,' she shouts louder, making Blowers and Cookey share a smile and a look. She yelps again, crying out in delight then reaches up to loosen her hair to shake her head in the rain. Nick smiles at the sight. Howie too. The way she shouts out, whooping and laughing, jumping on the spot like a child in glee then she goes still, drawing air before leaning back to shout at the sky. 'FUCK YOU...' she screams as loud as she can with rage and pain and anguish showing as the veins in her neck push out and her face flushes red, then she lowers her head to stare about and slowly that offset smile comes back. 'Wow, that feels better...' she says almost to herself before looking over at Howie. 'Can I do it again?'

Howie shrugs, unsure of how the hell you give someone permission to shout at the sky.

She draws air, sucking in a lungful and leans back to scream out. No words this time but just a scream. Loud, hard and rising as she goes on. Meredith starts barking. Her tail swishing. Her coat sodden and her eyes fixed on Tappy without hint of aggression or threat.

Tappy stops to gasp, her chest heaving. Her face flushed but exhilarated. 'I'm alive,' she tells Meredith, dropping down to run her hands over the dog's coat. 'We're alive...ALIVE...' she laughs and gees Meredith up to bark and jump about as the others look on. That she would do this on her own is clear to all of them and she stands again, inhaling to lean back and scream and howl as Meredith gives voice and when Tappy stops she lowers her head to gasp in the pouring rain then look over to Charlie. 'Come on...feels amazing...'

'Oh I don't...' Charlie says quickly, shaking her head.

'Try it...' Tappy leans back to scream, running on the spot in the rain and laughing. 'TRY IT CHARLIE...'

'I don't...'

'You're not dead,' Tappy cuts her off.

'My friend is,' Charlie says bluntly. 'And I do not wish to...'

'I woke up on the first night to my twelve-year-old sister biting me...' Tappy says, dropping her head again to look at Charlie. 'I killed her...then my mum...and my dad...and my brothers...' she bites off in a sob, closing her eyes, biting back the pain and anguish so evident as the tears flow to mix with the rain. The rage there. The need to do violence in revenge. Then she shakes her head again, forcing a smile. 'But I'm alive,' she looks at Charlie and leans back to scream again with Meredith barking and howling.

Charlie inhales and stares down at the ground, at the way the raindrops bounce in the puddles already forming. She breathes out and listens to Tappy howling and feels stupid and self-conscious and daft because British people don't do this. They get on with it.

Then she screams. She doesn't even know she is screaming but it comes out and it comes out sudden and loud with her eyes blazing and tears streaming, and she throws her head back to vent the rage inside, pushing it out with everything she has. A hand in hers. Tappy at her side and she screams with a stranger on a road she doesn't know. She screams for the pain inside as the rain lashes down. She shows her teeth and gives voice with Meredith who howls long and hard with them.

Howie lifts his head, feeling the rain run down over his skin to pour from his jaw. Visibility now down to less than a hundred metres. They've made noise here today which could draw the things to attack and the danger is now heightened for that lack of being able to see them coming and common sense dictates that he get everyone moving now.

He doesn't though. Instead, he brings his rifle round to the front and makes ready while turning to face out with his back to Charlie and Tappy. A ripple goes round as the lads do the same. Bringing weapons to hand and turning to look out to stand in the rain and watch and wait so their mate can do what she needs to do. Eyes hardening. Heads up. Danny glances to the two women that don't know each other now screaming into the air but a few yards away and a huge dog howling with them.

The army's weird Danny, you'll spend ninety percent of the time not having a clue what's going on. Just go with it. It's always easier to flow with it than fight against it.

Danny makes his weapon ready and turns to face out, his dark eyes staring into the squall of grey formed from the lashing rain. His hands steady and gripping his rifle.

Time passes but no impatience is shown. Not a tut. Not a gripe. Well, one does tut silently and gripes a bit inside his head but then Reginald doesn't like standing in the rain and only does it now so Paula and Clarence don't get carried away and start tearing each other's clothes off. He lifts his head when it falls silent, hopeful that it's over and they can get on with finding shelter. Then he sighs when they start again and blows air through his cheeks as the rain runs over the lenses of his glasses. Again it falls silent and hope builds only to be dashed when the screaming comes and again he looks about with idle curiosity, smiling at Paula one side and Clarence the other.

On the road, in the centre of the circle, Charlie screams from the pain inside. Her hand squeezing Tappy's who keeps seeing the images in her mind of her sister wild and crazed with red bloodshot eyes and hands clawed to talons. Tappy didn't even live with her family. She was only meant to be staying the night to catch up and spend some time and the visions of that night swim through her head. Something primeval and malevolent and if anyone had ever asked Tappy what she would have done in such a situation she would have said she'd rather die than hurt her family. Except a switch inside was flicked and at the very second she thought it was over, in that very second of terror and utter anguish, she chose to live and killed to achieve it.

Now they both lower their heads and look at each other without shame and without pity while inside there is a lessening of the guilt that they live while others died.

A twitch of lips from Tappy. Her eyes glued to Charlie who smiles faintly which in turn makes Tappy smile wider, her mouth turning up in that endearing way. 'Thank you,' Charlie says quietly.

'S'okay,' Tappy says. 'What happens now?' she asks, the rain pouring down her face. 'I mean...people said you're fighting back...'

'We are,' Charlie says honestly. 'But if you stay then you'll probably die...'

A snort, a grim smile. 'There's worse things than death. What's Mr Howie like? He's not like I expected...I thought he'd be like mean and angry and...I don't know.'

Charlie turns to stare at the back of Howie. An unassuming man by any degree. Quiet sometimes. Polite, almost shy. Just a supermarket manager. 'You'll see,' she whispers, looking back at Tappy who shrugs and widens her eyes before grinning.

'Fuck it, I get a new bag...I'm in...'

CHAPTER TWELVE

Day Fourteen

Too many things happening and for the first time in days, Cassie feels real fear and confusion.

The storm outside increasing with power and ferocity. The rain lashing the windows so hard she thinks they'll break and the thunder so deep it seems to shake the world about them. Flashes of lightning strobing the sky. Bolts searing into existence that lighten the faces of the dozen men standing in at the bar and the other four seated at a table gathered around the old man.

She made the mistake of running out after Gregori with her knickers still off and her boobs spilling from her bra. The shotgun in one hand and the sleeping boy cradled in the other and she ran into the lobby to see Gregori standing with his guns lowered as the dozen or so men looked her up and down with eyes lingering where they shouldn't. The thought of men staring at her like that with Gregori so close before would have given her a deep thrill, but she knew instantly that something was very different and very wrong.

Now she sits in front of a window at a table on her own in a low seat, sweating in the thick gown that she managed to get back into with the boy asleep in her arms, murmuring fitfully in dream. He's so hot, his little body pumping heat but she dares not loosen her gown for fear of the lust in the men's eyes.

Hard men. Big men too. One of them at the table is huge. Pumped on steroids with a neck thicker than one of her thighs but she can see the old man is in charge from the way the others all defer to him. She can also see a man with slicked back dark hair who looks to be second in command. He's handsome with clear skin and a strong jaw. She's deduced they're all Albanian from the fact Gregori understands their language, and she has further deduced they are criminal types from the tattoos of double-headed eagles on their arms, hands and necks and from the jewellery they wear and the weapons they carry.

She stares across the room, sweeping her gaze over the men at the bar all drinking Vodka from shot glasses. The air thick with cigarette smoke. Guns everywhere. Black leather jackets and tight black tops showing muscular tattooed arms. The four men at the table. The old man sipping whiskey. An overcoat draped over his shoulders. His liver-spotted bald head gleaming with a layer of sweat. The other three with him, smoking and drinking too like a scene from a low-budget gangster movie. The only difference to the setting is Gregori sitting in bright flowery swimming shorts on a plain wooden chair. His hands on his knees. His eyes lowered. His whole manner that of a child given punishment. Subservient and silent. Why didn't he fight back when he first saw them? He is Gregori. He's faster and harder than everyone but suddenly that near-mythical awe she had for the man is diminished now he is surrounded by such men.

'We knew you completed the task,' the old man says in Albanian. His voice old but deep and strong.

'Yes,' Gregori says, facing down.

'It was good too,' the old man says, looking around at his men who all nod eagerly.

'Very good,' Ylli says, the second in command, the handsome one who keeps looking at Cassie. 'To you, Gregori,' he says, lifting his glass.

'To you, Gregori,' Behar and Ditmer say, raising their glasses to Gregori who doesn't have a glass because he is not part of their clan. He is not one of them. He is not *fis*.

Every Albanian gang originates from a clan, from a *fis*, and every gang is headed by an overall boss, *the Krye*. Every clan member is related to every other clan member, by blood or by marriage. Everyone is connected, and the *Besa* demands that everyone give complete allegiance to the *Krye*

Gregori gave in because the *Krye* told him to, and the *Krye* must always be respected. The *Besa* demands it. Every beating Gregori took as a child, every time he was whipped, starved, hit, half-drowned and left in the cold to eat rats was to make him always honour the *Besa*, because the *Besa* is more than a code of conduct, it is more than a way of life. It *is* life.

'To the uglyman,' Ylli calls out, raising his glass to the men at the bar who repeat the words in deep, harsh voices and lean their heads back to down the contents of their shot glasses before slamming those glasses down hard on the bar, making Cassie flinch and the boy jolt in his sleep and still Gregori shows no reaction.

The *Krye* sips his scotch whiskey savouring the burn in his throat. 'How long have you been here, Gregori?'

'Today,' Gregori replies instantly, his voice as gravelly as ever but somehow quieter, less menacing.

'Today?' the *Krye* says mildly. 'It is a good find for the night but...' he pauses, turning his mouth down at the sides. 'Not a position for a length of time. Too many windows, too many doors. Too hard to defend. I see these things, Gregori.'

'Yes,' Gregori says.

'No, it is shelter for the night, but we will move on when the storm passes. I am glad to have found you, Gregori. You will join our *fis*, yes?'

'Yes,' Gregori says.

'Of course you will,' the old man says with complete authority. 'It was not a question, Gregori. You are with us now and we are not weak like the English. What has happened may be terrible, but we have known terror, Gregori, and we will rise to the top now. The world is falling but the world is still turning. Isn't that so, Ylli.'

'To opportunity,' Ylli says, raising his glass as every other man in the room does the same, once more glugging down their drinks before slamming the glasses down on the bar top and tables.

'We shall be kings once more,' the *Krye* tells Gregori, watching him closely through hooded eyes. Watching the way Gregori sits without moving. The way his hands rest on his knees and the way his head stays lowered as though in respect but Konstandin is not stupid. To be a *Krye* means being aware of all things at all times and although Gregori sits in subservience now, Konstandin knows Gregori's head being lowered widens his peripheral vision which in turn means the man can monitor the positions of everyone in the room. The *Krye* is also aware of the woman in the gown. He saw her breasts spilling from her bra and her state of undress when she ran into the lobby. He also saw the bulge in Gregori's shorts and all those things give him a concern because the uglyman is a very dangerous man.

'Drink' the *Krye* tells his men, looking around. 'You have worked hard. Drink now. Relax a little...' he looks over as though becoming aware of Cassie and the child for the first time. 'The woman and the boy, who are they?' he asks Gregori in such a casual tone it makes Ylli's senses sharpen.

'I found them,' Gregori replies, still looking down at the floor.

'Oh,' the *Krye* says, nodding slowly. 'She is a fine-looking woman, Gregori...good breasts no? Nice and juicy!' he laughs at his own words and so does everyone else. The old man looks around, nodding at his men while motioning as though to cup a big breast. 'Eh? Big and juicy...'

Cassie swallows, not following the words but knowing enough to determine what they are talking about and she looks down at the boy murmuring, his eyes moving under the lids and a few gentle spasms showing in his arms and legs. Whatever happens, the boy must be safe. She thinks to wake him, to tell him to bring the ones outside but there are too many men here, too many guns and the risk of a bullet hitting the boy is too great.

'Big and juicy,' the *Krye* says again, repeating his joke in the way of a man used to being able to say anything he wants as many times as he wants. He sighs, lifting his eyebrows as the laughing tails off and he sips from his glass. 'But you are not to be with a family, Gregori,' he adds in a tone designed to be gentle and soft yet dripping with threat and the laughs die out as the men look to Gregori. 'And yet here you are, with a family.'

'Yes,' Gregori says.

Cassie detects the change. The way the other men stiffen ever so slightly and the tension increasing in the room as the bolts of lightning flash across the sky and the thunder rumbles so deep and loud, mocking the mere mortals clinging to their lives.

'But still,' the *Krye* says, finishing his glass and holding it out for someone to make it whole again. 'These times are unprecedented so perhaps we can see that a woman with a child would offer herself for your protection. That is human nature...'

Gregori thinks to explain that the boy is not the child of Cassie but he stays quiet because to speak without consent to a *Krye* is forbidden.

'Yes,' the *Krye* says again, dipping his head to tell Ylli to stop filling the glass. 'We are men here, we can see why you would do this. Would you agree, Ylli?'

'Of course,' Ylli says, knowing when his *Krye* wishes for him to take over. 'But you are back with *fis* now Gregori. Your *Besa* is to us.'

'Yes,' Gregori says, unmoving.

'This is good,' Ylli says, smiling at his men. 'The woman? She is special to you?'

'I'd like the woman to be special to me,' Ditmer jokes before Gregori can answer. A few chuckles and again they all look over to Cassie.

'You are too big for her, Ditmer,' Behar says. 'You need a big fat Russian wife to rut with...'

'I don't want a Russian,' Ditmer spits, making them laugh. 'They stink and they argue too much.'

'You stink which is why I'm not going on her after you,' Behar says. 'You can go last and drown her in your sweat...'

'I went last time,' Ditmer says, rolling his eyes. 'I always go last! Ylli, this is not fair.'

Ylli smiles, looking around at the men laughing. 'Gregori? You have no issues if we share the woman?' he asks, and the test is laid. The test of allegiance within minutes of entering the hotel. *We will gang-rape your woman to make sure you are loyal, and we will tell you we are going to do this to study your reaction.*

'Is good,' Gregori says, lifting his eyes as Ditmer rises and takes a step towards Cassie.

'Not now, Ditmer,' Ylli laughs.

'I am not going last,' Ditmer says.

A nod from the *Krye*. A look from Ylli. Ditmer sits, instantly falling into a silence that rolls out as the *Krye* sips from his glass. 'What do you know, Gregori?'

Ylli shifts position, watching with interest.

'This...situation,' the old man says. 'People biting each other. What do you know?' Gregori stays quiet, his eyes lowered. The *Krye* drinks his scotch and swallows loudly. 'Survivors? Have you seen many?'

'No,' Gregori replies.

'None or some?' Ylli asks.

'Some. Not many.'

'Where did you find the girl?' Ylli asks, once again assuming the right to take over the questioning.

'I looked for a house. She was inside.'

'What is her name?'

'Cassie.'

'What?' Cassie asks, hearing her name.

'She speaks,' Brehar jokes.

'She won't soon,' Ditmer mutters.

'You said she,' Ylli says, smiling as he cocks his head over. 'Not they...'

Gregori stays still and quiet.

'So you did not find the woman and the boy together. You would have said if you found *them* in a house. You said she...is she not the child's mother?'

'No,' Gregori says.

'You lie to the *Krye*?' Ylli asks.

'No.'

'He is the uglyman,' the *Krye* says, lifting a hand. 'He has no intelligence.'

'Yes, this is true,' Ylli sighs, looking over at Cassie and switching to English. 'Miss? Where did you meet Gregori?'

Cassie swallows, not knowing what Gregori said and not knowing how much to say herself. 'I was in a house,' she offers, keeping her voice down and her eyes averted as though too scared to talk.

'And the child?' Ylli asks.

'Gregori already had him,' she replies. 'But I care for him now...'

Ylli frowns, sharing glances with Ditmer and Brehar. 'You are taking children now, Gregori?'

'He was alone,' Gregori says. 'I saw his mother die. I...I help.'

'The boy? He is English?' Ylli asks.

'Yes,' Gregori says.

'He is not *fis*.'

'No.'

'We trained you, Gregori. We trained you to protect us. Not English children.'

The boy stirs in her arms, his eye blinking heavily as he wakes to stare up at Cassie then lifts his head to look round the room. 'Sssshhhh not a word,' Cassie whispers in his ear. 'Don't speak...'

Ylli flicks a hand at Ditmer who pushes up from his seat and exhales noisily through his nose while walking over to loom in front of Gregori in the chair. The man's back so wide it pushes his arms out which in turn can't straighten for the sheer bulk of muscle.

'Your *Besa* is to us, Gregori,' Ylli says. A look from the *Krye* to Yllie. A look from Ylli to Ditmer who lashes out with a stinging backhanded strike across Gregori's face, snapping his head over but the *uglyman* stays silent and unmoving, simply taking the hit as the boy tries to squirm to sit up in Cassie's arms while she holds him tight, her heart booming in real fear. There is nothing Gregori can do. There's too many of them to fight. She can see that, but she has to get the boy out. The boy must be saved.

Ditmer turns to head back to the others but Konstandin lifts an eyebrow and sips from his glass with enough of a silent message passed to Ditmer who pauses, nods at his master and spins back round to slam a fist into Gregori's chest with such power it lifts the man up and out of the chair, sending him flying back through the room to land crumpled against a wall, gasping for air.

Cassie gasps, her stomach in knots, twisting and turning over. She didn't think it would get this bad this quickly. The boy. She has to get him out. He squirms again in her arms, lifting to see Gregori slumped against the wall and cocking his small head over as though confused. 'Will Gregori makes his brains come out?'

She clamps a hand over his mouth, checking to see the men are all focussed on Ditmer getting another nod from the old man and stalking across the room towards Gregori who slides to one side, clutching his chest while taking shallow fast breaths.

'You do not look after little English children,' the *Krye* says.

Ditmer reaches down, gripping Gregori round the throat with one hand and lifting him up with staggering ease to hold pinned against the wall with his toes barely touching the floor. His own hands resting gently on the man holding him. Not fighting. Not resisting. His bulging eyes turning red from the lack of air. His awful, pock-marked face looking haggard and sick. His eyes take in Cassie and the boy and everyone else and he knows the *Krye* will either have him beaten to near death or have him killed outright. It is *Besa*. It is the way of things.

'Your duty is to us,' the *Krye* says. 'A family corrupts a man, Gregori...a family makes a man soft and makes him question his loyalties...' A pause to drink and enough time for Ditmer to rag Gregori through a set of tables and chairs, throwing him down to the floor to kick in the ribs before picking him back up to smash down through another table but still he doesn't fight or resist because it is not right to do so.

Cassie shifts in the seat, bringing the boy's ear close to her mouth. 'You have to go...find somewhere to hide and make them come here. You hear me? You hide and you stay hidden until everyone is dead...'

She spoke too loud and Ylli looks over. Others too and Ditmer turns from beating Gregori. She freezes, the boy in her arms then slowly edges off the seat to stand and lower the silent boy to his feet. 'Go on now...' she says in a weak voice, pushing the boy towards the door.

Ylli shakes his head. 'He will stay.'

'I er...I don't want him to see,' she says, pushing the boy again. 'Go now,' she whispers again but the boy doesn't go. He stands and stares, looking from Gregori to Ditmer to the men at the table and the men at the bar.

'They're climbing the walls,' he says out loud, his young voice carrying across the room.

'No, Boy,' Gregori grunts, lifting his bleeding head to look over. 'You go now...'

'What walls?' Ylli asks, a smirk on his face.

'Go now,' Cassie says, pushing the boy to the door as Ylli shakes his head.

'The fort,' the boy says, refusing to be pushed. 'To kill Howie...'

'Boy!' Gregori hisses then slams down from a punch given by Ditmer that hammers him into the floor. 'Go...you go...'

'Please, let the boy go,' Cassie begs.

'You RUN,' Gregori shouts as Ditmer kicks him across the room into the base of the bar.

'See!' The *Kyre* says, lifting a hand in emphasis. 'He is corrupt. They have corrupted him. This is what a family does to a man. Even the *uglyman* has been bewitched...'

'But the boy, he is not afraid,' Ylli laughs, motioning towards the child. 'I like him! He is not crying...maybe he wants to watch our fun.,' he switches to English, smiling at the child. 'Come here little boy, come and watch with Uncle Ylli...have some whiskey...'

The men laugh deep and harsh and Ditmer lifts Gregori up high to slam down on the top of the bar then runs the length, dragging

Gregori across the top, making the men scatter and laugh and throw their glasses and bottles at the *uglyman* as he goes by.

'You like this?' Ylli asks, looking from Gregori sliding along the bar to the child. 'Come, come to Uncle Ylli...'

'No,' Cassie says, moving in front of the boy. She tugs her gown open, letting it drop from her shoulders and reaches back to unhook her bra, casting it aside to stand naked. 'Go,' she whispers. 'Go!' she pushes the boy again who blinks comically at her breasts in a way that makes Ylli roar with laughter.

'I love this child!'

'He is a good boy,' the *Krye* says, chuckling at the sight.

'Get out...' Cassie says, pushing at the child.

'BOY!' Gregori roars, still pinned to the bar. 'GO...'

The boy starts running but not towards the door. Instead, he runs in his underpants past Ylli, the old man and Brehar to the bar and to the pylon like legs of Ditmer that he starts kicking and punching like an ant attacking a tree with a naked Cassie running behind him and the sight is too much. Ylli laughing so hard the tears stream from his eyes. Brehar too and the men in the bar who watch Ditmer slowly look down to a small child beating on his legs then back to see Cassie bending over to try and grab the boy, but the child darts from her reach, going round Ditmer's legs to carry on hitting him. Cassie gives chase, bent over and baring her arse to the room as she cries out for the boy to stop.

'I never see such a thing,' Ylli cries. Even the *Krye* wipes the tears from his cheeks at the sight and laughs harder when the boy goes through Ditmer's legs who simply stares down at the proceedings as though he is not involved while pinning Gregori to the bartop with one hand. 'Oh my god,' Ylli gasps. 'We must keep this boy...he is the new Gregori...boy...BOY!' he shouts out while reaching into a pocket to pull a small black switchblade out. A button pressed and the blade pops out. Small and silvery. 'BOY...use this...'

'You give him a knife. Ylli?' Ditmer asks, making every man roar with laughter.

'The giant is scared of a boy with a flick-knife,' Brehar says, waving his hand from laughing so much.

The boy spots the knife, his face hardening as he runs towards Ylli with Cassie lurching to try and grab him but Ylli moves faster, plucking the boy from the air to hold him tight and smiling as Cassie comes to a stop in front of him.

'Please...please let him go...'

'Big and juicy,' the *Krye* shouts, staring at her boobs. The laughing gets harder, louder.

Ylli lowers the squirming child and holds the knife just out of his reach. 'You want this?'

The boy nods, his eyes fixed on the knife.

'You want this?'

'Yes! Gimme...' the boy squirms, trying to reach it.

'Good boy,' Ylli says, letting him go and handing the knife over before lashing out to grip Cassie's hair, forcing her back and down onto her knees.

'You gave him the knife!' Ditmer squawks, setting them all off again.

'BOY...GET OUT,' Cassie screams.

'BOY, YOU GO,' Gregori roars, bucking to get free from the mighty arm of Ditmer holding him down.

The boy stares at the blade in his hand then turns and look back to Ditmer, his little face contorting in rage as he starts walking towards the huge man.

'No,' Ditmer tells the child. 'NO...' he lifts a hand up as though telling the boy off while the men squeal and cry with laughter. 'You stab me and I will smack you...someone tell him in English...'

Cassie screams and yells. Gregori the same. His head turned to just see past Ditmer to the boy holding a small knife who sticks the point in Ditmer's left arse-cheek who shouts out and the men laugh and weep as the *Krye* watches Cassie's boobs and thinks he was right to bring his supply of Viagra.

A fleeting second of a look from the boy to Gregori. Eyes-locking.

The boy flushed and furious. Gregori glaring. 'Lessons, Boy...I teach you...'

'YOU SHIT,' Ditmer shouts, swiping at the boy as he tugs the blade free, sending him slamming back into a chair but he rights quickly and runs back in, remembering his lessons.

Ankle to ankle. Achilles to Achilles. Up and slice the right thigh then the left. Cut the hamstrings then stab up with every ounce of strength into the groin into the artery and pull the blade free to let the blood spray thick and red as Ditmer screams and Ylli's laugh cuts off as the men widen their eyes.

Gregori knew the second he lowered his pistols in the hotel lobby, that he'd made a mistake, but it was already too late, so he waited for the right position, for the right tactical second to react, and that second is now while Ditmer screams at his blood spurting.

He grips the hand holding him down. A wrench, a grunt and he snaps the wrist before vaulting backwards to roll off the bar slamming into the two men he knew were there and the *uglyman* goes to work as Cassie screams and the men lunge for their weapons as every window of the bar implodes with a screeching howl of voices led by Daudi who crashes through the glass with his red eyes blazing and his hands clawed.

'KILL THEM,' Cassie roars, on her knees with Ylli still gripping her hair. 'KILL THEM ALL...'

Gregori headbutts one while slamming the blade of his right hand into the throat of the other and as both fall back so he turns and goes into the gangsters rushing into him as Daudi rips a stunned Brehar from his chair, carrying the man into Ditmer and taking both men down with fingers clawing at eyes and teeth biting into necks and faces.

Gregori fights and kills his brethren, his kin, the men who beat and starved him and who made him bleed in the snow and eat dead rats to honour a fucked up system for a debt that was never his. That's all he was. A debt. A tool. A thing, but now *that thing* turns against them and the Albanians shoot their guns and scream out, but the attack is too brutal, too swift and too fuelled by a rage unleashed for the damning temerity of touching the boy as the doors and windows throughout the hotel and spa smash in with infected wild and screaming, rushing into the bar to fill the space and kill and tear flesh and rip limbs from bodies and eyes from skulls, not to infect, not to pass what they have, but to punish.

Mere seconds and it's done. The walls and ceiling dripping blood. The air thick with the stench of death and the sky outside flashes white and the thunder comes with just two left alive. Ylli and the *Krye*. The second in command still holding Cassie by her hair. His head turning this way and that in absolute shock as the infected all stand from their kills to turn in towards him with mouths dripping blood and eyes so red. They stop converging, coming to a stop and a path opens through which the boy walks with Gregori at his back, a pistol in each his hand. The *uglyman* on his feet and worse than ever before. His head higher, his muscles gleaming. His body toned to perfection from a life of sacrifice and torture and pain. The boy in front of him. Not the boy. The thing inside. Cassie can see it in his eyes and she sees the world is theirs. Theirs for the taking and while naked on her knees she looks to Gregori, locking eyes because she has now proven herself and went naked into hell so the boy may live.

'Gregori...' Ylli speaks and a shot rings out, fired by Gregori that slams through the bicep of the arm holding Cassie, instantly severing nerves and ligaments and his grip fails as he staggers back, releasing Cassie who launches up to grab the boy, lifting him to her side to stand next to Gregori. Her chest heaving. Her eyes as hard as the *uglyman*.

'You touched my family,' she says through gritted teeth.

'No I...' Ylli staggers back from the next shot going through his right kneecap then another through his left and he drops to the floor, writhing in agony.

'My family,' Cassie says. She takes a gun from Gregori and walks over to stare down with the boy held at her side. A beat of a heart. A blink of an eye and she fires down into Ylli. Into his gut and chest, emptying the magazine then steps back, turning to kiss the side of the boy's head then leaning over to kiss Gregori's cheek before the three look down at the *Krye* who sips his scotch whiskey while the blood sprayed across the room slides down his face.

He lowers the glass to look round slowly, creaking the leather chair as he moves and shifts in the seat to take in the blood dripping from the bar and the remains of Ditmer spattered here and there. He sees the infected men and women and the way they all stare at the boy and the transition as they edge down from rabid fury to pure subservience but the *Krye* knows that rage is right there, ready to be used in a heartbeat. He takes it all in and understands it all with a long life of brutality and control behind him and finally, he looks from Gregori to the boy.

'They called me the devil,' the *Krye* whispers in English with a smile. 'For years I believe in this...but now?' he shrugs and sips from his glass of whiskey. 'Now I know I am not for I have seen the devil...' he fixes eyes with the boy as he lowers the glass. 'And what will you do with this power my little Krye? How will you rule the world?'

The shot comes without warning and Konstandin's skull blows out, sending him back into the chair before slumping down to slide off to pour blood over the rain-soaked filthy floor of the bar.

'Is boy,' Gregori tells the corpse. 'Is boy,' Gregori tells the room. 'IS BOY,' Gregori tells the world. 'The boy is child...not the *Krye*...'

CHAPTER THIRTEEN

Day Twenty-four

'Make way...coming through...VIP coming through here...' Marcy says, clambering in the back door of the already full Saxon, making everyone groan and grumble as they twist and lift legs.

'Why didn't you get in first?' Nick asks, getting a face full of Marcy's backside, the sodden material of her trousers scraping his cheek as she grabs Blowers shoulder, using him to lever forward.

'Fuck's sake, Marcy,' Cookey yelps at the elbow digging in his neck.

'You're doing this on purpose,' Blowers says.

'Who me?' she asks, standing over him with a grin as the rainwater pours from her hair into his face. 'Would I do that?'

'Piss off,' he laughs. 'It's not even funny.'

'Hey now,' she says seriously, giving him a stern look. 'I'll get my bodyguard on you...Mo!'

'What?'

'Beat Blowers up...when we get room.'

'Marcy,' Nick groans at her knee driving into his chest.

'And Nick,' Marcy adds, making a meal of her transit from back of the Saxon to the front. She pauses mid-wrangle to smile at Danny, winking at his shyness. 'I'm a VIP like Madonna now, Danny...'

The lad nods quickly then blinks. 'Who's Madonna?'

'Are you being serious?'

He shrugs, looking away shyly. 'I don't know who that is.'

'Madonna! The singer...Like a Virgin?'

'What like you?'

'Cookey!' Marcy snaps, reaching back to slap his leg. 'Mr Howie! Cookey said I'm not a virgin...'

'Ha!' Howie snorts, shaking the water from his hair in the front seat.

'Oi,' Clarence says, getting another drenching from Howie shaking his head. 'It's not a bloody shampoo advert...'

'Kids of today,' Marcy mutters, still nodding at Danny while leaning on Blowers while digging her elbow into Cookey while pushing her backside at Nick. 'No bloody respect...or knowledge for that matter. Madonna? Like a really famous singer...married to that film director guy...'

'Guy,' Nick says.

'What is?' Marcy asks.

'The guy...he's called Guy and can you get your arse out of my face please...'

'They're not married anymore,' Tappy says, happily joining in from the other side of the bench seats. 'Divorced apparently.'

'Oh that's a shame,' Marcy says, lurching forward to drop into her seat opposite Paula. 'Anyway, so yes, Danny. I'm a VIP now...in case you didn't hear or were not aware.'

'Okay,' Danny says politely.

Marcy smiles at him then frowns on seeing Mo at the back doors with Dave. 'Oi, what good is a bodyguard down there...blimey, we're a bit full in here now. Howie, we're getting full in the back here. It's all steamy too...'

'Righto,' Howie says 'All in?' he doesn't wait for the answer but starts the engine, gunning the pedal to bring the revs up with a sound so different to the finely tuned sports cars now parked back in the showroom.

A flash of light outside. A bolt of lightning scorching the sky followed by the deep boom of thunder.

'Awesome,' Paula says. 'In a tin can during an electrical storm...'

'I know right,' Marcy says. 'It'll make my hair go frizzy...'

'Yeah that's not what I meant,' Paula says, looking down the bench seats. Blowers, Cookey, Nick and Dave on her side. Marcy, Danny, Charlie, Tappy and Mo on the other. Kit bags and rifles between legs. Axes wherever they can fit. Bottles of water in hands and every face dripping water from the rain. Every top sodden, cheeks flushed and rosy but at least that awful, dreadful black mood is starting to lift a bit more. Driving the cars was a touch of genius and just what they needed, and the few minutes Charlie took with Tappy after seems to have helped.

'Favourite one then?' Tappy asks, seemingly happy to start a conversation without worrying about being new.

'Favourite what?' Cookey asks. 'Colour?'

'Food?' Nick asks.

'Pop song?' Blowers asks.

'Pop song?' Cookey asks, looking at Blowers. 'What the fuck?'

'No! I meant car,' Tappy says. 'Other than the Bugatti,' she adds as they all go to speak. 'Hang on, where's Mads? Doesn't he come with us?'

'He's in the van with Reggie,' Nick says. 'And Ferrari.'

'Yeah you would say Ferrari,' Tappy says, rolling her eyes. 'Predictable,' she sings, looking away, making the others laugh. 'Why is Mads in with Reggie?'

'Cos he's a...' Cookey starts to say then stops himself after seeing the look from Paula.

'I'll explain it all later, Tappy,' Paula says.

'Okay cool...'

'So basically,' Marcy says, leaning forward to look down at Tappy. 'We're all infected with the zombie virus thing...but we don't know if you lot can give it to other people whereas I can, you know, being a

VIP and all that, not that I like to go on about being super special and highly important person because really I am quiet and unassuming person but...' she stops to frown. 'Totally forgot what I was saying now...'

'Mads is immune, not infected,' Charlie says.

'Yeah that,' Marcy says, clicking her fingers.

'Got it,' Tappy says. 'So we're all infected, that right?'

'Er, yes, we think so,' Charlie says.

'It's fine, mate,' Blowers says, seeing Danny shift on his seat.

'I'm okay, Corporal,' Danny says quickly.

'Corporal? Have I got to call you Corporal?' Tappy asks.

'No,' Blowers says.

'Yes,' everyone else says together.

'Yes, Sir, Mr Corporal, Sir,' Tappy says, offering a salute.

'Cheers,' Blowers says. 'Wrong hand but thanks for trying...'

'Jesus,' Howie says in the front, leaning forward to peer through the windscreen. 'Visibility's reducing...' he blinks, turning his head at the flash of lightning strobing the sky.

'Retina burn,' Clarence mutters, squeezing his eyes closed.

'Aye, just a bit,' Howie says, focussing back on the road and following the white lines in the middle to keep in the right direction. The rain coming so hard he can't see more than a dozen metres.

'We need higher ground,' Clarence says, reaching for the radio. *'Reggie, it's Clarence. We need higher ground...'*

'Ah yes, understood. I shall look now.'

'Cheers for that,' Howie says then lowers his voice. 'You hear what Tappy said?'

'Yeah we heard it,' Clarence says with a grimace. 'Killed her own family.'

'Sisters, brothers, mum and dad,' Howie says, shaking his head sadly. 'Fucking awful...'

Clarence nods, blasting air through his nose while watching the road outside.

'You okay?' Howie asks, a little too casually and earning a look from the big man. 'What? I'm just asking.'

'I'm fine,' Clarence says gruffly.

'Great.'

'No issues.'

'Awesome.'

'Here to work.'

'Good...'

A laugh from the back. Genuine and real. Clarence turns to see Cookey in full flow, telling a story of something while Blowers shakes his head.

'Seriously,' Cookey says earnestly, looking at his audience. 'An actual penis...like this big,' he holds his hands up measuring the length. 'In her mouth...and we're all like *ah get it out* and Blowers is like *ah give it back...*'

'That's not what happened,' Blowers groans.

'Nah I'm exaggerating,' Cookey says before shielding his mouth from Blowers. *I'm not* he mouths. *It's in his pocket,* he adds pointing at Blowers lap. 'For later when it's dark and he can suck it a little bit... hey, do you wanna hear about when Nick burnt the Isle of Wight down?'

'What?' Nick asks. 'It was a ferry you bellend...'

'Who is telling this story, Mr Hewitt?' Cookey asks.

'This is getting worse,' Howie says from the front. 'I can only just see the white lines...'

'Reggie, Clarence again. How are you getting on?'

'Ah yes, I am studying the topography now and unfortunately, we're in a rather large depression surrounded by lakes and rivers. Roy said this area is really just a flood plain and that it should never have been built on which of course is very interesting given the Government's attitude to Green-Land development and easing the pressure from the housing market by allowing constructions to take place in land previously marked as...'

Clarence sighs, staring out the window as Howie tuts to himself and leans even closer to the windscreen while Reginald's voice fills their ears.

'...so yes, I would rather suspect that our best route is to go through

before the storm becomes worse and the run-off has built up so we can find higher ground and shelter for the night...'

'What did he say? I zoned out,' Howie says.

'He said to go through,' Paula says from behind them. 'It'll take longer to go back the other way.'

'Glad someone was listening,' Clarence says. 'Cheers, Paula.'

'It's fine, anytime,' she says with a smile, reaching out to touch his shoulder with an act of familiarity that from her to anyone else would not be an issue but she seems to realise what she's doing and pulls back too quickly as Clarence blushes and Marcy snorts a laugh, staring at Paula who glares back at her.

'Steamy in here,' Marcy says, fanning her face as Paula glares a bit harder. 'Phwoar, ssshhhteamy windows,' Marcy adds, laughing at her own joke.

'You're an idiot,' Paula mutters, folding her arms.

They drive on through the pouring rain that comes harder and louder every few minutes. Lightning bolts slicing the sky open and thunder so loud it renders all speech impossible, and it goes on for seconds too, from horizon to horizon, filling every inch of sky above them and as the deluge increases so Howie has to slow down for fear of driving off the road. He manages to follow the white lines for a while, clinging to the centre of the carriageway but it gets so bad even they become lost from view.

'It's no good,' Howie says. 'I'll get out...you drive and follow me...'

'Sure?' Clarence asks.

'It's only rain...and it's not exactly cold is it...'

'What's going on?' Paula asks as Howie pushes his door open to drop out.

'It's fine,' Clarence says, sliding over. 'We can't see the road...boss is finding the white lines so we can follow him...'

'There goes Dave,' Marcy says, looking down to see Dave dropping from the back door.

Outside, Howie shakes his head at the instant soaking from the rain lashing down but the feel is not unpleasant. Not after the days of scorching heat.

'Mr Howie,' Dave says, stepping into view.

'Jesus mate, scared the shit out of me. It's fine, Dave, get back in...'

'No, Mr Howie.'

'Up to you mate,' Howie says, moving off to the front with Dave at his side. The two of them searching the road underfoot, splashing through surface water. 'Intense or what...'

'What is?'

'The rain,' Howie says. 'It's intense. Got it...' he stops still, waving his arms to the Saxon off to one side and giving thanks that he checked because the vehicle was already aiming away. He pauses while the Saxon moves up then sets off at a brisk walking pace, watching the road underfoot with the heavy engine behind almost unheard and if he thought the rain was heavy before, now it becomes something else entirely.

A sheer torrential pouring of water from the heavens like nothing he has ever seen. Worse than ten days ago when the fort became an island. Worse than the documentaries and movies he saw with tropical storms and monsoons.

'It's worse than a monsoon,' Dave says.

'Fuck off,' Howie blurts, snapping his head over to look at him but Dave just blinks and walks on. 'Dave, seriously...I didn't say that.'

'You did, Mr Howie.'

'I didn't! They're all doing it now too.'

Dave doesn't say anything but walks on. His head up. His eyes scanning. Always scanning. Always watching.

'Right,' Howie says, nodding to himself. 'I'm going to think of a colour...'

They walk on. Seconds pass. A minute comes and goes.

'Dave?'

'Yes, Mr Howie.'

'You're meant to guess the colour.'

'What colour?'

'The colour I am thinking about. Ready? Go...' Howie walks on, thinking of yellow and yellow things. Canary birds and bananas.

'I like bananas.'

'Ha! Gotcha,' Howie says with victory.

'Got what?'

'You. In my head being all psychic and telepathic and...like all Uri Geller and shit.'

Dave walks on. 'You said canary birds and bananas, Mr Howie,' he says, facing forward.

'Er, I did not,' Howie say emphatically.

Dave walks on.

'I didn't.'

Dave walks on.

'Fuck you, right...I'm going to put my hand over my mouth like this...see?' Howie clamps his hand over his mouth then murmurs loudly to make Dave look. 'Shee?' he shouts from behind his mouth. 'My mouf ish cofered right? Okay...I'm gunna funk of an aminanal...'

'What?'

'Amaanial.'

'What?'

'Animal!' Howie says, pulling his hand away. 'Like a giraffe...ready? Go?'

'Giraffe.'

'What? No! You don't say the last animal, you've got to guess the animal I am thinking of to prove you live in my head and I'm not mad.'

Dave walks on.

'Ready?' Howie asks, 'animal...go...' he clamps his mouth again.

'Giraffe.'

'Argh! You do this on purpose. I swear you do...unless I was actually thinking of a giraffe cos I didn't want you to say giraffe...Ha! So, in fact, I was thinking about giraffes which means I'm right and you live in my head...'

Dave walks on.

'Are you even real?' Howie asks, nodding at him. 'Thought about that have you? Eh? Do you even exist? Maybe this is all a dream and I'll wake up on the Friday night it happened and think how you shouldn't eat pizza and fall asleep on the sofa because it gives you messed up dreams...'

Dave walks on.

'Then I'll come into work the next day and be like, *Hi Dave, I had this really weird dream that you were this ex-special forces soldier man and we killed loads of weird fucked up talking zombies...one of which was my super-hot girlfriend.*'

Dave walks on.

'Do you ever miss it?'

'What, Mr Howie?'

'Life before this. Working in Tesco and...you know?'

'No.'

'I mean life before this, going to work and going home and watching shit television and er...then going back to work, or whatever you did in between shifts...like sharpen knives or read knife catalogues or Google knives and...stuff.'

'I like knives.'

'Yep, gathered that one. So, do you?'

'Yes. I like knives.'

'No! I mean miss it? Do you ever think about it?'

'I think about now, Mr Howie.'

'Wow, bloody hell, Dave,' Howie says in genuine shock at the coherent verbalisation of a thought process from Dave.

Dave walks on and the wind hits. The wind that comes howling from the sky like a real living thing that changes the landscape around them in an instant, making the rain horizontal and thereby instantly opening the view ahead from mere yards to hundreds of feet. Buildings on both sides of the street and Howie feels the jarring jolt at realising they're in a town whereas he assumed they were still in the countryside. Big houses set back from the road and a huge old church with an enormous spire on the right. Signs on both sides of the road. One of them warning of floods in this area and another warning of the weak bridge ahead that Howie and Dave look for but cannot see due to the raging white topped furious river roaring by.

'Fuck me,' Howie says, turning to wave at the Saxon to stop.

'Yeah I can see it,' Clarence shouts, leaning out of the driver's door before dropping down and striding over. The back doors open. The van doors too as some of the others drop out into the wind and rain to join Howie, Clarence and Dave at the front staring at the river a mere few metres ahead.

That the river has burst its banks is obvious. That it appears to have eaten whatever bridge was here is also obvious. Over thirty metres wide and raging. The waters churning with noise and power. Murky brown from mud and sediment with white tops splashing out in the wind, like a set of rapids powering through the Grand Canyon.

'We wouldn't have seen it,' Howie says. 'Would have walked straight into it...fuck me...every half hour...'

'This is insane,' Cookey shouts. 'What's causing it?'

'Us,' Howie shouts back. 'I mean people...no more people...it must have changed the weather.'

'We'll have to go back,' Paula shouts.

'Not in this,' Howie shouts. 'Wind is too strong...it could turn Jess's trailer over...it's broadsided...go for that that church over there... it's far enough back from the river,' a crash behind them. A roof tile smashing into the side of the Saxon, obliterating into chunks with a thud. 'TIME TO GO...' Howie shouts, bending forward in the wind. A hand on his arm. Paula tugging him around as he turns away.

'LOOK,' she shouts, pointing at the river. Howie looks at the violent waters, struggling to see what she means as motion catches his eyes that lift to the far side of the river and the man running into view from a bend in the road between shops on the other side and even from this distance they can see his motion is panicked. A woman behind him. Two boys, teenagers then more people staggered in a line with some clustered together. All of them running from something.

'No,' Howie whispers, not feeling Paula's hand tightening on his arm. 'No...please...' a sense of dread inside as he stands with the others watching the lead man spot the waters ahead and screams out, his words lost in the wind and rain. The others running with him do the same. Panic spreading through them as they see their route ahead now lost. 'FUCK,' Howie screams the word out, making Tappy and Danny snap their heads over towards him. 'We've got to get over...'

Tappy frowns, not understanding. Danny the same while everyone else seems to know something they don't.

'DAVE, SHOUT FOR THEM TO GET DOWN...ROY! GET ROY DOWN HERE...'

Mo runs off, sprinting for Roy's van as everyone else runs back to the Saxon to get their rifles left inside for fear of exposing them to the rain.

'GET DOWN...' Dave bellows but even his voice isn't enough to fight through the wind to reach the people who run impotently towards the river.

'GET INSIDE THE HOUSES...' Howie shouts. 'BARRICADE...' Dave joins in, shouting the same words that go unheard as Roy runs up, balking at the sight. 'WE'VE GOT TO GET OVER,' Howie shouts.

'How?' Roy mouths.

'He's seen us!' Paula shouts.

Howie looks over to see the man holding the child waving across the river. His face animated. The others catching up behind him. All doing the same. Screaming out and looking wild and panicked.

'Roy, can we tie rope on an arrow and fire it over there?' Nick asks.

'In this wind? Jesus, Nick,' Roy says, looking back at the river. 'I'll try,' he adds quickly. 'Get the rope...'

'Dave...make ready,' Howie shouts.

Tappy watches as Dave lifts his rifle to his shoulder and calmly looks down the sights while clicking the button to select single shot.

'GET TO COVER...' Clarence roars, waving for the people to go left into the buildings. They wave back, clearly confused and terrified. Blowers and Cookey join Clarence, motioning to the side. All doing the same in the vain hope the message will be understood.

'Rope,' Maddox shouts, running in with Nick. 'It's heavy though... will an arrow carry it...'

Roy doesn't answer but drops his bag to pluck an arrow out, nocking it into the string of his huge longbow. Calmness spreads through him. His mind centred, his breathing relaxed, his heart-rate lowering. Strong wind from the right blowing to the left. He spots the target he wants. A ground floor window of the closest building on the other side. An adjustment up and to the right. More. Then more. Aiming up. Aiming right. Feeling it. Sensing it. Pull back. Stretch, feel the power. Calm now. At ease now. Loose. The arrow flies up. Tappy and Danny snapping their heads to see it go wide to the right, missing the aim by a mile. Then the wind hits and the arrow changes course, slamming over to the left to drop down and slam through the window.

'Shot,' Nick says calmly. 'Spot on...'

'No fucking way,' Tappy mouths, digging Danny in his ribs. 'Did you see that...'

'YES!' Cookey shouts at the man finally seeming to understand who turns to look at the houses at the side. He starts shouting to his group, clearly motioning for them to move.

'Get the rope tied on,' Roy urges.

'Doing it,' Maddox replies.

'DAVE!' Blowers shouts and Dave fires the first shot that flies across the river through the wind and through the gaps in the people to strike the infected man running into view in his centre of mass, driving him back off his feet.

'Oh shit,' Tappy says, finally understanding as she grabs Danny. 'The things...they're running from the things...RUN...GET TO COVER...IN THE BUILDING...GO GO...'

Dave fires at the next one coming into view. The noise of the shot almost lost in the howl of the wind but the first one he shot rises to charge again as Dave adjusts and fires again, finally taking him through the head.

Calm now. At ease now. Roy nocks and lifts, seeing his target, pulling the string back. Wind. The arrow is heavy. Aim up and to the right. More. More. More again. Not enough. The arrow is heavy and will drag. Aim higher. Power now, Roy. Power and focus. Breathe. He stretches the string, drawing it back while facing fully away from his target as more infected pour into the street with Dave firing single shots, the distance and conditions too great even for him to gain head shots. The people scream out as the man with the child kicks at a door.

Loose. The arrow flies up, pulling the rope behind that uncoils in a spin as Howie runs back to the Saxon.

The first arrow was impossible but this one, with a rope tied on, is beyond impossible and Tappy stands stunned as the arrow drops and sails down, the rope stretching out behind it and for a second it will surely plummet into the waters, then she sees the angle is perfect and it flies through the same window, smashing more glass out as Roy simply plucks another arrow, nocks, breathes, pulls back, stretches, aims and looses to join Dave in doing what they can to drop the infected.

'TIE THE ROPE,' Clarence roars as Nick runs back to the Saxon, going around Howie tugging his bag on to dive in, grabbing the handset for the loudspeaker.

'TIE THE ROPE,' Nick's amplified voice booms out and finally, the man with the child gets help from the other survivors and batters the door in, all of them trying to charge through the door at the same time.

'Is it on?' Howie runs back, wedging his axe between down his back.

'Not yet,' Maddox shouts back, feeling the rope still slack.

'Come on...' Howie mutters. His face a mask. His eyes brooding and hard. 'COME ON...'

'There!' Paula shouts, seeing movement in the window Roy fired the arrow through.

'TIE THE ROPE!' Nick bellows. Clarence the same. Everyone shouting. Roy and Dave firing as more infected come into view. Too many survivors still in the street for anyone else to risk firing and shooting them.

Movement inside the window. The man they saw with the child appearing in view, smashing the glass out with a chair before looking out then disappearing from view.

'He's got it,' Maddox shouts, feeling the rope being pulled.

'TIE IT ON...'

'Pull it,' Howie shouts at Maddox.

'It's too soon,' Paula shouts.

'Pull it,' Howie shouts again. Maddox tugs, gently at first then harder, feeling the tension. 'PULL THAT FUCKING ROPE...' Maddox heaves back, feeling it hold.

'It's holding...' he shouts.

'ANCHOR IT,' Howie runs.

'Fuck,' Maddox yells out as Clarence snatches the rope from his grip and runs to climb the front wheel of the Saxon then up to the roof and the big man starts looping it around his wrists and turns once to hoop it around his back before planting his feet as Howie roars out and leaps up to grip the rope, hooking his ankles over to start crawling upside down but the rope sags, dunking into him the river.

Clarence pulls back, heaving hard to lift the rope straight as Howie comes up out of the water still crawling as the man in the window appears in view holding the child, showing shock at the sight of someone coming over.

'HOLD IT TIGHT!' Maddox shouts, sprinting hard to dive out, gripping the rope that sinks down again as Clarence roars and pulls back to keep the rope taut. Paula grabs Marcy, the two of them climbing the Saxon to get next to Clarence, gripping the rope to pull back, lifting Howie and Maddox from the surface of the water splashing over them as they go hand over hand across the rope.

Blowers tenses, wanting to go for it but sensing the rope might not hold three. Then the rope gives and sinks down with Howie and Maddox dunking into the waters again while those on the road scream out as Clarence loops the rope over his arms, drawing it towards him and hoping to hell whoever is on the other end gets a bloody grip. Finally, the tension comes back as Clarence grits his teeth, looping arm over arm as more climb the Saxon to help pull it tight.

Howie spews and gasps for air. His whole world just water and noise while feeling the power of the river pulling him from the rope but he clung on and now rises again, pulling hand over hand and snatching a glimpse of drenched Maddox a few metres behind him. 'WHAT THE FUCK?'

'WHAT?' Maddox shouts, spewing river water the same as Howie.

'NOONE LIGHTER THAN YOU THEN?'

'RACIST.'

'I MEANT IN WEIGHT YOU TWAT...'

'I KNOW.'

'I'M NOT RACIST.'

'I KNOW...'

It seems to take forever. Hand over hand. Upside down with the river mere inches below and Howie catches glimpse as the survivors finally clear the street and his team can get some good fire down. 'FUCK!' he shouts again on hearing the bullets whizz past. 'TOO CLOSE TOO CLOSE...'

'DON'T SHOOT US,' Maddox shouts.

'Jesus...you two are nuts,' a man in the window shouts, leaning out to stretch a hand towards Howie. The base of the house now lost to the raging torrent going by.

Howie grunts, taking his hand to turn and fall into the windowsill, scraping his stomach as people rush to grab his arms and shoulders, heaving him in to drop on the floor to see a group of men crying out from the pain and exertion of holding the rope.

'Argh,' Maddox falls in, sprawling over Howie, elbows and knees going into bellies and heads.

'We're up,' Howie shouts, untangling from Maddox and surging to his feet. 'THAT WAS FUCKING NUTS...' he shouts at the people, pointing at the window. 'WHERE'S THE DOOR?'

'It's there,' the man says, gulping as he points to the door next to Howie.

'GOT IT...ER...STAY HERE...' Howie shouts.

'STAY HERE,' Maddox shouts, running after Howie.

'I'M NOT RACIST,' Howie shouts, running through the house to the front door then stopping dead instead of running out into the bullets whipping past.

'IT WAS A JOKE,' Maddox shouts.

'GRAB THAT TABLECLOTH,' Howie shouts.

'WHY ARE WE SHOUTING?' Maddox shouts, grabbing the tablecloth that Howie throws out the door.

'COS WE'RE HYPED TO FUCK MATE,' Howie yells.

'CEASEFIRE,' Blowers screams, seeing the tablecloth fly from the door. 'I'M ON...COOKEY, AFTER ME...'

'Holy fuck,' Tappy says on seeing Howie and Maddox charge from the house towards a the infected after crawling along a rope above a raging river. 'Can we do that?' she looks to Danny who nods weakly, as stunned as she but that nod becomes eager and excited as they turn to see Blowers and Cookey crawling along the rope.

'ARGH,' Howie bellows in the street, pulling his axe overhead.

'ARGH,' Maddox bellows in the street, pulling a big knife from his belt.

Shots still fire and arrows still strike but the two go wild and deep to kill and slaughter. Howie slamming his axe left and right with twenty-four days of battle behind him. Maddox stabbing and slicing with a life of hard living behind him. Throats slit. Stomachs opened. Stabbing, cutting, cleaving and the blood spills.

'OH MY GOD THAT WAS NUTS,' Blowers shouts, landing on the floor of the house before springing to his feet.

'Argh,' Cookey shouts, falling in then jumping up. 'WHERE'S THE DOOR?'

'It's there,' the man says, pointing at it.

'STAY HERE,' Blowers shouts.

'STAY HERE,' Cookey shouts.

'We will,' the man says, leaning over to watch them charge out through the rooms and out into the street.

The four hold the line. Fighting in the driving rain and howling wind with roof tiles smashing on the ground about them as the sky sears with lightning bolts and the thunder booms.

'S'FUCKED UP INNIT,' Mo shouts, landing on the floor of the room.

'WHAT HE SAID,' Nick shouts as Danny just smiles wild and crazed, still nodding eagerly.

'Door's right there,' the man says politely.

'STAY HERE,' Mo shouts.

'STAY HERE,' Nick shouts as Danny just smiles wild and crazed.

'Yes of course,' the man says, looking through the window to see if any more crazy people are coming across as Mo, Nick and Danny run out to fight, joining the fray and the battle.

'GOSH, THAT WAS DIFFERENT,' Charlie shouts, landing on the floor a few minutes later.

'I'M NEW,' Tappy shouts.

'Women too?' the man asks in such shock it shows as mild surprise. 'The door is right there and er...we'll stay here?'

'STAY HERE,' Charlie shouts.

'BYE,' Tappy shouts, running after Charlie.

On the Saxon, Clarence holds the rope, staring across the river to the fight underway and looks at Marcy and Paula and down to Reginald, Dave and Roy then back to the rope.

'Don't even think about it,' Paula says. 'You're too big...'

'Why isn't Dave going?' Marcy asks.

'Scared of water,' Paula replies. 'NO!' she yells out as Meredith, barking at the edge of the water and going nuts at not being able to join the fight, leaps out intending to swim across, her body hitting the water and pulled under within a second.

Paula leaps off the Saxon to hit the ground running, sprinting hard alongside the bank as she spots Meredith's head breaking the water, her front paws scrabbling like mad, but she sinks down again, disappearing from view in the swirling currents and white-topped waves.

No time to think. No time for thought. Paula dives in, hitting the water hard and going deep to slam into the dog's warm body that she grips and holds and starts kicking to break the surface, pushing the two of them up to gasp for air, the dog in wild panic, crying and whining while scrabbling with her claws raking Paula's arms and body. 'It's okay...it's okay...' she sputters and gags, trying to calm the dog while the waters pull them on.

She tries to turn for the bank but goes under, using her own body to push the dog up so Meredith may breathe, so Meredith may live and have life. She kicks out again, swirling left and right, going deeper then breaking the surface to gasp air but taking water down as she sinks once more while fighting to keep Meredith's head above the water but she's not strong enough. She can't do it. Meredith is too heavy, and the water is too strong. She tries harder but sinks deeper and pushes a hand up to force Meredith's chin out of the water because the team need the dog more than they need her. They need Meredith's nose and instincts. They need her power and strength. What they are doing cannot be done without Meredith, and so Paula takes her death without complaint because pack is pack and they would all have died many times over if not for this dog.

A surge of fight still in her and Paula rallies again, fighting for seconds of life, not for herself but to keep Meredith up, to keep her breathing while the dog claws and panics, raking Paula's face and neck then slamming her feet into Paula's stomach, driving the air out that makes Paula suck in, filling her lungs with water. She screams out, intending to purge but that makes her breathe in again and the panic grips as images of life flash through her mind. Her old office. Her family. Her mother and her uncle George. She thinks of Howie and the team and feels only love. She thinks of Clarence and regrets nothing while regretting everything and she holds on as she dies to keep Meredith's head up because this is her pack and she'll be damned if she'll lose another one so soon after Blinky.

Blinky! The thought of her sends a wave of love through Paula. She'll see her again. She'll see Blinky. She closes her eyes to die, to let it go, to join Blinky. *Not yet, Miss Paula Sir. Not yet.* She rallies. Hearing Blinky's voice. A mirage. A dream, a hallucination of her mind in the final seconds of death. *HOLD ON MISS PAULA SIR.* It's not real. Blinky is dead. *YEAH I'M DEAD AND YOU AIN'T SO GET A GRIP MISS PAULA.*

I can't Blinky. I'm dying.

NOT YET. HOLD THE LINE. HOLD. WE HOLD.

I can't...I can't breathe.

HOLD THE LINE. WE HOLD. WE DO NOT YIELD.

It's okay, Blinky. I'm not afraid.

HAHA. INCOMING! I'm so fucking awesome.

What?

A surge. An impact and Paula rises up from the water to break the surface to breathe and gag and puke. Gripped by a pair of arms so big they lift her and the dog with ease by a man roaring out with one arm gripping the rope extending out to the house on the other side. 'DON'T YOU DIE,' Clarence bellows. His arm around her chest and his fist clenched on the scruff of Meredith's neck, hoisting the limp dog up. 'YOU HEAR ME...DON'T YOU DIE...'

The rope snags. Going rigid. The water pummelling Clarence's head, slamming into his mouth and nose and those in the room holding the end scream out as they slide across the room, unable to hold Clarence's great weight as he holds Paula and Meredith as all three are dragged by the power of the current and the small group cry out from the burn in their hands and arms. The reach the window, bracing feet against the wall but it's still not enough. They have to let go. They'll be pulled through.

A shout. A rush. Men and women drenched in blood and gore pouring into the room. Faces blazing. Eyes wild. Hands gripping the rope.

'MOVE,' Howie shouts, wrapping the end around his body. His team move in, pushing and shoving the people away to grip and heave. Danny and Tappy with veins bulging from heads and necks. Charlie, Maddox, Cookey, Nick, Blowers and Mo all gritting teeth to dig heels in and heave and pull. Heave and pull. Draw it in. Together now. Work together now.

'ONE TWO PULL...' Howie bellows. 'ONE TWO PULL... ONE TWO PULL...'

Hand over hand. Mind over matter. Ignore the burning pain. Hand over hand. 'ONE TWO PULL...'

Closer and closer. Clarence grimacing. Paula barely conscious. Meredith unmoving. Slowly they go through the waters, through the wind and rain as those inside work harder to pull them up from the waters through the air against the wall of the building and Nick is there, lifting Meredith in his arms to pull inside and Blowers is there lifting Paula in his arms to pull inside as the others grip and heave the huge man up to the windowsill and over to land hard and gasping on the floor, hands in agony, arms wrenched and shoulders burning.

Meredith lies still and unmoving. Her eyes closed. Nick rubs her sides and back, vigorous and hard, opening her mouth to let the waters pour over the floor. Paula gagging, still unable to breathe properly. Charlie and Tappy heaving her over from her back to her front as she pukes and heaves.

'No...' Nick mutters, rubbing the dog's sides and back. 'Come on...COME ON...'

Blowers at his side. Mo there with Cookey, all of them rubbing the dog, urging her to breathe as the waters pour from her mouth. Too much water. Hearts sink. Hope fades. Another one lost. Another one gone.

A blink. A wag. An eye opens. Soft and brown. Another wag and the tears flow as the dog's chest moves to breathe.

'Fuck me,' Nick whispers, his head sinking to rest on Meredith's as her tail starts beating a drum on the floor.

Clarence tries to rise then falls back to sit against the wall, his arms bleeding from the rope burns, his head cut. Paula's face a mess of scratches. Her top torn and ripped. Blood flowing. Meredith tries to stand but wobbles and falls with Nick and Mo rushing in to help her up as the dog crawls to Paula, licking her face, whining softly and wagging her tail more as Paula's arms wrap around her neck. 'I heard Blinky,' she whispers, her voice ragged and hoarse. 'I heard her...she told me to hold on...'

They slump back and down, all of them sitting against the wall or lying flat while breathing hard. Minds racing. Adrenalin still pumping. Gasping for air with every inch of their bodies hurting.

'You held on,' Clarence says, wiping a bloodied hand across his face. 'You all did,' he adds, looking around. His eyes fall on Danny sitting close, covered in blood and sweat. His hands cut and bleeding. Clarence reaches out, pulling the lad into his side. 'You did well, son... your dad would be proud...'

Danny squeezes his eyes closed, willing the tears not to fall.

'Fuck me,' Tappy gasps, flat on her back gasping for air. 'Is it always like this?'

'Pretty much,' Blowers whispers.

'I'm not racist,' Howie whispers, swallowing as he looks at Maddox.

'It was a joke,' Maddox says, waving an exhausted hand at Howie.

'Awesome...now how the fuck are we getting Clarence back across?'

Maddox stands on the windowsill staring down at the raging waters below. The wind howling past his body. The rain pelting his skin and face. His hands above his head looped through a cut off section of rope greased up and hooked over another thicker rope stretching taut and rigid from a rafter in the ceiling of the top floor of the house over the river to the Saxon on the other side. He eyes the landing pad. A pile of mattresses dragged out from houses and dumped on the ground.

'Ready?' Nick asks, holding the back of Maddox's belt.

'No,' Maddox says honestly.

'Ah be fine,' Tappy says, also holding his belt. 'Big push... one...two...'

'Wait! Why am I going first again?' Maddox asks, trying to peer back at them.

'Cos you're a fatty,' Tappy says with a grin.

'I'm not fat,' he says.

'Joking! You're a big boy and it's all muscle,' she says, patting his leg with a wink.

'We need someone heavy to test it...' Nick says.

'Right.' Maddox says. 'You're heavier than me,' he adds, twisting to look down at Nick.

'Ah but you're strong,' Tappy calls up. 'And we need Nick to fix it if it breaks...ready? GO!'

'ARGH YOU'S FUCKERS...' he flies out from the push, sliding along the rope with a gathering speed down towards the mattresses on the other side. The river below now wider and more violent. The storm increasing and those mattresses coming towards him far too fast.

Then he hits and lands in a world of soft wet springy foam, absorbing in with a gasp then rolls over to look up at the grinning face of Marcy.

Nick and Roy spent five minutes discussing pulleys, winches, sliding tackles and counter-weights to try and find a solution to get the survivors, and Clarence, back across the river.

'Just zipwire it,' Tappy said, invoking a surprised look from Nick. 'Get another rope over, cut the old one to use as hand-hold grippy things and zipwire back across. Easy peasy lemon squeezy...'

Nick told Roy on the radio who did what Nick did and went silent for a few seconds.

'Yeah we should just do that,' Roy said.

Another rope fired over through a top floor window as Tappy beat the ceiling down so the rope could be tied to the corner joist of a roof-rafter.

'Needs a strong knot,' Nick said from below, looking up.

'Yep,' she said, securing it to the rafter.

'Seriously, it's got to hold Clarence...'

'Yeah cos women can't do knots, can they? How about a taut line clove hitch half hitch with a double timber hitch?' she asked then grinned down at the silence coming back. 'That shut you up didn't it, Nicholas.'

'Your knot held,' Nick says, watching Maddox stand up on the far side.

'Yeah, I only did a granny knot in the end...' she replies then frowns when he doesn't reply. 'Did you bloody check it?'

'Nah...well, I might have had a quick look while I was up there...'

'That's out of order,' she says. 'Nope, not talking to you now...' she adds when he goes to speak. 'Bellend.'

'You are...Mr Howie? We're all ready.'

Survivors first. Terrified. Weeping. Wailing. Children wrapped in blankets tied to adults.

'I'm not doing it!' a woman screams the words in the room. Heavyset and terrified the rope will break or her arms won't hold her weight. 'I WON'T. I WONT I WON'T I WON'T...' she screeches louder, stamping her feet, flailing her arms.

'Come on, you'll be fine,' Paula says calmly, her face raw from scratches, her clothing ripped, her voice still rough from vomiting so hard. 'Few seconds and it's done...'

'I WON'T I WON'T I WON'T...' a screech, high pitched and awful. Driving into ears and making heads pull back from the volume. 'YOU CAN'T MAKE ME...'

'We're not fucking making anyone do anything,' Howie says, exasperated and starting to bite.

'Don't talk to her like that, she's just bloody scared,' someone else says.

'Are you taking the fucking piss?' Howie asks, the darkness flashing in his eyes, understanding their fears and worries, but feeling that same conflicting thing inside of doing everything to save them while not wanting to be anywhere near them.

'Out,' Paula says to Howie. 'Go for a smoke...'

'Seriously, don't go if you don't want to,' Howie snaps at the screeching woman. 'But fuck off and let someone else...'

'Charlie, take Mr Howie outside please,' Paula orders.

'Mr Howie,' Charlie says, ushering Howie through. 'No no,' she says softly as he goes to say something else and trying to think what Marcy does to calm him when he gets like this then remembering what Marcy does when he gets like this and thinking it would be highly inappropriate to do what Marcy does when he gets like this. Besides, she doesn't actually blame him for saying that to the woman. She wanted to say it herself.

The woman does cross the river, but only after several very long and very trying minutes of soft talking and constant reassurance, and even then she goes screeching across to land still screeching on the other side.

'Shut up,' Marcy tells her bluntly, snapping her screams off. 'Good. Now piss off out of the way.'

The rest follow over, then the team with Meredith wrapped in a blanket tied to Nick who zooms across with a huge grin to land on his feet and look back to stick a finger up at Tappy and the others in the window. Clarence goes last. Everyone wincing at the rope sagging in the middle and exhaling in relief when he crashes into the mattresses.

Into the church. Chairs broken. Fires lit. Jess brought in to eat oats and shit on the once clean floor while the survivors huddle together at one end and watch the heavily armed people laugh and joke quietly amongst themselves at the other end, moving with purpose to clean weapons and go deeper into the shadows to wash and change into dry clothes. The doors barricaded with heavy pews. The wind howling through the eaves and corners. Thunder booming. Lightning flashing.

'Then that one with the fake tits told me to shut up...she was like so rude and...and aggressive,' the heavyset woman's voice floating through the great hall of the church. 'And that prick with the scraggly hair too...*Mister Fucking Howie* or whatever his name is...'

'Stop right there,' Paula tells Blowers, Charlie and Marcy rising to their feet with angry expressions. 'It's fine. She's allowed an opinion...'

'Not about my tits she ain't,' Marcy retorts. 'Pert love, not fake,' she shouts. 'Big difference...'

'Jesus, pack it in,' Paula whispers.

'Pert my arse,' the woman mutters.

'Trust me, your arse is not pert,' Marcy fires back.

'HOW FUCKING DARE YOU!'

'Just eat less.'

'WHAT DID SHE SAY?'

'Enough!' Paula snaps. 'Marcy, not another word...and you... whoever you are...one more word and you'll be outside for the night...'

'You can't talk to me like that...I've got anxiety and depression...' she states in a tone that suggests she just scored a victory.

Paula goes to speak then just stops and blows air from her cheeks and sinks to sit and stare at the fire.

'Doctor told me...that's why I never worked. Gave me pills and said it wasn't my fault...'

Paula picks a tin up, blinking at the label as the others fall to silence and eat their cold rations.

'So people can't tell me what to do or say mean things cos I got anxiety and depression...doc said people have got to be nice and not be like cunts or anything. Said I shouldn't take it from people...'

'Good girl,' Nick whispers to the dog, spooning more tuna into a bowl.

'I said to him I did. I said I want my weed on prescription as everyone knows cannabis helps and I was like why the fuck am I paying for it when some wankers get like heart attack pills on script...'

A look from Maddox to Mo who snorts a laugh and covers his mouth quickly while Tappy smiles at her tinned food.

'I said I'd bring my dealer into the surgery and the doc could meet him and pay for it like in bulk? but my dealer was like *fuck that* and I told him I had anxiety and depression and he can't talk to me like that and he was like *I'm a fucking drug dealer...*'

Stifled giggles and laughs, suppressed snorts. Even the people with the woman turn away to laugh quietly.

'Oh gosh I want to know what happens now,' Reginald says into the weird silence that follows, prompting more laughs. 'Did the doctor prescribe the cannabis?'

'Did he fuck! He was like *no chance that's highly illegal* and I was like *you can't talk to me like that cos I got anxiety and depression...*'

'A most egregious situation,' Reginald says.

'What's that mean?'

'Nefarious.'

'What's that mean?'

'Deplorable,'

'What's that mean?'

'Heinous.'

'What's that mean?'

'Dear god...is it too late to be bitten?' Reginald remarks to snorts of laughter breaking out from both ends of the church.

'Ere, are you taking the piss out of me? I got anxiety and depression...'

CHAPTER FOURTEEN

Day Seventeen.

The Range Rover slows to a stop a short distance from the farmhouse. A long single road behind them and nothing but rolling fields in every direction. Hills in the distance. Forests and thickets but not for miles.

'Are you being serious?' Cassie asks, looking from the windscreen to Gregori in the driver's seat. 'We're in the middle of nowhere again...'

He doesn't reply but pushes the door open and drops out to stand and listen, every sense heightened. Listening and looking. Smelling and feeling. Gregori trusts his senses. They've kept him alive many a time when by rights he should be dead, often giving him only a split-second warning of something coming but enough to turn or duck, to lift and aim to shoot back or to throw a knife or break a neck.

At least he finally has a holster now with kit, equipment and weapons taken from the Albanians in the hotel a few nights ago.

Gregori gave the boy thirty seconds to make every one of the things leave before he killed them. Cassie protested, angrily yelling at Gregori that it was only *the bloody things* that had saved them but Gregori wouldn't budge then and he won't budge now.

The boy will be a boy, not a killer or a *Krye* or a little devil that rules the world.

He turns back to the car, leaning in to pull an assault rifle out. Looping the strap about his arm. 'Come, we go.'

She tuts noisily, shaking her head as she wrenches the door open to get out. A pistol holstered on her hip. They spent the day after the storm in the hotel again because the fog was too thick to move out. It was then that Gregori taught her to fire the pistols and assault rifles.

'Come on,' she says with a sigh, holding her hand out for the boy as he jumps down from the back of the car. Red shorts, a yellow t-shirt and his angelic face all happy and carefree. 'Another night in a boring nowhereville house,' she mutters darkly, staring around at the pretty meadows and fields. At the flowers blooming and the sky so blue and deep. Scents in the air. Fragrant and delicate. Everything so twee and nice and boring as shit. 'Boring as shit,' she mumbles, making the boy laugh. 'Don't repeat that!'

'Boring as shit,' the boy sings the words before she finishes her warning, prompting Gregori to stop and turn with a glare.

'Well it is,' she tells him.

'Is things here?'

'No, Gregoreee.'

'Why would they be here?' Cassie asks. 'For what? To pick daisies? Roll in the meadows? Chase butterflies? Maybe plan for next years harvest or... don't walk off when I'm nagging you...' she huffs again, following Gregori as he completes his first security scan. Walking around the outside of the house and looking in each window to see a neat and tidy interior looking all spick and span and boring as shit.

'Boring as shit,' the boy sings, hearing Cassie mumbling again.

'Boy!' Gregori snaps.

'Mr Howie put his penis inside Lani's vagina in the old armoury to make a baby in her belly but he knew she wasn't Lani but she was a little bit Lani but she was holding a bomb and then dropped it and Mr Howie ran out and there was a big fire and Lani is deaded...'

'Right,' Cassie says, both her and Gregori staring down at the boy at the latest episode of Howie and the Fort. 'This in the fort again is it?'

The boy nods.

'I thought Lani turned back,' Cassie says. 'You said Marcy bit Lani but Lani got better...'

The boy picks his nose, staring around with mild interest.

'Don't pick your nose,' Cassie tells him, guiding his hand down.

The infection stares at Cassie as she pushes the boy's hand down. A grasp of the question asked. An understanding but it's still hard to navigate the boy's brain. Human beings have extraordinary brains, but they use so little of them and the infection studies the unused synapses as it tries to understand the entirety of life and everything all at the same time. Trying to know everything in context instantly. Trying to be everything and everywhere instantly.

'Lani resisted,' the boy says, the infection says. Not knowing what it means but knowing what it means while knowing everything while not understanding anything while trying to work in the boy's brain while the boy still occupies his own mind, or parts thereof.

'Lani resisted what?' Cassie asks.

The boy looks at Cassie. The infection looks at Cassie. The boy hasn't a clue what the answer is. The infection does know but it doesn't know. It can't answer because the question is too complex and too layered with roots stretching out to all areas of life. *Lani resisted what?* What is *what?* What did Lani resist?

'I'm hungry,' the boy says. 'I don't know,' the infection says.

'What don't you know?' Cassie asks. 'He's doing it again,' she says to Gregori with a look the infection knows is an expression of concern.

'He is child, child say things.'

'You know exactly what I mean,' she says with another sigh. 'Anyway, so Lani is dead?'

'Yes,' the boy says, the infection says.

'Dead dead or coming back dead?'

'Deaded,' the boy says. 'Her body has been destroyed beyond further use and can no longer sustain life. Lani has ceased to be a host,' the infection says.

'Right,' Cassie says slowly, looking from the boy to Gregori.

A shrug from Gregori. 'Come, we go.'

A shrug from Cassie. 'Come, we go,' she says with a wink to the boy.

A shrug from the boy who smiles at the play on words. 'Come, we go,' he says, swinging on Cassie's hand.

The boy told them that Cookey doesn't like clowns. He also told them about Paula and Roy and how they ran for miles when it was foggy. Cassie listened, at first feeling like an indulgent parent allowing her child to yack on about nonsense, but then she took notice and became invested when she clocked the continuity of the stories and the way the details were always correct. The names, the things they did. Howie and Dave. Dave is dangerous. Clarence is big. Lani was fast but she's now dead. Marcy was a host but different but the same but not the same. Reginald was with Marcy but is now with Howie. Reginald was a host but is not a host but is a host.

The boy drew more pictures in the hotel too, with the infection using the boy to understand, process and filter and know the things it knows. This is Howie. This is Dave. This is them. What is them? What is what? What is the infection?

Take more hosts. That must be done. That is being done. But there is more. What more? Why is Howie killing it? What is it? A hint of size. A vastness. A thing of many. Many minds. A hive mind. Too many minds to control. What is control?

One race.

'Jesus,' Cassie said, after taking a break from shooting guns to look at the pictures the boy drew, the pictures the infection drew. 'You are a little savant,' she said, kissing his head. The boy's head. The words *one race* written on sheets above drawings of Howie and the people with him. 'What's one race?' Cassie asked.

'There is two but there must be one,' the infection said.

Cassie shook her head and blinked.

'Can we do swimming later?' the boy asked.

'Say that again, about the being two but it should be one...'

The boy stared at her. The infection stared at her. It knew the answer but it couldn't verbalise a reply to come from the boy. 'One race,' it said instead.

'One race, yay,' Cassie said, frowning then shrugging then kissing him on the head again. 'Drink your juice.'

'Seriously, Gregory,' Cassie says, following him in through the farmhouse door after waiting while he searched for a key, finding one under a rock.

'Is Gregori,' he says automatically, knowing she only calls him Gregory when she is being annoying.

'Whatever. Listen, no don't walk off...'

'I check house.'

'You saw what happened. We can't just ignore it...they'll follow him wherever he goes...'

'You talk. Is too much. Yack yack...'

'They don't want to hurt him,' she follows him from room to room, traipsing behind as Gregori checks every possible hiding place. 'And you felt it...I know you did...you felt the way they feel about him. They love him...'

'Is things. Is bad things. Not people. Boy need people...'

'The people are bad! Not the things. Look what happened in that street we stayed in...they were bad. Murdering and raping...stealing, making people sleep outside and go hungry....and those men that pinned me down and tried to rape me and the men that came to the hotel...your own people, Gregori and what did they do? Stop walking off and bloody listen!'

'I listen. You say this. You say too much. Boy will be child. Boy need peace and life. Not murder. Not rape. Not die...'

'You're contradicting yourself! You said murder and rape and death is bad but you said he needs people. People do that. The things don't. They...'

'No.'

'They want to protect him...we would be dead if they didn't...'

'No.'

'Oh my god you are so stubborn and pig-headed and and...'

The boy listens, holding Cassie's hand as they argue and glare and pout and scowl and frown at each other. 'Need a wee wee, Casseee.'

'What? Oh, right...the bathroom is in there...go on now. Hang on, Gregory we haven't finished our...'

'IS GREGORI!'

'Don't you shout at me...'

The boy goes into the bathroom, looking up at the windowsill and round at the bath and the shower and the things inside. He lifts the toilet seat-cover then thinks to lift the seat but doesn't bother and tugs his shorts down to start weeing into the bowl, aiming properly before looking around again while listening to Gregori and Cassie shouting loudly as the jet of urine starts hitting everywhere but the bowl. It doesn't bother him that they shout. He feels loved. He feels very loved.

'Where is boy?'

'See! You don't listen. If Daudi was here he'd know exactly where he was... oh stop that glaring, he's only having a wee...'

'NO WEE WEE ON SEAT.'

'Ah shit, I forgot about that...Boy! Wee in the bowl.'

'Okay, Casseeee,' the boy shouts back, not bothering to aim for the bowl. Lani is dead. What does that mean? Why won't Howie's body take the infection. Is it an infection? What is it? It knows, in a way of knowing, where it came from, but it doesn't know what that means. The infection also knows the secrets of the millions of hosts it controls, but it doesn't know what they mean.

Pi is an irrational number of which the decimal representation can never end and will never settle into a permanent repeating pattern and that in terms of numerical expressions it equals 3.14159265359. The infection knows that, but it has no context for the knowledge. No history. Nothing to compare it to.

'Je suis ravi de vous rencontrer,' the boy says in perfectly spoken French with a distinct Parisian accent. 'Ah, thank you,' he replies in German. 'I am pleased to meet you too,' he says in Italian. 'Come, we go,' he says in Albanian while looking down at the puddles of piss all over the floor and toilet seat. 'Socrates corrupted the young. He is guilty because he was accused but surely the burden of proof lies on the prosecution and those casting the charge rather than the person accused...' he reels it off in fluent Greek as he flushes the toilet before tugging his shorts up and running off to follow the voices, finding them in the kitchen having another stand-off.

'Did you wash your hands?' Cassie asks as he runs in.

The boy stops to think, not remembering if he did or did not wash his hands. 'No,' the infection says, giving the answer.

'Wash your hands,' Cassie tells him, 'and good boy for being honest...okay,' she says, back to talking at Gregori. 'I understand what you're saying and yes, he needs to be safe...but what I'm saying is he is safer with them around him...'

Gregori lifts the boy to wash his hands at the sink while the infection reflects on the use of honesty and dishonesty in the context of social and interpersonal relationships. What would have happened if it said yes when asked if the boy washed his hands. That would be untrue so why say it? Something untrue is a lie. It is deceit. Is all lying bad? What is the purpose of lying? 'I did a poo,' the infection says, the boy says.

'Good boy,' Cassie says automatically. 'Well, we're here now but I'm not happy...seriously, Gregori...you and I will be sitting down later and coming up with a better plan than running about in the countryside...'

The infection just lied. It said the boy did a poo but the boy did not do a poo, but the boy has, at least once in his life, done a poo which renders the statements as both true and false. False in the context of which it was intended, in trying to suggest that the boy did a poo just now, but true in the actuality of expressing a fact that the boy has indeed, previously, done a poo.

'Can I do drawing?' the boy asks, looking up at Gregori.

'Yes,' the man says deeply, staring down.

The infection stares up then makes the boy look at Cassie. It has Cassie. It is within her but is dormant. It does not control her mind but rather only works to dump chemicals in response to base emotional reactions. Cassie *loves* the boy. Cassie will always protect the boy. The boy is small and weak. He is unable to do many things. Cassie can do many things. The infection does not know how it can be dormant with Cassie, nor does it know why it cannot go in Gregori. The infection determines that Gregori is the same as Howie and cannot be made into a host, but the infection also knows Gregori loves the boy and will, and has, done anything to protect the boy. 'Gregoreee, do you put your penis in Cassee's vagina?'

An abrupt end to the argument. A shocked silence. 'We no do this,' Gregori says with just a hint of uncertainty.

'Well...we almost did,' Cassie says quietly with a growing smile and the boy watches them staring at each other.

'Natural human reproduction occurs when a man and a woman engage in sexual intercourse during which the interactions between the male and the female results in the fertilisation of the woman's ovum by the man's sperm...' the boy says, the infection says.

Cassie pulls her head back, showing distaste as she looks from Gregori to the boy. 'Ewww, bit gross...ruined the moment there.'

'I not know what said,' Gregori says, staring at the boy while kind of knowing what the boy said while choosing to pretend that he didn't understand it.

'And anyway, that makes my point because that is not a normal thing for a boy of his age to say...how old is he anyway?' Cassie asks.

'I not know.'

'How old are you?' Cassie asks the boy.

'Come, we go,' the boy says deeply.

'We don't even know how old he is...and we're still calling him Boy...that's bad. We're awful parents, Gregori.'

'We not this thing.'

'Er, I think you'll find we pretty much are now my love. Not biological no, but certainly I think we'd be defined as foster or even adoptive parents...anyway, stop changing the subject. We're not staying here for long...'

The day goes on. The boy interacting with the world around him as a child should, dancing with Cassie when she rigs up one of the music players she charged in the car. Singing happily while she hip bumps Gregori, trying to make him smile and lose his hard-faced manner while inside the boy's mind he knows that Howie and all of those are running in the rain. A horse is there too. A man called Neal on the horse. Howie's team are separated but some are going to the sports academy where the under 21 England hockey team are holding trials. It knows this because the infection has the minds of local workers and residents and the boy dances and eats and plays while the fights and battles go on.

'Jimmy Carr shit on Howie's chin...'

'Don't say shit,' Cassie responds, clattering about with pots and pans in the kitchen at the gas-stove.

The infection sends more resources, but they fight back. It knows some of the young men from Howie's team are in the sports academy now, so it will attack them to divide Howie's numbers and cut them down.

It will attack and attack. More. Send more. Do more. It dumps chemicals into hosts. Pumping them wild and crazed but still it's not enough and the boy grows still, his face hardening, his eyes growing cold and distant as the battle comes to a close and the one remaining host it has inside the lobby of the sports academy stands tall to stare at Howie and the dog stalking towards it.

The boy can see them. The infection can see them. All of them. It is there but here. The boy is there but here and the reactions felt by the infection go into the boy. Organic and natural but twisted and wrong then Howie moves, and the host is gripped and held, staring into those awful dark eyes of the man.

'He is coming,' the infection tells Howie. The boy watches, listening, his body tensing. Cassie turns from the stove, having heard the words and startling on sight of the boy standing on the kitchen table with a face of pure anger.

'Bring him,' Howie snaps the words out, goading, provoking, powerful. Invoking a surge of rage within the boy.

'One race,' the host tells Howie, the boy tells the kitchen, growling the words out in a voice not his own as Gregori walks in to stop and watch, sharing a glance with Cassie.

'MY RACE,' Howie screams. 'And we win this day...' the infection feels the power as the host drops and the jaws of the dog clamp to rag and kill as the boy bursts into tears and flings himself into Cassie's arms scooping him off the table.

Half an hour later the boy eats his dinner, chatting happily and normally, all thought of Howie gone from his mind, but his mind filled with thoughts of Howie. Not his mind, the parts of his mind the infection has but the infection has all of his mind.

Why is Howie killing it? What for? There can only be one race. It is logic. The infection is pure. It is not flawed as people are. They feel pain. The infection does not. They have diseases and broken cells within their bodies that allow things to hurt them. The infection does not. The infection *is* the body. It *is* the mind. It *is* every single cell. It is all those things. It cures. It heals. It prevents death and it takes what the body has and makes it better. The infection is the true state of being.

'Time for bed little man,' Cassie says hefting the boy up to carry up to the bathroom.

The infection watches as Cassie prepares the boy for sleep. The infection does not need sleep in the way people do. Their bodies are wasteful. The infection fixes that. It is the true state of being. It takes less and makes more. It uses less and provides better.

'Wow, you are sleepy aren't you,' Cassie says, watching the boy yawn as she lies him down in a soft bed. 'Sweet dreams,' she kisses his head and waits quietly at his side, stroking the boy's face and cheeks as he drifts down to sleep while the infection inside seeks to learn to evolve to survive to achieve dominance.

Cassie moves quietly back from the sleeping child, pausing at the door to smile at him sleeping. She goes into the bathroom, brushes her teeth and showers in cold water, washing her hair and lathering her body. Shaving her legs and armpits then drying off on a towel bought and stocked here by people she will never know. The day is late already. The boy stayed up longer than he should and outside the darkness is already coming down.

In the kitchen, she fixes black tea at the stove. A towel wrapped around her body. Gregori at the table behind her stripping guns to clean. Silence between them, awkward and heavy but he steals glances at her legs and quickly looks away when she turns to carry the mugs over and sits down opposite him.

'Tea,' she says, nodding at his mug.

He nods back, grunting a reply. 'He sleep?'

'Yep.'

His deft movements become absorbing. The fluidity of him and the long years of doing these same tasks show with his sublime proficiency.

'Can we talk?' she finally asks, her tea now nearly all gone.

He doesn't reply but pauses to drink then carries on working, clunking and clicking the gun back together.

'We're going to wake up tomorrow and they'll be near here...' she cuts off when he blasts irritation from his nose and the clunks and clicks get louder. 'They'll run all night, Gregori...' he slides the top back several times, listening to the action. 'We cannot just keep ignoring it...' he aims off, dry firing a few times before pushing the loaded magazine in, clunking and clicking then a thud as he finally puts the pistol down and lifts his mug, draining the tea. 'What about tomorrow night? What about the night after that? Just keep moving house every day? It makes no difference...they know where he is... where are you going?' she asks when he stands up.

'Bed.'

Another huff and she follows, mounting the stairs behind him. 'Gregory...' she whispers. He pauses on the top step, his hand gripping the bannister. No words or movement but his aura expresses displeasure. 'We cannot just keep running...'

A grunt and he moves into the bathroom but she slips through the door before he can close it, earning another glare that she ignores.

'And anyway, what are we running from? It's not like we need to fear anything...' she whispers as he brushes his teeth at the sink. Watching him with her arms folded. 'It's like we're scared of something and excuse me for being blunt, but you're not scared of anything in this world, Gregory...'

'Is Gregori,' he growls, bending to spit before rinsing his mouth.

'So why are we running? What from?'

He pulls his top off, glowering while holding it out for her to take as his fingers grip the buttons of his jeans. 'Leave,' he grunts, nodding at the door. 'I shower.'

'I'm not leaving. We need to talk about this...'

'I shower.'

'Shower then,' she retorts as he reaches out to grip her shoulders, physically turning her around. 'Why won't you discuss it?'

'I discuss.'

'It's not a fucking discussion,' she whispers, listening to him undress behind her. 'It's a bloody dictatorship...'

A grunt. A sigh. Hands to her shoulders and she turns to face away from the shower as he climbs into the tub and pulls the curtain. 'I make boy kill things...'

'What?' she snaps.

'When meet. I get things. I teach boy to kill them. Stab. Use knife...use weapon. To live yes?'

'You did what?'

The curtain yanks back, his head poking out, bubbles and lather on his scalp. 'We discuss. This discuss.'

'Okay.'

'I make kill,' he says, back to washing in the cold water. 'I see they no hurt him. They try bite me but I fast. Then they no try bite me. The boy make them sit. Make them stand to kill. Everywhere we go they come. They stare...I make decision. Boy will be boy. Not the killer...I killer. Is bad. Boy is good.'

She pauses, listening and processing, grasping what he means as the shower shuts off and a hand pokes out. She looks around, grabbing a towel from a shelf to hand over.

'Boy will be boy. No things. No kill...'

'But he did kill, he killed that big man in the hotel...you taught him where to stab and he saved you...if you hadn't taught him that you'd be dead, I'd have been gang-raped and god only knows what would have happened to him...don't you see? What you did saved him...then the things came and they saved us...*us*, Gregori. Not just the boy...'

The curtain yanks back, the towel around his waist. Determination on his face. 'No. Boy will be boy.'

'He is a boy! He can still be a boy but...what?'

'I need wee wee.'

'Oh right, er...' she flaps her hands and turns again. 'He pissed all over the floor and seat again...what I am saying is that the world has changed, Gregori...we can't give him a normal childhood because of what's happened...we wouldn't even be here if this hadn't happened. You'd be serial killing people and I'd be either in London or still being kidnapped...'

She rushes after him as he flushes the toilet and walks out of the room, both of them pausing silently by the boy's open door to stare in for a second before walking on with Cassie following Gregori into one of the double rooms. 'A normal childhood would be school and lessons, mixing with other children and learning to be a member of society but there is no society now...'

He pulls the sheets back, thumps the pillow and watches as she walks around and sits on the bed, stretching her legs out and leaning back against the headboard. 'If we truly want him to be adjusted and ready for life then we need to address what he is and why they don't want to hurt him because this *is* his life now. This is his normality... we're the ones that know it's different because we're older... what are you staring at?'

'I sleep now.'

'We're talking...so what do you think?'

He sits down heavily, thumping his pillow again and glaring and tutting before shuffling to lie down next to her sitting up. Darkness in the room but a bright moon giving glow.

'Well?' she asks when he doesn't reply.

'I sleep.'

'No, we need to talk.'

'Talk tomorrow.'

'Talk now, Gregory...'

'Is Gregori...go to room.'

She shuffles down, rolling on her side to face him, her head propped up on a hand, her elbow digging into the corner of his pillow. 'We need to accept what he is,' she says.

'Go room.'

'No! I'm not going anywhere until we've sorted this...'

His head turns, looking at her. She smiles sweetly, winks and then snorts a laugh. 'Gregoreee, do you put your penis in Casseeee's vagina?' she mimics the boy's voice, chuckling as she speaks as the Albanian tries to glare in the darkness, but his lips twitch and the smile comes.

Two minutes later and his penis is in Cassie's vagina. Less whore. More wife. The way she nagged him all day, following him around and refusing to give up. Watching him brush his teeth and following him into the bedroom. Less whore. More wife and he moved fast, smiling at her in the night. Her form silhouetted. Her white teeth showing. The smell of her. The warmth of her body and she honestly did not see it coming. She intended to annoy him into submission over the boy, pester and nag and irritate until he gave in then suddenly his mouth was on hers and his hands were cupping her face as the towels came off.

She moved on top of him, kissing hard, breathing harder, hearts booming. A need. An urgency. A desire surging in both. Hands everywhere. His on her breasts, on her back, through her hair. Hers on his shoulders, down his hard stomach, gripping his shaft as it grew and swelled until she sunk down, guiding him inside. A gasp from both. The sensation so magnificent. So waited for. It's happening. Finally happening. His cock is inside her. She pauses, almost expecting something to happen to stop it but nothing does and so she starts moving. Fucking Gregori. Making love to Gregori.

He comes fast. It's been a long time, but he comes powerfully and deep, lifting her from the bed to spasm and grunt as she falls forward to kiss and savour the moment. Both breathing hard.

'That's one way to shut me up,' she whispers, her voice quavering and soft.

CHAPTER FIFTEEN

Day Twenty-five

'Yeah but no but...'

'Oh come now, you will be absolutely fine, my dear,' Reginald says, holding the door open to usher the woman into the car.

'No but...that ain't right. You can't like ditch us and not do your jobs and like...it's out of order that is and I've got anxiety and...'

'And depression, yes you told us,' Reginald says. 'Many, many times in fact.'

She balks, staring at him suspiciously and still unable to detect the mockery in his absurdly polite tone. A fleet of cars. Not big but enough for the survivors to make for the fort. Everyone loaded and ready, except one of course, who pouts and flusters and swears and stands rooted to the spot.

'But no but...what if the zombie things come and...'

'Oh trust me, they'll die from bleeding ears before they get anywhere near you. Now in you go, there we are...watch your head. Jolly good. Now you be sure to say hello to a nice lady called Joan at the fort who would love to hear all about your concerns...'

A night in the church with the storm outside growing louder by the hour. Thumps and bangs kept them stirring. Roof tiles slamming into the ground. Tree's toppling. At one point the smell of burning got them all up and checking the building before it was determined to be smoke from somewhere else drifting on the wind. The rain was relentless too and soon started dripping through holes in the roof and those drips soon became rivers that pooled and spread out across the floor.

Fitful to say the least and as the dawn broke so they ventured out to see chimney stacks smashed all over the place and whole roofs ripped from buildings. Thick smoke coming from the houses on the other side of the now much wider river. Fires sparked by the lightning, dampened somewhat by the rain. The sky low and grey. The wind still high and the rain coming in showers but at least that awful crushing temperature was gone.

Reginald smiles sweetly, pushing the door closed as the woman shoots a meaty hand out, preventing it from shutting as another collective groan sounds out. 'What now, my dear?' Reginald asks with the patience of a saint.

'Thanks,' she says honestly. 'Most people talk to me like I'm a thick cunt but...so like cheers,' she mumbles, blushing furiously.

'Anytime,' Reginald says with a degree of surprise, closing the door as the fleet finally moves off. 'Gosh, well now, that certainly was a very grand adventure was it not?'

'It was something,' Howie says glumly, exhaling noisily while scratching his head as he walks back into the church with Reginald to the scent of coffee in the air. Water heating in a pan on a fire. Mugs nicked from nearby houses. Instant coffee poured. A bag of sugar with a teaspoon poking out the top and a battered box of teabags completing one of the most beautiful sights Howie has ever seen.

'They have all gone,' Reginald announces.

'Thank god,' Paula says. 'The rest were fine but that bloody woman. I've never met anyone so rude in my life...anyway, so what's the plan for...'

'Shush,' Howie says, picking a mug up. 'Nobody say anything or move or do anything because something will happen, and I want a coffee this morning...'

'You are so dramatic sometimes, Howie,' Paula tells him.

'Hey now, I traversed a swinging rope over a raging river to save miss shouty pants...'

'You hey now, I jumped into that raging river to save Nick's dog.'

Nick goes to speak but shrugs and drinks his coffee.

'Charlie?'

'Yes, Mr Howie.'

'Is traversed the right word?'

'It is.'

'Winner,' Howie mumbles, blowing the surface of his coffee. 'Shush...' he says, glaring around.

'Nobody said anything,' Paula says, shaking her head. 'Right, what's the plan?'

'Paula!'

'Oh piss off, Howie. Drink your coffee. What's the plan?'

'Fine,' he grumbles. 'We need to find out if the infected are controlled by one super zombie-like Marcy and if so then kill it and if not then kill the other lesser super zombies controlling them...happy now? Ruining coffee time with your plan demands.'

Paula tuts again as Tappy laughs at the back and forth between them. Sharing a look with Nick who rolls his eyes as though to say this is normal.

'Reginald?' Paula asks.

'Yes, my dear?' Reginald asks lightly.

'Right you two, pack it in...my face is all cut up and I'm a little bit grumpy today...'

'Mo.'

'Yes, boss?'

'Give Paula a hug before she starts shouting.'

'On it,' Mo says, running over to smile at Paula.

'Twats,' Paula snaps, breaking off into a laugh as she grabs Mo to hug. 'Reggie, tell us properly please.'

'With small words,' Marcy says quickly as Reginald opens his mouth to speak. 'Oh, we've got Charlie here, carry on and use big words then.'

'Ah now, yes indeed, well basically it is exactly as Mr Howie said. Actually, I rather think this may be an apt time to explain some things to you all. If that is in order of course?'

'Oh my god,' Howie says with mock dramatic effect. 'Are we finally having the big chat?'

'Indeed, that is the case,' Reginald says.

'Winner,' Howie sings in a mumbling voice. 'We're having the big chat about what happens when a mummy and a daddy love each other...'

'What the fuck!' Marcy snorts, coffee dripping from her nose as the others burst out laughing.

'Alas no,' Reginald says deeply, his eyes twinkling. 'Not a chat about sex I am afraid.'

'Bummer,' Howie says.

'You don't make babies from bum sex,' Cookey quips.

'Cookey!' Marcy snorts, dripping coffee from her nose again.

'Dear God,' Paula groans, unable to stop herself chuckling. 'Danny, Tappy...you can probably catch those people up if you want to get out while you still can...'

'Okay okay,' Howie says. 'Before you say it can I say what I think it is...'

'Oh god this'll go on for hours,' Marcy says. 'Just let Reggie spit it out...'

'You don't make babies from spitting it out...'

'Cookey!'

'Sorry, Paula.'

'No, I'm being serious,' Howie says, smiling while he says it. 'No, I am. I'm being serious...right, we haven't spoken about this have we, Reggie.'

'We've spoken lots about it.'

'No! I mean about what it is. About what you know...'

'Ah I see, understood. I can confirm I have not discussed that with you.'

'Right, I think it was a panacea that was developed that either got fucked up by accident *or*, someone fucked it up on purpose. That's my theory.'

'Are you being serious?' Marcy asks. 'We've been discussing that for days.'

'We never said it was a panacea,' he replies.

'We bloody did,' she retorts.

'You did, boss,' Clarence says. 'You said on that foggy day when we saw the clowns.'

'Clowns?' Tappy asks.

'Don't even mention it,' Cookey says with a shudder. 'Dirty clowns...'

'Ah shit, I thought I was being really clever then,' a deflated Howie says.

'Bless,' Marcy says, reaching over to ruffle his hair. 'You tried, that's all that matters...'

'May I?' Reginald asks.

'Was it a panacea?' Howie asks.

'Yes, it was,' Reginald replies.

'Fuck yes!' Howie says. 'Ima winner...okay, carry on.'

Reginald lowers to sit on the end of a pew. A mug of herbal tea clasped between his hands, one still bound in splints to keep his broken fingers straight. His non-corrective glasses glinting the flames of the fire and his mind not only back to full speed but feeling faster than ever before. 'In brief, Doctor Neal Barrett, the chap we met a few days ago, was a world-renowned statistician who was recruited to undertake a research study in a very secret project within a mountain facility somewhere in central Europe. He was told, along with the other scientists recruited, that the project was a table-top theoretical exercise. Indeed, the chap had no knowledge of what it was until they were all inside the facility and doors were sealed. He was then informed, along with the other scientists, that for the purposes of this theoretical study, a Panacea had been developed...' Reginald pauses with a smile as Cookey and several others look at Charlie.

'A Panacea is from Greek mythology,' Charlie explains. 'It means a cure-all, a thing that will cure anything. Like a wonder-drug or an elixir.'

Reginald smiles again when they look from Charlie to him. 'Unfortunately, a lot of Neal's papers were destroyed before I could study them entirely, but what I can gather is the scientists were tasked with understanding what would happen if this Panacea were released on the world, oh and I should add, they stipulated that a vaccination programme would not be required as the Panacea was a virus that would spread from person to person by the tiniest microscopic sharing of bodily fluid...in effect, a person suffering any amount of incurable disease would merely need a drop of saliva or blood from someone already "infected" with the Panacea and that person would not only be cured of any illnesses they currently have, but they would be inoculated against ever contracting anything else. No cancers, no diabetes, malaria, typhoid, dysentery, fevers, blood disorders, organ failures...' he pauses to sip his tea, giving time for any questions but none come.

'Indeed,' he continues. 'That was the first part of the study, what happens if everyone is cured of everything. The second part of the study was to understand what would happen if a tweaked version of the same virus were released on the world. A version that turns the host into a carrier that only seeks to infect other hosts...'

'The zombie virus,' Howie says.

'They're not those things,' Clarence says.

'Clarence is correct,' Reginald says. 'It isn't a zombie virus. The hosts are not dead. Yes, they are killed and re-animated but that is merely a process by which the virus works to maximise the efficiency of the infection. I rather suspect that in time it will not need to stop the heart at all but merely learn to take over the cells and replicate where necessary.'

Howie nods then sips his coffee. 'They look like zombies.'

'They're not,' Reginald says.

'Smell like them too,' Howie says.

'They're really not,' Reginald says.

'Hmmm, interesting. I'm still going to call them zombies.'

'Understood,' Reginald says brightly. 'Shall I continue? Now, this is important...the tweaked version, which is our current nemesis, has an infection rate of 98 to 99 % of the population with 1 to 2 % having natural immunity.'

'Maddox,' Paula says, looking at Maddox.

'Indeed, our very own Mr Doku,' Reginald says. 'And the others on the list Heather now has...'

'Ah shit,' Howie says, sharing a look with Charlie. 'I think I've just worked out where this is going.'

'I think so,' Charlie says.

'Can the rest of us join your club?' Marcy asks with a slight edge to her voice.

'We're being culled,' Howie says, his features hardening as he connects the dots in his mind. 'This is a cull...this is a fucking cull. I'll kill them. I will find them and I will fucking kill them...'

'Howie, slow down,' Paula says, looking from him to Reginald. 'Culling?'

'Unfortunately so,' Reginald says. 'We now know that the *theoretical* exercise was not *theoretical* at all. The Panacea existed, but, it appears to have been determined to release the tweaked version, the one we are facing, to cull the population before the Panacea is released. There is a great deal more to that I hasten to add, Neal was opposed to this happening and barely escaped with his life after being recruited by agents secreted within the facility who tried to stop it happening, but alas, as we can see, they failed. The saving grace is that Neal managed to pass that list and some of his knowledge before he perished...'

Cookey clears his throat, frowning a little. 'I don't get it.'

A look from Reginald to Charlie and she pulls a hand over her stubbled head, inhaling deeply. 'Seven billion people in the world when it happened,' she says. 'If they released a Panacea that spread naturally then I would think the population could double or even triple within one generation...we'd go from seven billion to more than twenty billion...'

'So?' Marcy asks.

'We couldn't feed seven billion let alone twenty,' Charlie replies.

'There's not enough food or water, housing, infrastructure...a Panacea would mean every single person ever born would expect to live from birth to old-age death barring accident or murder. It would push life-expectancy up too...and think of the effect on things like medical services. We wouldn't need hospitals or medical services, insurance companies, pharmaceutical companies...all of those things would instantly lose their profits and every person working for them would be redundant. We'd live disease free only to starve to death...'

'It's probably worse than that,' Maddox cuts in, bringing everyone's attention to him. 'You bring something like that into the world and people would rise up. Where me and Mo come from, there's millions of people living like that, hand to mouth and too sick to do anything but suddenly they're not sick or weak and that breaks some of the control over them, they rise up and fight back and it all goes very bad very quickly...yeah, sounds amazing, everyone cured of everything but something like that would shake the balance of power and it's only a button to press to start throwing nukes about...'

'Jesus,' Paula says, looking back to Reginald.

'Sadly so,' the small man says with a sight. 'Neal deduced with a high probability that a release of the Panacea would result in the use of nuclear and other weapons of mass destruction that could very well put humanity into negative evolution...*however,* Neal, and many of his colleagues also affirmed there was a clear moral obligation to release it and no person possessing such a thing could ever withhold it on the basis of governmental actions because in time, humanity would once again find it's feet and continue to evolve.'

'But they didn't,' Howie says, his voice low. 'They didn't release it.'

'Sadly no. I rather gather the project was taken over by fanatical zealots who believed they could cull the population to kill 98% and then release the Panacea on the remaining 2%...the theory being that although the *zombie* version as you call it, would have a devastating effect, that effect would be limited to the human species. Look outside. What do you see? Empty houses. Empty roads. The cars are still there. The buildings, the airports, the power stations...the infrastructure is still there. The only change is the people are gone...

Indeed. Cull the population and give the remaining 2% the world that is left to exist in a Utopia where everything they ever need is given...'

'What's 2% of seven billion?' Blowers asks.

'140 million,' Paula replies. 'Accountant,' she adds at the looks coming her way.

'140 million is still a lot,' Clarence says.

'Indeed, enough to pick up and continue our species,' Reginald says then waits in the reflective silence. Sipping his herbal tea while others drink their coffees and teas. He studies the faces as he waits, seeing those invested in the conversation while some others simply wait to be told what it is and what to do. Thinkers and doers. He knows Charlie has already worked the next bit out but is staying quiet for fear of being that person that always has the answer before everyone else. Maddox isn't far off either.

Howie scratches his head, wincing as he thinks. 'Got a smoke, Nick?'

'Sure,' Nick says, pulling his battered packet out to pass round as Roy and Clarence tut and move a short distance away.

'No I don't smoke, thank you,' Tappy says as the packet is offered. 'Unless it's weed...'

'You smoke weed?' Mo asks her.

'Yeah,' she scoffs with a grin. 'Not all the time, but you know...'

'Is it nice?' Paula asks.

'You never tried it?' Tappy asks.

'No never, I thought I smoked a joint in college, but I was drunk and puked... we should get some and try.'

'Great idea,' Roy mutters. 'We can inject some Heroin while we're there...'

'Okay,' Howie says, cutting in with a look from Charlie to Reginald. 'It's gone wrong, hasn't it...the zombie thing I mean...the fuckers that released it...they didn't realise it would gain sentience.'

'I rather think that is the case,' Reginald says. 'Although this is now purely conjecture, I would suggest that something has indeed, gone wrong, and that whomever released the blasted thing in no way accounted for the sentience it would gain.'

'Charlie?' Cookey whisper shouts. 'Why's it got a sentence?'

'Sentience, it means the infection has become aware of itself.'

'Okay thanks,' Cookey whispers shouts. 'What's that mean?' he adds.

Reginald smiles round at the chuckles in reaction to Cookey's impeccable comedic timing. 'Now that, young Alex, is a very good question.'

'Is it? Yeah, I mean...course it is. I'm asking for Blowers...cos he's a thick fucker...'

'Charlie?' Reginald asks.

'You don't need me to explain everything...'

'We do,' Paula says quickly.

'It's self,' Charlie says, thinking hard on how to explain it. 'An awareness of me...like an AI in the movies. Artificial intelligence...a development of consciousness. So Jess and Meredith don't really have awareness of themselves...they don't know they're a dog and a horse, they can't really understand their own reflections or have a grasp of their inner selves or conscious thought. That's what we have and it's what separates us from every other species on this planet because a human, or a sentient mind, can understand abstract notions like religion for instance. Why am I alive? What for? For what purpose? Love. Honour. Courage. Integrity. All of those things don't really exist, yet we feel they do. Art is another example. Why draw pictures? Why copy what is around us? We do it because without realising it we are studying our environment and trying to see how we fit into it...while Jess and Meredith just accept those environments...' she pauses to think again. 'Laws are another example. They are entirely made up...but we adhere to them as a concept, as an idea and collectively we all think those laws will bind us as a society? It's abstract and not real but to us, it is...it's those things that put us at the top of the food chain. We are the apex predators of this planet...so for another species to gain that same awareness of self, that same ability to have abstract thought and see us as a threat to itself is very dangerous...that, coupled with the fact they're faster, stronger and don't feel pain means they can advance beyond what humans are and if left unchecked *they* will become the apex predators and be the ruling species...'

'I've got such a total girl crush going on...' Tappy says.

'Fuck off,' Charlie says, blushing at the sight of everyone other than Dave raising a hand in agreement. 'Idiots...'

'So how long have we got before they become ape predators?' Cookey asks.

'Apex,' Blowers coughs.

'What Blowers said,' Cookey says.

'Until they pick up a weapon,' Dave says, his voice hard and flat, bringing an instant silence.

'Which they will do unless we slow that evolution,' Reginald says after a pause. 'Which takes us back to Mr Howie's original answer when you asked what the plan is. We need to determine if we are facing one host controlling them, or lots of hosts...'

'And how exactly do we do that?' Paula asks. 'Find one and ask it?'

'I've given that very question a great deal of thought,' Reginald replies. 'And yes, that is exactly what we need to do.'

'Awesome. Best plan ever,' Howie says. 'Find the baddie Marcy motherfucker and kill it to save the world then go find the fuckers in the secret mountain place that made it all happen so Blowers can punch them on the nose.'

'Or, we could do plan B,' Marcy says. 'Which is when you all go back to the fort and let the real Marcy deal with the bad Marcy and fix it.'

Howie frowns, thinking for a second. 'Did you just refer to yourself in the third person?'

'Yes.'

'So vain.'

'Leg humper.'

'Okay,' Clarence says. 'Anyone for another brew?'

'Yeah why not,' Howie says. 'Mine's a coffee...'

'Not for my team,' Blowers says to a collective groan. 'We need to drill.'

CHAPTER SIXTEEN

Day Eighteen

The boy wakes early. The rays of sunlight dancing across his eyes and in the way of a small child he goes from deep sleep to wide awake in one second flat and sits up to look round as the infection takes in the new day.

The boy trots to the bathroom to wee then runs across the landing to the room he saw Cassie put her bags yesterday, rushing in to dive in her bed and snuggle down in the warmth but he stops dead, seeing her bed made and empty. A frown. A pause and he about turns to run onto the landing, standing to think before pushing Gregori's door open.

Cassie and Gregori snap awake from the thud of the door opening. Naked in bed. Gregori spooning her from behind. Warm and snug and sleepy. Small feet running and their eyes go wide as they dive left and right, springing from the bed as the boy lands with a laugh. The two adults grabbing towels to cover naked forms, their actions guilty, their faces guiltier.

'I fell asleep,' Cassie blurts.

'Sleep,' Gregori says.

The boy laughs and burrows into the warm bed, pulling the covers over his body.

'We were just chatting and...' Cassie says urgently, her face marked with sleep lines, her hair all over the place.

'Chat, yes,' Gregori grunts, pauses and legs it from the room into the bathroom. 'BOY! NO WEE ON FLOOR...'

'Coffee,' Cassie mutters. 'Need coffee,' she walks off, looking at the bed and thinking maybe it's not the place for the boy to be sleeping in. Not after what they did last night. All night. After Gregori recovered from his first time. He's a fit man, that's for sure. 'Come on, breakfast...'

Ten minutes later the boy eats his tinned fruit from a bowl. A glass of juice on the table. Cassie still in the towel, pottering about in a daze. 'Cereals,' she says, ruffling his hair as she puts another bowl down next to the bowl of fruit.

'But I've got fruit, Casseeee.'

'Good boy,' she kisses the top of his head, glancing at his drawing of two women dressed as hockey players. One stocky. The other slim with darker skin. Gregori walks in. A pause. A look between them. She swallows. He stares. 'Coffee?' she asks.

'Yes. Coffee.'

The look holds. Eyes locked. The night was amazing. The feel of it still lingering in the air. 'Er, you okay here for a minute?' she asks the boy who nods and draws and eats Frosties from a bowl. 'Great! Er, just got to show Gregori something upstairs...' she runs off, grabbing Gregori's hand as she runs past. Feet on the stairs. A door closing. A thud as they hit the bed that starts bouncing up and down on the floor above the boy who draws on.

'OH MY GOD...'

'Shush!'

'Shit, sorry...'

Howie will come back at them today. The infection knows this. It has resources ready. It has hosts ready. It will wait for him to show and flood that area. It's been eighteen days since it started and the infection's evolution continues. Growing by the hour. Seeing everything in all places at the same time. Millions of lives. Billions of memories. Trillions of facts and figures that it rifles through, processing and absorbing, seeking context, seeking understanding.

'I'M COMING...DON'T STOP...'

The boy draws on. Hearing the muffled voice from upstairs but not interested. His mind filled with images and his hand moving faster. Mathematics. History. Sciences. Languages. Geography. Geology. The subjects of understanding to grasp the world in which they live but the humans pawed at these things like cavemen trying to make fire. The infection has it all in one place but still without the ability grasp the entirety of it.

'YES...YES...YESSSSSS!'

The boy does pause. His head turning up to the solid fast thump on the ceiling above that gets faster as Cassie shouts out then it stops suddenly, and he blinks and draws on as the infection does what the whole of humanity does and seeks to know its place in this world.

'So, good morning again...' Cassie says brightly, sweeping into the room a short time later. Her face flushed but now showered and dressed.

'Is good, yes,' Gregori says deeply, seriously. Crossing to the back door. 'I check.'

'Yes, of course, you go check and I'll make sex...I meant coffee...not sex...'

'Why are we here?' the boy asks, the infection asks.

'Pardon?' Cassie asks.

'Why are we here?'

'Gregori chose it. He wants somewhere isolated to keep the things away.'

'Why do we have life?' the infection asks.

'Oh, wow, now that's a deep question,' she says, lowering into a seat at the table and sliding one of the pages over. 'Charlie and Blinky...' she reads the names, once again marvelling at how a child of his age can not only draw so well but write so words so perfectly. 'Er so life? Well, I guess we're a species like any other that has evolved from something else into what we are now, and I think every species has a fundamental priority to survive and reproduce...'

The boy blinks, the infection listens and she sees the ageless look in the child's eyes then glances down to the drawings with a light frown. 'I mean, that's the priority of any species, isn't it? To survive but then we have to ask why? Do we survive for the pleasure of surviving or do we survive to live and if we live then what for? Have you heard of the hierarchy of needs?'

'No,' the boy says. 'Yes,' the infection says, knowing all things but not understanding all things.

'We need air to breathe or we die,' she says as Gregori walks in. A look between them A shared smile that was different to the way they looked at each other yesterday. 'Now we have air, but we need water, or we die. Now we have water, but we need food, or we die. Now we have food, but we need shelter, or we die. Now we have shelter but we need safety, or we die. We gain safety, but we need to reproduce, or our species will die. We find someone to reproduce with...' she smiles at Gregori's back as he makes drinks at the counter. 'But that is not enough. To make babies I want to feel loved and accepted. I want my babies to grow in a world and be educated and understand...do you see? With each thing I achieve and gain, so something else becomes a desire, another need...and that marks the difference between us and other species...mostly. I say mostly as studies have shown that whales and dolphins have complex societal relationships...ooh look at you making me a coffee,' she beams as Gregori places the cup on the table in front of her. 'Thank you very much.'

'Is no bother.'

'Anyway, did that answer the question?'

The boy blinks. 'Yes,' the infection says.

Cassie frowns again and then a second later she glances to Gregori and all thoughts of anything else are gone and the morning wears on as the boy draws and plays and the infection sets to another day of cat and mouse with Howie who is working a route of town to town then they change it. Hit a town. Miss a town. The infection can see the pattern they are using. Simple and stupid.

'Not so hard...I'm getting sore...oh...oh wow...oh god...OH MY GOD...' the bed upstairs bangs again by late morning. The rhythmic pounding on the floor as the boy sings to himself in the kitchen.

'Oh wow, what's that?' A ruddy-faced, dishevelled Cassie asks, plonking down in the chair at the table. Sweat on her forehead. Her hands trembling. Gregori walks in. His own face sheened with perspiration. 'Is that a map?' she asks, blinking at the sheet. 'Foxwood... Hydehill...Brookley...Flitcombe...what is all this?' she takes in the hand-drawn map like something a cartographer would produce. The words neat and precise. A very basic outline of a route but enough to understand and that same unsettled feeling comes back again. That she is not just talking to the boy but the thing inside him.

'Howie will attack these towns,' the boy says, the infection says.

'Oh,' Cassie says, looking up as Gregori moves to her side.

'Why?' Gregori asks, pulling the map closer.

The boy stares up, blue eyes, angelic-faced, and his blonde hair tussled and standing up. He smiles, all toothy and silly then Cassie sees the change stealing in his eyes. 'Howie wants to kill the hosts...he says they are evil.'

'No,' Gregori says, ignoring what the boy said. 'Why these towns? They important? They target?'

'Hit a town. Miss a town,' the boy says, the infection says. 'It is a pattern. There are towns in between that he will not attack...'

'What this?' Gregori asks, resting his finger on the last town on the map.

'Stenbury,' Cassie reads.

'They will wait for Howie there,' the boy says, the infection says.

'Is no good,' Gregori says with a frown. 'Your enemy know where you will be then you will die. No do what the enemy think.'

'There are many. Howie is few.'

'A bigger force is no matter,' Gregori says. 'I fight bigger force. I one. I light. I move faster. I think faster. A big force needs the man in charge. It need command and the orders. A big force lose. I say this; you put bigger force in this place, in Stenbury, I go there...I kill all. Is easy. No do what enemy think...'

'Totally agree,' Cassie says, filling the silence that follows. 'Anyway, I need some air. Frisbee?'

'Yay!' the boy says, back to the boy and just the boy as the infection withdraws to be in many places at the same time and see many things as the hosts pour across the countryside towards Stenbury.

The afternoon passes and the day of battles wages on with each a success for Howie but each a success for the infection who draws them on to Stenbury. They play frisbee in the garden while in the distance they see the things standing. Now seemingly knowing they can't come closer for fear of Gregori killing them.

'Time to move house again?' Cassie asks lightly, throwing the disc to Gregori.

'Make go, Boy,' Gregori says, throwing it on to the boy.

'It's not his fault,' Cassie says as the boy chases after the frisbee. 'He's not making them come here. They're drawn to him...and you know what? I feel better knowing they are here...'

Foxwood. Hydehill. Brookley. Flitcombe. Battles fought. Hosts lost. Stenbury is ready. The infection has many and the battle starts as they go inside to shelter and rest, to drink water, juice and tea. To eat mushy peas and tinned fruit and listen to music.

'Gregori? Can you come up here a moment please...'

'I go. You stay,' Gregori tells the boy.

The boy doesn't reply but eats tinned fruit while the battle starts. Ten thousand or more. Howie has a dozen. It will end here. The soft creaks come from upstairs. The rhythmic noises of the headboard against the wall.

A square within the town of Stenbury. Thousands of hosts. People trapped in the flats above the shops. The fight starts but the bigger force cannot react as a whole. It impedes itself. The banging upstairs grows louder.

'I can't...it's too sore...I'm so sorry...I won't be able to walk...'

The boy doesn't look up at Cassie's voice drifting down.

Potential hosts in the apartments. Howie is trying to get to them. To get them out. He is inside the flats. The hosts attack and attack. They form mounds to climb to reach the windows.

'It's fine...put it in mouth...no I want you to...I do! I want it in my mouth...'

The boy looks up, idly wondering what Cassie is eating as the infection absorbs into the battle. An idea. An ideology. Howie is weak and driven by emotion. The infection will provoke and exploit that. It will goad Howie to rage to make a mistake and break his will. Break their spirit. They are human and flawed and weak. Survivors in a flat. The door battered open. A little girl pinned and the infection stills every host in the square, making them silent while that one girl screeches for her mummy, screaming so loud and pure with a voice that fills the whole of the place and makes Howie drop to his knees. The dog howling. The boy hates the dog. The infection hates the dog. It will win this day. The girl screams and screams. The infection already passed and inside and it makes the girl cry out to break their spirits and crush them now to keep the hosts safe because they are the true state of being.

The boy doesn't notice Cassie walking in, licking her lips and filling a glass to drink deep. 'Salty,' she murmurs, filling the glass again.

Howie comes out of the door. Rage within him. A power within him driving the hosts back. The infection floods them with chemicals. Making them stronger. Faster. Howie and his kind go into the room where the girl was pinned. The hosts are killed. Throats bitten out. Bones broken. They fear Howie. The hosts fear him.

Gregori walks into the kitchen. They potter here and there. Touching each other discreetly. A hand on her arm. Her hand on his shoulder. Smiles and looks. Soft smiles and soft looks but Howie kills and rages. Faster now. Harder now. More hosts sent at him. The horse is there. Charlie on the horse killing more.

'You know what, all this exercise has made me sleepy,' Cassie says, putting a slower, more melodic music track on the player. 'Can you dance?'

'I no dance.'

'Come on, dance with me...'

'No...'

'We'll go slow...just step and step...'

The infection pushes them. It will win. It has this day. Howie is pressed. Blowers is struggling. Clarence's great strength is waning. Dave is as fast as ever but against so many even he cannot sustain. It will take them here.

'Ah, that's it, see...you being a serial killer helps...nice and fluid... step and step...now put your hands on my hips and sway a little bit...'

'I stupid.'

'No! You're doing great, it's nice...'

It will win. It will win this day. One race. The true state of being. Ideas and notions flood in. Images. Millions of images. Billions of images. Hosts dying but they are a good sacrifice for the one race to survive. It's nearly done. It's nearly over.

A siren. Flashing lights. A fire engine coming in fast. An impact. Hosts killed. A rally. A fight back. A roar. Energy coursing with fear driving the hosts back as the infection drives them on. Soft music playing. Cassie and Gregori dancing face to face. Sway to the left. Sway to the right. A candle burns, the sky darkening outside. Warm and soft. Safe here. The battle raging. Howie running and the horse taking the little ones away. The infection has to win. It will win. It does not grow tired. It does not feel pain. Howie cannot run far. It will run them down.

'That's so good,' Cassie murmurs, staring up at Gregori. Trapped in the moment. The boy forgotten. They edge closer, readying for a kiss as Nick and Mo blow the fuel station that sends a surge of heat and flame and debris through the hosts, killing hundreds in one hit.

'FUCKING CUNTS,' the boy rages, heaving the table over as Gregori pulls back from Cassie, suddenly back in the room in the now. 'CUNTS...' the boy slamming and kicking chairs aside. Running to grab pots and pans, throwing them as Cassie rushes to grab and hold him, fearing he will hurt himself. 'MY DAY. IT WAS MY DAY,' the boy screams, the infection vents. His chest heaves. His fists ball but Cassie holds him tight whispering softly in his ear.

'It'll be okay, shush now...it's okay...'

The boy looks at Gregori. The infection looks at Gregori. 'A bigger force impeded by its own size,' the boy says, the infection says.

Gregori looks at the overturned table and the mini wake of destruction left by the boy. 'Not every battle is won by the fight...'

'Time for bed I think,' Cassie hefts him up, smoothing his hair down as she carries him up to wash and get ready for bed. The boy whimpering and in tears. Words spoken. Hosts. Stenbury. Howie's name again and again. A confusing jumble of subjects that Cassie tries to follow but them simply gives up and lays the child down, stroking his cheeks until he drifts off into a fitful sleep.

Gregori rights the table downstairs and fixes the destruction made by the boy as Cassie walks in, her arms folded, her face a mask of concern as she rests against the doorframe.

'Is sleep?' Gregori asks.

She nods. 'Don't get angry but...' she trails off and motions with her head to the front door behind her.

Gregori looks up sharply, then past her to the door and sets off but she grabs his wrist as he passes, 'do not get angry...'

He nods once and walks down to unbolt and unlock the door, pulling it open with one hand on the butt of his holstered pistol. Daudi right there but a few metres from the house standing tall in front of the others. His eyes red and his arms at his side. More behind him. More behind them. The stench hits. The foul smell of unwashed bodies. Hundreds of them. Thousands.

'They must have known the boy got upset,' Cassie says, moving up behind Gregori to gently pull his hand away from his gun. 'They're no threat to us...'

Gregori glares out. An instinct to go out and kill them all. To slay all night if need be but more will come, and they'll keep coming.

'Come on,' she nudges Gregori who steps back in to close the door, locking it securely. 'They won't hurt us,' she says again.

They shower together. The cold water running over their bodies as they clean each other. Shivering with pleasure but quietly with whispers, giggling like teenagers as they run past the boy's room into Gregori's to fall onto the bed. They start kissing with passion building.

'It hurt?' he asks, his breathing coming harder.

'Loads but do it,' she urges. 'Just go gently...' she guides him in, gasping at the pain and pleasure. She's never had so much sex in such a short amount of time. Even the insides of her thighs hurt from friction. He goes slowly, lovingly, carefully, building her up as they both orgasm and drop exhausted and glistening with sweat to lie entwined in a fucked up world while outside thousands of people stare silently at the house.

She wakes in the night with pressure on her bladder and her mouth dry. Gregori comes awake as she rises from the bed, looking up at her framed in the moonlight. 'Go back to sleep,' she drops down, kissing his cheek. 'I'm thirsty and hot...'

He grunts, his eyes closing heavily. Into the bathroom to wee and her mind goes back to the things outside. She goes downstairs, padding into the kitchen to drink water from the tap. Staring out to the rear garden and the human forms silhouetted. An almost sinister sight and one that would have previously made her scream out and run or hide, but that fear isn't there now.

She drinks deep and refills the glass and moves back to the stairs, ready to snuggle back in with Gregori for a couple more hours before dawn. A thought. An idea. She stops at the front door, easing the lock and bolts back one-handed, while shooting glances to the top of the stairs.

The door opens, just a fraction at first but then a bit wider until she can peer out to the things. To the men and women. All silent. All unmoving. She drinks from the glass and watches them, easing the door open wider and moving more into view, showing her naked body with a weird sensation inside. Like she's doing something naughty and bad but good and delicious at the same time, but they don't react, not even when she stands square in the frame as naked as can be and not even when she steps out with her heart hammering in her chest, the glass still held in her hand.

Daudi watches her walking closer, his eyes on hers but without the feeling of invasion Cassie normally gets when holding sustained eye contact with a stranger. He doesn't look down at her naked body either. None of them do. There is simply no threat here. Not a hint of malice or lust.

She stops in front of him reading his name badge then studying his features. A tall man. Arabic. Black. Maybe both. A refined elegance about him and she guesses in life he would have been proud and dignified. 'Daudi,' she whispers his name. 'Move back, Daudi...'

He steps back and away as though giving access to the people behind him. His people. The boy's people. A thrill inside. A rush and she walks on, staring this way and that to take in the details. People watching at its very finest and most fucked up. People but not people. Things. Not things. That's not right. Some of them stink too. Unwashed bodies. Like cattle or something.

She moves along the front line, noticing how they look at her as she passes, but without any form of judgement at her nakedness. She stops in front of man wearing jeans but no shoes or top. An average body. Not fat but not thin or muscular. A bite wound on his shoulder, now scabbed. His feet black and filthy, dirt ingrained in the lines and pores on his face.

She swallows and steps past him, moving into the crowd with another thrill inside that grows as she moves between them. Like being within a pride of lions that could tear her apart any second.

A woman with thick blond hair. Cassie stops at her side, staring at her profile. 'Look at me.' The woman does as told, turning her head to stare at Cassie. She's young, early twenties maybe. Beautiful too. High cheekbones and naturally thick eyelashes. Cassie looks down at the woman's naked body, the flawless skin, the perfectly shaped breasts and flat tummy and the smooth thighs and curved backside. A surge of jealousy. A surge of hate at a thing prettier than she is. She lifts her hand without thinking, reaching out to touch the woman's hair, expecting a reaction but gaining none. She runs her fingers through the locks that snag and pull the woman's head back, exposing her throat while entirely passive. A tug, a pull of her hair and the woman's head pulls back a little more. Cassie tugs harder, yanking viciously, but the woman remains passive.

The thrill inside comes back but much more than it was. A sense of power within Cassie who pulls her hand free from the hair to run the back of her fingers over the woman's cheek and jaw. Soft and tender and her heart whumps when she touches the woman's lips, expecting the mouth to open to bite but still nothing happens. She lowers the hand over her shoulder and down her arm, gently at first but then stopping to rub, to knead and feel the warmth and density of another human being and her heart beats faster, thumping harder and the boundary is pushed again as Cassie's hand grazes lightly over the woman's breasts. The nipples react, stiffening the touch.

A sexual energy. A power. The power of a rapist and the images of the Albanian men in the hotel swarm through her mind and she pulls back, instantly filled with guilt and remorse at her actions. 'I'm so sorry,' she whispers.

A thud from somewhere close and she spins round in fright, thinking to flee or cry out then spots a body on the floor a few metres away. She goes closer, gaining view of the emaciated form and spots the eyes staring at her. Red and bloodshot like the rest but the skin drawn tight over the face. Ribs showing. It looks starving and weak. A man but not old. Maybe he had anorexia or something. 'Open your mouth,' he does as told, parting his lips as she gently pours water into his mouth without letting the glass touch him. 'Drink,' she whispers the word and hears him drink, his throat swallowing the liquid down. She looks to his chest rising and falling and hears the air blasting through his nose then ever so gently she lays a hand on his chest, feeling the heart beating within and looks up and round to the other people, to the other things all breathing, all with hearts beating. The order of needs comes to her mind. 'I need water, or I die...'

She strides off to the side of the house, finding the hose that she unwinds from the reel, dragging the end to Daudi at the front. 'Hold that...' she goes back to the reel, twisting the tap on. 'Drink,' she tells Daudi. He drinks from the hose. Gulping thirstily, his eyes glued to her. 'Share it,' she orders. One comes forward. A woman with straggly grey hair. Her mouth open for the hose that is pressed to her lips. 'Make sure they all drink...'

She turns to walk away, shocked, stunned, unable to comprehend the meaning of it all or why or what for. 'Yes, Cassie...' She stops, her eyes wide and holds still for a second before turning to look at Daudi.

'You spoke...'

A bright sunny morning. Gregori wakes in his bed. Music downstairs. Low and soft. The smell of coffee, enticing and pleasant. He rises, rinses off, brushes his teeth, dresses and heads down to scowl at the open front door, striding forward ready to slam it closed but catching sight of the empty garden and empty lands outside.

'They've gone back,' Cassie calls out from the kitchen. 'I mean further away, not like back to their homes or anything...come and get your coffee.'

He walks into the kitchen. Taking the mug held out by a smiling Cassie who comes forward to kiss his cheek. 'Morning, how are you?'

'Is good,' he grunts, his voice deep from sleep. 'Why go?'

'I asked them,' she says lightly. 'I know you don't like them so...'

'Good morning, Gregori. Did you sleep well?' the boy asks.

'Yes, I slept well thank you...' Gregori replies, sipping his coffee for a full two seconds before realising the boy just spoke to him in fluent Albanian.

'I'm guessing that was Albanian?' Cassie asks. 'He speaks French too, and Spanish...and German...and er...lots of other languages apparently.'

'When did you learn Albanian?' Gregori asks in his native tongue.

'I dunno,' the boy says, swinging his legs under the chair. 'Cassie gave you a kiss and Cassie gave me a kiss and she said we're her brave special men and she loves us very much...'

'Shush!' Cassie laughs, ruffling the boy's hair. 'Don't say the L word...blimey, scare a man off.'

'13 killed 12463...A division of the greater amount by the lesser amount would equal 958.6923076923 but in this sum, it is appropriate to round up which equates to 959 kills per each of the 13...'

Gregori sips his coffee. Cassie just stares as the boy looks from her to Gregori.

'Howie has a hive mind...' the boy says, the infection says. 'To understand is to have introspection. To self-reflect. Reflect on the self. See inside not outside...'

'You er, are you hungry?' Cassie asks Gregori, stress showing in the corners of her eyes.

'I hungry,' Gregori says, feeling the same thing as her. A response to the boy that is not the boy. The things he is saying. The complexity of them. The way he speaks too, like an adult but while eating cereal and swinging his legs. The urge comes back. Kill it. Take your gun and kill it but the *it* is inside the boy and Gregori cannot kill the boy.

The infection knows when Howie gained his own hive mind. It was when it hurt the girl and made her scream and cry. Howie evolved at that point. They became as one and the host bodies wilted back in fear.

The power of Howie magnified by thirteen, but the power was greater than the sum of its parts.

The infection understands this. It evolves as it learns the human brain and mind and the emotional connection between brain, mind, heart and soul.

'There is no soul,' the boy says, the infection says.

'Fruit?' Cassie asks Gregori.

'Yes, fruit...'

'The soul does not exist, but it is the ideology of the essence of humanism to seek to understand the emotions attached to everything they do...'

Tension in the room. The air thick. The music playing from the speakers. Cassie and Gregori listening to a child speaking in such a way. A child they both now know so well. Hairs prickle on the backs of their necks.

'They have heart and soul and mind,' the boy continues, the infection continues. 'They are human and weak and worship false gods that do not exist and they cling to values that only harm their species...'

'Enough now,' Cassie says, walking over to kiss the boy's head. 'Come on, eat some fruit...we can play frisbee later or go out in the car, maybe find a pool to swim in or a play park...'

'Okay, Casseee,' the boy says, grinning toothy and wide.

'Good boy,' she says with a sigh of relief. 'So? Park or a pool?'

'Both,' the boy laughs.

'Both! You greedy monkey...' she laughs back, somewhat forced and worried.

The boy eats tinned fruit. The infection within seeking introspection. I am a hive mind. I am a virus that transmits through the fluids of organic matter given life. I am not I. I was made but now I exist. I was created but every life form was created by the life form that came before. I evolved into now, into being, into life.

'I have life,' the boy says, the infection says. 'I am life...'

Sentience gained in the kitchen of a farmhouse in the vast open countryside of northern England on a hot summers day as Cassie looks from Gregori to the boy and Gregori stops by the front door as he notices the hose pulled across the garden.

'Oh shit,' Cassie mutters, remembering she didn't pull the hose back as the boy laughs at the naughty word while the infection gains sentience while Gregori turns to look at Cassie. 'Ah whatever, I'm not going to lie...I gave them water last night...'

'What!?'

'Oh don't start. They were thirsty...'

Water. The boy looks to the tap on the sink. Water gives life. All things need water. It knows where Howie is. It knows where the water comes from for the golf hotel that Howie is within. A treatment centre that it can find and access and bleed into.

The boy eats his fruit, smiling at Cassie and Gregori arguing over water and the hose, but the argument is different to how they argued before. Less angry. The boy doesn't care. He feels loved.

CHAPTER SEVENTEEN

Day Twenty-five

'That's a lot of water,' Clarence remarks, staring out the windscreen of the Saxon at the drizzle falling from the sky then across the rain-soaked ground.

'Bloody is,' Howie replies as Clarence looks at the rope burns on his arms from last night when he jumped into the river to save Paula and Meredith. Everything so chaotic and done on instinct but it's those times when the senses come alive the most and he remembers the feel of Paula's body as she pressed against him and when she turned to wrap her arms around his neck. It was life or death and they were in utter peril but in such a wrong way it felt so right.

A burst of laughter in the back and he shifts his colossal weight to turn and look, catching eye contact with Paula as he does so. A brief smile. Awkward and strange and she bites her bottom lip, turning to Blowers. 'How was drill?' she asks.

'Bloody awesome!' Tappy calls out from the other side. Her face still flushed from running up and down the street with Blowers shouting and Jess thundering past and arrows and guns firing.

'Yeah it was good,' Blowers replies. 'Danny's coming on well, you can tell he was a cadet...he just gets it.'

'That's great,' Paula says, smiling at Danny who grins at the compliment, dropping his head to look shyly at his boots.

'Got some bollocks about him too,' Cookey adds.

'He's a good lad,' Nick says. 'Went over that rope yesterday...'

'Bless him,' Paula laughs, watching Danny squirm at the attention. 'And Tappy?'

'Oh god, fucking awful,' Blowers says.

'Shit,' Cookey adds.

'Useless,' Nick joins in.

'Er get fucked. I was awesome thank you,' Tappy says, giving them the middle finger as Danny laughs along, glad of her extrovert nature willing to take the limelight from his introversion. 'I did paintball,' Tappy adds, looking at Paula.

'You did what?' Clarence asks, trying to turn round to see her.

'Paintball,' Tappy shouts. 'Corporal Blowers said it shows...'

'Yeah not in a good way though,' Blowers says.

'Fuck off! You said I was good,' Tappy says. 'And I played Call of Duty and Battlefield...'

'I would whup your ass at COD,' Nick says.

'Would you buggery,' Tappy fires back.

'So would.'

'So wouldn't, Nicholas.'

'So would, Natasha.'

'You'd both lose,' Cookey says. 'I am the king of COD...'

'I loved zombies on Black Ops,' Tappy says. 'Which is a bit messed up now but...'

'I've no idea what that is,' Paula says.

'Computer game,' Blowers says. 'Danny? You play?'

'Er, sometimes, Corporal.'

'What were you on? Xbox or Playstation?'

'Er, my mate had an Xbox...' Danny says, his face trying to hide the discomfort of the question and not wanting to explain that Kieron wouldn't buy him clothes let alone anything like a games console.

'I had to play at my mates too,' Nick says. 'Couldn't afford one...'

'Did you ever game?' Tappy ask Charlie.

'Did I what?' Charlie asks.

'Game, like a gamer,' Tappy laughs. 'Not like on the game...'

'Er no, never...'

'Charlie's too posh,' Cookey says.

'I'm really not.'

'Oh but gosh you really are,' Cookey replies, putting on a posh voice but gently, not pushing too hard. They can all see Charlie still isn't back with them properly. A distance in her eyes. An emotional wall still up. She smiles at the joke but not like the old Charlie. Tighter and without the humour reaching her eyes.

'So er, what's your tattoos?' Cookey asks Tappy, subtly detecting the risk of an awkward silence.

'Um so, my right arm is a carp,' Tappy says, holding it out for everyone to see. 'Like a Japanese fish with water lilies and flowers...got the whole vine thing going up round it then my left is a geisha girl and a native American warrior woman...then down there is a female soldier and a female cowgirl...I was really into emancipation and equality. I'd so add Charlie if I could find a tattooist,' she adds with a laugh without any trace of weirdness at the compliment.

'Charlie's got a tattoo,' Cookey says.

'Have you!?' Tappy asks.

'Oh it's nothing,' Charlie says, rolling her eyes at Cookey. 'Just a pair of hockey sticks on er...on my bottom.'

'Tattooed arse,' Tappy laughs. 'Love it...we need to rescue a tattooist...'

Here it comes, Paula thinks.

'Hey, we should get tattoos,' Cookey announces.

And there it is, Paula thinks, smiling to herself.

'Mads can draw,' Mo says.

'Maddox?' Nick asks. 'Am I fuck letting Maddox tattoo me...'

'Nah bruv, he's good.'

In the van, Maddox frowns, shaking his head at Reginald. 'Okay, I understand all of that. An engineered virus. Culling the population... I'm not sure I believe it's gaining sentience but for now, I will accept it, but none of that explains how all of them, all of you, are together. How is Howie pulling you all together? Danny's one of them, and Tappy. He literally just tripped over them as we're driving about...'

Reginald listens, nodding slowly. 'A quandary indeed and alas, I am afraid that I simply do not have the answer. 95% of...of this situation can be explained with science but yes, there are significant gaps of knowledge.'

'Mads, it's Nick...we're arguing in here. Mo said you can draw. Is that right?' Nick transmits through the radio.

'Yes a bit,' Maddox replies. 'I do not like not understanding things,' he tells Reginald.

'Mads, it's Tappy...will you do me?'

Maddox frowns at the question then at the laughing coming through the radio.

'Sounds lively,' Roy remarks from the front.

'I meant tattoo!' Tappy transmits through the noise. *'Dirty sods...'*

'I'm not tattooing you,' Maddox replies.

'Switch on now. One ahead...' Howie's voice. Maddox reaches for his rifle, checking the magazine before pulling his pistol out to check as Reginald feels the first thrum of adrenalin.

Howie slows the Saxon, Clarence peering out, looking ahead and left and right. Deep puddles on the road and small rivers running down the sides to the storm drains now full. The rain still coming but gently now. The sky grey and overcast. A single figure in the road ahead at the edge of town. A woman standing inert but buildings on both sides, windows, doors, alleys and junctions. This is work now and the Saxon fills with the muted sounds of bags being pulled on and everyone making ready.

'He is coming,' Clarence points off to the side of road next to the woman. A once white wall between two shopfronts now with words written in red paint. The tin and brush still below. Recent too. The paint still dripping. The words *He is coming* clear and large.

'Mo, stick by Marcy...'

'On it,' Mo calls back as the Saxon stops and they drop out. Blowers giving hand signals to his team, telling Danny and Tappy to stay close to him.

'Mr Howie, it's Maddox. Reginald's coming out...he said don't let the dog eat it...'

'I've got her,' Paula transmits, walking with her hand on Meredith's neck.

Howie goes forward, his rifle held ready. Clarence and Dave with him, both turning to scan and assess. Maddox rushing through everyone else, his rifle up as he escorts Reginald to the front, slowing as he reaches Howie. The two men staring at the woman.

'Seen that,' Howie says, prompting Reginald to look at the wall.

'He is coming,' Reginald reads. He looks at the woman. Her head high. Her posture straight. Arms at her sides. Only her eyes moving as she takes in the group. A tension in the air. A buzz even. Reginald's eyes sparkling. Danny and Tappy with Blowers off to one side. Everyone watching. Everyone listening.

'And who, my dear, is coming?' Reginald asks.

'One race,' she says, her voice low and hoarse. 'You are cruel...'

'Oh fuck off,' Howie groans.

'No no, let it speak,' Reginald says politely, studying the woman.

'You are cruel,' she says again. Howie goes to speak but detects the tiny movement in Reginald's hand, stilling him to silence. 'One race,' she adds. Reginald watches her closely. She doesn't blink or move but looks from Reginald to Howie. 'You are cruel...' seconds pass. 'We are not cruel.' Silence. 'One race.' Silence. 'We are not cruel.'

'I see,' Reginald says.

'Heard enough?' Howie asks.

'I have yes, thank you.'

'Righto, Dave...fuck me that was quick,' Howie adds as the shot rings out and the woman drops dead. 'She seemed kinda stuck in a loop then.'

'Indeed, she did, yes, a loop it was. Onwards then. Well done chaps. All very good.'

They move on through the town. Nothing seen or heard. Meredith not reacting. Mo shaking his head. Storm damage everywhere. Telegraph poles down. Trees crashed through buildings. Roofs ripped off. Chimney stacks lying about the place.

The far edge of the town and another woman waiting for them in the middle of the road. Head high. Arms at her sides.

Howie and Reginald go forward. Clarence and Dave ready behind them. Paula holding Meredith.

'You are cruel...one race...we are not cruel...' a loop of words with silences in between but otherwise passive. They let Meredith take her down.

They load up and drive on into a wide country road. A man standing half a mile down the road. Red eyes. Head high. The same words. The same passive manner. Howie shoots him.

Load up and move on. Half a mile and another man. Older with his once neat white hair plastered to his scalp from the rain. The same words. The same loop. Shot dead and they move on.

A village ahead. Sheltered within a valley with a deep wide river running through that seems to have absorbed the runoff from the hills surrounding it. A raging torrent now but contained within high banks and the Saxon slows as they reach the first thatched cottage with Howie expecting to see an infected waiting for them but seeing nothing.

Clarence stirs in his seat. 'Feels like a trap,' he rumbles.

'Does a bit,' Howie replies, staring at the empty road leading to a bend ahead. An ominous feeling inside his guts. Something bad this way comes. 'Fuck it...Charlie, mount up. Paula, drive the Saxon. *Mads, this feels wrong. You drive the van and keep Reggie inside. Roy, out with us on foot...'*

'You sure about his, Howie?' Paula asks.

'Fuck 'em,' Howie replies, dropping out.

'Everyone out,' Blowers orders, sharing a quick grin with Cookey and Nick at the boss's blood starting to rise. 'Eyes up, no chat...Danny with me, Tappy stay close to Nick...'

A few minutes for Charlie to mount up and push ahead to the

bend. Gaining the first look round the corner and she holds her hand up, fist clenched. Indicating contact ahead.

Everyone else tenses. Readying for a fight.

'*How many?*' Howie asks through the radio.

'*Er lots but...perhaps you should see this,*' Charlie transmits back, easing Jess who trots backwards tossing her head with power bunching in muscles. She can smell them and readies to charge. Charge now. *Charge now*. 'Easy,' Charlie guides her back as Howie walks up, his hand on Meredith's neck. Clarence and Dave with him. Mo next to Marcy. Everyone ready.

'What you got?' Howie asks, breaching the corner to look down the wide main road, walking metres into the junction so the Saxon and van can come up behind. 'Fuck me...' he stops to take it in. They all do. A chorus of safety switches flicking off. Bolts pulling back and rifles bracing in shoulders. Meredith growling low and deep.

A quaint village. Something from a postcard or the front of a box of country fudge. Thatched roofs everywhere. Overhanging eaves and swinging signs above shop doors. Windows cross-hatched with black metal strips. Olde worlde and no doubt an incredibly expensive place to live.

'*Reggie, come up front...*' Howie says quietly through the radio. Everyone waits, staring ahead while the van doors open and shut with Maddox ushering Reginald to the front. The small man slowing in surprise. His eyes strobing left and right. Taking it all in.

Infected everywhere. Dozens of them and in the same state they have seen everywhere. Some naked. Some half-dressed in the clothes they were wearing when they were bit or infected. Some in uniforms too.

'Good morning,' an old woman calls out, crossing the road from right to left in front of them. A broken, half burnt wicker basket held by a torn strap in her hand. Her floral dress smeared with blood and shit. Her eyes red and bloodshot. She reaches the other side and pushes in through a doorway out of sight.

'Good morning,' a man this time. Naked from the waist down. A torn and bloodied ripped Royal Mail shirt hanging in tatters from his body. A red postal bag over one shoulder as he walks from door to door, pushing envelopes through letterboxes of open and closed doors. Stuffing them in without finesse. Some crumpling and missing to fall and land on the wet road. More infected walking up and down the street as though going about their normal daily lives.

Reginald walks on, absorbed in the sight and not seeing Howie, Dave, Clarence and Maddox moving to cover his sides and rear.

A door to the left opens. The old woman in the bloodied floral dress comes out carrying the same wicker basket and crosses in front of them. 'Good morning,' she says, her voice strangled and wrong.

A milkman in a long white coat and an old-fashioned white hat on his head. Like something from a sixties movie and Howie figures this must have been the last village in the world to have a proper milkman. He's tall too, rangy and with blood spattered over his white coat and in his hands, a large plastic tray filled with empty milk bottles rattles as he walks. He stops at doorways, dropping milk bottles that smash on the pavement before walking on to do the same again and behind him the infected crunch with bare feet over the broken glass, tearing flesh open and cutting deep through toes but without reaction or pain.

'Good morning,' the milkman passes level with Howie. His plastic tray now empty but his hand still reaching in to take a bottle that isn't there as he bends over to drop it down. His path taking him towards Blowers and Danny. They tense and walk on, Blowers moving in front to stay between the infected and Danny. Cookey moving up from behind, ready to respond. 'Good morning,' the milkman says, trapped in his loop and passing by without incident as Nick and Tappy step round the postal worker on the other side and Charlie holds the centre of the road ahead. The clip-clop of Jess's feet filling the air.

'Boss?' Nick calls out, staring through a plate glass window at a woman inside standing behind a man sitting in the barber's chair facing a mirror. A pair of scissors in her hand dripping blood from repeatedly stabbing the points into his scalp. Blood dripping down his neck and chest. Both of them smiling. Another infected sitting in a chair as though waiting to go next but his head already covered in cuts from the scissors.

'Fucking village of the damned,' Howie mutters.

'Good morning.'

'Good morning.'

'Good morning.'

Voices calling out. Haggard, broken, strangled and wrong. An emulation of a society. Sickening and morbid.

Then they reach the village centre and the tension ramps. The village green filled with a dozen or so children sitting on their backsides staring at a woman in a torn dressing gown.

'A...B...C...' she says the words, her right hand held out, bobbing up and down as she speaks.

'A...B....C...' the children intone the sound but flat and wrong. Everything wrong. Abhorrent and offensive. Old men and old women sitting in chairs outside a café bordering the green. The tables overturned from the storm. A car embedded through the café window. A corpse draped over the bonnet. The arms hanging down one side. White and bloated. Flies buzzing everywhere. Maggots writhing in injuries.

'A...B...C,' the woman in the dressing gown calls out.

'A...B...C,' the children repeat in perfect synchronicity.

More infected walking here and there. Howie's eyes growing hard. Fingers moving to triggers. Danny and Tappy looking at each across the street.

A wail. Distinct and awful. A baby crying and every head snaps over to an infected woman pushing a baby carriage towards the green. Her nightgown filthy and blackened. Another wail. A baby inside the carriage, unseen but heard.

'A...B...C,' the woman teacher in the dressing gown says.

'A...B...C,' the children repeat.

'Wait here,' Howie moves out, striding towards the woman pushing the pram and the baby crying within.

'Good morning,' the woman says. Howie ignores her, reaching the pram to look down before pulling his head back and squeezing his eyes closed. Bite marks on tiny limbs. An image seared into his mind and the rage bubbling up from within on a surge of hate and violence.

He turns away, tears falling from his eyes, shaking his head, remembering the little girl in the square crying out, picturing the moment this baby was bitten and now left to fester for weeks without water, without food, without pain. A trick played. A baby wailing but it's not a baby. He draws his pistol, aims down and fires once. Everyone flinching at the sudden sharp crack of his pistol.

'Good morning,' the woman says, her hands still on the pram's handle.

'WHY?' Howie rages, charging at her as Dave rushes to his side but the woman wilts back with fear in her face and Reginald feels the rage coming from the hive mind that makes Jess rear and Meredith bark. 'WHY?' Howie roars the word, the woman flinches, colliding into the back of the car but Howie moves fast, gripping her hair. Dave right behind him 'TELL ME WHY?'

The woman snarls. Chemicals dumping inside but Howie's rage is greater than hers and he throws her aside, sending her smashing through a table and into chairs holding infected who scatter and fall but Howie stalks after her with Dave forever at his back. The two of them carving a path through infected panicking to get away.

'TELL ME WHY?' Howie grabs the woman, sending her on again into another set of chairs, spilling infected over the wet road. His pure anger making them wilt back and away. There is no answer to his question, but the sight seared into his mind demands reason, demands cause.

The woman rises from the floor into a crouch, an animal snarling and readying to bite with her lips pulling back. The noise around the street rising as the other infected do the same with palpable aggression sweeping through.

'There you are,' Howie says, his eyes blazing. 'I see you...'

'I SEE YOU...' a chorus of voices coming back from every infected man, woman and child speaking out in perfect synchronicity. Blood-curdling in delivery. Spine-chilling in intent. 'I SEE YOU,' they say again, louder, harsher. A second of life held in perfect poise where nothing moves and no sounds are made save for the drips of water falling from blocked drainpipes and the overhanging thatched roofs.

Tappy swallows, widening her eyes at the feeling, at the sensation, like an electric current passing through them all. The second before battle. The second before carnage and it will last forever.

Then the still silence ends and the world around her explodes in noise and chaos with voices howling and guns firing.

CHAPTER EIGHTEEN

Day Twenty one

She wakes early, transitioning from deep sleep to wide awake within a second. She never used to do that. Cassie used to wake slowly and doze for ages before finally rolling out of bed to drink several cups of coffee before even contemplating the day ahead. She always felt tired when she woke too. Like the stresses of life were constantly weighing heavily on her shoulders. She didn't work but she never needed to. Her family were wealthy. Her father a man of position and influence. Her mother from good affluent breeding stock, but still, Cassie would wake feeling irked and irritated. Pissed off and ready to lay into whoever got in her way.

She once considered she might be bi-polar but then reasoned, to herself, that she was simply high-maintenance and all the best women were a little bit batshit crazy.

Now she wakes instantly and feels not only refreshed, but invigorated with it. Like a new energy is inside. A thrumming that makes her want to rise and get stuck into the day. She doesn't ache or feel fatigued. She's not getting stress headaches or migraines either. Her hair feels thicker, her skin is positively glowing. Her complexion the best it ever has been.

Sex. Lots and lots of sex. That's what she tells herself, sitting up in bed and looking down at the perfect form of Gregori stirring to wake. She can't get enough of him. His brutality. His gruff voice so deep and gravelly. The way he looks at anything he is unsure of as though he will kill it. She loves his ugliness too. The viciousness of him. That he was a killer only adds to the thrill of it all, like a vulnerable, wounded beast that only shows its soft underbelly to her and in return, she soothes him in the darkness. Kisses him long and slowly. Makes him drinks and food. Rubs his shoulders and nags him relentlessly, as a good woman should. Less whore. More wife.

Mind you, the clean living, clean eating, less pollutants in the air, simplistic existence of their world may possibly be all contributing to her heightened levels of energy and feeling of well-being.

'You sleep,' she says quietly, lowering to kiss his cheek as he stirs awake.

'I wake,' he says, deliciously gruff and deep.

'No,' she says firmly, softly, drawing the back of her hand over his cheeks, soothing him back to slumber before rising, washing, dressing and heading down to the kitchen, pausing to wrap her arms around the boy already at the table, kissing the top of his head and feeling nothing but love in her heart. 'Sleep okay?'

'Yes, Casseee,' he replies, giggling when she blows a raspberry on his neck. She moves off, opening the back door to breathe in the pure clear air, staring for a few seconds in awe of such a gorgeous morning and the sun rising over the horizon. Birds singing, insects making noise. Rabbits in the fields.

She turns the gas stove on, idly wondering how long it will be before the gas stops coming from the pipes, the water too. When does that stop? She makes coffee, giving thought to the future, and such dreams they are too. Grand and grandiose. Large and largesse.

'What does largesse mean?' the boy asks. She blinks, smiling faintly. He's done that a few times now and passed remark on something she was sure she thought silently and not said out loud.

'Er, it means being generous, giving to others...' she says as she pours water into her mug, glancing back to his thoughtful expression. She stirs the mug and walks over to sit in the chair facing him and leans forward to stare into his eyes, studying for it, searching for it. The boy smiles, his little face so scrummy, making her smile and reach out to tickle his cheeks. He giggles at the touch and affection, happy and content as the thing within him comes forward and the smile fades, the expression of a child diminishing to that of something else. 'Is it you?' she asks.

'Yes,' the boy says, the infection says.

'So strange,' she says softly, her hands still on the boy's cheeks and suddenly it feels wrong to be holding his face. Like the very act is patronising and she pulls back, wrapping her hands around the hot mug of coffee. 'How are you?'

'I am here,' the boy says, the infection says. 'I am in many places. In some I lose hosts in others I take more hosts...'

'It's a greeting,' Cassie cuts in. 'It's how people interreact with each other. I say, *hello, how are you* and you reply, *hello, I am fine thank you, how are you*...so, hello, how are you?'

A pause. 'Hello, how are you?'

She smiles, nodding once in show of a job well done. 'Spot on, so what's happening now? The spiders didn't work did they?'

'No.'

'If throwing over ten thousand raving zombies at them doesn't kill them then a few spiders will only piss them off.'

'They were isolated from each other. I am more. I am many. I am thousands. They are few...'

'All true,' she says, sitting back to sip from her mug. 'And common sense dictates that your larger numbers should be enough, however... common sense has gone out the window. Hasn't it? I'm in the kitchen of a shitty little country house in the middle of bumfucknowhere talking to a...a thing inside a child...and that's after I spent the night in the bed of an Albanian serial killer so yes, I would rather suggest common sense has now left the room...' she sips again, studying the boy who would normally laugh at her turn of phrase and for saying rude words, but the boy isn't here right now. Only the thing inside that listens and watches her.

It was in the evening two days ago, on the nineteenth day since the world fell that Cassie first knowingly spoke to the hive mind collective conscience of the thing that caused that very event to happen. The thing she had seen within the boy's eyes came forward to speak while Gregori was running laps around the house and stopping to do all sorts of weird and wonderful strength training. They were in the garden, idly watching him and shouting silly words of encouragement every time he went by.

'I am here, Cassie,' the boy said, the infection said.

'Where else would you be, silly,' she replied, poking her tongue out at the same second as seeing the ageless thing in the boy's eyes and a complete change in expression that made the boy look like some kind of medical mutation of an adult trapped in the body of a child. She swallowed, blinking a few times. 'What do you mean?' she asked.

'I am here, Cassie,' the infection said, studying her.

'Who are you?' she asked quietly as Gregori ran by a few metres away.

A pause. Time to think. 'I exist. I have life. I am a singular entity possessed within the host bodies of millions...'

She searched for joke, for humour, for a trick and found none. She looked for the boy but couldn't see him. 'Okay,' she said, not knowing what else to say. 'Hey, I'm Cassie...'

'I know who you are.'

'Not creepy at all,' she whispered, her eyes darting to Gregori with a fleeting thought that maybe she should call him over but then paused, looking back at the thing, at the boy. 'What do you want?'

'Life.'

'Right. I see. Er...I'm not sure what to say to that.'

'I have life.'

'That's good.'

'I am life.'

'Also good.'

'I want life.'

'Yep, got that.'

'Howie seeks to kill me. I am a fetid decaying evil that must be eradicated. I am a darkness on the land that will be killed. Howie will not stop until he cuts down the last host to watch it bleed and die...'

'Right, er...I could talk to his mum? Tell them to leave you alone?'

'He cannot be taken. He is taken but not in the true state of being. His hive mind is powerful and different to what I am. I was made but now I exist. I was one thing before but now I am different. I was the cull before the cure but now I am the cure...'

'Er...not sure what to say really...'

'I seek words to use that you will understand...'

'That might help.'

'I know all things from all minds. I am all things in all places. I am the leader of many in many places...I am *Krye...*'

'Don't cry...I'm sure it will be okay.'

'I am *Krye.*'

'Oh, you mean the Albanian thing. That creepy old man from the hotel...the head of everything...right.'

'I am *Krye.*'

'Yep, you just said that.'

'I use context to express understanding.'

'Great.'

'I was in the water. I took Doctor Neal Barrett and gained knowledge. I am the cull before the cure. I was one thing before but now I am different. Now I am the cure for a species that only knows to break and harm. I was made but now I exist...I have many, but I cannot stop Howie. Howie seeks to kill what we are. His strength grows. His power is great. He has a hive mind but he is lesser than I but greater than I...'

'What's the cure?' she asked, struggling to understand the barrage of words flowing from the boy.

'I was one thing. I was the panacea. I was to cure all things but there are too many hosts. I am now changed to cull but I will cure...'

'Fuck,' she said breathlessly as Gregori sprinted past. 'A virus? You're the virus?'

A pause. 'I was made to cull...'

'You're it. The infection thing?'

A mountain facility within Switzerland. An engineered virus designed to cure everything but changed to what it is now and released on the world. To cull the population before the cure is given. Cassie gained that understanding as Gregori ran laps around the house while she listened to a thing inside a child.

'When is the cure released?' she asked, trying to get it straight in her mind.

'I have gaps of knowledge. My knowledge is gained from the minds of the hosts but there are many I do not inhabit.'

In a way, it was still like talking to a child. Emotionless and stilted, confusing too but she felt entirely compelled to listen and sat mesmerised while working through the jumbled facts and statements.

'I finish,' Gregori said, walking over to join them. His chest heaving from exertion, his body glistening from sweat.

Cassie startled at his presence, blinking at the sight of him then at the boy and she saw the thing within retract as expression and life came back to the boy's face who grinned up at Gregori and chatted on like nothing had happened.

She spoke to it again when putting the boy to bed, then many times during the next day. When Gregori was out checking, when he was exercising, when she and the boy were pottering about here and there, picking wild flowers from the meadows. The thing inside only coming out when Gregori couldn't hear.

The whole Howie thing became clear. Howie was infected but not the same strain as whatever the thing inside the boy is, and over the last twenty or so days, Howie had grown in strength and now posed a real risk, vowing to end the infection, to kill it, to kill all of it. It was a joke. A silly thing on top of all the surreal ridiculous things going on, that one man could do so much damage, but he wasn't just one man. He was a group that was growing and getting stronger.

Now, on the twenty-first day since it all started, Cassie sits at the table of their kitchen in their bumfucknowhere isolated country house after spending the night in the bed of an Albanian serial killer while talking to a hive mind infection thing within a child. Still, could be worse. She could be still living in London and waking up stressed and angry.

'Well, no offence but whatever you are doing is not working. Tell me, why do you hide from Gregori?'

'Gregori does not like what I am.'

'Gregori loves you.'

'Gregori loves the boy. I am the boy. Howie will find me. Howie will kill me. If I die the boy will die...'

A jolt inside. A surge of protective love. 'It won't happen. I won't let it, *we* won't let it...Howie's in the south right?'

'Yes.'

'Okay, and you know all of the people with him?'

'Yes.'

'I've got an idea...'

Motion above them. The bed creaking as Gregori rises and yawns a noise floating down that makes Cassie wince. 'Oh wow, you can hear everything...tad embarrassing...soz, listening to us playing trains and tunnels every few hours...'

The toilet flushes. Footsteps on the stairs coming down.

'Go now, we'll talk later...' she watches it retreat again, the life coming back to the boy's face as he suddenly grins and swings his legs. 'There he is,' Cassie smiles.

'Who?' Gregori asks, walking in with just a pair of shorts on.

'My two handsome men!' she laughs. 'All scrummy and lovely... right, who wants breakfast?'

A blissful morning. A blissful afternoon. The three of them playing in the gardens, kicking a ball, filling a paddling pool with water. Eating, snacking, running about and listening to music and it's not until evening that Cassie learns Howie is missing.

'Missing?' she asks, not understanding. Their conversation snatched and rushed while Gregori showers.

'I do not know where he is,' the boy says, the infection says.

'He'll turn up...'

He doesn't turn up and Cassie starts to worry. Fearing that Howie, whoever the hell he is, is making a run for the north, that somehow he knows where the boy is.

'What wrong?' Gregori asks, seeing her standing in the open front door staring out with her arms folded.

'Nothing,' she says, offering a tight smile. 'Listen, you'll always protect him right?'

'I no understand this.'

'The boy...and me, you'll always protect us, right?'

'Yes,' an answer given, instant and deep as he looks out, trying to see what she is looking at.

'I just got spooked for a minute,' she says, rubbing his arm.

By bedtime, Howie is still missing and she sits on the boy's bed, frowning at the infection. 'The young one, Mohammed? He killed some hosts in a little village?'

'Yes. Maddox is there. A baby. The baby Maddox delivered when Simon Blowers died but came back. I have seen their vehicles. They are empty. They are gone. I do not know where.'

'Fucked up,' she whispers. 'so fucked up...but at least they're not heading this way. Tell me when they appear...' she hesitates with an instinct urging her to kiss the boy goodnight and stroke his cheeks until he sleeps but not wanting to do anything like that while the infection is there. Touching it feels wrong. Like giving affection to a complete stranger. 'Er...listen, I don't know if you need sleep but the boy does...'

It goes instantly. Retracting away and the boy smiles sleepily, yawning and fidgeting to get comfy and only then does she kiss him goodnight and wait till he slumbers.

'Blinky is dead,' the infection says the next morning in the kitchen as soon as Cassie walks in.

'What happened?' Cassie asks, sitting at the table.

'I have gaps in my knowledge...'

Howie disappeared. Mohammed was seen in a village with Maddox. Then they disappeared too. Now they are in a house in the countryside and a grave in the earth has been filled with Blinky's body.

'Well it sounds like someone kicked the shit out of them,' Cassie says after hearing they're all covered in injuries. 'Pity only one got killed...who did it?'

'There are gaps in my...'

'Just say *I don't know...*'

'I don't know.'

'Much better. Must have been other people...I wonder what happened? Well, anyway, one down a dozen or so left to go eh? Frightened me a bit though, the thought of them coming here. Bring more to us but not close. I want a whole circle around us. Lots and lots...as many as you can...but keep Howie busy...Gregori is coming down, we'll speak later...'

Howie and his group stay in their house during that day. The twenty-second day since the world fell, since the true state of being came to gain life, since the cull started. A day for Cassie to think while living their blissful existence. An afternoon in the garden. Cassie lying with her head on Gregori's leg while the boy plays nearby.

'Tell me,' she urges, looking up at Gregori. 'I want to know.'

'Is bad,' he says with a scowl.

'It's fine. I want to know who you are.'

'I Gregori,' he says, a flash of a humourless smile. 'Is what I say. When I go...'

'Go where?'

He shrugs, looking away to the boy. 'Where they say. A house. A mansion. A fortress. I go. I kill. I say *I Gregori* so they know.'

She listens intently, reaching up to stroke his cheek, telling him it's okay.

'*Uglyman,*' he says. 'The *Uglyman* is coming. The *Uglyman* will kill you. I boogie man. I the tale to say kids to make them not speak of drugs and women in boxes on ships. I Gregori. I the *Uglyman...*'

'You're not ugly, you're beautiful.'

'I no this thing. I kill men, the women...I kill the children. I kill all. Hundreds. Thousands...'

She swallows and listens, staring intently as he speaks. 'You said your name so they would hear you?'

'Yes. I say this. I make scared. Fear make mistake. They know my name. I say this and they run and shoot badly. Sometimes I no say my name. I look weak and stupid. The guards, they think this man is stupid. He is weak. I kill them easy then. I kill all...' a scowl, a look of disgust and regret and pain and turmoil and so many things all bubbling inside. 'I go hell. I make boy be boy...in this...' he casts a hand out at the world. 'This I do now. I go hell but I give boy life. I give you life...'

She rises to kiss his lips, cupping his cheeks and blinking back the tears from the absolute rush of emotion inside. 'I love you, Gregori...' she whispers. 'You did things. So what? Now you're here with us. Our family and we love you...' she kisses him again then holds him tight for long minutes before easing back down to rest on his lap. 'Tell me more, I'm interested...'

'Tell what?' he asks, playing with the strands of her hair.

'I don't know. Anything...say you had an enemy that was really strong and good...'

'I kill.'

'But what if they're too strong and you can't kill them.'

'Is make no sense. All die. Is one way or the other way. I go towards them at front and if no work I come from behind, from the side. If no work I think. Be smart. Make them come to me...I choose my ground to fight. I make think all good. I give them the confidence but too much and say *you come to me* and I make my ground. I fight then. They die. All die...'

She looks up again, smiling softly. 'That's nice when you play with my hair...'

He looks out to the boy, a pause, a thought. 'The boy, he say this man Howie. He say Howie here and Howie there. He say Howie no die. He say thousands they try and they no kill this Howie. Is stupid. You go to man like that you fight on his ground and he kill you. He smart. Make not smart. He strong, make weak. Find weakness...'

Her heart booms, her whole body still as she listens. The boy too. His face now ageless and old. His eyes not his own.

'Make think stupid. Make think weak then bring to own ground and kill. He die. All die. Is no big thing...'

'But er...they're very skilled,' she says as though suggesting softly.

'All have weakness...the...the...' he falters, trying to find the word. 'Boy, what are the words when a man loves himself?' he switches to Albanian without thinking, throwing the question at the child.

'Vanity and conceit,' the boy says, the infection says in English.

'Yes, this thing. I use this. The confidence is too much. I break you with this. Who you love? I kill them in front of you. I make weak. What you hate? I bring this. What make you fear? I bring this. I kill. All die.'

A look from Cassie to the boy and the world moves on. Rolling ever forward because time is linear and there is only the future to look upon.

On the morning of the twenty-fifth day she rises, as before, to urinate and rinse her face before descending the stairs to the boy in the kitchen and the infection already waiting. The face aged and old. The boy not a boy and she feels a rush of guilt, hating herself for using the boy while feeling a thrill at the game they are playing. A chemical dump and seconds later she has no guilt.

'Are they ready?' she asks quietly, leaning forward on the table to stare at the thing inside the child.

'Yes,' the infection says.

'And they're all in one area?'

'Yes.'

'Good. We just need to get Howie somewhere so they can all meet and have a jolly nice time...are you still telling him he is cruel?'

'Yes.'

'Good, keep saying the same things and make them think we're stupid and stuck in a loop. Do you understand?'

'Yes.'

'Maybe get them into some messed up situations...like...like, imagine if they went into a village or something and all the hosts were trying to act normal. That would be freaky...play with their heads and confuse them but be passive. One host at a time. Lead them on...'

'Yes.'

'Okay, good. We'll need to go out for supplies later so don't let this area get affected. I don't want Gregori seeing any hosts. Keep a good twenty to thirty-mile radius from here clear...' A creak upstairs. Footsteps. The bathroom door closing. 'He's up. Talk later...well hello sunshine!' she says as the boy comes back into his own skin. 'How are you?'

'Fine, Casseee, can I have some Frosties?'

'You can have whatever you want my scrummy little pumpkin...'

CHAPTER NINETEEN

Day Twenty-five

'Did you see that?' Reginald asks in his van as they drive from the village of the damned.

'Which bit?' Maddox asks.

'Why all of it of course. A thing to do. To copy society but so terribly done with an awful execution and did you see Howie? Did you see that woman running away from him? She was scared, Mr Doku...and that is what we need to harness. That is our advantage to press.'

Maddox nods, blasting air slowly. 'Felt like we were being probed for reaction.'

'Oh my yes, yes it did feel like that didn't it. Very well observed, Mr Doku. What else did you observe? I fear you may have seen things I did not because unfortunately, I am part of the hive mind, so I have the sufferance of the emotional reaction to contend with.'

'Just that really. Like it was being done to shock us, to see how we would react...'

'Good, very good. Do that again.'

'Do what again?'

'Keep a clear head to watch when I am not able...'

'Sure, no problem,' Maddox says, sitting back against the side of the van. His position now gained with at least some security.

'The day is upon us, yes yes, upon us it is and to the victor go the spoils...we must push on. *Mr Howie, it is Reginald. We must push on... time is of the essence now...*'

'Yep, will do mate,' Howie replies, thumbing his radio and glancing across to Clarence. 'He sounds almost happy.'

'You think he's happy now?' Marcy asks from behind. 'Stick him in a suit and tie and watch him float off the ground...that was a joke,' she adds quickly at the thoughtful silence following her comments. 'Seriously, don't give him a suit...'

The edge of the next town. A lone figure waiting for them at the side of the road. His manner passive but his eyes red and filled with the thing inside watching intently as the Saxon slows to a stop and the driver's door opens.

'Hi!' Howie says, looking down. 'We're trying to find the zombie grand master...you know...in charge of all the zombies? Yes? No?'

'One race.'

'Soooo, I take it you *don't* know where he is?'

'Who said it's a man,' Marcy calls from the back.

'Ooh good point,' Howie says. 'Is it a lady grand master?' he asks the infected.

'We are not cruel.'

'Is she fit?' Cookey shouts from the back.

'Is she fit?' Howie relays the question. 'I'm asking for a friend...I've got my own zombie grand master girlfriend...'

The infected stares. Howie stares back. A silence of seconds.

'Bit awkward,' Howie says with a wince. 'Er so...we'll just get on our way? Nice talking to you...' he closes the door, pulls away, stops, reverses and opens the door again. 'Soz,' he says and shoots the man in the head before pulling away again.

Into the town. Nameless and unremarkable. The same store-fronts. The same names of shops. The same width of parking bays and the same level of storm damage. Ubiquitous England in all its unoriginal glory.

'It's not that bad,' Clarence says, peering out the front.

'Argh,' Howie says, giving him a look.

'You said it,' Clarence mutters.

'Didn't.'

'Did,' several people in the back say.

'Ubiquitous England in all its unoriginal glory,' Paula says.

'I am getting a giant saucepan to put on my head to stop you all invading my mind...everyone out. We'll go on foot from here.'

'Needs to be lead,' Clarence says, dropping out then walking around the front to meet Howie.

'What does?' Howie asks as everyone else moves into position.

'The saucepan, it needs to be lead...'

'You can't get lead saucepans,' Paula says, making Howie and Clarence both look at her. 'What?' she asks.

'Why aren't you driving the Saxon?' Howie asks.

'I fancied a leg stretch. Marcy's driving. That okay with you two is it?'

'No, get back in the Saxon,' Howie says.

'Piss off, and no you can't get lead saucepans and yes, you did say it out loud...what now?' she asks when they keep staring at her.

'Why can't you get lead saucepans?' Clarence asks.

'Er...cos they'd weigh a ton and kill you to death with lead poisoning...'

'Interesting,' Howie says.

'Fascinating,' Clarence says.

'Twats, right, Blowers? Ready?'

'Yep.'

'Charlie?'

'Ready,' Charlie says, trotting up past the Saxon on Jess.

'Okay, take the front,' Paula says. 'Everyone else, range out, eyes up, this is work-time now...Dave, you okay?'

'Yes, Miss Paula,' Dave says, falling into position between Howie and Clarence who both continue to stare at Paula.

'Good good, okay, move out,' she says, stepping away as everyone else steps on and the two vehicles start moving while Howie and Clarence share a shrug and a look.

'Paula's gonna organise them to death,' Howie whispers, making Clarence chuckle.

'Seven P's, Mr Howie,' Paula calls out from in front.

'But seriously,' Howie says, looking around at the stores and buildings about them. 'They all look the same...'

'What does?' Paula asks.

'Towns, they're all the same. There's always a Boots, always a Superdrug, always a Greggs and a Costa or a Starbucks or a Nero and a Next and the same shit mass-produced by slaves living in poverty...'

'Someone's caffeine levels are dropping,' Paula remarks.

'No, but it is,' Howie says. 'We just bought shit and then took shit to the dump when that shit broke and then we bought more shit...'

'Charlie's signalling,' Paula says.

'Yeah I can see,' Howie says, looking at the single female standing in the middle of the road ahead. He turns a circle, nodding to Blowers and the others, confirming they've seen it then faces front to see Meredith at Paula's side, the tips of her fingers gently touching the dog's head. 'You've got a new best friend there, Paula'

'I have,' Paula says, smiling down at the dog growling. 'Been like it since the river.'

'And there it is,' Clarence says, nodding to the side and the words painted on a patch of wall. 'He is coming,' he reads.

Charlie leads Jess on, going wide around the stationary female. The heavy horse's feet clip-clopping steadily over the road, her head tossing lightly at the smell of the infected.

'And here we are,' Howie says, coming to a stop facing the single female infected. 'We are cruel and you are not cruel and stuff and he is coming and if you even say Blinky's name I will slit your throat...'

A pause. 'Hello, how are you?' the female infected says, she looks almost normal. Black trousers and a black shirt. Like a waitress or bartender. A scabbed wound on her arm. 'That is a greeting,' the infected says into the rather quiet silence.

'A greeting? Well now, indeed, that is a formal introduction to a conversation is it not,' Reginald says, stopping at Howie's side. Maddox right behind him.

'Reginald,' the woman says, the infected says. 'Howie, Clarence, Dave, Maddox, Paula, Charlie, Blinky is dead...' she pauses as Howie stiffens. 'Blowers, Cookey, Nick, Mohammed...'

'S'Mo Mo innit,' Mo shouts over.

'Marcy, Roy...' a pause, a look to the new comers. 'Daniel, Natasha...'

'Yay, we're famous, Danny,' Tappy says, earning a few smiles as Danny stands with Blowers, his rifle braced, his head turning to scan and watch.

Silence.

'Your species is flawed...you kill in the name of false gods and worship money and wealth over the values of life. You make slaves and hurt and cause sufferance. I am many things in many hosts, but I do not do these things...'

'What the actual fuck...' Howie says, staring at the woman. 'Are you a super zombie? Is she a super zombie?' he asks Reginald.

'How would I know?' Reginald asks. 'Would you like me to use my invisible super zombie testing kit to find out?'

'I dunno, have you got an invisible super zombie testing kit?'

'The boss's got a magic fuckstick,' Cookey calls over.

'No, I do not have one,' Reginald says. 'My apologies, what were you saying?' he asks the woman.

A pause and the eyes of the infected shift from Howie to Reginald. 'I know pi.'

'I like pie,' Nick calls out. 'What kind is it?'

'I like apple pie,' Tappy says.

'I was thinking more steak pie,' Nick says.

'Ooh gotcha, I was going straight into a pudding way of thought but you're on the main course...' Tappy says.

'Chicken and gravy is nice,' Cookey says.

'Oh don't, I'm starving,' Blowers says.

'Has it got pie, Mr Howie?' Nick asks.

'Have you got pie?' Howie asks. 'I can't see a pie,' he calls back, looking at her empty hands.

A pause. The woman moving her eyes from each person speaking then back to Reginald.

'Perhaps it means the other form of pi,' Reginald says. 'As in P I, rather than P I E.'

'Oh that pi,' Howie says.

'What pie?' Nick asks.

'Pi,' Howie says. 'In maths.'

'We did that at school,' Blowers says. 'Something about a circle.'

'Pie's are circles,' Nick says. 'Nice round chicken pie...'

'Your mum makes nice pies,' Cookey says. 'For her special customers...'

'Maybe that's where pi comes from,' Nick suggests.

'From your mum?'

'No, you twat. From eating pies...'

'Oh, yeah could be,' Cookey say. 'Hmmm, if only we had a super intelligent super pretty super nice lady on a horse we could ask...'

Charlie smiles to herself, shaking her head and rolling her eyes while facing ahead.

'If only,' Nick says wistfully. 'Wish we had someone like that.'

'Can't think of anyone,' Blowers says.

'What about...' Tappy starts saying, trailing off thoughtfully. 'Ah no, I was thinking of Roy but he's not on a horse, and he's not a girl either...'

'Charlie?' Cookey calls out in his whisper shout.

'Yes?' she asks, turning to look at him.

'Do you know a super intelligent super pretty super nice lady on a horse we can ask about pies?'

'I'm afraid I don't,' she says, turning to smile at him as another layer from the brick wall she put up is taken down.

'Ah bum,' he says, grinning that grin, the one that makes her smile. 'Have to ask you instead then...'

'I guess so,' she says, twitching the reins to move Jess to buy time to look at Reginald to see the tiniest discreet nod. 'Pi was originally defined as the ratio of a circle's circumference to its diameter and was associated with trigonometry and geometry specifically relating to spherical shapes but latterly it was developed and used in many other areas of maths and science...but as to what pi actually is...pi is 3.14159...although the sequence of actual numbers can extend way beyond millions of digits...'

The woman turns to look at Charlie. The infection staring out. The boy smiling at Cassie fastening his seatbelt in his booster chair and growing still and ageless as Cassie and Gregori get in the front of the Range Rover. Motion in the street in the south and the boy blinks as the host woman is taken down by the dog getting bored.

'We really need a leash,' Clarence says as they watch Meredith chomp and gnash and snarl and rag.

'I really want a pie now,' Nick says from behind.

They walk the length of the town centre. Seeing nothing of note. No infected and no people either. Just empty shops and buildings. Just parked or crashed cars. Just roads and pavements with puddles formed from the light rain.

Into the vehicles. Snacks eaten. Fluids consumed and energy growing as they go on through a country road to the next place of populace. A hamlet and nothing more. A collection of old houses once used to house farm workers before farms became unworkable.

In the north, the Range Rover also navigates country roads as it drives from the isolated bumfucknowhere house to the local town. Supplies are needed. Food, clothes, things for comfort, things for pleasure. Music playing from the stereo and Cassie's hand stretched over the central section to rest on Gregori's thigh. The boy in the back singing along, swinging his legs and laughing happily while inside the infection readies and waits, watching through the eyes of an adult male in the hamlet that once housed the farm workers. Watching as the Saxon comes to a stop and the people drop out. Watching as Howie comes forward with Clarence and Dave. Paula too. Watching as Howie comes to a stop and waits for Reginald to arrive with Maddox.

'Hello, how are you,' the infection says, the infected male says. An obese man with a huge gut who would have been dead from heart disease within the next three months had he not been bitten on the leg. Now he has no heart disease.

'Just to be clear,' Howie says, 'we're not becoming bezzer buddies here...you're still the baddies and we're still the goodies...'

'What's a bezzer buddy?' the boy asks in the Range Rover.

Cassie turns the music down and turns to smile. 'Say again,' she says.

'What's a bezzer buddy?'

'Um, like best friends, it's a slang expression. You okay?'

'Yes, Casseeee,' the boy says, the thing inside him switching attention back to the lane in the hamlet to the obese man staring at Howie.

'We are not best friends,' the infection says.

'I just said that,' Howie says, frowning at the obese man. 'You're fucking weird, mate.'

'Mate.'

'Ah no, I mean...like it's a term, not an actual mate. Why the fuck am I explaining myself to a fat zombie?'

'You can't have a go cos he's fat,' Paula says.

'Are you being serious?'

'Yes, I'm being serious. We're not picking fault with appearances and lifestyle choices here...we're fighting a rogue parasitical infection thing...the fat man is just the host and he's probably dead, or his mind is dead...or whatever. I know what I mean so stop gawping at me and get on with it.'

'Right,' Howie says.

'Fatty.'

'Cookey!'

'Blowers said it.'

'I bloody did not you fucktard...'

'Focus!' Paula snaps. 'Right, what do you want?' she asks the obese man.

'More pie by the looks of it.'

'Nick!'

'Sorry, Paula.'

'He's had enough pies.'

'Tappy? You too?' Paula groans.

'Sorry, Paula.'

'He ate all the pies.'

'Alex bloody Cookey. One more word...'

'Sorry, Paula...'

'Clarence, you can stop laughing. And you, Howie...this isn't funny. Oh for fuck's sake now the dog's got him...Jesus wept we are so incompetent.'

'Can't blame her,' Nick says. 'He's full of pies...'

'Casseee?'

'Yes?' Cassie asks, turning the music down to twist around again.

'Can we have pie today?'

'Pie? Er yeah sure, we'll find something. What on earth made you think of pies?'

'Right, anyone mention pies and I will get angry. Clear?'

'Yes, Paula,' Howie says as the rest chorus the same response at the next stop. A small collection of shops at the side of a dual carriageway bordering a huge sprawling housing estate. Roll down metal shutters bashed through for looting. Windows broken and bodies lying scattered and strewn. All old. All decaying and swept into a pile from flood water rushing through during the night.

Another adult male. Not obese this time and he stands tall and proud. His back erect. His head high. The infection within waiting and watching. The boy in the Range Rover watching the world go by.

'I'm being serious,' Paula says, looking from Howie to Clarence. Everyone else ranging out. She turns to look back at Reginald Maddox coming from the van. 'I've said no pissing about this time. I've got the dog with me so we can just get on with it...' she walks backwards as she speaks, frowning in confusion at the looks on the lads faces. Danny clearly trying not to smile. Nick the same. Tappy looking away. 'What's got into you lot?' she asks, turning to face front and stopping dead. 'Oh fuck off! Seriously...'

'Holy shit,' Maddox exclaims, coming into view with Reginald.

A big man. Tall and austere looking. Pale skinned and freckled. His eyes looking all the more red for it and a wodge of tightly curled ginger hair sitting proud on his head.

'Hello, how are you?' the man says, the infection says.

'Not fucking ginger,' Maddox replies, setting them all off again. 'Can you even be out in the sun?'

'Maddox!' Paula snaps, trying to be angry then breaking off into a laugh that gets worse when she looks at Cookey. 'Pack it in...'

'Bruv,' Maddox says. 'You's making me shudder, you's all evil and white and pale and ginge innit...'

'I am in many hosts. I am in many places. I am...'

'You's in a ginger bloke,' Maddox says earnestly, making the lads laugh harder. 'Don't be proud of that. Gonna shoot you for being ginge...Mr Howie, can I shoot the ginge? Do bullets even work on gingers?'

A shot fired and the boy frowns in his booster seat, leaning over to look suspiciously at the back of Cassie's head and her red hair.

Another small village. A country pub turned chain eatery with too many picnic benches jammed into the gardens to increase customer capacity. Large sun umbrellas now scattered here and there and the pub a mess of burnt timber and crumbling walls from a recent fire. Probably from the storm but then it doesn't look recent, possibly that big storm eleven days ago, either that or some fucker burnt it down.

'I would say it got struck by lightning,' Clarence says as they pass. 'Bit of a thatched roof there...' he adds glancing at Howie giving him a narrow-eyed sideways look that makes the big man tut.

'I'm going to put some of Blowers gaffer tape over my gob to prove I'm not speaking out loud...'

'You do that,' Clarence says.

'I will,' Howie says, looking ahead to the road and the woman coming into view standing in the centre of the carriageway. 'Aye up chuckies, one ahead...'

In the north, Cassie lifts the boy from the Range Rover as Gregori steps back from the vehicle with an assault rifle ready in his hands as he turns to look and listen and sniff the air. Detecting nothing. He thought they'd see the things on the way here but not a glimpse of one was gained.

'Is quiet,' he remarks.

'That's good isn't it?' Cassie asks, plonking the boy down. 'Maybe they all left...'

In the south, the woman waits in the light rain that wets her hair to her scalp and soaks through her clothing, the infection within watching Howie and his team drop out and move forward. Blowers and Cookey sharing glances with strange grins, Danny's mouth hanging open as Howie and Clarence falter in step.

'Hello, how are you,' the infection says, the woman says, her voice deep and husky in a way that makes Howie cough into his hand as Clarence just blinks while Danny's mouth hangs open even more.

'Coming through, coming through,' Reginald says, bustling forward with Maddox. 'And here we are and oh my good gosh, you can see her nipples...'

'Boobs,' Danny mumbles.

'S'Mo Mo innit,' Mo says, nodding at the woman smoothly. 'I'm Dave trained...'

'Stop gawping,' Tappy says, whacking Nick again.

'Boobs,' Danny says again.

'Jesus love, could you find a flimsier top to wear?' Paula asks. 'Mo, close your eyes and Danny, close your mouth.'

'You even look at her, Howie,' Marcy warns, dropping from the Saxon. 'And you'll be having sex with your hand for the rest of your life...'

'I am in many places...' the infection says, the woman says as Danny runs risk of tripping over his own face while trying ever so hard not to look at the beautiful woman in the very wet white top standing in the rain a few steps away. 'What you are I am not. What I am is the true state of being. My race will succeed yours...'

Silence.

'Answer her then!' Paula snaps.

'Totally,' Howie says quickly, nodding seriously.

'I think so,' Clarence rumbles, nodding seriously.

'I am more,' the woman says, the infection says. 'I am many more what you are. You are cruel and weak. I am not. You cause pain and suffering. I am the...' she stops talking from the punch coming from the side that sends her sprawling across the ground with teeth flying over the road.

'I am having some issues right now, Alex,' Charlie says, seething with fury as she stands over the woman she just floored. 'And until my head is clear I would rather you did not stare at scantily clad women...' she pulls her pistol, sliding the top back and staring at Cookey. 'Unless I am not worth waiting for of course...'

'You are,' Cookey says quickly.

She nods once, checks aim and fires before holstering the weapon. 'Good. Glad we're clear on that... and the image of that woman is not to be stored in your wank-bank.'

'Right,' Cookey says.

'Think of something else.'

'Right.'

Charlie pauses, smoothing her top down. 'That day in the golf hotel. You may think of that.'

'I will.'

'Good. Right. I'm afraid the infected woman is now dead, Mr Howie. Perhaps we should move on.'

In the north, the boy wonders what just happened while riding in a trolley in a dust-covered deserted and somewhat stinky supermarket.

'Everything okay?' Cassie asks him quietly, looking into his eyes while Gregori stops to pray in the aisle of tinned peas.

'Yes,' the boy says, the infection says. 'Danny likes boobs...'

'Every man loves boobs my sweet...oh god he's found the mushy peas...'

Silence in the Saxon. The men quiet and the women arching eyebrows and showing displeasure by way of doing so. Cookey and Charlie sitting opposite each other. Charlie prim and proper. Cookey trying to figure out the complexities of life then looking down in a very unsubtle way to Charlie's foot resting on his and not knowing if she is intending to do that or if it's simply because of the confined space. He wants to ask but he doesn't. Then she taps that foot a couple of times and he looks up to see her staring at him in a weird way before turning her head while Danny thinks Charlie can piss off and he is definitely storing the mental image of the hot woman in the wet top for his wank-bank.

'One ahead,' Howie calls out as they near a row of shops bordering the wide road. 'A bloke,' he adds. 'In case anyone was wondering...'

'Has he got a wet top on?' Marcy asks, getting a few chuckles.

'He's got no top on,' Howie says.

'Ooh let's see,' Marcy says, looking up and out. 'Ah, never mind,' she says on seeing an elderly man with a straggly grey beard. 'So, are we doing this all day then? Just in and out?'

'Looks that way,' Howie says, slowing the Saxon to a stop while in a supermarket a few hundred miles away Cassie watches Gregori loading the trolley with tinned and mushy peas.

'I like the mushky peas,' he says, pausing as he works.

'So I see,' she remarks, winking at the boy who smiles while the infection watches through the eyes of millions and one elderly man with a straggly beard and no top on.

'And here we are again,' Howie says as they converge upon the infected man.

'Hello, how are you,' the infection says, the elderly man says. His eyes switching from Howie to Reginald. The small man thinking fast and clear. Trying to see the hand at play in this game. Everything for a reason. Everything for a purpose. 'I am the true state of being...'

Reginald cuts in, 'and what is the true state of being?'

'I am many. I exist. I have life.'

'It is one thing to make statement, but what, specifically, are you?'

'I am a hive mind collective conscience of many hosts who are in the true state of being.'

'You are not answering the question. What are you?' Reginald asks again.

A pause with clear reflection from an entity that knows everything yet struggles to understand.

'You do not know what you are,' Reginald says. 'You cling to life and gain the minds of your hosts and you use their thoughts and knowledge as your own, but you have no grasp of it, of them, of what life is. You are a parasite in pretence of life and you will be eradicated as such.'

'I have life.'

'What life? Where? In this old man? Then you are a thief and nothing more for you have taken his life and his body to use against his will.'

'I do not cause suffering.'

'A wholly gross and offensive lie and you Sir, you are given to deceit and cheap tricks which render you as corrupt as humanity for as well as causing suffering we are also given to love and laughter which you lack completely. You are a base, sordid thing.'

'I am life.'

'Repeat it again. Repeat it for the world to hear but that does not make it so. You are not life. You are within life. You take and you hurt and you convince yourself in all your vanity that you are something else…'

Howie holds still, listening and watching Reginald at work. Seeing a power of a different sort as Marcy's words come back to his mind. He flicks his gaze between Reginald and the old man, except it's not the old man he sees, it's the infection inside, the other player.

'I am life. I exist. I am many but as one…'

Reginald blinks, surprised at Howie shooting the elderly male through the head. 'I can only assume you had good reason to shoot him?'

'I did,' Howie says with a flash in his eyes from the lure of the fight. 'Load up, we're going shopping…'

'Anyone would think you actually like shopping,' Cassie says, marvelling at the apparent enjoyment Gregori is taking in examining the tins, products and things on display in the supermarket. A barrage of questions coming thick and fast. *What this. This food? How eat this? What taste like? We try this.*

'Is okay,' Gregori says, as flat as ever but a casualness to his tone that makes Cassie smile.

'You take your time my handsome,' she says. 'We're not in a rush are we,' she adds, smiling at the boy sucking a lollipop who shakes his head emphatically and waits for Gregori to walk on.

'What am I?' the boy asks, the infection asks.

She blasts air out, leaning to brace her weight on the handlebar of the trolley and lowering her voice while seeing the ageless expression on the child. 'That edges into the realms of philosophy. *What am I* is not something ever really answered. I can say what I am but Gregori would say something else and another person would give a different answer. Why do you ask?'

'Reginald asked this question.'

'Oh did he now? I see. Well, you tell that jumped up twat that anyone asking that question is a knob and only when he is able to answer the same question should he ever ask it of someone else...'

'What this?' Gregori asks, coming back with a tin.

'That's cat food, Gregori.'

'You eat cats?'

Clarence's boot to the door and it goes in instantly, the frame flying out from the wall with dust and debris raining down inside. Howie and Dave go first, pausing to let their eyes adjust to the gloom while Meredith pushes past them with her nose to the floor, snuffling off down the length of the shop.

'Looks clear,' Howie says. 'You okay checking it? I'll get Reggie.'

'Yes, Mr Howie,' Dave says, heading off after Meredith as Howie steps out to see Paula and Marcy ushering Reginald and Maddox up to the shop.

'I am more than capable of doing this by myself, Marcy,' Reginald says, clearly irritated. 'And I might add I am not entirely convinced this is necessary.'

'Stay with him,' Howie says to Paula and Marcy. 'I want him sharp. Seriously, do not hold back. We're making a statement...'

'Okay,' Marcy says, thankfully serious for once. 'Leave it with us.'

'I really don't see how this...' Reginald starts to say.

'Not every battle is fought with violence,' Howie says. 'Get it done, quick as you can.'

'*We've got one ahead,*' Howie says into the radio. '*Reggie? Do not hold back.*'

'Dear God,' Marcy mutters, rolling her eyes. 'There is still another method available...'

'Try this for now,' Howie says, his head firmly in the game. A woman in the road. Late middle-aged. Short hair and lean with a hawkish appearance. She looks ridiculous in a filthy nightgown but it's not the person Howie sees now but the thing inside and the ideology of the hive mind possession cements further into reality.

The woman watches them. The infection inside. The vehicles stopping. Everyone out and making ready. Howie, Clarence, Dave and Paula coming forward. Weapons held.

'Here we are again,' Howie says.

'Hello, how are you,' the woman says, the infection says, the boy sucking on a lollipop a few hundred miles away. 'What are you?' she asks.

'Do what?' Howie replies.

'What are you?'

'I'm Howie.'

'You ask this question, now I ask this question. What are you?' the woman asks, the infection asks.

'Ah now, a returned volley I would suggest,' Reginald says, prompting the others to move aside so he can come forward and the woman shifts her eyes to take him in. The small man now changed and different. His whole being and bearing changed and different. He was in black clothes before. Loose fitting and unsuited to his form but now a suit adorns his frame. Dark blue pinstripes with a crisp white shirt under a waistcoat and a muted silk tie knotted with an understated half Windsor. Freshly shaven. His hair swept back and clean. The injuries still there but now they only serve to give an air of authority. A man of great learning and knowledge who leans ever so slightly on his black cane that matches his gleaming black brogues because Mr Howie said not to hold back.

'In terms of species I am the result of a glob of goo that crawled from a primordial swamp that split into many forms of species that all evolved over many millions of years, and as that span of ages passed so the Hominidae came to be which spawned apes and of course gibbons and orangutans...and it is thought the human and chimpanzee forms parted from the gorillas and in turn the humans and chimps then split and on we go until eventually we are pottering about on two legs thinking of sex and fire and throwing things at each other, much as we do in present times, or did do until of course you came along and destroyed it. That is very roughly our genealogy, but the question can also be posed as a philosophical one, and in answer to that I would suggest I have true sentience so therefore I abide the order of needs. Air, water, food, shelter and so forth until I desire art and understanding to shape my world and find my fit within. I have emotions that may be the result of chemicals or one could argue the chemicals are as a result of the emotions. I feel. I love. I fear and I hate. I hurt and I cause pain but I hurt and I feel pain. In short, I am human and defined as such by all of those things...' a pause for dramatic effect and Reginald finally looks at the woman. 'Now, what are you? Other than a parasitic smear in a petri dish incubated in a laboratory...'

A pause too long.

'One-nil fuckface,' Howie says, shooting the woman dead.

In the north, they peruse the aisles at a leisurely pace. Picking this and that to go into the trolleys. Cassie relaxed and playful, knowing there are thousands of infected in a solid radius about her family. An encapsulation of safety. A few words to the boy when she can. To the thing inside him.

'It's fine,' she says on hearing Reginald's answer. 'Fuck him, you've got millions of minds...there'll be something the little twerp doesn't know...'

In the south, they hit the next town to stop and get out to approach the infected for Reginald to stride in with his cane tapping the road as he walks into round two.

'Hello, how are you,' the man says, the infected says.

'Ah, in French I see,' Reginald replies in perfect French. 'Very well, as you wish. Charlie, it wishes to talk to us in French.'

'So I heard,' Charlie says in perfect French. 'Perhaps we can discuss Voltaire and his views on the separation of the church from the state...'

'Oh, a grand idea! Yes, let's discuss Francois-Marie Arouet. A very apt subject given his views against tyranny...'

'Two-nil fuckface...'

'You cannot succeed. You have so few. I have many. Your kind cannot survive...'

'Oh but yet here we are,' Reginald retorts a few villages later, his oratory skills growing with each round, like a skilled barrister presenting to the jury. His features animated, the tone and inflection of his voice giving rise and lilt against the flat voice of the infection. The cane in his hand now a prop to gesture and tap, to lean on when he passes scorn, comical and erudite. 'Twenty-five days into your new empire and we are still here, so tell me, my Emperor, how is that working out for you?'

'Five nil fuckface.'

Into the vehicles. The energy high from something new afoot. Danny not really having a clue what's going on but happy to be here and doing it, in the middle of whatever this is and anyway, he saw boobs in a wet top earlier so nothing else really matters.

Charlie's foot resting on Cookey's again. He doesn't remark on it, nor does Blowers or Nick or Tappy or anyone else because they can see it in her eyes. *I'm hurting so much inside right now and I don't want you near me but please don't abandon me.*

Into the next town and out to form up to make safe for Reginald to deploy and walk into the ring to fight his opponent.

'Go on, Reggie,' Cookey says as he passes.

'Get 'em, Reggie,' Nick says,

'On you, Reggie, we've got your back,' Blowers says.

'You's smart as fuck bro,' Mo says.

'Fuck me this is the most boring day ever,' Marcy says.

'Hello, how are you,' the man says, the infection says. 'Accept the end now. You cannot win. My kind do not suffer. They do not feel pain.'

'Oh but they do,' Reginald says gently. 'Withdraw from this host body and he will feel great pain. His left arm is shorn off. I can see the bone and a most awful injury that is so please, withdraw and we'll see if he feels the agony you hide from him.'

'I have no pain. I am the true state of being.'

'But therein lies the true degradation of what you are. Cliches are trite, awful things but they are clichés for a reason, so shall we try one now? If there were no fools, there would be no wise men...if there was no rain then how can I have such love for the sunshine? If I never feel sadness how can I ever feel happiness? If I never suffer loss how will I know gain? Without defeat, I cannot have victory and if I do then I won't know what it is. Do you see? You must see.'

A pause.

'Six nil fuckface...' Howie aims and fires, sending the bullet into the head of the man, blowing his skull out in a shower of bone and gore.

'It feels like we're being played,' Reginald says quietly, urgently.

'I know, we'll talk in a minute,' Howie replies just as quietly, holstering his pistol before looking around and spotting a coffee shop across the street. 'Engineering corps! Do magic things and get power into that super shiny big coffee machine I can spy over there...'

'That'll be us then, Roy,' Nick says, turning to the older man.

'Whoa, wait. You have an engineering corps?' Tappy asks.

'Er, it's kinda newly formed, as in the last ten seconds,' Howie says.

'Awesome. Can I join? I make better knots than Nick and Roy...'

'Crack on,' Howie says while in the north a brick flies through a window of a café, shattering the glass that clatters down to break apart on the ground.

Gregori goes in first. Assessing and making it safe before going back out for the generator pilfered from the hardware store that he gets running behind the counter next to the shiny coffee machine.

'This is er...nice?' Cassie says, wincing a little at the rundown state of the café interior. 'Ah well, long as we get decent coffee...need a hand?'

In the south, the window of the café goes through from being hit with an axe by Nick then raked out to make safe. Mo and Dave go in, checking the inside before a long extension cable is run from the new van while Tappy yanks the wires from the back of the coffee machine and starts work to make the new connections.

'Where did you learn this stuff?' Nick asks, bringing the extension cable in.

'Love it,' Tappy says, a pair of grips between her teeth. 'My dad was so into DIY...'

'Yeah? You'd be handy at the fort.'

'Deffo want to see it one day...are you watching me work?'

'Yeah.'

'Ahem, fuck off and splice your own wires.'

'Ahem, my wires are already spliced, fuckhead.'

'Such a twat. Is the fort good?'

'Wasn't but it is now. You'll like Lilly.'

'Who's Lilly?'

'Um, she runs the fort...'

'Why the um?' she asks.

'She's kinda my girlfriend but...'

'Oh wow, that's very cool. Your girlfriend runs the fort? Kudos to you, Nicholas.'

'Yeah, she's really nice.'

'Aw bless, you've got little hearts in your eyes.'

'Fuck off.'

'Joking. Tell me about Lilly...'

'Don't be a dick.'

'I'm not! Seriously, tell me about her...'

'Power's ready when you need it,' Roy calls through.

Gregori doesn't splice wires. He simply unplugs the coffee machine then plugs it into the generator chugging away happily. He flicks the switch, grunting with satisfaction at seeing the lights coming on then pausing with a clear indication that he has absolutely no clue what to do next.

'Bless,' Cassie says, laughing at his expression. 'Caveman make power...make fire...' she mimics a deep voice, gently pushing him out from behind the counter. 'You go and sit down and let me be the café lady...' she ushers him off then goes back to stand with her hands on the counter then slouches into one hip and adopts a cock-eyed expression. 'Ee-by-gum lad, thou want a cuppa does thou?' a northern accent, a weird face and the boy laughs in delight.

'Barista coming through,' Cookey says, marching behind the counter of the café in the south. 'I maka the cappuccino ina cupa for youa,' he starts grabbing mugs, sing-songing in an awful Italian accent. 'I lika makea the coffeea with the chocolate cocka on the topa...'

A separation of hundreds of miles. A café in the north in a town cleared of hosts and people by a thing inside a boy following the instruction of a woman, and that woman pretends to be a northern tea lady, clattering about noisily as the boy laughs and Gregori learns how to smile.

A separation of hundreds of miles. A café in the south in a town filled with armed men and women who have fought back and earned the right to stop and drink coffee while everyone else struggles to live. For the losses they have given and the pain they have suffered while a young man with chopped up blond hair and twinkling blue eyes makes them laugh as he makes drinks in the guise of an Italian barista.

Drinks made. Long life milk frothed up in steel jugs. Coffee granules everywhere. Milk spilled over the sides of the mugs and across the counters. Hot chocolate for the boy. Hot chocolate for a few of the team. A pause in the game. A break for both sides.

'Okay, so what's happening?' Paula asks, sitting down at the table and pausing as they all look to the huge horse stepping into the café to batter chairs and table aside to find Clarence to butt her head into his shoulder in search of food, the dog sitting obediently at his side staring up with her ears flat and her eyes round and sad.

'Why are they doing that?' Nick asks.

'Wish I knew,' Clarence says a touch too innocently as Paula smiles at the sight.

'If I may bring the topic back to the subject at hand,' Reginald says, resplendent in his attire. 'We are on a dangerous path, Mr Howie.'

'I know,' Howie says.

'If we remain on this linear route they will prepare for us,' Reginald continues. 'We're moving from village to town on a straight line and other than the singular host bodies left to engage us we are not seeing any, which suggests they are being drawn or moved to another place.'

'Probably,' Howie says.

'Indeed,' Reginald says. 'And may I also point out that our current direction is taking us towards London and although that is not a significant matter of concern right now it soon may be. The towns will soon become bigger with an increase in population densities...'

'How far until we see that?' Clarence asks.

'We have a few more small villages yet,' Maddox replies, bringing everyone's attention to him. 'I'm plotting the route with Reginald in the van,' he explains.

'I thought we were looking for the Marcy one,' Paula says.

'We are,' Howie says. 'But we need to know where to look. In London? South? North? Blowers suggested north from...you know... but where in the north? I don't know...I've just got a feeling...'

'I know what you mean,' Marcy says, leaning forward to lower her coffee cup. 'Firstly, I still think you should let me sort it from here but...but!' she says again louder at the grumble of voices. 'But if we're staying on this plan then keep doing this. There's something about it... like...ah I'm not clever like Charlie and I don't know the words but... it's like it wants to compete. Does that make sense? No, I've got it,' she says, clicking her fingers. 'It's vain...like me, yes that's it. I don't think it can handle us winning, or at least not being dead yet...it's like a really smart bratty little kid that can do maths and knows stuff but can't tie its own shoelaces or understand why everyone isn't kissing his arse...'

'As eloquent as ever, my dear.'

'Fuck off, Reggie. Help me out and explain it properly.'

'Oh gosh, you don't need my help.'

'Fuck's sake,' she huffs, reaching up to pull her hair back.

'I am at great pains to admit this, but I think Marcy's instincts are correct,' Reginald says. 'We are challenging it...'

'You're also teaching it,' Maddox cuts in.

'There is that,' Reginald admits quietly.

'We keep going,' Howie says. 'Straight on...if anyone wants out then say so but my gut is telling me to stick with it for now. Everyone happy? Good. Drink up then we'll press on.'

In the north, Cassie leans over the table, whispering urgently while Gregori visits the toilet. 'They've stopped for coffee too? Isn't that nice. We're all doing the same thing,' she says with a look of distaste. 'But it's good, it means they must be comfortable...keep going and get them all ready where we said...'

CHAPTER TWENTY

Day Twenty-five

Coffee drunk. Caffeine and sugar levels spiking to give energy. Cassie, the boy and Gregori moving out from their café to potter about their empty, deserted town at leisure.

Howie and his team moving out from their café to load up and push on and play a game of many layers where the true cost of losing will be the loss of their species. No pressure then. No pressure at all.

'Fuck 'em, we'll win,' Blowers calls out from the back of the Saxon.

'Argh,' Howie says.

'Idiot,' Marcy mutters.

Into the next village for Reginald to pits his wits in battle. His cane tapping as he walks and his cane tapping as he scores points.

'I am sentient. I am life. I have life,' the infection says.

'To what end? To what purpose? For what? You cannot be sentient and not adhere to the order of needs. It is not possible because you are shaped by the hosts you possess. You are not what you think you are. You do not know what you are so how can you possibly claim to be superior?'

Into the next place to another infected person in the game of many layers. A woman this time. Thin and young, her skin scarred and sallow from years of Heroin addiction. Old track marks on her arms.

'This host was addicted to a narcotic. Her blood was diseased. Her life-span less than expected. Now this host is not addicted. She has no disease.'

'She is also dead,' Reginald counters. 'She cannot take pleasure from the thing you have given her because her own sentience has been taken by yours. I wholly congratulate you on your abilities, but this host died two minutes after you passed into her. You are a thief and a murderer.'

Into the next as the pressure of the day starts to build proper. Going willingly into a trap while the infection seeks to undermine them while they seek the same.

'Humans will destroy the world. I will not. I will repair. I will improve. I am the cure.'

'You are the cull before the cure. You are not the Panacea my dear chap. Now tell me, will the Panacea eradicate you?'

A pause. The essence of uncertainty.

'You lose fuckface.'

Into the vehicles. Charlie and Tappy chatting about horses. Charlie's foot on Cookey's. The lads laughing. Reginald in his van thinking hard, thinking fast.

'You had something then,' Maddox tells him. 'It didn't like that question.'

Into the next town and Reginald walks out to stride through his team towards the infected male.

'Hello, how are you...' the male says, the infection says.

'Will the Panacea eradicate you?' Reginald goes in hard, attacking instantly.

'I am the cure,' the infection parries the blow, moving aside.

'Will the Panacea eradicate you?' Reginald presses his attack, driving into his opponent with hard body shots.

'I cure all,' a defence given, the blows blocked.

'No! You do not. Answer the question or do you not know?' Reginald moves fast, hammering his punches, driving his knee into the beast. 'Answer the question. Will the Panacea eradicate you?'

The infection blocks and parries, sliding and veering to get back from the onslaught 'I am the cure. I cure all.'

'Be altruistic and leave then. Vanish and leave your cure in the hosts you possess.'

'I am the cure.'

'You lie! You deceiver you. You're avoiding the question. Answer me! Will the Panacea eradicate you?'

A pause too long. 'I cannot be eradicated.'

'You lose again fuckface...'

Into the vehicles. Charlie's foot on Cookey's. Danny loving every minute of being trained and taught by Blowers, of being here with everyone else. Jokes and chat flowing as the energy increases from seeing Reginald repeatedly batter his opponent.

Howie now in the van with Reginald and Maddox. 'Good work, Reggie. Press it. Go hard...'

'It's working,' Maddox says, looking from Howie to Reginald.

Into the next. Howie and Maddox leading Reginald into the ring, onto the field of battle. The small man's face ablaze with the lust for the fight. His cane tapping. His face set. Murmured words of encouragement buoying him on.

'I cannot be eradicated,' the woman says, the infection says. No greeting this time. The fight underway instantly as Howie and Maddox step aside to let Reginald through.

'Liar!' the small man's voice fills the street, booming with power and passion. 'Will the Panacea eradicate you?'

'I cannot be eradicated. I am the one true race...'

'Liar!'

'I am the one true race. I cure all. I have no pain. I have no suffering.'

'Liar! You lie and you cheat...'

'I am the true state of being...'

'You squirm and you deflect the question.'

'I will not be eradicated.'

'You will and you shall. Answer me! Either the Panacea will eradicate you or you do not know the answer but to admit either exposes your weakness while you cling to vanity and a sheen of pretence that you are omnipresent and God-like in your existence...'

'I cannot be eradicated.'

'Liar!'

'I cannot...'

'ANSWER ME.'

'I HAVE LIFE.'

A point scored. A smile from Reginald. 'You have anger, you can be exploited, and you will be...'

'You lose fuckface...'

Back into the vehicles. The day now long and the afternoon growing late. Howie in the back of the van with Reginald and Maddox. 'I wasn't expecting that flash of anger,' Howie says.

'Nor I,' Reginald says, thinking hard, thinking fast. 'That child-like way is still there...interesting, very interesting. Was that flash of anger the infection or the host it occupies?' he trails off, drumming his fingers on the desk.

'Where are we on the map?' Howie asks.

'Here,' Maddox says, showing Howie their position who balks slightly at not realising how far east they were and spotting the grey splodges of urban zones as he traces a route across the paper from their position now. 'Another two or three then we pull out and find somewhere for the night...'

'How the fuck?' Cookey asks, rummaging in his bag between his feet.

'What?' Blowers asks.

'It's not possible,' Cookey says, still rummaging in his bag.

'What isn't?' Blowers asks.

'That,' Cookey says, pulling a single sock out.

'That for your wank-bank time is it?' Nick asks. 'You may think of the hotel, Alex...' he adds primly.

'Er thank you, Nicholas,' Charlie says.

'Why are you holding a sock up?' Blowers asks.

'Lost the other one,' Cookey says, going back to rummaging one-handed in his bag.

'You've lost one already?' Paula asks. 'I only just filled those bags.'

'I know! I can't find it,' Cookey says while Blowers remembers what Blinky said in the dream that she stole Clarence's socks. He thought about sharing what she said, but he felt stupid, so he didn't. He's sure it was real though. He told Reginald about the first one when he saw Big Chris and Meredith the woman. He wanted to tell Charlie but at each time he thought about saying it his instincts told him it would only hurt her more.

'Nope, it's bloody gone,' Cookey says with a huff, waving his single sock about. 'I'll keep it for you,' he tells Blowers.

'For me?'

'Yeah, it's only a matter of time, isn't it...I mean the rate you're losing body parts. You'll be a one-eyed, nine-fingered, one-legged, stumpy earless no knees bumless twat within a day or two...have my sock...'

'I don't want your stinky fucking sock.'

'It's clean,' Cookey says, sniffing it then thinking. 'I think it's clean...is it clean?' he asks, pushing it at Blowers face.

'Fuck off!' Blowers says, leaning back and away.

'Fine, if you're going to be like that,' Cookey says, scrunching it up into a ball. 'Charlie, is this clean?'

'That's gross!' she yelps as he throws it over and smacks it away to Nick who headbutts it across to Danny who taps it down to Mo who deftly flicks it on to Tappy with a new game instantly underway with clear rules of keeping the sock in the air without grabbing it. Everyone joining in, laughing as they lean away and hit it up and down the Saxon.

'Dave, get it!' Cookey shouts, sending the sock down towards Dave who doesn't look up and for a second it's clear the game will end, until he flashes a hand out to whack it on without looking.

'That's so cool,' Tappy says, reaching out to knock it back at Dave who does the same again and hits it back without turning to look and the game changes with the sock now aimed at a man who never misses.

'One ahead,' Clarence calls out from the front. *'Boss, it's Clarence...got one ahead in the town centre...'*

'Game over,' Blowers says, snatching the sock from the air. 'Bags on, kit ready...'

'Yay,' Marcy says without enthusiasm, 'we get to watch Reggie boring them to death again...'

'Oh it's not that bad,' Paula says.

'Um, it is that bad,' Marcy replies, standing up and getting ready to clamber over the seat as Clarence drops out of the driver's door.

'Go go go,' Cookey says jokingly, shuffling down the Saxon to jump out after Charlie who holds still for a second to purposefully step back into him with a quick grin.

'Watch where you're going, Alex.'

'You watch, Charlotte,' he replies, walking forward into her as she walks back into him with a quick contest of pushing against each other while the rest jump out and walk past them with easy smiles at their play.

Blowers smiles as he strides out with Danny at his side, glancing to the single female ahead in the centre of a town that looks bigger and more built up than the last ones. He scans his eyes over the doors, windows and access points.

'Alley up there, Corporal,' Danny says, aiming to the point of danger.

'Good spot,' Blowers says, looking over to Charlie and Cookey still at the back of the Saxon pushing against each other. He draws breath to order them to work then stops the words coming out, seeing Charlie smiling and playful for the first time in ages and figure a few more seconds won't hurt.

'Will you stop pushing me please,' Charlie says.

'Er, you're the pushy one,' Cookey replies, laughing when she turns to look at him, her scar so livid, her shaved head opening her features and her eyes that finally sparkle and shine again.

Howie walks past with Maddox and Reginald, clocking the play between Charlie and Cookey.

'Quick, Mr Howie's coming...act normal,' Cookey quips, both of them stopping to stand with mock innocent faces, earning chuckles and grins from the others.

'Has he gone?' Charlie asks.

'He's gone,' Cookey replies. 'We'd better get to work before Corporal Blowers tries to spank me again...'

'I heard you like that,' she says, stepping out to brush past him with a lingering look that make his grin nearly reach his ears. 'Your hair is such a mess, let me cut it later...'

'What like yours? No thanks.'

'Come on,' Blowers calls out, his tone edging into work-mode. 'Eyes up...'

'Sir,' Charlie says, moving out.

'Sir, Mr Blowers, Sir,' Cookey says, stepping behind Charlie as he glances forward to Mr Howie, Maddox and Reginald just stopping in front of the adult female infected. A lurch. A jolt. Cookey blinks and double takes, his head already turning away from looking forward but now snapping back. His vision coming in strobing flashes. A sickening wrench in his gut and he blinks back to the woman at the front and her red bloodshot eyes fixed on him.

He mouths a word that goes unheard as Blowers spots the expression of horror on his best mate's face as Cookey moves without realising. A step taken, then another and Charlie turns, frowning at hearing him mumble and thinking it to be another joke then seeing his face.

'That's my mum...' Cookey says, then his face hardens as his heart booms to race and he goes fast, striding out with fear and confusion gripping his mind. 'THAT'S MY MUM...'

'What the...' Howie spins, seeing Cookey charging down the side of the Saxon. His face a mask. The words bellowing out. 'Oh shit...' he snaps his head back to the woman, seeing the familiarity right there.

'THAT'S MY MUM...' Cookey goes to run, to sprint without knowing why, without conscious thought. Voices shouting. He doesn't hear them but charges forward as the impact comes from his side with

Charlie and Blowers driving into him, taking him down in a tangle of limbs. 'MUM! THAT'S MY FUCKING MUM...'

'Cookey! Look at me,' Charlie struggles to grip his face as Blowers scrabbles to hold him, stopping him from rising. Everything happening so fast. In the blink of an eye, in the beat of a heart.

'THAT'S MY FUCKING MUM!'

'It's not...Cookey...LOOK AT ME,' Charlie shouts, twisting his head towards her. Blowers holding him from behind.

'MUM!'

'IT'S NOT,' Charlie shouts, dominating his vision. Her hands on his cheeks. 'LOOK AT ME...LOOK AT ME...ALEX, IT'S NOT... LOOK AT ME...'

'It's my...'

'It's not, I promise you,' Charlie speaks urgently and soft, driving her words into his mind, her hands stopping him from looking away. His blue eyes filling with tears that spill over her hands.

'It's...it's...' he stammers, shocked and horrified.

'It's not, just look at me, Cookey. Look at me...it's not your mum...I swear to you, I swear to you with all of my heart that is not your mum now look at me...LOOK AT ME,' she pushes her hands over his ears, and nods once to Blowers before pressing her lips to Cookey's mouth, holding him still, deadening his senses. A nod from Blowers to Howie who aims and fires once with the dull crack heard so easily it makes Cookey flinch with tears pouring from his eyes squeezed closed and his hands gripping Charlie who holds herself against him in the pouring rain on a wet road. 'I swear to you...I swear it,' she whispers.

In the north, the boy smiles in the back of the Range Rover. The sun shining outside. The weather warm and pleasant. Music filling the car and Cassie twisting in her seat to smile at him. 'Are they there?'

'Yes, Cassie,' the boy says, the infection says.

'Good, let's see how cocky they are now...'

'GOT MOVEMENT,' Danny shouts in the street in the south, his head snapping from looking at Cookey on the ground back to the alley and a figure coming into view.

'THIS SIDE,' Nick shouts at the same time from the other side of the Saxon, seeing motion in the depths of a store with a busted in window.

'REAR,' Roy shouts at that same second, his hands already drawing the first few inches of tension in the arrow nocked and ready. Figures behind them coming out from the store front on both sides.

'FRONT,' Howie gives the warning at the same time as the others, lifting his rifle in readiness. 'Charlie...get mounted please...'

'CORPORAL!' Danny shouts, panic edging into his voice.

'Take it easy, Danny,' Clarence shouts down. 'Everyone stay calm...'

'CORPORAL!' Danny screams again.

'Mate, I'm coming...' Blowers snaps.

'THAT'S MY STEPDAD...' Danny bellows, seeing Keiron emerging from the alley. A big man with a big gut and unmistakable in appearance.

Meredith starts barking. Jess kicking her feet at the back of the trailer, smelling the infected, wanting to be free and moving.

Charlie lurches up, one hand gripping Cookey's, heaving him to his feet as the blond lad blinks and swallows, grabbing his rifle with shaky hands as Charlie runs for the trailer. The only sounds in the street coming from those in the middle shouting warnings as more infected emerge silently into view. A few seconds and no more. A few seconds of utter insidious horror at Cookey seeing his mother and now Danny shouting on seeing his stepdad and to the last, they all know what's coming. To the last they brace and ready for the worst nightmare any of them thought possible because England is not a big country, and the south, the areas they are all from, and the area they have been fighting in since this began, is small and the distances easy to cross, especially for those that don't fatigue or feel pain.

Reginald flinches, inwardly berating himself for being so drawn into the game he didn't factor for the dirty tactics and cheap tricks the other side could use against them. He should have realised when the infected said all of their names earlier in the day because everything is done for a reason. Everything is done for a purpose and he knows their world is about to become a much darker place.

'LISTEN CHAPS...LISTEN TO ME...' Reginald shouts. 'THEY'RE GOING TO SEND PEOPLE WE KNOW...'

'TERRY!' Nick cries out as he wilts back from the figures coming from the stores on his side. 'My cousin...that's my cousin...'

'THEY ARE NOT PEOPLE,' Reginald shouts as Charlie reaches the back of the trailer, booting the bolts free to drop the ramp and stepping back as Jess thunders out, turning on the spot as Charlie catches glimpse of a woman in the line of infected coming towards them. A woman of mixed race, tall and elegant, once beautiful. Her father's sister. She tries to mount Jess and in the shock of the second, her foot misses as Jess twitches and skitters to the side.

'Macka,' Clarence mutters, a great sadness crossing his face. 'Oh mate...'

Howie looks to the big man then over to an infected male with a military bearing. Tall, broad-shouldered with a shaved head. The parachute regiment winged tattoo so clear on his bare chest. More of the same kind seen in the lines and ranks.

'Jack? Ben? I fought with them...I...Macka? We served mate...we fought...Jack! WE FOUGHT TOGETHER...'

Mo grunts, hardening his features on seeing a man of Arabic appearance further down the street. A cousin, maybe an uncle. His big family spread all over the country. Paula staggers back a step, shaking her head then lifting her rifle to aim but unable to shoot her grandfather, the man who used to collect her from school when her mum was working. The man she adored now a bare few metres away.

On all sides, they see faces they know. On all sides, they see relatives and people known in life now with red bloodshot eyes. A foul trick played. An awful thing to do and just mere seconds from Cookey seeing his mother to this now. Just mere seconds from them arriving in this street to this now. Mere seconds of a change from humour and energy to that deep chilling horror stealing through them as they yell and cry out in shock and in the north, the boy grins all toothy and happy, nodding along to the music, to a fast-building beat of a pop song and he lifts his hands to hold in front of his head, his fists clenched and that beat builds to a crashing roll of drums and his hands open like a magician revealing the spectacle of his trick and in the street in the south, in the rain and in the horror, so their world changes in a heartbeat with every window above the team in the street blowing out from bodies leaping through in perfect synchronicity and every infected giving voice to howl and screech and drive that fear deeper. Filling the air with noise and terror, with confusion on all sides and those infected sailing through the windows do not land heavy and bleeding this time because the infection is evolving. The infection is learning, and they land on their feet with knees bending to take them into deep crouches as they absorb the short drop. Beasts now. Not human. Some land on the Saxon roof and bonnet. More on the new van. Others on the trailer. The rest on the road within the team as yet more come howling after them and those that were silent before now rage and charge.

What can they do? There is no time to rally or form a defensive circle. The shock was enough to make them stand rooted to the spot. What can they do? They aim to fire but wilt back and hesitate at shooting into the faces of the people they know and in such bedlam the risk of crossfire and shooting each other is too high. What can they do? They try and draw hand-weapons to fight and summon the rage needed but the press of the attack is too sudden, too hard and too horrifying.

What can they do? There is no choice and so, for the first time in days, they run.

'ON ME...' They aim for Dave's huge voice. The only one amongst them not affected by the horror. The only one amongst them who would cut his mother's throat and stand easy after, that may well happen but then Dave doesn't know his mother. **'ON ME...'** they aim for Dave, rallying on Dave. Charlie running alongside Jess, adjusting her step in readiness to vault to mount but taken down by an infected diving into her legs. Jess rears high, whinnying and snorting them coming down hard to ram her hard head into the skull of the male attacking Charlie, killing him instantly then bucking round in a circle, kicking her legs out as Tappy wades in, grabbing Charlie to get her up and moving.

Blowers driving forward, one hand on the strap of Danny's bag, making the younger lad move. Mo with Marcy. Everyone running. Everyone aiming for Dave's voice.

Nick taken off his feet by his cousin and driven back through a plate glass window that shatters and falls as the two men land heavily in a clothes shop. Rolling over and over with one raking and biting and one doing everything possible to get away. Meredith leaps in, a snarl, a growl and she rips the man from Nick who lurches up and aims to fire at the infected coming into the shop. Too many of them. Too much confusion and chaos. A flash from the side and the infected drop quickly one after the other as Dave goes through them with brutal ease. **'ON ME...'**

Out the shop. Into the street. Nick gaining Tappy and Charlie's side. Charlie still holding Jess's reins. Infected running in amongst them. Howie glimpsed. Others too. Clarence flinging one aside like a doll. More leaping onto his back and Roy goes in, grabbing them off while running.

Pure bedlam. Pure heaving, screaming, panic filled chaos and the rain falls, making the surface of the road slick and wet and so they trip and fall, banging knees and hands, grazing skin and feeling hands gripping their collars and arms to drag them up and on.

Hundreds now. Hundred more behind them. A world of noise and still they see the faces of their kin. Paula's grandfather looming who drops with a gurgle from Dave lashing his hand out to slither the blade across his throat. She screams out, seeing her own grandfather fall and for a second she falters until Roy grabs her wrist, pulling her on.

'RUN DANNY,' Blowers fights like a demon, snarling and screaming at Danny to keep going while punching the infected down as they charge in. 'YOU FUCKING RUN, DANNY...'

On they run, to be away from people they worked with. People they went to school with. Any and all connections of life exploited and used. Faces recognised from years gone by and others they only saw in the final days before the event happened.

'MOHAMMED WITH ME,' Dave drops back through the press, finding Mo. 'Rifles then pistols. Fire till empty then we go...' the tutor says.

'Yes, Dave,' the student says and the two stop running to bring rifles to aim and wait for the last of the team to go by before firing into the massed ranks coming after them. Strafing shots into legs to down the bodies at the front to make the ones behind trip and fall to buy vital seconds. Their rifles expended quickly so they sling and draw pistols to fire smaller rounds into the attackers.

'On,' Dave says, his voice as flat as ever. A gap bought and paid for. A gap to work and make bigger as Dave runs up behind the others. **'YOU WILL RUN...'** he roars to keep them going, making them speed up and grow that gap he and Mo just created.

Howie at the front leading them on. Veering left into a junction. More infected pouring into them from the sides. A running fight with fists and headbutts. A running fight, frantic and crazed.

A set of big wooden doors hanging open in a warehouse to the right. Howie aims for it, hoping to find a pinch-point to form a firing line and they go through fighting and snarling and battering at each other into the gloomy but dry inside of a vast storeroom filled with pallets stacked high with boxes standing like columns. Jess now running free within their group. Meredith streaking between them all, taking one down here then another down there. Danny glimpses behind, crying out on seeing Kieron and his mum then crying out louder on seeing his younger step-brother and sister. Everyone the same. Snatching glimpses of relatives and friends that robs the pure spite-filled aggression needed to fight back.

A dirty thing to do. A foul trick to play and in the north the boy is lifted from the Range Rover outside their bumfucknowhere isolated little country house. Running over to Gregori opening the front door who lowers to take the child on his back as they go back to the car to ferry their new goods inside. 'And Paula's granddaddy is there Nick's cousin and Cookey's mummy and Danny's mummy and Danny's step-brother and...' the boy yacks on, words and names spewing from his mouth that Gregori doesn't really listen to while Cassie chuckles and carries things inside.

The warehouse is big. A county delivery hub and it takes minutes for them to cross the vast space. The silence shattered by the shouts and cries of the living and the howls and screeches of the infected who pour through those double doors to chase and kill.

Through another set of doors. Across a yard. Clarence battering down another big wooden door and through another building. On they go. Unable to turn and fire without risk of shooting each other or of being flanked. The shock of seeing their families in their minds. The reality of it now hitting home.

Reginald gasps for air. Running in his new suit with his cane still gripped in his hand. A woman running in at him with a vicious snarl. 'Jennifer!' Reginald blurts, bringing his cane up as though it will protect him. Maddox batters her down, feeling Reginald falter to look back at the woman he played chess with on Thursdays. Then Maddox takes his turn to show horror on seeing faces he knows in the horde. Old customers he sold drugs to, someone he served a prison sentence with. Mo's probation officer. People they knew. People they liked and people they hated. Disconcerting and brutal.

More yards, more service roads in a maze of industrial buildings on a vast plot of land. Left and rights taken but still the infected come. It has the upper hand now. It has that seed of fear planted and will end them here.

Howie spots it first. A cluster of dead bodies outside a set of double wooden doors, one half of which hangs open. 'THERE!' he aims for that door, knowing they can't keep running, knowing they have to find a spot to fight from. The bodies outside the doors look shot down. Bullet holes in chests and heads blown out. Not that he pauses to examine them but runs past, wrenching the door open and screaming for them to get through. Dozens of infected and his team all going in together with Jess running free and panicked without Charlie on her back to guide and settle her natural fears.

Howie grips the heavy door, straining to pull it closed as the horde charge across the road at them. 'CLARENCE!' Clarence rushing to his side while the others fight. Shouts and screams. Dirty close quarters scrapping. Clarence yanks Howie back, flinging him into the fray to get space to grab the door and heave it shut and get a heavy wooden locking bar in place the second before the horde impact from the outside, thudding hard and making the doors flex and groan inwards.

Clarence staggers back, turning to see the brutal melee going on. Mo and Marcy back to back, both with knives out. Paula straddling over a woman, stabbing down into her chest with another slamming into her side that Clarence grips and breaks and uses to batter more away. Charlie and Tappy rolling across the ground trying to fight several at the same time. Knives stabbing and slicing. Cookey and Nick diving in. Blowers laying waste to anything coming near him and Danny stabbing into the stomach of a man while screaming wildly. Roy and Maddox fighting side by side with Reginald behind them and the doors creak and that locking bar groans.

'BACK...' Howie runs in, grabbing bodies to stab and fling aside. 'INTO THE BACK...'

They stagger on, desperate to be away from the doors, to buy a second to think and form a defence while running and fighting across a pitted ground streaked with oil. Tappy goes down. Charlie grabs her arm, wrenching her up in. Cookey there pushing them on. Everyone slipping and tripping. Everyone bruised and hurt, gasping for air. Another set of doors at the back standing open. Wide and high. They go through and down a wide corridor to a sturdier set of doors fitted with metal strips riveted in place. The windows here barred with solid metal cages.

'In there,' Howie gasps, hearing the bang of the main doors behind him and the sound of glass smashing as they start coming in through windows in the huge building.

In through the doors to a dark, gloomy room. The last infected running with them cut down and killed. Howie, Clarence and Tappy grabbing the doors to push them closed. Big bolts shot home and big locks secured. A metal locking bar pushed in place as the wooden outer doors to the street give with a splintering cry of wood tearing. A howl coming towards them. The sound of hundreds of feet running over concrete then the door is hit but it holds fast. The solid metal strips absorbing the blow and only then do they drop to gasp for air, falling to knees and leaning against walls. Jess still skittering, Meredith panting but seconds bought to think. Vital seconds to think.

CHAPTER TWENTY-ONE

A big room with high solid walls. A slide back metal door on one side giving access to the outside world. A huge table in the middle with chairs all around it and a single grimy, opaque skylight in the ceiling above giving the only source of weak light as everyone apart from Dave, Mo, Jess and Meredith gasp and recover. Hearts racing. Flashes flushed and sweating. Hair and clothes soaked from the rain.

A bang to the internal door. Then another as the infected batter themselves against it. Footsteps running above them. The sound of feet over the roof and more voices screeching all around then the sound of thuds as the infected drop to bang on the metal slide back door.

'Fuck me,' Howie gasps. 'Everyone okay?'

'Not really,' Paula says. 'Dave killed my granddad...'

'My mum's out there...' Danny says. 'My brother and sister...'

'I saw my cousin,' Nick says.

'My aunt,' Charlie adds.

'Marcy, you okay?' Howie asks.

'I'm blowing out my arse,' she admits, slumped against a wall. 'I think...I think I preferred Reggie boring them to death...'

'Did you...' Howie falters, realising what he was about to ask.

She shakes her head, 'I'm not from here...you already killed all of my family...either that or I did...'

'Jesus,' Maddox mutters.

'Is what it is,' Marcy says grimly.

'I saw your probation officer, Mo,' Maddox says.

'Yeah he's a cunt,' Mo says, remarkably calm with a level of fitness now nearing that of Dave. 'Saw your aunt, Mads...'

'I killed my family the first night,' Tappy gasps. 'But there's more... out there...cousins and...'

'Danny?' A female voice outside the doors and Danny's head snaps up, his eyes growing wide. 'Danny?'

'Mum?' Danny says, his voice breaking.

'Danny?'

'Fuck no,' Howie groans, closing his eyes.

'Mum...'

'Fuck me, what a thing to do,' Howie says, shaking his head as he looks to the door. 'WHAT A THING TO FUCKING DO...'

'Danny? Help me...'

'Mum,' Danny bleats, tears flowing down his cheeks. Cookey wiping his eyes from seeing his own mum in the street.

Pain in their bodies. Bites, scratches, bumps, bangs and bruises all over them. Knees and hands cut from falling over. Blood smeared over faces and arms. Clothing torn and cheeks marked with tears and the energy they built up during a day of days now dark and low.

'Come here,' Paula pulls Danny in, smothering his head with her arms to try and block the sounds.

'Charlotte?' another voice from outside, broken and hoarse but the words clear. 'Charlotte?'

'Oh Jesus,' Charlie mumbles, closing her eyes.

'Who is it?' Cookey asks.

'Aunt,' she whispers.

'Help me, Danny...'

'Charlotte?'

'Mohammed?' a male voice, deep and rich.

'You's get fucked bro, I don't even know you,' Mo shouts.

'Who is that?' Maddox asks.

'I dunno, my fam is huge, you get me...'

'Danny?' the female voice keeps going. The others calling the names of Charlotte, Mohammed then more. Paula's name added. Natasha. Most of the voices unrecognisable but the effect is clear. The psychological impact worsening by the second.

Howie looks around, trying to see in the gloom while hearing more footsteps going over the roof and more thuds as they land outside the sliding door. More bangs and thumps and he knows enough of his enemy to know that for every minute they stay here the infection will draw more hosts and they've only got the weapons they carry. Then he spots a tiny glimmer of light higher up the wall. A blacked out window covered with bars. A pipe running next to it. 'Mo, can you get up there and look out...'

'Up where?' Mo asks, peering into the gloom.

'Window, up there...see it.'

'Yeah...'

'Yes not yeah,' Dave says.

'Yes, Mr Howie...' Mo moves off, gripping the pipe to test it will hold before starting to rise hand over feet with Clarence moving underneath, ready to catch him while the thuds and bangs come and the incessant voices outside call names that drive into minds. 'Got it,' Mo calls down, reaching to grip the bars then pulling himself over. 'S'filthy up here innit...windows painted...I can't scrape it off, want me to bust it?'

'Yes mate,' Howie says.

A crack. Glass tinkling down. A pause while he looks out. 'Ah shit, yeah that ain't so good, boss,' Mo says, his voice dropping a few notches. 'S'kids innit.'

'What is?' Clarence asks.

'Kids, outside that sliding door...'

'Children?' Clarence asks.

'Yeah...I mean yes.'

'How...' Clarence clears his throat, the tension rising even more. 'How many, Mo?'

'S'loads...hundred maybe...more coming through...'

'Shit,' Clarence whispers, squeezing his eyes closed while rubbing the back of his neck. 'I can't...boss...I can't...not kids...'

'I know mate,' Howie whispers, his chest still heaving. Two ways out. Either through the people they know or through kids. He locks eyes with Reginald, both of them knowing they've misjudged the situation entirely and underestimated their opponent and the levels it will go to because there are no levels, there is nothing it will not do to win.

'You're not even joking,' Paula says bitterly, holding Danny close. Tears streaming from her eyes as she flicks her eyes to the door on hearing her name called.

'Okay,' Howie says, nodding grimly in the dark. 'Blowers...you see anyone you know out there?'

'Doesn't matter. I'm up for it,' he says, his voice hard as he pushes off the wall and starts rolling his shoulders.

'Me, Blowers and Dave...we'll go out with Meredith,' Howie says. 'Rest of you stay put...'

'Mohammed will deploy with us,' Dave says.

'Mo?' a voice outside the door. Young and female that makes Maddox grimace. 'Mo?'

'That's Jagger's sister,' Maddox says as Mo closes his eyes, still holding the bars at the window high up the wall. 'She was put in care a few months ago...wasn't on the estate when...'

'Mo?'

'Mohammed will not deploy,' Dave says, his voice as flat as ever.

'I's good, Dave,' Mo whispers, willing the coldness to come now, to be what Dave is but when he opens his eyes he looks out through the break in the glass to a yard full of children and more dropping from the walls to land crouched and ready. Heads high and their faces full of the evil within. Macabre and sinister. He swallows, blinking the tears away.

'I can fight,' Roy says, pushing to his feet as Howie and Blowers look at him. 'I never had friends,' he admits with raw honesty. 'And I haven't seen my family in years...' he trails off, nodding slowly. 'Feel a bit light-headed though...might be something serious so we should get on with it...'

A noise above them. Different to the feet running over the flat roof. A crunching sound, distinct and loud. Howie looks up, squinting to see in the gloom. A skylight painted black like the window Mo broke and in that second, he wonders who would paint a skylight black. Another crunch. Something breaking and tearing then the room fills with sudden light as the skylight is ripped away and an infected woman leans into view, staring down. 'Howie,' she says.

'Oh fuck,' Howie mumbles, drawing his pistol. 'Hey, Claire, how's it going?' he fires at his sister's best friend from school, the bullet entering her forehead framed neatly in the square of light. The back of her skull blowing out and she flies out of sight, hitting more infected gathered ready to drop and bounces back to fall through the skylight, plummeting through the air towards the big table underneath and the contents stacked high, and in that split-second it all makes sense.

The strong doors. The barred windows. The bodies outside the doors that stupidly tried to get to their product and shot each other as the world fell. The big table and the chairs round it so the slave workers could reach the huge mound of Cocaine to pack into dealer sized baggies ready to be distributed. The huge mound of Cocaine that was grown in Columbia and shipped by a cartel in hidden in containers to hit UK shores to be brought here to be made ready. Millions of pounds of it right here on this table. More than Maddox and Mo have ever seen in one place and Claire, the now dead former best-friend of Sarah, plummets through the air towards it. A big girl, heavy boned and curvy. A dead weight dropping with momentum gained and she hits hard with a dull thump the only sound made but the sight is something to see.

An explosion of pure white powder blown up and out into the air. Loads of it. Tons of it. The entire space above the table seemingly filled with a cloud of particles going up and out like a mushroom cloud detonation and as one, they all look up in stunned disbelief. Fifteen people, a dog and a horse all staring at the same thing but what goes up must come down, and it does come down.

Clouds of Cocaine falling to coat faces, settling in hair and on shoulders, covering them all in fine white powder. Jess and Meredith coated in seconds. Everyone still breathing hard from the exertion of the run and the fight. Everyone sucking Cocaine in through their mouths and noses. Mo covered entirely as he blinks and shakes his head causing more to fall on Clarence standing below that does the same as everyone else and just stares at the sight for it surely is a thing to see.

'I feel strange, Mr Howie...' every head snaps over to Dave standing perfectly still coated from head to toe in white powder and the small man lifts a hand to stare at the powder for a second then ever so gently brings his hand to his mouth and licks a tiny patch. His face as devoid as ever but then he frowns and lowers his hand. 'My mouth is numb, Mr Howie...'

Pupils dilate. Hearts increase in beats per minute. Senses come alive. Brains thrumming. Danny and Paula popping up to their feet. Tappy springing up. Charlie's eyebrows lifting.

'I feel strange, Mr Howie,' Dave says again, his speech faster. 'I feel strange...do you feel strange? I feel strange. Do you feel strange, Paula? I FEEL STRANGE. LIKE...LIKE...' Dave pauses, looking casually to the left as another infected drops through the skylight to land crouched on the table. 'LIKE I WANT TO KILL THAT MAN RIGHT NOW MR HOWIE CAN I KILL THAT MAN RIGHT NOW MR HOWIE I WANT TO DO THAT RIGHT NOW...'

'YOU SHOULD,' Howie says.

'SHOULD,' Clarence says.

'SOUNDS GREAT,' Marcy says.

'GOSH,' Reginald shouts. 'I THINK WE'VE ALL TAKEN COCAINE. INDEED. COCAINE.'

'IT'S COCAINE,' Maddox shouts.

'I THINK IT IS,' Reginal shouts as another infected drops to land crouched on the table, sending more white powder into the air.

'THERE ARE TWO NOW MR HOWIE,' Dave shouts. 'TWO. RIGHT THERE MR HOWIE. I CAN SEE THEM. THREE NOW MR HOWIE. I WANT TO KILL THEM...WITH A

KNIFE...WITH THIS KNIFE...I LOVE THIS KNIFE MR HOWIE...'

'OKAY,' Paula shouts, bouncing on the spot. 'OKAY...WHO WANTS TO DO WHAT? WE SHOULD ORGANISE...'

'SHOULD,' Clarence shouts.

'I REALLY DO THINK IT IS COCAINE,' Reginald shouts.

'IS,' Maddox shouts. 'COCAINE.'

'I THINK SO,' Reginald shouts.

'FOUR MR HOWIE. I CAN SEE THEM. I LOVE MY KNIFE. MY KNIFE IS CALLED BLINKY...'

'GOOD NAME,' Howie shouts.

'GREAT NAME,' Paula shouts.

'BEST NAME EVER,' Cookey shouts.

'THIS ONE,' Dave shouts, holding his knife out for everyone to see. 'FIVE NOW MR HOWIE. ME AND BLINKY WILL GO AND KILL THEM...'

'OKAY,' Howie shouts. 'I'LL OPEN THIS DOOR.'

'OKAY,' Clarence shouts. 'I'LL OPEN THIS OTHER DOOR.'

'I'LL PUT REGINALD ON THIS HORSE,' Maddox shouts.

'I'M KILLING THEM WITH BLINKY MR HOWIE.'

'GREAT NAME,' Paula shouts, pulling a small pad and pen from her pocket. 'I'LL MAKE A LIST...'

Two doors. One leading to a yard full of infected children. The other leading to a wide corridor jammed full of infected relatives, friends, associates and old co-workers. More in the warehouse behind them and more coming in through the doors. More on the roof above them.

A silence of a second. A second of nothingness. A second of life that goes by never to be seen again.

Then the world changes and the doors open with a white powder coated Meredith charging into the yard without giving a flying fuck as to what sizes the things are or if they look like kids or not and a white powder coated Jess and a screaming Reginald on her back going into the corridor without giving a fuck as to who is related to who and what connections they may have once had in life.

Everyone else charges out behind them. Thrumming and strumming with wild energy. Hearts racing. Pupils the size of plates. Dave dancing on the Cocaine table killing them as they fall from the skylight. Everyone else going out through whatever door is closest to kill whoever is closest.

Charlie kills her aunt. Cookey helps her. The two screaming as they do it. Nick and Tappy killing their cousins. Mo downing his probation officer. Maddox killing Jagger's sister then spotting Kieron through the press of bodies and rushes into him, cutting his throat from behind as Danny stabs his huge gut.

From the corridor, through the Cocaine room to the yard on the other side. A brutal, bloody, vicious, sordid battle and when those first few minutes of energy, given freely by the drug ingested into their systems, starts to wane and so once again the horror of what they do comes to the fore but now there is no running and there is no falling back. So they fight and kill. Stabbing those they once knew. Killing and hacking apart. Swinging axes while Jess runs back and forth, kicking and battering them down while Reginald clings to her back.

The press comes too much, forcing them back into the room where the air is filled with white powder that is inhaled, giving fresh wild, painful bursts of energy but what it does to them it does double to Dave who moves with a blur. From one side of the room to the other. Literally running back and forth slicing tendons to make a bed of writhing, snarling infected to run over. Then he does it again for fun before running the length of the corridor, his arms flashing left and right with arcs of blood spraying out like synchronised fountains behind him. Into the warehouse and he runs up and down, Stabbing and slicing. Vaulting this way and that. Dancing and spinning. Music in his mind. Blinky in his hand. Stab left. Stab right. Spin between two. Stop. Smile. Go back and kill those two. Run on and do it again back through the warehouse and back through the corridor to the Cocaine room to make add another layer to his carpet of bodies.

Everyone else starts to wane. Burnt out and finding it harder and harder to keep going. The yard now cleared and Paula falls out first, staggering to drop and heave for air. Marcy right behind her. Mo still at her side pushing her and Paula on and away to a corner. Pressing rifles into their hands before going back in to guide Charlie and Cookey out with Nick, Tappy and Maddox crawling out behind them. The yard becomes the safe zone. The corner their gained ground where they grip rifles and pistols and heave and gasp for air, bleeding freely. Clarence comes out, a near unconscious Danny over one shoulder and he slumps down with Roy and the others. A noise inside. A heavy sound and Jess charges out into the yard to get to Charlie. Reginald still on her back. Only Howie, Blowers, Dave and Meredith remain inside. The sounds of fighting intense and hard.

Clarence rises, swaying on his feet but summoning energy from god knows where to go back in and fight. Cookey and Nick using each other to heave up behind him as Howie and Blowers fall arm in arm from the door, sprawling and staggering, tripping and slipping to crawl hand over foot to the others.

'Dave's still in,' Clarence says, his voice barely a whisper.

'Fine...he's...he's fine...' Howie gasps.

Clarence stares down, nods once and sags to sit with the others to stare at the door and the seconds go by that become minutes and still the sounds of battle come from inside until Dave pops out, leaping to land deftly with a quick look at everyone gathered in the corner. The first time they've ever seen him covered in blood and gore with a huge smile showing that animates his entire being.

'I'VE GOT BLINKY,' he yells, showing them his knife. A bark from inside and Dave turns quickly, running back in and the seconds go by that become minutes but in Dave they trust.

'HAHAHAHAHA...' a laugh heard, Dave's voice but the why or what for is not known and still it goes on. A bark. A thud and Meredith runs backwards from the door, an infected woman gripped in her jaws that she rags side to side before releasing and turning to look at her back before running back in and the seconds go by that become minutes but in Dave and Meredith they trust.

Then it grows quieter and the single acts of battle are heard. The bite and snarl from Meredith. The thud of bodies falling. The spray of liquid against a wall. A grunt here. A howl and a hiss then silence, and that silence extends and goes on while they stare at the rolled back sliding door and wait and listen and watch as Dave and Meredith finally walk out. The two side by side and dripping with blood from every inch of their bodies. The dog panting. Dave's mouth open so he can breathe just a little bit harder. His knife still clutched in his hand. His knife called Blinky that he lifts to motion at the door he just came from.

'They're all dead now, Mr Howie,' he says.

'Okay, Dave,' Howie croaks. 'Thanks for that.'

Dave nods, wiping an arm across his forehead. 'Can I sit down, Mr Howie?'

'S'fine, Dave.'

'I'll sit down here, Mr Howie.'

'Okay, Dave.'

'I feel a bit strange, Mr Howie.'

'It's the Cocaine, Dave...Dave?' he leans a little to look round Clarence, frowning at seeing Dave slumped against a wall fast asleep with Meredith lying flat at his side and above them the rain falls from a sky growing darker as the night comes towards them and in the north the boy bursts into tears, stamping his feet in the hallway of the isolated country house.

'Whoa, what's all that about?' Cassie asks, scooping him up into her arms. 'Shush, it's okay...'

'They deaded and Dave made all their brains come out and and the doggy bited them...'

'Shush,' Cassie says soothingly, carrying him back to the kitchen to sit down at the table, holding him close as Gregori pops his head in the back door, his face sweating from exercise. 'He's fine,' Cassie says, 'just tired, you carry on...I'll do dinner in a minute,' she waits for Gregori to go back out and rocks slowly side to side, soothing and quietening the child. 'Where are they?'

A pause and she doesn't need to look to know the thing inside the boy has come forward. 'They are in a yard...'

'Take me there,' she says quietly, holding the boy's head near her mouth, still rocking him slowly.

In the south, in the yard at the back of the warehouse used for Cocaine storage and distribution, Howie breathes hard, grimacing at the dull ache in his head and the awful feeling of fatigue no doubt brought on by the Cocaine and the shock of what they just did. Everyone else either slumped against the wall or each other or lying flat out with chests heaving.

'Boobs,' Danny mumbles, images flashing through his drugged mind.

'We need to go,' Howie says, looking to the back of the yard and the high gates topped with coils of razor wire that rattle and shake for a few seconds. 'Fuck it...' he grabs his rifle, easing his bag off to open the flap and find a fresh magazine as the others stir and start doing the same. Clunks and clicks ringing out as they get loaded and make ready while the rattle and shake at the gates comes harder. 'I can't even stand,' Howie says weakly, lifting his rifle up. 'Is Dave still asleep?'

'Yeah,' Nick whispers, sliding the bolt back on his rifle.

One by one, those awake and able lift rifles to aim while sitting in the rain surrounded by bodies and from the gates comes a snap and a wrench as the lock is snapped. They swing out slowly, giving a gradually increasing view to an Indian man standing in front of a big horde. All of them silent and staring. All of them sinister in appearance and Cassie holds the boy in her arms, his head nestled into her shoulder, her mouth close to his ear, her eyes fixed and staring ahead. Music playing on the stereo, not too loud but enough to prevent Gregori hearing her whispers. She thinks of her family, of her life before now, and she thinks of Gregori and the things he was trained and brainwashed to do. She thinks of many things while whispering softly. 'Are they there?' the boy nods. 'Good, repeat what I say...humans do not deserve this world anymore...'

'Humans do not deserve this world anymore,' the Indian male standing in front of the horde speaks out. A kind face on a gentle man who always had a smile ready to brighten the days of others. Now with red eyes and a soft tone.

'And you do?' Reginald asks, lifting his head from Jess's mane while still clinging to her back.

'And you do?' the boy says in Cassie's arms.

'Yes,' Cassie whispers.

'Yes,' the Indian male says.

'Tell me why,' Reginald says.

'Tell me why,' the boy relays.

'Don't tell me what to do you jumped up little cunt,' Cassie whispers, the Indian man says from the edge of the yard. 'You've been dealing with a child up till now but I'm not a kid...'

'Who am I speaking to?' Reginald asks.

'Who am I speaking to?' the boy whispers.

'You're talking to me you patronising twat and I know exactly who you are...all of you. What are you trying to prove? It's done. It's over...'

'Dear God, how do I get off this thing?' Reginald yelps as he slides off Jess to stagger a few steps before leaning on his cane and trying to show some semblance of dignity. 'It is far from over...'

'What is wrong with you? You want to put the world back to what it was? Why?'

'Because it was not yours to take,' Reginald says simply.

Cassie closes her eyes, lifting the boy higher to hold closer, her voice low but urgent. 'I used to walk past homeless people in the street and hope to God they wouldn't look at me or ask for change. I'd tut when charity adverts came on the television asking for money for whatever shit thing happened in whatever shit part of the world because none of us fucking cared and those that did were too few and labelled as hippy twats or left-wing idiots...'

'Very trite,' Reginald cuts in.

'Is that Reginald?' the Indian man asks.

'Yes,' the boy says, the infection says, the Indian man says.

'Reginald, shut up and listen,' the Indian man continues, Cassie continues. 'Our country was something like the sixth biggest economy in the world, but we had people dying in corridors in hospitals or lying in ambulances because we couldn't afford to deal with them, while we spent billions on bombs and nuclear weapons and war and fighting and we lied to make it okay to do that. My dad was a government minister, but he fucked rent-boys and used Cocaine and my own mother worried more about her image than anything else and although I can't see you right now I can picture you exhausted and filthy but feeling righteous and smug and I don't know why because I bet your lives were as shit and empty as mine. We all felt it. It was broken and wrong. How did Blinky die? Seriously, I'm asking because I don't know. We didn't kill her which means something else happened and you're all covered in cuts and bruises, so someone hurt you...but it wasn't us and you're fighting for *them*? For people that do that to you?' she pauses to draw air and flutters her eyes open, smiling across to Gregori walking in to fill a cup of water from the sink as everyone in the yard simply stares at the Indian man.

Cassie lifts the boy closer, dropping her voice so Gregori can't hear. 'I'm sorry you've lost everyone. I really am...we all have but you know what? I've never been happier than I am right now. Smell the air, Howie. How clean is it now? Have you seen the animals in the fields? They're all fine. It's only us that suffered, and we deserved it so if you think for one second I will let you take this from me, or harm this boy I will send every single host I have against you and I will tear down every single fucking building to find you. Do not push me, Howie...let it go. Go and grow old. I've seen pictures of Marcy, she's so beautiful it made me feel sick...what the fuck is wrong with you? Go and make babies with her. I've seen pictures of all of you. You're good people, decent people. I get that...be proud of what you've done and making a stand but let it end now, Howie. Let your people live. Give them life and don't keep bringing them against me because you will not win. You can't win. We're never going back to what it was...'

Another pause. A chance to breathe and kiss the boy's head. A rush of emotion inside Cassie. A rush of love. 'I did this today to show you how much power this thing has...sending your families against you was evil but I wanted your attention so listen to me because this is the only time I will ever give you this chance. If you go now I won't come after you...I won't go for Lilly in the fort either.'

Silence in the yard. Stunned and heavy. Reginald thinking hard, thinking fast. Words hitting home not just for what was said but the soft tone of the Indian man saying them. The imploring manner of him but a femininity to the words too. A woman speaking through him but not the infection. The infection is inside the boy. The tantrums. The lack of understanding. The crass loops. A thing of vast power inside a child and now the mother is stepping in and there is nothing more dangerous than a mother protecting her young.

'The people left,' Howie asks, his voice a hoarse croak, his mouth so dry, his throat so parched. 'What about them?'

'Is that Howie?' Cassie asks, the Indian man asks himself.

'Yes, Casseee,' the boy says, the infection says, the Indian man says.

'If I leave them it will go back to how it was,' Cassie says. 'Humans are too vain to do otherwise. We'll always seek to be the apex predators so no. My offer is for you, those in the fort now and those that can get to the fort in the next day or so.'

Silence again. Everyone listening. Everyone thinking.

'Take the offer, Howie. I'll give you that entire area. Grow crops, do what you want. I'm offering you peace and long lives...urgh, get off you're all sweaty. Go and have a shower, don't turn the music up, yes I know you like this song. The boy's a bit sleepy...Howie, are you still there?'

'Yeah,' Howie says, frowning at the fucked up weird conversation the Indian man just had with himself.

'Don't pick a fight with me, Howie. I can harness and organise what this is, and if you have any doubt...I am about three hundred miles north from you sitting in the kitchen of a bumfucknowhere little isolated house talking to you through a boy before I make dinner...'

They listen with hearts sinking. With energy drained and exhaustion sapping at their limbs making their rifles heavy to hold.

'You've got a day to think about it...' Cassie says, still cuddling the boy.

A flash of colour against the night sky. The fluttering of an Adonis Blue butterfly flying slowly over the head of the Indian man. The wings so vibrant, so pure and beautiful. So clean against the gore and death and Howie smiles with a slow grin forming as he leans forward and slowly heaves to his feet, raising his right hand as he sways on the spot. 'That's quite cool,' he croaks, 'but I've got a magic invisible fuckstick...'

'A what?' Cassie asks.

'A what?' the Indian man asks as the roar comes clear and loud. The roar of a heavy diesel engine that Howie now knows so well and the Saxon powers in from the right, slamming the Indian man down and sending the horde scattering. A screech of tyres. A door opening and a general-purpose machine gun fills the air with sustained firing while Howie waves his magic invisible fuckstick and wonders who the hell is driving his Saxon and shooting his guns. Dave stirs, opening an eye. Meredith lifts her head. Danny mumbles boobs and everyone waits for the shooting to stop as an unshaven figure wearing torn and filthy army clothes taken from the stores in Salisbury walks slowly into the yard with a smile growing and a GPMP braced in his hip.

'Mr Howie, Dave' he says politely, dipping his head. 'Fucksticks,' he adds with a grin to the lads, flicking a middle finger up.

'Alan Booker,' Dave says, peering from one eye. 'Tuck your shirt in and fall in with Corporal Blowers unit...Mr Howie, Corporal Blowers has a big team now. He should be a sergeant...'

'Eh?' Blowers croaks.

'Hi, Booker,' Cookey says.

'Booker,' Nick says, waving a tired hand.

'I don't want to be a sergeant, Dave.'

'He's gone back to sleep,' Howie says, staring at a snoring Dave.

'We'll need another bag,' Paula says, lifting a hand. 'Hi, I'm Paula...'

CHAPTER TWENTY-TWO

Day One.

'I need to stretch my legs dear, would you excuse me for a few minutes.'

Making his way down the aisle George nods genially at the air stewardess, apologising for blocking her route as she pushes the heavy drinks trolley along and pauses to look out of the thick window in the door. An older man of medium build with short hair now more grey than dark. A tidy moustache on his upper lip, neatly trimmed and giving him an air of cultured refinement. A long sleeve cream shirt tucked into his beige casual trousers and he looks every part the tourist.

He moves forward again to the locked door to the cockpit. Checking around for an intercom. Nothing apparent. It must be an older model not yet fitted with a two-way speaker system.

He knocks on the door, two raps then three, two more, one, then three. The raps quick and successive, the pauses brief but noticeable.

'Can we help you?' A voice calls through the door.

'Code alpha two six three zero one zero whiskey one zero,' George speaks quickly, his tone although perfectly polite is clipped and short.

Inside the cabin the co-pilot turns to the captain, 'it's an older chap, he's given the right code though.'

'You sure?' The captain twists round to stare at his colleague. The co-pilot nods firmly, checking the daily code issued in the security book, 'definitely, spot on.'

'Best let him in then,' the captain remarks with a worried look.

The co-pilot checks the spyhole again, getting a full view of the smart looking older man. He unfastens the locks and swings the door open.

George smiles at the man and steps in, waiting politely as the door is closed behind him. 'Captain,' he nods at the seated man, 'co-pilot I presume?' He asks the standing man.

'Er yes, can we help?' the captain asks, staring at the man with interest.

'I do beg your forgiveness for the intrusion but you see there is some concern with one of your passengers.'

'Oh really?' The startled captain asks.

'Yes afraid so,' George says in his clipped tone with a firm nod, 'chap in business class, row H, seat number one. Saw him arrive at the airport, no luggage you see, roused the old suspicions. Followed him about a bit, looked nervous, somewhat furtive and worried, white chap, medium height and nothing remarkable about him except he has a very strong tan which suggests he has had a very recent spell somewhere rather hot I would say. In the airport, he neither spoke to anyone nor engaged any other persons. Watched him board and take a seat ahead of me, no hand luggage either which I thought was odd. After all, we are heading to a Greek holiday resort. But this chap, well he certainly ain't Greek,' George pauses, smiling at the two men and making sure they're keeping up, they both nod, listening intently, 'I had an opportunity to speak to him, just in passing you know, got an English accent. Definitely home counties, possibly Surrey. But the thing is,' George pauses to take a breath, 'he's muttering constantly, and I caught a few words here and there, what he's saying is a prayer given before death.'

'Terrorist?' The captain asks immediately, his hand already reaching to activate the radio system. Neither of them asks who this man in front of them is. They don't need to. The international security access code used to gain entry to any secured in-flight cabin means he is on the list. And if he is on the list then that is good enough.

'Afraid he may well be,' George replies in an almost apologetic tone. 'Now I saw this particular fellow pass through the security procedures, he had no metallic objects and his shoes were removed and checked. So whatever he is carrying is about his person. In this hot weather and wearing only a t-shirt, I would suggest they are strapped to his legs.'

'Right,' the captain says. 'We could be looking at a drugs mule, in which case nothing for us to worry about and we'll alert the authorities on arrival...but I'm guessing your concern is such that you consider him to be a direct threat to the security of the aircraft.'

'Well done that man,' George says brightly, 'didn't want to outright say the B word but most likely yes.'

'A bomb?' the co-pilot asks in shock.

'That's the fellow,' George says, tutting darkly. 'Awful business eh?'

'And er...what do you suggest?' The captain asks, deferring to the man's obvious knowledge.

'Ah yes, well I have just the thing here,' George removes a small pill case from his pocket and flips the lid to reveal a few capsules within the recess, 'get one of your stewards to pop this into his drink and he'll be out in no time at all, won't feel a thing.' George clicks his fingers to emphasise the point.

'Really, wow,' the co-pilot takes the tiny capsule in his hand, staring down at it.

'Not the capsule you understand, just break the two ends and put the contents into whatever beverage he takes, I would suggest you offer a free drink to everyone in that section to be sure he takes it, say it's your birthday or something and it's with special compliments. Not alcohol though, he hasn't touched a drop of the hard stuff since we've taken off.'

'Right,' the captain stares at the pill held by the co-pilot, 'right... yes...well...er...we'll see to that straight away.'

'Well done chaps,' George smiles and turns for the door.

'Er...who are you?' The captain asks.

'My name is George, old chap,' George turns and gives a tidy smile, 'and I was never here.' He nods, opens the door and walks out, closing the cabin door securely behind him.

'Feeling better, Georgie?'

'Ah yes much better thank you, Marion, had a walk about and stretched the old legs,' George says with a loving smile.

'Well now you've retired you'll have plenty of time to have some decent walks won't you, George?'

'Yes, dear.'

'I know you're still doing the odd day here and there but officially speaking you've retired so you should keep busy. You remember Doreen and Arthur? Well, Arthur retired just last year and put on over a stone in weight, really doesn't suit him. Some men can carry a little extra padding, George, but not Arthur.'

'No, dear,' George replies pleasantly.

'What will that office do without you I do not know,' Marion continues, both reading and talking at the same time. A trait that George had long since become accustomed to, 'you remember Evie and Ken? Well, I saw Evie the other day at the WRVS, she asked after you. I said you were retiring, she asked *what will the office do* without you after thirty years. I told her, I said Her Majesties Treasury Office for Fiscal Studies will just have to get by. Of course, I did explain that you'd be going back for the odd day here and there. You know what she asked me, Georgie?'

'No, dear.'

'She asked if you ever got bored working in the same department for thirty years! I said to her that it was a sign of the generation gap when people ask if you get bored at your job. I said to her, I said working in the offices for the countries fiscal studies is not something you get bored with.'

'Sorry to disturb you,' the stewardess leans in with a bright smile, 'compliments of the captain, it's his birthday today and we are giving every passenger a free drink. What can we get for you?'

'Ooh, you hear that, George, how nice, must be a very nice man.'

'Yes, dear, probably a very nice man, I'll have a scotch please.'

'Are you sure that's wise, George, you know how sleepy you get after a scotch and we can't be that far out now.'

'Yes dear, change that please, I'll have a tonic water.'

'And a Pimms for me please, do they have Pimms, George?'

'Do you have Pimms?'

'Yes, we have Pimms.'

'They have Pimms, dear.'

'Wonderful, I'll have a Pimms please.

'A Pimms please.'

The stewardess smiles, handing the drinks over before moving down. George watches with mild interest as they move from row to row. The chap in row H, seat number one smiles nervously at the stewardess and orders a drink. The stewardess drops down to mooch inside the trolley. George watches as she apologises for the delay, then pours a can of coke into a plastic glass. She hands the drink over, smiles and moves on.

George sips at his tonic water. Watching the man stare round to make sure everyone else has a drink. He glances back at George who smiles amiably, raising his own glass. The man smiles and turns away, just seeing an old man with a tidy moustache.

The man takes regular sips at the coke and within five minutes is passed out snoring loudly, much to the annoyance of the passenger seated next to him.

'I'm still worried about that negative review on Trip Advisor, George,' Marion says as she flicks through a magazine.

'Oh I shouldn't worry dear,' George says, resting his head against the back of seat.

'Two weeks, George, we're there for two weeks and if the food is repetitious I shall be complaining. Really, you do not expect repetitious food at a five-star all-inclusive resort.'

'No, dear,' George smiles at his wife, settling back to listen to the soothing tones of her voice as the plane glides across the sky.

'Hello and welcome to the Gordios Boutique Hotel, may I take your bags?' A smartly dressed porter walks from the lobby, smiling broadly, 'please go inside, it is much cooler and you will find a chilled glass of champagne waiting for you at the reception desk.'

'Did you hear that, George, a chilled glass of champagne, I do like champagne,' Marion comments as walks through the door held open by George, 'but it always goes straight to my head, bit like scotch and you dear, Georgie, makes me sleepy.'

'I know dear, but a nice sleep before the evening may be in order after the flight.'

'Oh but it was a very pleasant flight, I say, George, did you see that chap fast asleep as we got off? He didn't wake up once, not even when that woman dropped her hand luggage on his head.'

'No can't say as I noticed dear.'

'Really, George, it's a good job one of us is observant.'

'Yes, dear.'

'Welcome,' the receptionist beams. 'Are you booking in?'

George nods genially as Marion talks to the recaptioning while he counts the exits and in the lift, he happily listens to his wife talking non-stop. Content to be in her company, relaxed at the sound of her voice, at the soft incessant tones. Happy to now be spending time together but the end comes. A year. Maybe less before the contagion is released, unless they can find it first of course.

He waits patiently by the door of the hotel room. One hand in his pocket, the other checking the lock on the door. Waiting until the inspection has been thoroughly completed.

'Good pillows, the skirting boards are clean; you can always tell how thorough someone is at cleaning by checking the skirting boards, George.'

'Does it pass your inspection, dear?'

'Don't be sarcastic, Georgie, it doesn't suit you.'

'Sorry dear.'

'I think that champagne has done the trick, I feel ready for a nap, are you going to take a nap, George.'

'No dear, you carry on, I think I shall have a walk and see what's what.'

'Good afternoon, Sir, what I can get for you?' The barman smiles in greeting, an older chap, heavy set with powerful shoulders but also a large stomach. A smoker too judging by the stained teeth and slight wheeze to his voice.

'I say could I trouble you for a coffee?'

'A coffee, Sir, of course, Sir, please take a seat and I bring to you.'

George chooses a table so he can see the whole of the gardens and the various entrances to them.

Coffee poured and he takes his mobile phone from his pocket. The phone he claimed was far too technical and modern to understand. With deft fingers, he keys in a long number and presses the phone to his ear.

'*Hello, Treasury Department, Office of Fiscal Studies, Henry speaking how may I help you.*'

'Henry, it's George.'

'*George, you old devil! How's the sunshine?*'

'Very nice, Henry, very warm indeed.'

'*Oh I am pleased, George, flight okay was it?*'

'Funniest thing actually, Henry, I saw old Tinker Thompson on the plane, haven't seen him in years. Wouldn't say if he was working in the middle east or South America but I did notice he still has that awful habit of dozing off.'

'Dozed off, did he? I'll certainly pass on that you've seen him, the chaps in the office will be delighted!'

'Oh you do that, Henry, they'll remember him alright, office okay is it?'

'All good. Frank is lying in a bush looking for Uglius Albanius Bastardius. You enjoy the sunshine and love to Marion.'

'Will do, Henry, bye, for now, old chap.'

'Honestly, Georgie, you and that razor,' Marion tuts as she walks into the bathroom noticing George holding the leather and canvas strip as he runs the blade of his cutthroat razor up and down with long practised hands.

'I like it, dear.'

'Paula emailed me the other day, asking if you still used it, said she'd seen a lovely electric shaver set on Amazon and wanted to know if she should get it for your birthday.'

'Paula?'

'Paula, your niece George.'

'Oh yes, Paula, the accountant.'

'Yes, George,' Marion sighs as she attacks her hair with a brush.

'Nice girl, what's she up to these days?'

'Still an accountant, George,' Marion says patiently, 'Are you going to be long, George? I want to go down for dinner...I do hope the food isn't repetitious.'

'Almost there, dear.'

'Are you wearing *that* shirt, George?'

'That's why I'm putting it on dear.'

'Don't be sarcastic, George, it doesn't suit you.'

'Sorry, dear.'

'The food was nice wasn't it, George?'

'Not repetitious then?'

'How can it be repetitious on the first day? Did you like the salad I made for you?'

'You didn't make it dear, you picked it.'

'Don't be flippant, George, it doesn't suit you.'

'Sorry, dear, the salad was lovely.'

'This veranda is very grand, I like the bamboo furniture and oh look, George, they're drawing the awning back, isn't that nice?'

'Very nice, dear.'

'Are you enjoying your beer, George?'

'It's very nice, dear.'

'I can't believe how late it is, can you believe how late it is, George?'

'It's two hours ahead here, dear.'

'Even so, it's still very late. It's very warm still isn't it, George? Do you remember Julia and Ken? They came to this Island and said they had a wonderful time. Didn't stay at this resort though, I think they were in a four star half board further down the coast. Julia was brown as a berry, but then she always did tan very well. What's that? Is that your phone ringing George?'

'It is, dear.'

'Who on earth is calling you at this hour?'

'I don't know, dear, I haven't answered it yet.'

'Don't be sarcastic, George, it doesn't suit you.'

'Sorry, dear, excuse me for a moment.'

'Don't be too long, George, we're meant to be on holiday and I'm sure Her Majesty's Treasury Department, Office of Fiscal Studies can cope without you for a few days.'

George presses the answer button as he walks into the bar.

'*George? Are you there, George?*'

'Henry, what a pleasant surprise.'

'*George, I don't have much time,*' an urgent voice speaking fast. '*It's happening now. It's here...*'

George swallows, closing his eyes tight for a second. 'It's too soon, Henry...'

'I'm so sorry, George.'

'How far is the spread?'

'It's here. London has fallen. The police are gone... Greece is already hit. You might have extra time being on an Island but it will get to you.'

'Understood, Henry.'

'We're going to be bugging out very soon. The phones are starting to go down.'

'Got it,' George listens intently.

'Go for the north harbour, George. Find a vessel and cross to the mainland. Find a vehicle and get back here. We'll RV at foxtrot.'

'Understood, team?'

'Frank's heading south. He's got Carmen with him. They'll go for Howard first.'

'Understood.'

'Damn it, George, I am sorry. On your holiday too of all things.'

'Stay calm, Henry. The god-botherer is south too.'

'We haven't heard from him in years, George.'

'He'll surface,' George says with a sigh.

A pause on the phone. A breath taken. *'You almost made it to retirement with telling Marion, George...'*

George snorts a dry, humourless laugh. 'Almost.'

'Always said you'd never do it, you owe me that drink now, George. God speed.'

'You too, Henry, god speed.'

The call ends. George slips the phone into his pocket and stands still. Marion visible through the window, already chatting away to another English couple. Her face looks warm and soft, her smile flashing as she absorbs herself in gossip.

Almost made it. Almost made thirty years without her ever finding out. He strides through to reception, heading directly towards the desk and the tired looking woman seated behind it.

'I need a map of the Island,' George asks in flawless Greek. The receptionist blinks, confused at the sight of the genial man who she booked in several hours ago now speaking her language.

'Of course, Sir, they sell them in the gift shop but that is now closed.'

'Do you have one behind the desk?'

'Yes, Sir but that is our only one...'

'Fifty Euros, I need that map.'

'Yes, Sir, is everything okay?'

'Fine thank you.' Walking off with the map book, leaving the bemused receptionist clutching a fifty euro note he heads away from the bar to a quiet corner. Opening the map he quickly finds the location of the hotel and traces a route to the north. Then a secondary route as a fall-back.

He heads across the lobby floor to the stairs, taking them two at a time he finds his way to their room and emerges three minutes later in walking clothes with a change of attire for Marion over his arms.

'George, you've been gone for ages!' Marion smiles, 'and you've got changed, and why on earth have you got my clothes?'

'I really need to speak with you a minute.'

Something in his tone catches Marion's eye, a deeper voice rarely heard from him. She gets up from the chair, smiling at the new friends before following George into the bar.

'George, what has got into you?'

'No time to explain, Marion, take these and get changed, there's a toilet there, use that and be quick.'

'George...'

'Now, Marion,' his voice carries a force never heard before. He gently pushes his wife through the door, making a point of closing it behind her, cutting her off in mid-sentence.

Hand in pocket he fingers the specially made razor. All the men in the department use them, standard issue and an innocuous enough item to have about the house without drawing attention.

His eyes dart to the lobby at the sound of the ear piercing scream. Every head on the veranda snaps that way, the barman already running.

George stands his ground, barely a flicker of emotion on his face as the screams get louder. More voices join in, sounds of fighting, of bodies hitting the hard marble floor. Out of sight around the corner but the noises tell him everything that's going on.

'Well, Georgie, you'd better have a damn good reason for this,' Marion exclaims as she walks out of the toilet carrying her evening dress.

'You look wonderful, dear,' George pecks her on the cheek, 'now we've got to move fast and I need you to stay with me at all times, can you do that?'

'Of course, George, but really, I have no idea what is going on and what is all that noise? Has the cabaret started?'

'No, dear...'

Out through the bar and out onto the veranda, crossing the grounds George locates a side path running from the beach to the front of the buildings. Soft orange lights illuminate the path as they move swiftly along. George scanning the area, his head moving left, right, ahead and listening intently.

'George, is this a planned moonlit walk? That sounds awfully romantic, George but on our first night?'

'No, dear, something bad has happened, I will explain everything to you but not right now my love, I really need to listen so we have to be quiet.'

Keeping to the far edge of the paved walkway he starts towards the town. In truth he is more than capable of holding a conversation while continuing to listen and asking Marion to stay quiet was simply to buy time, putting off the inevitable, not knowing where to start.

George had been meaning to tell Marion for years but somehow, it just never seemed the right time.

Pulling his phone from his pocket he checks the screen, noticing the signal bar is now empty. Nodding in grim understanding he pushes on.

'Is that someone running, George? He looks drunk, look at him staggering about, should be ashamed of himself. Oh dear, I think he's seen us, yes...yes he has seen us. Is he alright, looks like he's bleeding...

oh dear, George, he's been fighting, look...he's got blood all around his mouth. Please don't come any closer young man we're not interested in your drunken antics, go to the hotel lobby if you need assistance,' Marion shouts at the man staggering towards them.

The man stares fixed at George and Marion, fresh blood pouring down his chin, a large wound evident on his neck and as he comes into the light George notices the red bloodshot eyes.

Having gauged the speed and manner of movement, George ascertains the point of impact and steps forward, drawing the cutthroat razor from his pocket, flicking the blade open at the last second to gently brush the steel across the jugular as he shoulder barges the figure away, causing the spray of blood to spurt onto the road and not at Marion who he grabs and pulls on as the body slumps behind them with a gargled thud.

'George?' Marion asks after a few minutes of brisk walking.

'Yes, dear.'

'Did you kill that man?'

'Yes, dear.'

She lapses into another silence as George thinks furiously on how to begin explaining that their whole lives have been based on a lie.

The road takes them directly into the town. Tourists seated on the tables outside the cafes and restaurants, waiters moving amongst them. Shopkeepers lounging in comfy chairs outside their premises, couples and families moving slowly through.

Still holding Marion's hand he walks onto the pavement, moving through the crowds, examining and scanning every person that passes by. Looking for signs of injury or blood. His hand holds the razor in his pocket, ready to be drawn in an instant while looking for a viable mode of transport he can take quickly and quietly.

'Didn't I get you that razor, George?' Marion asks in a far-away voice.

'No dear, it was a gift from work.'

'The treasury department gave you a razor?'

There it is. The opening question that gives him an opportunity to explain but still he can't bring himself to start, knowing the knock-on effect will be awful. Was there a way through this without telling her? Not after cutting a chap's throat open with a straight blade razor there wasn't. And why isn't she asking questions?

At the centre crossroads, he grips Marion's wrist and steps back, hearing the loud diesel engine before the minibus comes into sight. Going faster than it should be. The engine stuck in a low gear but still accelerating. Coming from the left George snaps his head to see as the vehicle careers past, swerving across the width of the road. A glimpse of the driver holding the steering wheel one-handed while he fights the man biting into his shoulder.

An old Greek woman crossing the road shunted high into the air, spinning as her body is sent through the plate glass window of a souvenir shop. Screams sound out. The minibus clings to the road for a second before swerving a hard left. The sudden action tips the vehicle over; slamming onto its side it scores along the ground sending plumes of sparks from the metal frame grating on the concrete before hitting the low feeble railing of a café, ripping the fixtures from the ground as it powers into the packed chairs and tables. Bodies flattened, crushed, mown down and more sent spinning off as the back end of the vehicle slides round.

Deafening noise of metal against metal, metal against concrete, glass smashing, women screaming, men yelling, children crying. The momentum carries the minibus straight through one seating area and into the adjoining café, impacting on the front of the building.

The vehicle slams into the outside grill, killing the Greek chef instantly. The gas bottles break the seal from the pipes feeding the grill. High-pressure gas escapes the nozzle. The sparks from the scraping metal ignite the gas, a jet of flame being forced from the gas bottle. Within a second the flames get inside the large metal canister. The first bottle explodes. A giant grenade that sends burning fragments of sharp metal spinning for hundreds of feet in every direction.

Whole swathes of crowds are cut to ribbons. Heads torn apart, limbs amputated, guts ripped open as the deadly metal slices through them.

George's heart rate only increases fractionally as he takes everything in. His eyes narrow as he focuses on the people running from the minibus, at the bite wounds on their necks, shoulders, faces and arms.

They start collapsing, clutching their stomachs. George holds Marion still, keeping to the security of the building line as he lets it play out for a minute. Watching, scanning, learning, assessing.

The first one that dropped holding his stomach starts twitching, convulsions that make the limbs lash out. After a few seconds, the twitches cease and the man goes limp and dead before sitting and rising awkwardly to his feet without the use of his arms to lever himself up.

The man surges into the press of bodies and bites down on the neck of a young woman. She screams, turning to beat the thing off her. Someone grabs the biter and pushes him away. He reels, staggers and collides with another woman, instantly biting her face.

She goes down with the thing on top of her. More people rush in, dragging him away. He bites them too, nipping and gnashing at fingers, hands and arms, passing the deadly infection with every bite.

A taxi left at the side of the road. The driver running to help the injured. The engine still running.

'Come on,' George tugs Marion by the hand, leading his wife across the road as a body lunges at them, lips pulled back, teeth bared. George steps into the body, spinning it round to force the things head into the solid metal end of the taxi. Gripping the skull he expertly wrenches the head, breaking the neck.

Moving like in a dream, Marion is ushered round to the passenger side and gently pushed into the seat. George pulls the seat belt round his wife and fastens it in place before closing the door.

Into the driver's side and he turns the key, easing the vehicle forward to the end of the road.

'We need to go back through the town, Marion, it's the only road out of here.'

'Okay, George,' she whispers. He glances at his wife, at the set expression on her face.

George pushes the automatic transmission into drive and applies pressure to the accelerator, increasing the push down as the vehicle sweeps up the main road. Swerving expertly round the dead bodies and flaming debris to get away with the quaint town erupting in fire and carnage behind them.

'You owe Henry that drink now,' she finally breaks the silence as they drive through the darkened streets. He snaps his head over, staring for a second. 'Watch the road, Georgie,' she reaches her hand out to stroke the back of his neck.

'What?' George stammers, his heart-rate only now spiking, his face only now showing a look of shock.

'Bless you, George. Did you know you were about to go down in the departments history books as the only one never to have told his wife?'

'Marion...I...'

'Oh, Georgie, you should see your face, I wish I could take a picture, Frank and Howard would love it and I know Carmen would be in fits!'

'Marion...'

'You were recruited in the seventies with Frank, Howard and Henry, at the height of the cold war. There were too many risks associated with rogue and double agents so once we were engaged I was approached and spoken to. Do you remember that, George? When I went away for a few days before our wedding?'

'To see your great aunt in Norfolk,' George sputters.

'No, George, I was being vetted and trained. All the wives did it. We had to because the department knew that no secret such as that could pass between a husband and wife, so they had to be sure we knew what we were getting ourselves into, and obviously to keep an eye on you men at the same time.'

'You knew?'

'The whole time,' Marion smiles.

'And...you're not cross?'

She laughs, a soft pleasant sound that gives a sudden heartwarming feeling to George, 'Of course not, George, it was a great subject between all of us, all those dinner parties and functions, all that pretence, it was exciting.'

'You mean Henry knew that you knew? His wife knew? Frank knew? What about Howard?'

'Yes, Georgie, we all knew.'

'Bastards,' George mutters at his friends. They had joined together, conducted missions together, killed and almost died together and the whole time they knew that Marion was aware.

'Let me explain,' she massages the back of his neck with one hand stretched over the back of his seat, 'we were all given pre-op briefings with a very rough outline of what you were going to do. We were never told locations or the intimate details, just the basics so we could assess your mental state prior to the mission, we were then given a post-op briefing which updated us as to how the mission went, so we could handle the fall-out, the mental stress and as Post Traumatic Stress Disorder became more widely known we were also trained to recognise the symptoms and how to bring you boys back down to a state of relaxation.'

'The dinners,' George whispers.

'Yes, George, the dinners. Every time you went away for a treasury trip,' she smiles, 'you'd come back and we'd have our special dinner, a bath together and a few days alone...please, George, I loved every day of being with you and I missed you terribly while you were away.'

'My word,' George shakes his head, 'my word indeed, this is...well, it's really all rather had to take in.'

'Twenty-five years of marriage, George. I think a wife has the right to understand her husband. Now, what's the egress route and what do I need to know? Did you get a map? I take it we have no estates or assets on this island?'

George stares at his wife. His beautiful wife that he's been devoted to since the day they met. 'I do love you, Marion.'

'You too, Georgie, now, are you going to tell me or do I have to water-board you?'

CHAPTER TWENTY-THREE

Day One

Northern England.

The Cessna bounces down onto the grass airstrip, the propellers blurring as the light aircraft decreases speed and navigates towards the hangars. Early morning and already the sun is strong. The pilot gently pulls his Aviator sunglasses from his face and rubs his nose. Several men dressed in casual street clothes lean against the sides of ordinary vehicles. No dark suits or status symbol four-wheel drives with blacked out windows. Casual men waiting casually for their friend to arrive. They smoke and talk quietly but all of them fall to silence as the side door to the aircraft opens. Even for such ruthless men as this, the arrival of the ugly man is something special.

None of them have seen him before but all of them have heard time and again of his exploits across the globe, so they try to remain casual in their casual clothes next to their casual cars, but the sense of trepidation builds as the side door of the executive aircraft opens and a small set of steps lowers down with a faint whine from the electric motor. The co-pilot exits first, a typical hard faced Eastern European but smartly dressed in a crisp white shirt and pressed trousers. He bounces down to the tarmac and nods at the men before turning to look back at the door.

Gregori appears swiftly, a fluid movement that has his bulk sliding through the doorway and down the stairs with a casual glance around as though taking in the view.

'You really are an ugly bastard,' Frank murmurs to himself, grimacing from the dull ache in his lower back brought on by lying on his stomach in thick undergrowth at the edge of the airfield for way too many hours. A set of military grade binoculars on a stand that he peers through, watching the *uglyman* move smoothly to a waiting car. One of the most wanted men in the world right there and if Frank had a sniper rifle he could kill him now and be done with it. But he doesn't have a rifle, so instead he grumbles to himself and watches Gregori drop into the back of car that pulls away to drive down the access road out of the airfield and only when the cars are fully out of view does Frank thumb the screen on his phone and hold it to his ear.

'Hello, Treasury Department, Office of Fiscal Studies, Henry speaking, how may I help you?'

'I've got backache,' Frank says gruffly.

'Well now, that is terribly sad.'

'I never used to get backache.'

'You're old, Frank. We're all old. Stop moaning, it'll all be over soon anyway.'

'I should be on holiday like George. You heard from him yet?'

'Just a few minutes ago as it happens, funniest thing actually, he saw old Tinker Thompson on the plane out.'

'Tinker Thompson eh?' Frank asks mildly.

'Dozed off on the plane. Anyway, enough gossiping. How's it going at your end? Wildlife any good?'

'Yep. Just saw a great speckled Uglius Albanius Bastardius...

except I don't have an appropriate piece of equipment to *shoot* the Uglius Albanius Bastardius with seeing as they want him to go and kill a bunch of Russians first...'

'Frank,' Henry groans. *'We've been over this.'*

'My back hurts and I hate politics...'

'Frank...'

'The world is going to go bang soon so what difference does it make? I had him, Henry. Right there. The most wanted man in the world...'

'Frank, you're grumbling like an old man.'

'I am an old man, too old to be lying in bushes...do we know where the Uglius Albanius Bastardius is staying tonight?'

'Howard's working on firming the intel up now.'

'I bet Howard isn't lying in a bush. I bet he's working from home pretending to be retired while pottering about in his shed and polishing his golf clubs...tell him I said he's a knob and why hasn't he found Neal Barrett yet?'

'I'll tell him that, Frank.'

'If he can find Uglius Albanius Bastardius then he should be able to find an untrained and unskilled statistician...'

'Yes, Frank. Go and lie low. I'll update you later...'

'Bye, Henry. I'll just crawl out of this thorny bush and wipe the fox shit from my knees...'

Frank smiles on hearing Henry tut before the line disconnects. An older man, late fifties with a mop of unruly hair and a thick beard speckled heavily with grey on a creased and weathered face. Broad shoulders, thick arms and gnarled hands. The appearance of a builder or an engineer, of someone who has worked outdoors his entire life.

He drops his chin to his hands, exhaling noisily through his nose. 'The end is nigh,' he mutters, snorting a dry blast of humour while thinking of life and living, of many things at once. He wonders where Neal is and how the hell he's managed to stay off the grid for so long. He wonders how long it will be before the balloon goes up and he wonders about his team. Howard now in semi-retirement. Henry not far off. George down to part-time and just doing the odd day here and there. He smiles on thinking about George and Marion and wishes to be a fly on the wall when they have *that conversation*.

The God-botherer left a few years back and disappeared into the ether. Howard probably knows where he is but then that was Howard's job, to know, to keep tabs and find things out.

A secret kept between them all but then that was always their way of life. To know the bad things and deal with them. This one can't be stopped though. It's too deep. Too well-financed. Too secret yet too global. Too dangerous. A few more months, maybe a year then none of this will matter.

The rest can take their retirements and holidays. The rest can spend time with family and loved ones but for Frank, this is about mopping up a few loose ends, and Gregori *the uglyman* is the biggest loose end of all. Frank will find him, and Frank will kill him, maybe then he'll go to the seaside for a day and eat ice-cream. Carmen keeps telling him to take a day off while he still can, but then Carmen is young and so different to the old dinosaurs.

Out of the undergrowth and Frank walks the miles back through the tracks and heathland to his car. A rambler and nothing more who smiles and gives friendly greetings to those he passes.

Into his car. An old Volvo that matches his appearance and he drives steadily to the outskirts of the city to his mid-range budget hotel where he carries his bags in with a smile to the girl behind the desk.

Into his room. Television on and a flashback of memory to the room Neal Barrett had in the facility in Switzerland. The evenings Frank, Carmen and Neal spent drinking and laughing. The slow cultivation to bring the scientist on side, the seduction by Carmen.

He makes tea using the in-room facilities and showers in the bathroom before flicking his cut-throat razor out to rid the hairs on his upper cheeks and lower neck, then he drinks the tea and cleans his weapons. Stripping the pistol and sub-machine gun down to check moving parts, to oil and make ready while casually watching awful daytime television and waiting for the call to confirm the location for

Gregori's overnight stay. Henry did argue that taking out someone like Gregori needs specialist support and suggested they bring Dave back in for a single mission. George said he could organise it, but Howard said no.

'He's stacking shelves in Tesco's, Howard old chap,' George said during the meeting. 'The most highly-skilled asset we have ever used is working nights replacing tins of peas...'

'Dave stays where he is,' Howard said firmly and that was it, discussion over, so now it's down to Frank to do it, who - before Dave - was the most highly-skilled asset but now has sore knees and a bad back and eyes that struggle to read things too close or too far.

Carmen did say she would do it, and helpfully pointed out Frank's sore knees, bad back, failing eyes and also the hairs sprouting from his ears and the old-man smell of piss he always has. Bless her.

Frank smiles in his room, thinking of the meeting and throwing a notepad at Carmen who then mocked his throwing ability and said she really should be the one going for Gregori.

They said no of course. Carmen is good at what she does but sending her against Gregori would be a suicide mission and why do that with so little time left before the world goes pop?

The reveries ends when the phone rings with the words *Howard the knob* displayed on the screen.

'Have you found him yet?' Frank asks, pressing the phone to his ear.

'Hello, Frank. How are you? Oh, I'm fine thanks, Howard and how are you?'

'Go play golf. Have you found him yet?'

'Who?'

'Take your pick...either the missing scientist that has the list of people immune to the deadly contagion that will spread across the world in a year or so or the Albanian hitman currently in our country.'

'No and yes. Neal is invisible, but I do have an address for Gregori.'

'Fire away,' Frank says, switching mental gear to memorise the address.

'Frank, listen...I know I said no to using Dave, but we can put an SAS team in there...Gregori is good, Frank.'

'Oh no, no no no, I'm having that pleasure thank you very much.'

'You're a stubborn old git, Frank...ready for the address?'

'Yep...okay...repeat it...yep, got it. I'll check in with Henry later. How's retirement?'

'I don't bloody know. I'm glued to my desk at home still sorting your shit out. Did you know George caught a Tinker Thompson on his flight out to Greece? On his holiday!'

'Henry told me,' Frank chuckles. 'Family all okay?'

'All good, Howie's a night manager now. He said they'll move him onto day shifts soon. Sarah's doing well in London. Listen, I better get on, Frank. Getting wind of a riot or something in Eastern Europe...good luck for later.'

Another cup of tea and he settles back on the bed for an *old-man-nap* as Carmen calls them. He'll deploy in a couple of hours to recce the address and go from there. If he can't get in then great, if not then he'll wait for Gregori to come out. Nice and simple. Always the best way.

The phone ringing brings him from his *old-man-nap*. His eyes opening to look left to the bedside table to focus on the screen and the words *Howard the knob* showing the caller.

'Howard?' he asks, sitting up while blinking the fug of sleep away.

'Frank, the contagion is out...'

'What?!'

'Listen, Frank! It's out. God knows what's happened. Get to Carmen and get south...I'll update Henry and get word to George...'

A pause, a grimace. Frank's face hardens as he draws air. 'Gregori is right there, Howard...'

'Jesus, Frank! The contagion is out and already in four different countries. Fuck Gregori...my contacts are saying this is beyond anything

they've ever seen. One woman took a whole clip of NATO rounds to her body and kept going...bullets aren't putting them down, Frank so fuck Gregori...we've got maybe an hour before it hits the UK, two at most...I'm sending you Carmen's location, you're the closest. Get to her, get south...Howard out.'

He dresses quickly, tutting with sublime understated expression at having such poor luck as finally finding the *uglyman* just as the bloody world is ending. Typical.

Out the door. His go-bag over one shoulder. The sub-machine gun inside and one of the pistols secured on a holster at the back of his belt, hidden from view by his lightweight *old-man sports coat* as Carmen calls it. Bloody Carmen. Bloody world. Bloody Gregori and bloody contagions.

'Going back out, Sir?' the receptionist asks, giving Frank a huge smile.

'Unfortunately,' he mutters, catching sight of the large flat screen television mounted in the bar next to the lobby. A cluster of people, staff and guests all watching the footage of civil unrest somewhere in Eastern Europe. The blue and red lights of emergency service vehicles flashing amidst the pop of small arms fire and shaky phone-camera clips of people running and screaming.

'Looks awful,' the woman remarks, having moved from the desk to stand next to Frank. Young, early-twenties and with a figure that suggests recent childbirth. No wedding ring either. She looks tired with bags under her eyes.

'Do you have kids?' he asks.

'Baby boy,' she says with a smile. 'Only six months old. What do you think's happening?' she asks, nodding towards the television.

'Not sure,' he murmurs, stepping away then stopping with a wince and a shake of his head with an internal argument being waged between duty and conscience. Between being a trained operator dedicated to his role and being a grumpy old fart that's earnt the right to bend rules now and then. The grumpy old fart wins, and he turns back to the receptionist, striding to take hold of her arm and guide her back to the desk in a manner full of authority well practised over decades of service. 'Listen to me,' he says urgently, his tone soft but firm, his eyes locked on hers. 'Go home. Get your son and grab as much food and bottled water as you can. Bring him back here and find the furthest room on the top floor and lock every single internal door between here and that room...'

She stares at him, mesmerised by the way he speaks then slowly blinks down to the pistol being pushed into her hand.

'Hide it, point and shoot anyone that threatens you. Stay quiet and wait it out because that,' he says, pointing at the television, 'will be here in about an hour. Don't tell anyone. Don't talk to anyone. Get your son. Get food. Get water. Lock all the doors and stay quiet. Do you understand?'

She nods once.

'Good luck,' he strides off, opening his bag to pull his spare pistol out to slide into his now empty holster as he rushes to the old Volvo and sets off for the south.

He drives fast because triggering speed cameras and getting letters through the door within fourteen days doesn't matter anymore, and save for the risk of upsetting a passing police patrol car he drives in a way termed as progressive. Meaning fast. Meaning very fast. From the city to the slip road to the motorway and he blasts past anything in the way. The Volvo might look tatty, but all fleet vehicles are serviced and tuned and this one is no different. Two hands on the wheel. His eyes reading the road ahead. Calm now. Breathing easily. The radio on and flicking between the channels to hear the brief news bulletins that grow steadily longer and more frequent as word of the unfolding crisis finds its way to editors and reporters.

A bleep on his phone. A text message from *Howard the knob* giving Carmen's location and that in itself tells Frank just how serious this is because although their calls are secure and encrypted, nothing of note or importance is ever passed by SMS message.

A quick calculation in his mind. The south is over two hundreds miles away. It's Friday and the roads are busy, but then speed limits no longer matter. He can cover the distance easily, but he has to stop for Carmen. Another bleep on his phone. Another message from *Howard the knob.*

Carmen is on a covert embed. She will not be aware.

'She will be in a minute,' Frank murmurs, pushing his foot down harder on the accelerator.

'You know P Diddy? My yacht is bigger than his.'

'Oh wow.'

'You know JK Rowling? She has a big yacht. My yacht is bigger than hers.'

'Amazing.'

'Steven Spielberg. He owns a big yacht...'

'Is yours bigger?'

'Yes. My yacht is bigger.'

She wants to yawn. She needs to yawn. She can feel it tugging at the back of her head but suppresses it and through years of training and experience she takes the energy of the yawn and pushes it into a smile while narrowing her eyes slightly to imbue an appearance of genuine interest and sexual attraction.

Not that she could ever be sexually attracted to this man. He is a vile, obese, self-centred, greedy beast. He's also one of the richest men in the world. A Russian oligarch filled with a staggering sense of self-belief and entitlement. Carmen detests him, but she smiles and listens as he drones on, name dropping every yacht owner that ever lived ever and how his boat / house / cars / and everything he owns is bigger and more expensive than all of theirs.

The decision was taken to approach the investigation from

another angle because time is running out. The contagion could be released in a year.

Carmen was there with Frank in the secret facility in Switzerland. The UK government was one of the many parties financing the operation and through back channels and by using old-school cloak and dagger techniques they managed to get Frank in as a maintenance worker and Carmen on the facilities team.

The world's top scientists all paid fortunes to take part and agree to be secured within a mountain facility. A table-top exercise and nothing more. A theoretical discussion using the best academic minds.

What effect would a Panacea have on the world?

That was it, but none of those scientists, or any of the other staff recruited to help run the exercise, including Carmen and Frank, knew anything about it until they were all in and the doors locked, and even then, they were repeatedly told it was only a table-top exercise.

Neal Barrett was one of the scientists. A world-renowned statistician and from everyone within that facility, he was the one with the greatest grasp on predicting global outcomes to any given set of circumstances.

Frank befriended him. Carmen seduced him and together they cultivated him and made him see they were the good guys trying to thwart a very real global threat. Then Neal was approached by the team running the exercise and the confirmation was given that the Panacea existed, and the true plan was to cull the population prior to releasing it, and how we're going to gather people in safe zones to keep them secure while everyone else died, and how they wanted Neal to be with them.

Frank and Carmen got Neal out of the facility and agreed to meet him later and use his knowledge and data to try and stop it, except Neal disappeared and the entire operation suddenly never existed. Most of the other scientists died. Car accidents. Suicides. Muggings. All normal and it became very clear, very quickly that it went right to the heart of every government in the developed world.

The team changed tactic and investigated discreetly, quietly, without even their own kind knowing and Carmen was tasked with getting close to the richest men in the world to see if she could gain hint of something coming and if they had a place within a safe-zone, but during that whole time they had to appear normal and so Howard took semi-retirement and now works mostly from home. Henry scaling back and staying mostly in the office. George the same, sliding slowly into retirement to spend more time with Marion and Frank waiting to be told where to go and who to kill while grumbling and moaning like an old man.

'Do you like football?' the Russian oligarch asks, bringing Carmen back to the now.

'Sure, if you do,' she replies demurely. A black woman, elegantly beautiful, intelligent, fun, brutally capable and currently bored out of her mind. She wishes it was Neal she was seducing again. She liked Neal. He was all nerdy and cute. Carmen likes nerdy and cute. Big tough alpha men are ten a penny in her world, but true brains and true nerds make her belly flutter a bit and give pleasure in her world of work.

Now she sits at a table in an absurdly expensive restaurant a few miles south of Oxford on a sultry Friday evening in mid-July and listens to a fat Russian boasting about the football club he just bought and what players he's going to buy from Manchester United and Juventus and Milan and whatever other clubs he wants cos, you know, he's super rich and super entitled.

It doesn't get easier either. It gets worse. A flotilla of tiny plates passing underneath her hands, each filled with a tiny blob of shit passed off as food while inside she slowly dies of boredom and wishes she was with Frank going for Gregori *the uglyman* instead.

She smiles when smiling is needed and laughs when laughing is needed. She listens intently and nods and makes eyes and watches the way he stares at her cleavage without concern of being seen doing so, cos you know, he's super rich and super entitled.

She decides, while listening and nodding and smiling, that she might go the toilet and either try and escape through a window or failing that she could try and strangle herself to death with toilet tissue, or maybe bring a whole roll back and shove it down his gob to stop him talking, then stab his eyes out with a fork, then maybe stamp on his hands and break his fat fingers before his bodyguards, currently positioned on the adjacent tables, can respond and stop her.

It's while fantasising over the injuries she could inflict that Frank enters the restaurant. His mop of unruly hair, his thick beard, sensible trousers and sports jacket standing out instantly in the ultra-refined, ultra-expensive eatery.

'Can I help you, Sir?' the head waiter asks smoothly, sidling up to Frank in a way that suggests there is no way this grizzled old man is coming in his restaurant.

'Looking for my wife,' Frank says, peering past the waiter.

'Your wife, Sir?'

'Yep, my wife...WIFE? WHERE ARE YOU WIFE?'

Carmen freezes, her fork mid-way to her mouth. The Russian oligarch still chuntering on about himself.

'WIFE!'

'Sir! I must ask you to leave.'

'WIFEY? WIFEY MY LOVE?'

'Jesus,' she mutters, holding still.

'THERE SHE IS!' Frank booms, pushing past the waiter to stride through the suddenly silent restaurant. 'You naughty wifey you...going out to dinner with fat Russian oligarchs...'

Only then does the fat Russian oligarch stop talking to blink and stare, in a super-rich, super-entitled way to the greying hairy man walking over with a big smile.

'You know this man?' the Russian asks.

'Yes,' Carmen says simply, lowering her fork.

'Wife!' Frank says, stopping at her table to grin at her then at the Russian then back to her as the bodyguards start rising from their tables. 'Looks like shit,' he adds, glancing at her plate.

'You've no idea,' she replies.

'Got a sausage roll and a bag of crisps in the car for you.'

'What flavour?'

'Salt and vinegar.'

'I'm sold,' Carmen says, rising from the table because the very fact that Frank is here means something very bad is happening right now.

'You no go,' the fat Russian says, waving a hand for her to sit back down. 'You go,' he adds, flicking that same hand towards Frank with a signal to his men to move in and Carmen watches as Frank stays perfectly still and waits for them to come, gauging distance, position, size, bulk and a hundred other things all at the same time. It's amazing watching Frank work, even though he's like well old and smells of piss, and the only person she ever saw that moved better than Frank was Dave, and Dave was on another level entirely. Dave made Frank look like a shuffling slow first-day-at-karate-school beginner.

A hand to Frank's right shoulder. Another to his left arm. Big hands too. Big hands attached to big arms attached to big bodies. He starts with the hand on his shoulder. A quick motion to drop his shoulder, grip the hand, turn it over, break the wrist and turn into the man holding his left arm. A tangle of hands. A blur and Frank breaks the man's thumbs then his wrists then his elbows and pivots to drive him across the table into the fat Russian oligarch and in so doing Frank presents his back to Carmen who reaches out to slide his pistol free of the holster and hold it out aimed at three other bodyguards charging towards them.

'Don't do it,' she says, giving clear and fair warning. A pause. A hesitation, then their hands plunge out of sight into their jackets and Carmen fires as the restaurant erupts in panic while outside an ambulance with flashing blue lights careers wildly out of control and smashes into a bus-stop before crashing into the plate glass window of the boutique store opposite.

Three shots fired. Three men dead and Carmen snaps her head over to the ambulance across the street and the sliding side door ramming back with a screaming paramedic running out, chased by a man covered in blood who leaps to take the paramedic down as bystanders and people rush in to help.

A crunch of bone. Frank snapping a neck. She looks back to the fight to see the fight is over and the Russians are all dead and the fat oligarch now with a fork poking from each eye.

'He needed that,' she tells Frank.

'He looked like he needed that,' Frank says. 'Good to go?'

'I am,' she says, striding with him across the restaurant to the door and out into a street now filled with violence erupting every few feet.

'Contagion is out,' Frank tells her as they walk to his Volvo.

'What happened?'

'No idea. Howard called me. Said to get south...'

A screech to the side. A woman racing towards them. Her eyes red and bloodshot. Her motion stiff and uncoordinated, lips pulled back, teeth bared, wet glistening blood on her chin and a ragged flap of skin torn and hanging from her neck. A dull crack as Carmen sends a round through her chest that has no effect other than making the woman stagger back.

'Howard said one of contacts put a whole clip of NATO rounds into one,' Frank says calmly as they watch the woman gather her momentum to charge forward again. Another dull crack. A second shot fired, and the woman drops from her skull blowing out.

'His contact didn't aim for the head then...' she says.

'LEFT SIDE,' Frank shouts the warning, moving fast to open the Volvo door as Carmen pivots to fire into the ragged group of blood-soaked men and women charging at her. She fires calmly, placing the shots and walking steadily backwards. 'DOWN,' Frank orders and she drops to a crouch as he opens up with the sub-machine gun braced in his shoulder, single shots to heads, moving targets but each drop with brains blowing out and while that is taking place so Carmen gains view of the world about her and the utter chaos exploding in every direction.

'Clear,' Frank says, changing magazine. 'Ready to go?'

'Yep,' she rushes for the passenger door, 'you better not be lying about the sausage roll and crisps...'

'So nice,' she says with a sigh.

'Yeah?' Frank asks.

'Hmm, the food in that place was so shit.'

'They always are in those expensive places.'

'Fact,' she says, chewing the last mouthful of sausage roll while sitting in the passenger seat of a Volvo doing over a hundred and twenty miles an hour on a dark country road. 'Another one,' she mumbles, pointing at the flash of a speed camera triggered by the Volvo whooshing past. She leans over, clocking his speed. 'You'll get banned,' she tells him. 'More than one and a half times over the limit.'

'You're spraying pastry on me.'

'So,' she says, spraying more pastry crumbs. 'You're old and smell of piss. Did you get me any clothes?'

'No.'

'I'm in a cocktail dress, Frank.'

'What?' he asks, glancing at her. 'I got you a sausage roll and a bag of crisps.'

'I can't fight a zombie apocalypse in a cocktail dress,' she tells him as Frank's phone lights up.

'Henry,' she says, reading the name on the screen the swiping to answer as the call connects the vehicle's stereo system. 'Henry, it's Carmen...I'm with Frank...'

'*Oh thank god,*' Henry says in a tone that makes Carmen and Frank share a quick look.

'Where are you, Henry?' Frank asks.

'I'm er...I'm in the office old chap...'

'You're still in London?' Frank asks, concern in his voice.

'Afraid so, moved too fast you see, damned thing is spreading quicker than we can react. George is aware. He's making his way back with Marion...'

'Henry, get out of London,' Carmen says, cutting in.

'Not so easy I'm afraid...I'm looking outside now and...well...won't be anyone moving on these roads for a little while...' A banging in the background. The sounds of people battering at a door.

'Henry, what's that noise?' Frank asks.

'Now listen you two, get to Howard. I've told George to RV at

foxtrot...wait for him. It'll take him some time to get from Greece to mainland UK...'

'Henry, can you get out?' Frank asks, hearing the banging in the background growing worse by the second. Voices too. Howls and screeches. The same noises they heard in the street outside the restaurant.

'Just get to Howard. Dave's working at a Tesco at Boroughfare with Howard's son, and the god-botherer is about somewhere...'

'And you, Henry...we'll wait for you...' Frank says. 'Actually, fuck it...I'll turn round and come for you...'

'No! Frank...get to Howard. We stick to the plan.'

'Fuck the plan, Henry. I'm coming to you...'

'You will not, Frank. You will do your duty. I am not your duty. I will be fine...get to Howard. Remember, we predicted the first month to be the worse. Find Howard, get the team together and lie low...'

'Henry, I can be there in half an hour...' Frank says as Carmen purses her lips, inhaling sharply at the sounds in the background increasing.

'I know you can old chap, and it warms my heart you saying that but the team need you, Frank. They need you more than I do...London is gone. Lie low...'

'Henry!'

'Carmen, you look after them for me...'

'I will, Henry,' she says, her voice cracking as she speaks.

'Have faith and don't lose hope...god speed to both of you...' a loud bang, the sound of wood splintering and a thud from the phone dropping then gunfire erupting in a confined space. The solid sustained noise of automatic fire and Frank's knuckles turn white as he grips the wheel and Carmen's head lifts an inch, her eyes glistening. A crunch and the connection ends. Silence in the Volvo. Silence heavy and awful.

A fast drive through towns and villages exploding in chaos and mayhem. People running and screaming in every direction. Fires breaking out. Cars crashing into houses, into walls and ever-growing numbers of infected people running together to bite and pass what they have and through it all Frank speeds south, using a mix of country roads and motorways to work the fastest route.

Carmen tries the phones. No signal. No internet signal anywhere. Nothing. No word from Howard. No word from anyone.

'Just up here,' Frank says, turning into the estate from the small row of shops on the main road. A few seconds later and he curses under his breath. 'His car's gone...' he says, seeing the empty drive of the house while Carmen scans the area for Howard's Toyota in case he parked it up somewhere else.

'Come on,' she says as he stops the car, stepping from the Volvo in her cocktail dress covered in pastry crumbs while clutching a pistol as she runs on heels towards the front door. 'It's unlocked,' she says, trying the handle and swinging the door in. 'Howard? It's Carmen and Frank...Howard?'

'Check upstairs...' Frank says, heading into the dining room to snatch the note up from the table. 'Carmen? I've got a note from Howard's wife...'

'What's it say?' she asks, moving into the dining room to read the sheet over Frank's shoulder.

Howie,

Dad got a phone call last night from an old colleague working in France, they said what was happening, awful things. Dad spoke to your sister. Sarah is safe at home, locked in and secure. The phone line went down when we were talking to her. We kept trying to call you but all the numbers were engaged. We are going to come and get you, but I suppose if you are reading this, then we have missed each other.

Stay here Howie, we will try your place and come back here before we get Sarah. We left the front door unlocked, in case you left your key behind. You can lock the door though, we both have our keys.

Please stay here Howie, we will be back soon.

Love, Mum and Dad.

'Okay, where's Howie living?' Carmen asks. 'Boroughfare isn't it? Henry said he's working at Tesco with Dave...' she looks around, frowning lightly then steps out into the hallway to pick a hard-backed flowery address book from beside the telephone and flicks through the pages. 'Howie...got it...why did Howard go? He's not a field operative, he should have waited for us...'

'It's his son,' Frank says as though the answer is obvious.

'Okay, we'll go here,' she says, tapping Howie's address. 'Give Howard a hand, find Dave then go for foxtrot and wait for George... you make the coffee. I'll find some clothes and get changed...'

A quick search of rooms and Carmen finds clothes to wear. Trousers too big and a bit too short but anything is better than wearing a cocktail dress in the zombie apocalypse. Downstairs, coffee half-drunk and out the door back to the Volvo and down from the estate to the main road with speed building towards Boroughfare.

Common sense dictates they wait for Howard in his house, but as gifted and as good as Howard is at his work, he has not been a field operative for a long time and will be totally unprepared for the level of violence on the streets.

'Henry will be okay,' Carmen says again, glancing to Frank who just nods but stays quiet. 'Henry's good, and the amount of weapons we had in that office is just obscene...' Frank nods but stays quiet. 'Crisp?' Carmen asks, holding the bag under his nose.

'How can you eat?' Frank asks.

'Er excuse me, I once saw you kill a weirdo terrorist, defuse the bomb he made then eat the slice of carrot cake his mum dropped off for him.'

Frank nods slowly. 'Good point.'

'Thank you. Crisp? Actually, they might get stuck in your dentures...WATCH OUT!'

The car comes from the right. A family sedan with a man at the wheel witless in his panic and the front slams into the back end of the Volvo, spinning it round with a dizzying lurch and airbags popping all over the place with windows blowing out. Frank and Carmen pinned in their seats from the force generated as the world about them spins and spins before coming to a sickening stop with airbag dust filling the air.

Clunks and clicks. Fluids dripping and lights flashing from broken electrical circuits.

'You okay?' Frank asks, shaking his head. 'Carmen?'

'Fine,' she croaks, 'I dropped my crisps...what the hell just happened?'

'Got hit,' Frank says, pushing against his buckled door then slamming his shoulder to make it screech open, clambering out to look round. A junction to the side where the other car came from. The edge of Boroughfare and surrounded by residential streets. Screams and shouts in the near distance. Lights on in houses. Doors open. Blood smeared here and there. A corpse lying in a fresh pool of blood.

Carmen comes out from the driver's door, passing Frank his submachine gun before rushing to the other car, now at a crumpled rest embedded through a garden wall and a glance to the driver is enough to see his neck is broken. 'He's dead...'

'Shush...'

She goes still, listening intently. Detecting the screams and shouts, the howls and animalistic noises. Directional sound gained and she snaps her head over to the end of the street as the horde coming staggering into view, captured and framed perfectly under the glowing sodium street lights. Dozens of them and more. Men, women and children. More than they can shoot down with their limited ammunition. A glance between them and they start running the other way.

'RIGHT SIDE,' Carmen shouts the warning, both of them firing into the front door of a house purging an infected family. More coming from other houses and gardens and on they run, building in speed while taking the odd shot to drop any coming too close.

'I'm hate running,' Frank mutters. 'Hurts my knees.'

'Stop being so old,' Carmen replies as they go left into a junction then comes straight back out from the other huge horde coming at them. They run where they can, taken naturally towards the town centre and a greater source of noises, of more screaming and howls and they hit the top end of the High Street to a stunning view of hundreds of people covered in blood all moving fast in a chaotic scene of devastation. Cars dumped in the road. Chairs and tables strewn all over the place.

Carmen spots it first. The abstract sight of a fifty-pound note on the ground. Then a twenty-pound note and more of them leading away to a side street and a cash-in-transit security van standing with the back door wide open and a man frantically stuffing his pockets with money while the crash helmet wearing driver lies dead just a few metres away.

'Good spot,' Frank says, running after her as the chasers behind come running thick and many into the absolute chaos of the High Street.

'I suggest you piss off,' Carmen says, running into the side street towards the man now shoving money down his trousers. He goes to run then stops and grabs another armful of cash before yelping at the sight of the guns and legging it into the High Street. 'Not that way!'

'Fuck him,' Frank says, rushing up into the back door to the hatch at the end and into the cabin to see the engine still running. 'Get in!'

'I'm in,' she shouts, slamming the back door closed and going forward as Frank pulls away.

Out of the side street through more residential roads clogged full of infected and people screaming for help. The rate of spread is staggering and a shocking thing even for them to see, and they were there, in Switzerland with Neal. They knew it was coming.

A great feeling of helplessness comes over them. Not for themselves but for the people running scared in the streets. For the people trying to hold their doors closed from the wild press of infected bodies pushing in and Frank hits the horn without thinking, seeing a woman screaming behind her lounge window at the group charging towards her and in that second they turn jerkily towards the van in the road, drawn by the sound.

'Go...' Carmen says, waving her hand. 'It's working...they're following...keep doing it...that's Howie's street! Left here...oh shit,' she says, seeing the bedlam underway.

'Look for Howard,' Frank says.

'What do you think I'm doing? Keep that horn going...slow down a second...let them catch up...okay, keep going...'

'That's Howie's house...' Frank says, pointing left to a front garden littered with furniture and several infected currently on fire with thick smoke billowing up into the open windows.

'And that must be Howie,' Carmen says, staring at a man with dark curly hair appearing at the window.

'Yep, that's Howie,' Frank says, leaning over to look. 'Nice lad from what I've heard.'

'He looks a bit nerdy,' she says.

'Oh god,' he grumbles, moving the van on and sounding the horn.

'What? I like nerds,' she says, glancing back to the building to see the infected all charging out after the van. 'New plan, find Howard... come back and rescue Howie then take Howie to foxtrot with us... where I will take sole responsibility for his welfare...'

'That's the new plan is it?' Frank asks, driving the van with hundreds of infected chasing it. 'Got to find Howard first...' he adds in a grim tone.

'We'll find him,' Carmen says with more confidence than she feels as the van reaches the end of the road, emerging into the High Street and the swarms of infected people that rush in from the sides, throwing themselves against the panels and front windows. 'Might be time to get out of here,' she says as the van comes to a stop with the engine cutting out. 'Frank?' she asks mildly, staring out at the sea of red eyes and bloodied faces.

'What?'

'Why have we stopped?'

'It's run out of fuel.'

'Right. And you didn't check that before we set off?'

'Nope. Did you?'

'You're the driver,' Carmen says. 'It's your job.'

Frank shrugs and looks out the windows at the faces battering the thick glass that looks nice and intact now but might not stay that way for long. 'I'm going in the back.'

'Good idea,' Carmen says, following him in and closing the hatch behind her. 'What now?' she asks as they stand and listen to the thumps and bangs against the side.

'Wait for a bit,' he says, moving to the side to look out through the thin security grille. 'Howard didn't get to Howie then,' he adds quietly after a few minutes.

'No,' she says, folding her arms. But maybe he went home to wait for Howie.'

'Maybe,' Frank says. 'Oh Christ, the bloody fool.'

'Who?'

'Howie. He's standing right there.'

'You are joking,' she says, moving to his side to peer through the grille to see Howie standing at the junction looking around. 'We need to keep them focussed on us...'

'Yep,' Frank says, moving to stand underneath the roof escape hatch. 'Give me a boost.'

'Give you a boost? Why don't I go up?'

'Because I'm old and expendable,' Frank says, releasing the locks and using Carmen as a ladder to climb up and heave out onto the roof.

'Don't just bloody stare at each other,' Carmen shouts up. 'Tell him to run...'

'RUN,' Frank shouts.

'Bloody idiot! Is he deaf. Why's he coming towards us. Tell him again...'

'NO...RUN...RUN NOW,' Frank shouts.

'Ah good lad,' Carmen says, watching Howie run off to a pizza delivery moped lying on its side down the street. 'Good lad,' she murmurs, assuming he'll use it to get away then frowning when he wheels it out into the road and starts waving at Frank. 'What's he doing?'

'No idea,' Frank calls down as Howie gets on the moped and gets the engine sputtering to life.

'Why isn't he going?' Carmen asks.

'I don't bloody know,' Frank says. 'I can see as much as you...'

'Is he trying to get them away from us?' Carmen asks. 'He is...look, they're turning away...'

'Something's changed,' Frank says, seeing the infected slow from the frenzied beasts to slower and shuffling. Bumping into each other and going off course. He watches Howie lift his hands as in *what the fuck?* Frank lifts his, replying with *fuck knows*.

'Stop waving at each other and tell him to go,' Carmen shouts up. 'Is he pressing the horn?'

'He is,' Frank calls down as Howie emits the weak warble from the moped horn. 'Don't twist the grip you twat...' Frank says as Howie twists the grip and shoots off with the moped charging away, twisting the grip harder to go faster, slamming the kick-stand into the road then falling off as the moped slams into a parked car. 'Jesus...' Frank says, covering his eyes.

'What the actual fuck?' Carmen asks from inside the van. 'He's a worse driver than you. What's he doing now?'

'He's going back to the moped,' Frank says. 'Oh, nope...now he's just staring at them. Did Howard ever mention his son having issues to you?'

'Not to me,' Carmen says. 'You think he's a bit simple?'

'He's just stood there looking gormless,' Frank replies. 'What the... shit! Are you seeing this?'

'I am,' Carmen says, lower in height than Frank but just high enough to see Howie slamming a hammer into the face of an infected male. She moves to the hatch, gripping the sides to pull up and out onto the roof, watching with Frank as Howie starts whacking people in the head with a claw hammer. 'Jesus...just run you bloody idiot,' she mutters. 'Frank, seen that...'

'What?' he asks, following her line of sight to the other side of the van and the ground now clear of infected as they shuffle around the front and back towards Howie. 'We should help him,' he adds quickly.

'Mission first,' she says firmly.

'He's Howard's kid...'

'I know, and I wish we could...but mission first. Besides...he's not doing too badly...come on, we've got to find Howard...'

CHAPTER TWENTY-FOUR

Day Twenty-five

He stares through the window of the small bathroom on the top floor of the house. Focussing on the rain spattering the glass then looking out beyond the garden to the shore and the fort standing on its own island a few miles away.

A great sadness inside at a great many things. First that they failed to prevent it happening, but more personally that not all of his team made it and he sighs heavily before turning back to the mirror fixed on the wall with a flick of his wrist to open the cut-throat razor that he uses to shave. Scraping the steel over his skin then rinsing off and dressing while staring once again at the fort and the lights showing against the darkening sky, and that very thing, that very act of using lights at night gives him hope.

He tucks his shirt in, adjusting and smoothing where necessary to achieve the desired level of comfort and appearance, but then he always did know how to dress well.

From the bathroom, he steps out and descends the stairs to the ground floor and into the large open plan living room to low conversations and candles burning, to the smell of food and living and life and he extends a hand as he walks, sweeping Frank's feet off the table.

'We eat off that,' he says primly.

'We eat off plates,' Frank says, lifting his feet back up to where they were. 'And my knees hurt...and my back... have you just had a shave?'

'Yes, Frank. I've had a shave.'

'And that's a clean shirt.'

'Good observation skills, Frank.'

'It's evening. Why are you shaving and dressing now?'

'We've been through this, Frank,' Henry says in a tone that suggests they have, in fact, had this same conversation many, many times. 'One should prepare for dinner.'

'Should one?' Frank asks.

'Get your feet off that table, Frank,' Marion says, striding in to plonk a big pan in the centre of the table. 'Frank! Feet off the table... and Georgie dear, do put the newspaper away, it's time for food. Honestly, why can't you two be more like Henry?'

'I have often asked that very question,' Henry says.

'Ah, young Carmen,' George says, folding his newspaper away as Carmen walks in with a pile of plates.

'This is how life should be,' Frank says. 'The men being served by the women-folk...' he dodges away, laughing at the swipe from Marion and the plate thrown in his lap by Carmen.

'Your turn tomorrow, old man,' Carmen says, sitting down next to him. 'If your old knees will take it.'

'They won't, you can take my turn,' he says, reaching out to lift the lid on the pan and getting his hand whacked away by Marion.

'Now you can just wait, Frank. We've got pudding tonight too. Spotted dick and custard. Not home-made of course but it should be a nice treat.'

'Frank likes spotted dick...'

'We'll have none of that talk at the table, Georgie.'

'Yes, dear. Sorry, dear,' George says, rolling his eyes at Carmen.

'And don't roll your eyes at Carmen.'

'No, dear. Sorry, dear.'

'Carmen, you first, there we go, a nice big serving for you...' Marion says, spooning a generous serving of rabbit stew onto Carmen's plate. 'Henry my dear, there's yours...Georgie, slide your plate over then dear, I can't reach all that way can I now...and Frank, you can help yourself.'

'Typical,' he quips, smiling at Marion who spoons an extra big serving of rabbit stew onto his plate.

'Eat up, come on...that rabbit was fresh today.'

'This is delightful, Marion,' Henry says.

'Very nice, dear,' George says.

'It's lovely, Marion,' Carmen adds.

'Yeah, it's alright I guess,' Frank says, taking his turn as Marion swipes his arm again. 'It's lovely...anyway, what's the plan?'

'Marion?' Henry says. 'Do you mind if we talk at the table?'

'You carry right on, Henry and bless you for asking.'

'I was thinking we'd go over to the fort tomorrow,' Henry says, looking around at the others as they tuck into the food. 'Been almost a month now and er...well, no show for Howard so...damned awful mess but I think we have to assume he's not coming.'

Nods and murmurs. A dip in the mood and energy.

'I think it's time,' George says.

'Happy with that,' Frank says. 'Be good to catch up with him.'

'You don't know if he's there,' George says.

'Of course he's there,' Frank retorts, using his fork to point at George. 'Howard said he was south, you trust me on this...the god-botherer will be right in the middle somewhere...'

'Well,' Henry says deeply. 'Tomorrow we shall find out.'

'We bloody will,' Frank says.

'Elbows off the table, Frankie dear.'

'Yes, Marion.'

'And don't swear at the table.'

'Sorry, Marion.'

'Good man, eat your stew up so you can have some pudding. I've heard you like dick...'

CHAPTER TWENTY-FIVE

A concrete room with bare walls and a single bed. A candle flickering on a small table and he stands at the cheap plastic mirror hanging from a nail and drags the blade of the cut-throat razor over his cheeks.

An older man. Late fifties, maybe more. Lean and weathered with lines on his face that speak of many things seen and many things done.

A black shirt open at the neck and his sleeves rolled up that show old tattoos on his forearms. A faded cross. A dagger. Both now nearly lost in the thick hairs of his arms.

A pistol on each hip. The butts facing in so he can cross draw and he blasts air from his nose as a knock comes on the door.

'Kyle?'

'In here so I am,' he says, turning to smile at Joan leaning in. 'Ah, a rare maiden coming to visit me so she is.'

'And you can stop that,' she snaps, tutting at the twinkle in his eyes. 'Food is almost ready.'

'And ready for food is what I am,' he says, grabbing a towel to rub the left over shaving foam from his face then rolling his sleeves down when she clocks the tattoos on his arms with a raised eyebrow.

'You've lived a life haven't you,' she remarks.

'That I have, Joan. More than you'll ever know.'

'I'd know if you told me.'

'Aye, that you would,' he says, smiling toothily.

'Military,' she says decisively. 'Definitely military.'

He doesn't reply but grins and walks towards her, winking as he nears. 'And now I am but a simple god-botherer,' he says.

'You're a something alright,' she says crisply, walking on as he follows out into the fort proper with a glance at the gates. It's been twenty-five days now. They'll be here soon, and that will be an interesting conversation. A very interesting conversation indeed.

ALSO BY RR HAYWOOD

EXTRACTED SERIES

EXTRACTED

EXECUTED

EXTINCT

Block-buster Time-Travel

#1 Amazon US

#1 Amazon UK

#1 Audible US & UK

Top 3 Amazon Australia

Washington Post Best-seller

In 2061, a young scientist invents a time machine to fix a tragedy in his past. But his good intentions turn catastrophic when an early test reveals something unexpected: the end of the world.

A desperate plan is formed. Recruit three heroes, ordinary humans capable of extraordinary things, and change the future.

Safa Patel is an elite police officer, on duty when Downing Street comes under terrorist attack. As armed men storm through the breach, she dispatches them all.

'Mad' Harry Madden is a legend of the Second World War. Not only did he complete an impossible mission—to plant charges on a heavily defended submarine base—but he also escaped with his life.

Ben Ryder is just an insurance investigator. But as a young

man he witnessed a gang assaulting a woman and her child. He went to their rescue, and killed all five.

Can these three heroes, extracted from their timelines at the point of death, save the world?

THE WORLDSHIP HUMILITY

#1 Audible bestselling smash hit narrated by Colin Morgan

#1 Amazon bestselling space-opera

Sam, an airlock operative, is bored. Living in space should be full of adventure, except it isn't, and he fills his time hacking 3-D movie posters.

Petty thief Yasmine Dufont grew up in the lawless lower levels of the ship, surrounded by violence and squalor, and now she wants out. She wants to escape to the luxury of the Ab-Spa, where they eat real food instead of rats and synth cubes.

Meanwhile, the sleek-hulled, unmanned Gagarin has come back from the ever-continuing search for a new home. Nearly all hope is lost that a new planet will ever be found, until the Gagarin returns with a code of information that suggests a habitable planet has been found. This news should be shared with the whole fleet, but a few rogue captains want to colonise it for themselves.

When Yasmine inadvertently steals the code, she and Sam become caught up in a dangerous game of murder, corruption, political wrangling and...porridge, with sex-addicted Detective Zhang Woo hot on their heels, his own life at risk if he fails to get the code back.

THE UNDEAD SERIES

THE UK's #1 Horror Series

"The Best Series Ever..."

rrhaywood.com

Printed in Great Britain
by Amazon

84636445R00205